Splatoon™

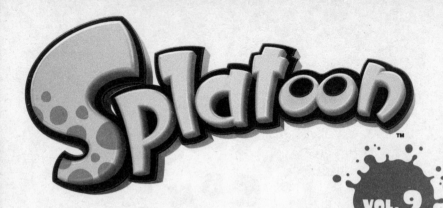

VOL. 9

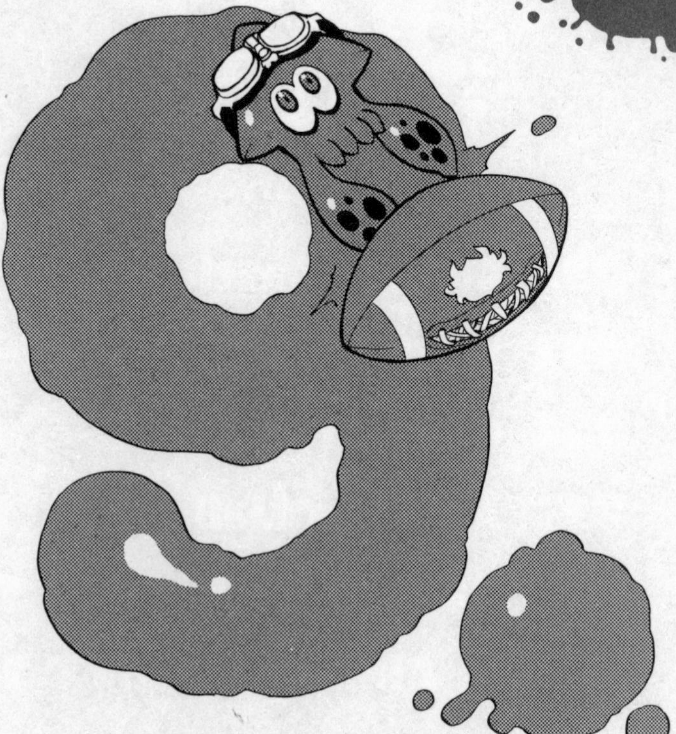

STORY AND ART BY

Sankichi Hinodeya

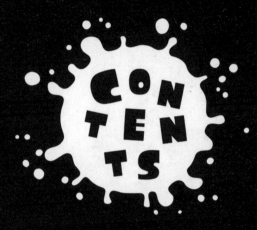

CONTENTS

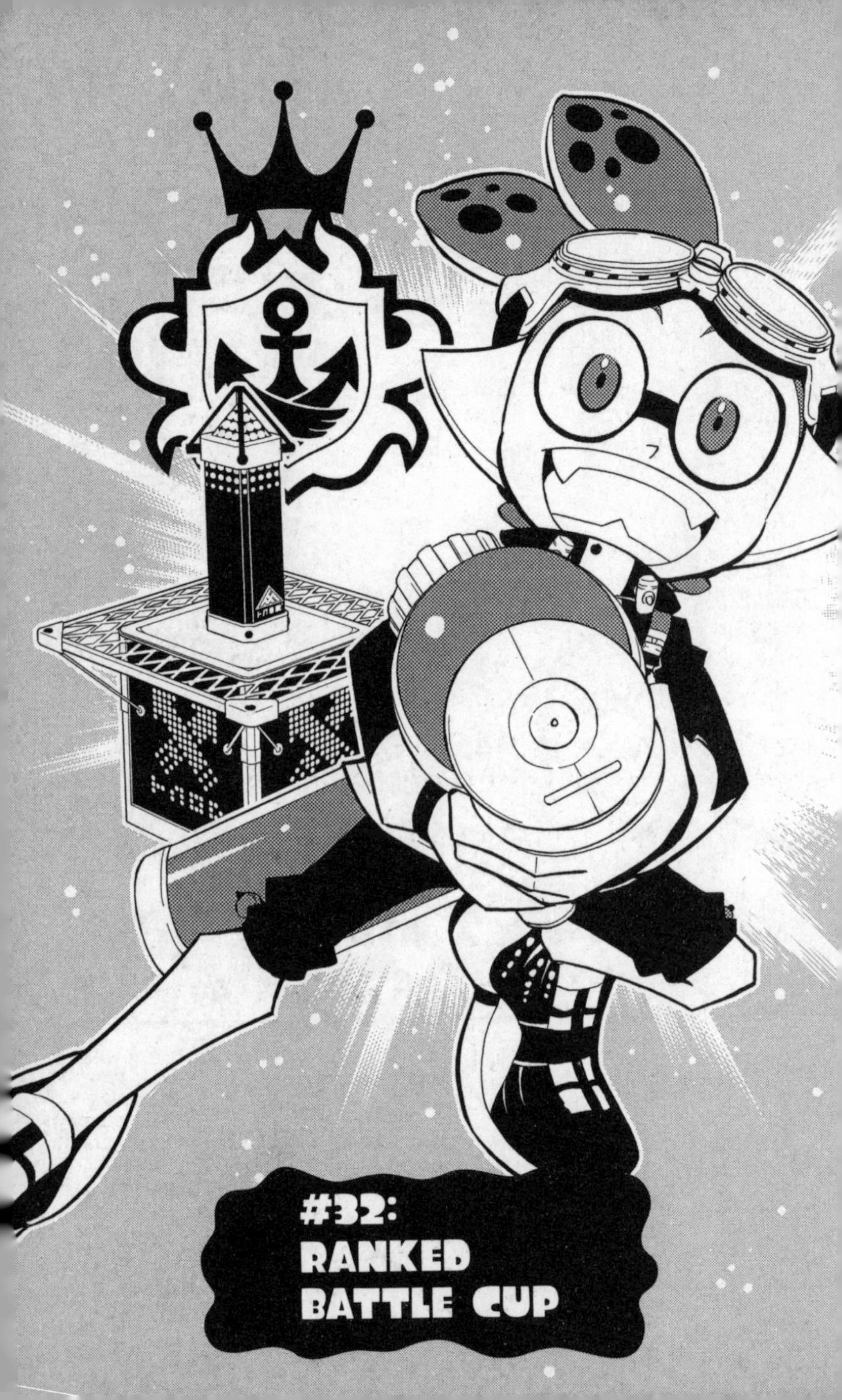
#32:
RANKED
BATTLE CUP

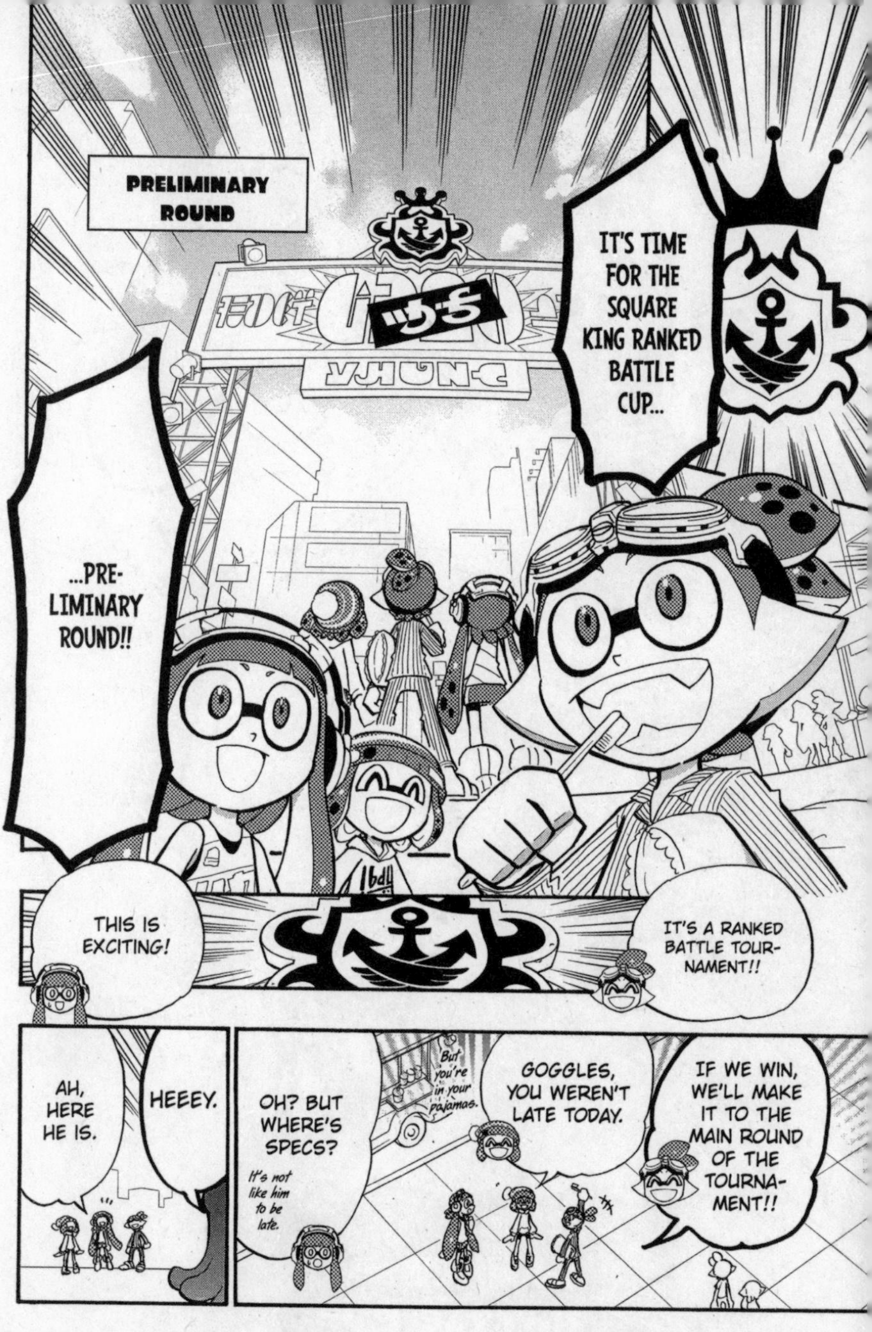
PRELIMINARY ROUND
IT'S TIME FOR THE SQUARE KING RANKED BATTLE CUP...
...PRE-LIMINARY ROUND!!
IT'S A RANKED BATTLE TOUR-NAMENT!!
THIS IS EXCITING!
IF WE WIN, WE'LL MAKE IT TO THE MAIN ROUND OF THE TOURNA-MENT!!
GOGGLES, YOU WEREN'T LATE TODAY.
But you're in your pajamas.
OH? BUT WHERE'S SPECS?
It's not like him to be late.
HEEEY.
AH, HERE HE IS.

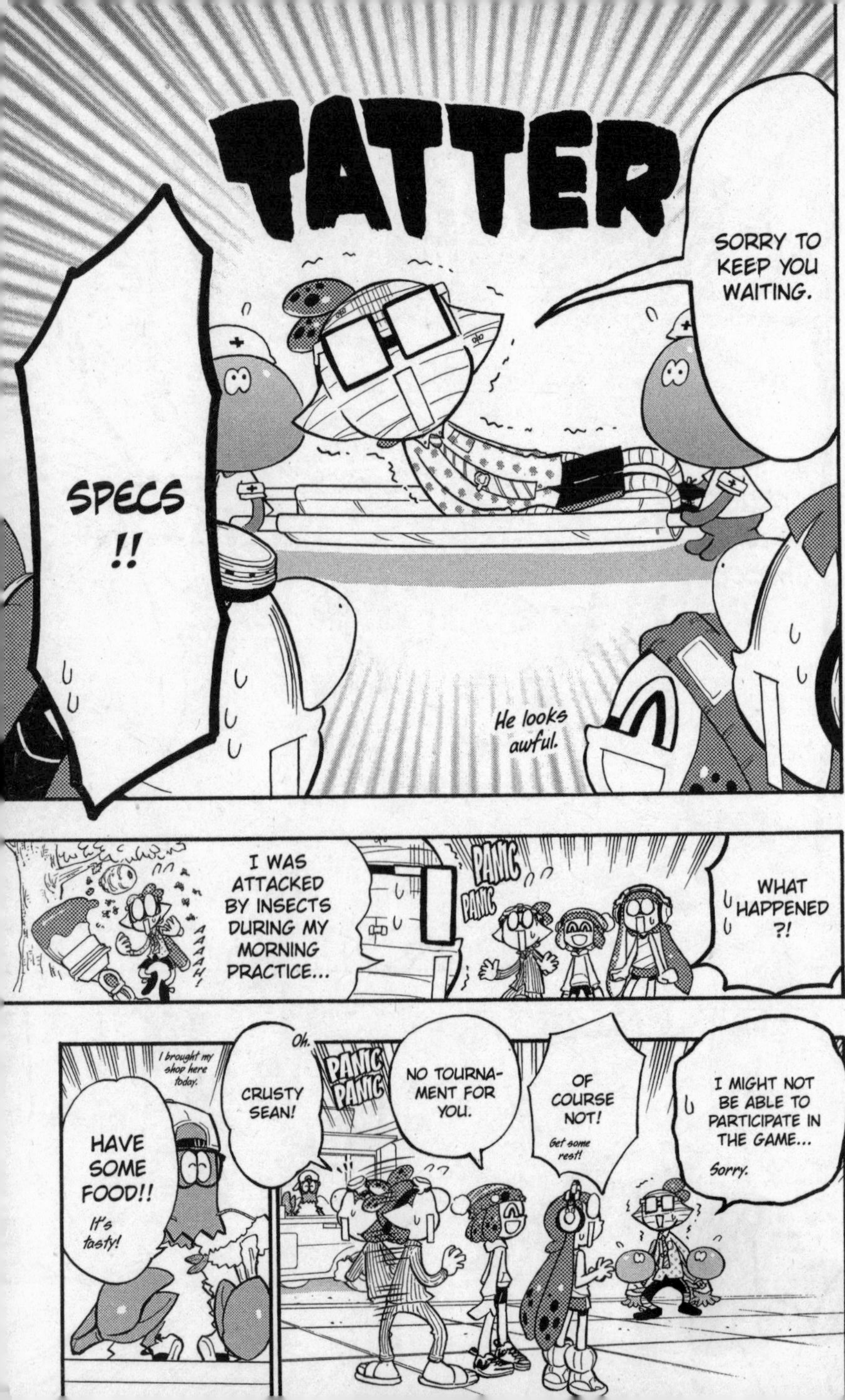

TATTER
SORRY TO KEEP YOU WAITING.
SPECS !!
He looks awful.
WHAT HAPPENED ?!
PANIC
PANIC
I WAS ATTACKED BY INSECTS DURING MY MORNING PRACTICE...
AAAAAH!
I MIGHT NOT BE ABLE TO PARTICIPATE IN THE GAME...
Sorry.
OF COURSE NOT!
Get some rest!
NO TOURNA-MENT FOR YOU.
PANIC
PANIC
Oh.
CRUSTY SEAN!
I brought my shop here today.
HAVE SOME FOOD!!
It's tasty!

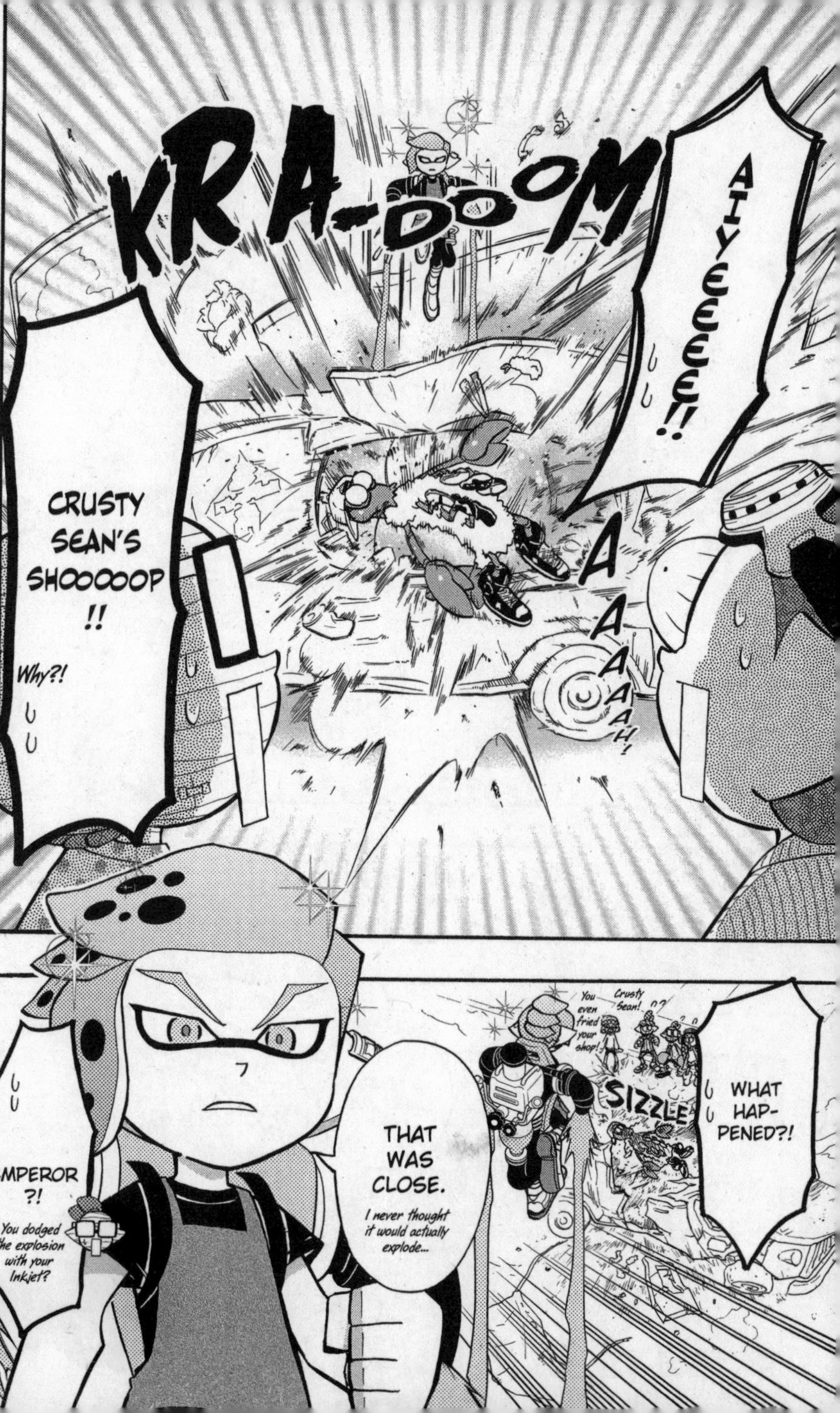
KRA-DOOM
AIYEEEEEE!!
AAAAAH!
CRUSTY SEAN'S SHOOOOOP!!
Why?!
Crusty Sean!
You even fried your shop!
WHAT HAP-PENED?!
SIZZLE
THAT WAS CLOSE.
I never thought it would actually explode...
EMPEROR?!
You dodged the explosion with your Inkjet?

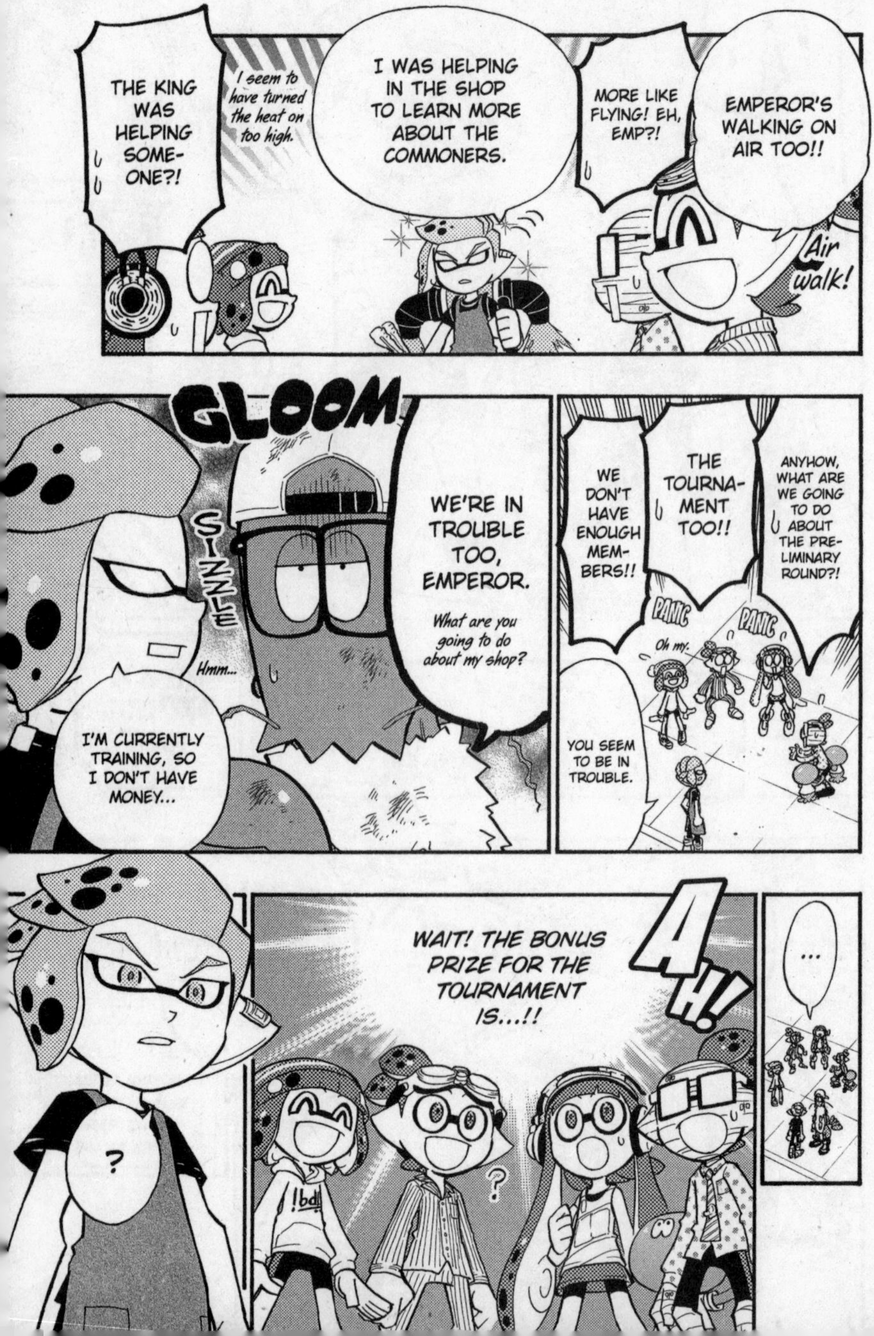
EMPEROR'S WALKING ON AIR TOO!!
Air walk!
MORE LIKE FLYING! EH, EMP?!
I WAS HELPING IN THE SHOP TO LEARN MORE ABOUT THE COMMONERS.
I seem to have turned the heat on too high.
THE KING WAS HELPING SOME-ONE?!
ANYHOW, WHAT ARE WE GOING TO DO ABOUT THE PRE-LIMINARY ROUND?!
THE TOURNA-MENT TOO!!
WE DON'T HAVE ENOUGH MEM-BERS!!
PANIC
PANIC
Oh my.
YOU SEEM TO BE IN TROUBLE.
GLOOM
WE'RE IN TROUBLE TOO, EMPEROR.
What are you going to do about my shop?
SIZZLE
Hmm...
I'M CURRENTLY TRAINING, SO I DON'T HAVE MONEY...
...
AH!
WAIT! THE BONUS PRIZE FOR THE TOURNAMENT IS...!!
?
?

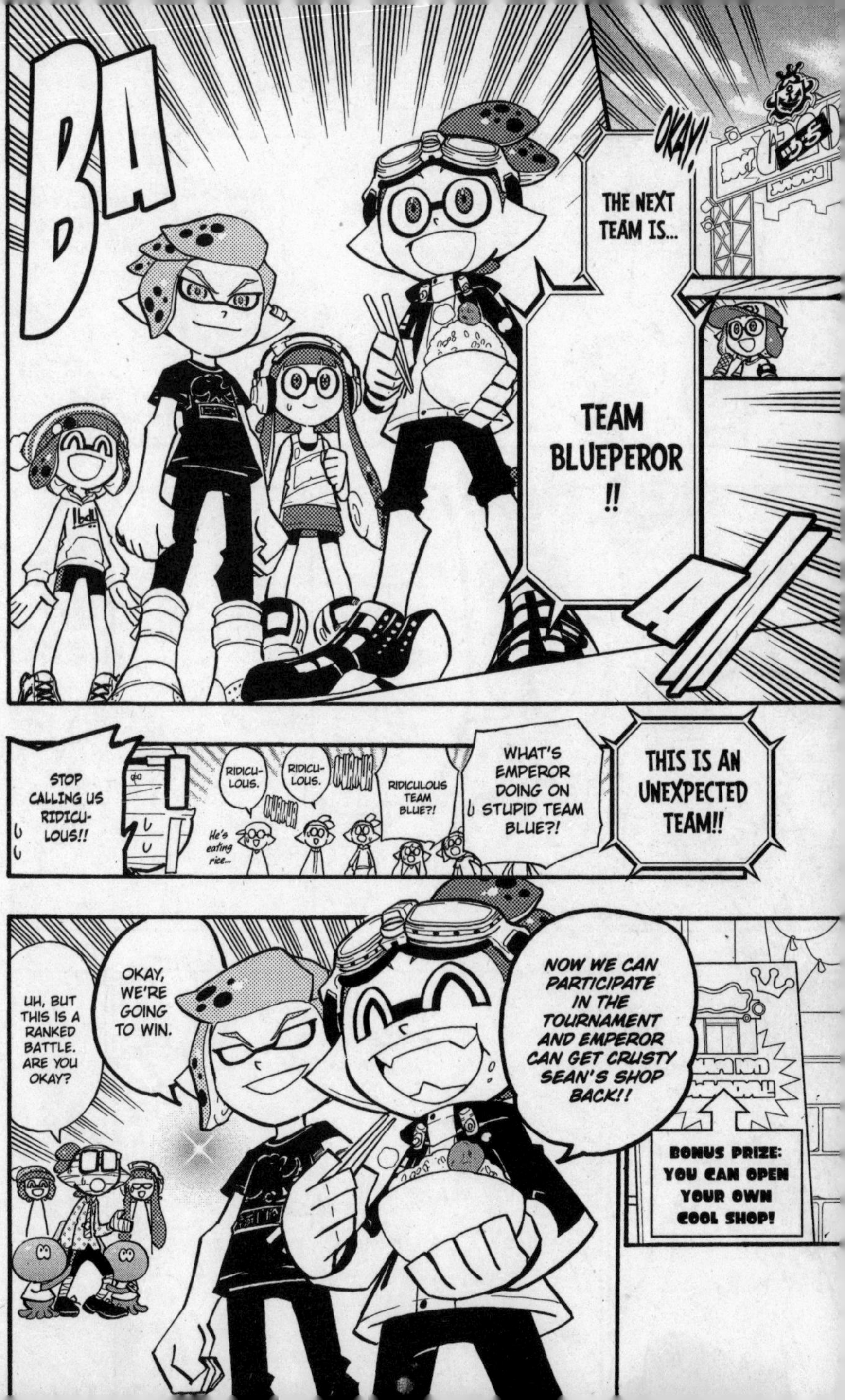
OKAY!
THE NEXT TEAM IS...
TEAM BLUEPEROR!!
BA
THIS IS AN UNEXPECTED TEAM!!
WHAT'S EMPEROR DOING ON STUPID TEAM BLUE?!
RIDICULOUS TEAM BLUE?!
RIDICU-LOUS.
RIDICU-LOUS.
He's eating rice...
STOP CALLING US RIDICU-LOUS!!
BONUS PRIZE: YOU CAN OPEN YOUR OWN COOL SHOP!
NOW WE CAN PARTICIPATE IN THE TOURNAMENT AND EMPEROR CAN GET CRUSTY SEAN'S SHOP BACK!!
OKAY, WE'RE GOING TO WIN.
UH, BUT THIS IS A RANKED BATTLE. ARE YOU OKAY?

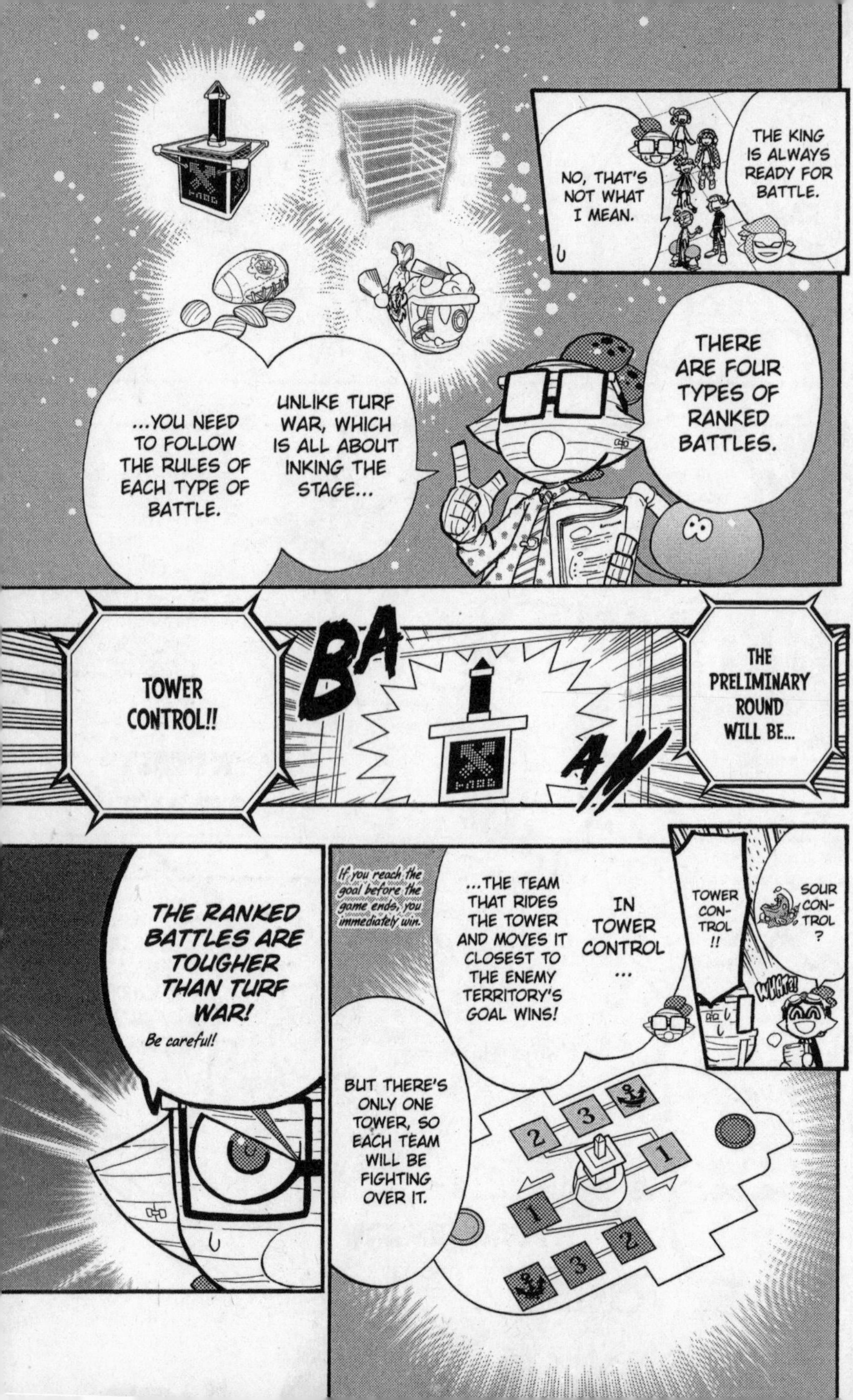
THE KING IS ALWAYS READY FOR BATTLE.
NO, THAT'S NOT WHAT I MEAN.
THERE ARE FOUR TYPES OF RANKED BATTLES.
UNLIKE TURF WAR, WHICH IS ALL ABOUT INKING THE STAGE...
...YOU NEED TO FOLLOW THE RULES OF EACH TYPE OF BATTLE.
THE PRELIMINARY ROUND WILL BE...
BAAM
TOWER CONTROL!!
SOUR CON-TROL?
TOWER CON-TROL!!
WHAT?!
IN TOWER CONTROL...
...THE TEAM THAT RIDES THE TOWER AND MOVES IT CLOSEST TO THE ENEMY TERRITORY'S GOAL WINS!
If you reach the goal before the game ends, you immediately win.
BUT THERE'S ONLY ONE TOWER, SO EACH TEAM WILL BE FIGHTING OVER IT.
THE RANKED BATTLES ARE TOUGHER THAN TURF WAR!
Be careful!

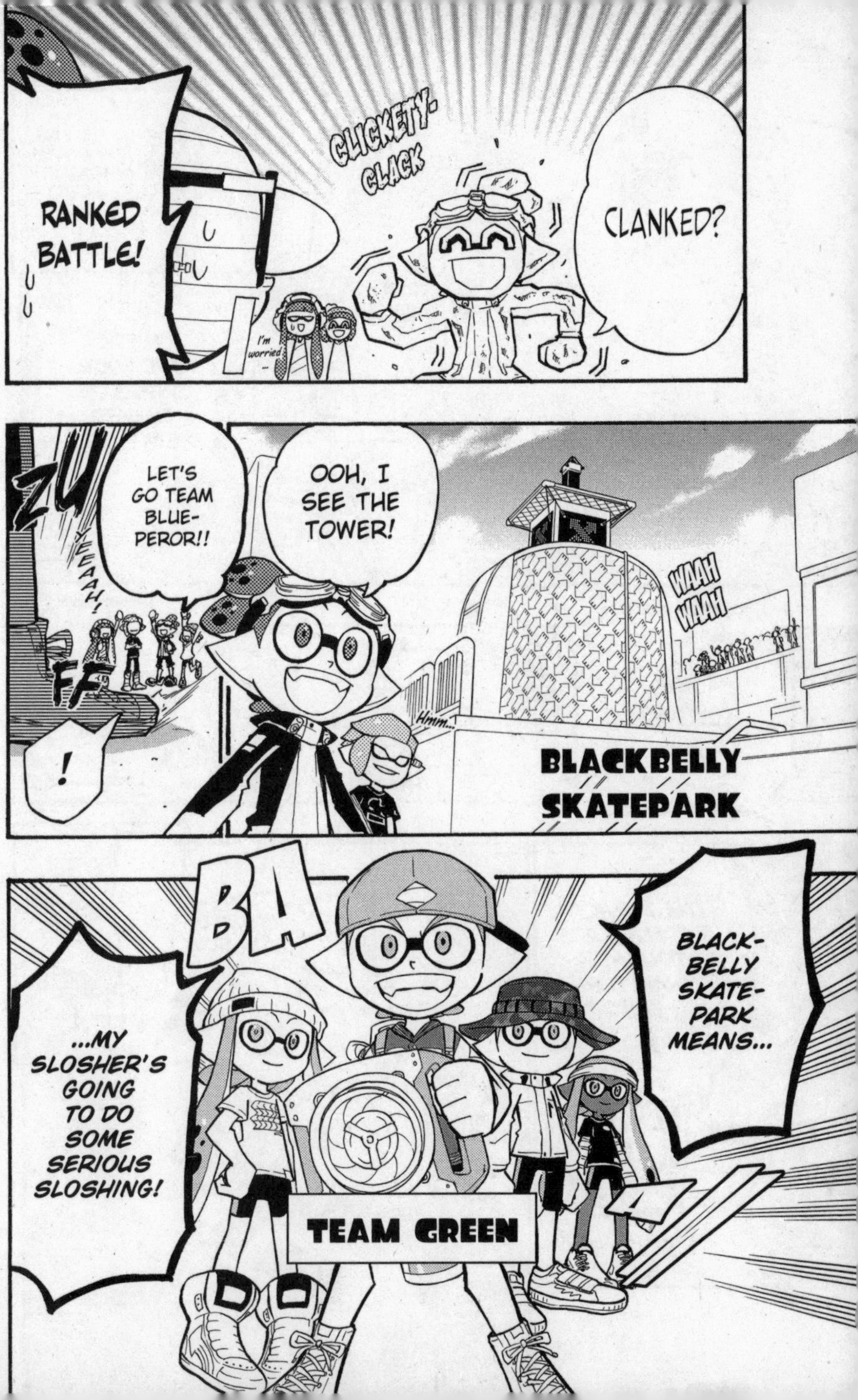
CLANKED?
CLICKETY-CLACK
I'm worried...
RANKED BATTLE!
BLACKBELLY SKATEPARK
WAAH WAAH
Hmm...
OOH, I SEE THE TOWER!
LET'S GO TEAM BLUE-PEROR!!
YEEAAH!
ZU
FF
!
BLACK-BELLY SKATE-PARK MEANS...
BA
TEAM GREEN
...MY SLOSHER'S GOING TO DO SOME SERIOUS SLOSHING!
DO

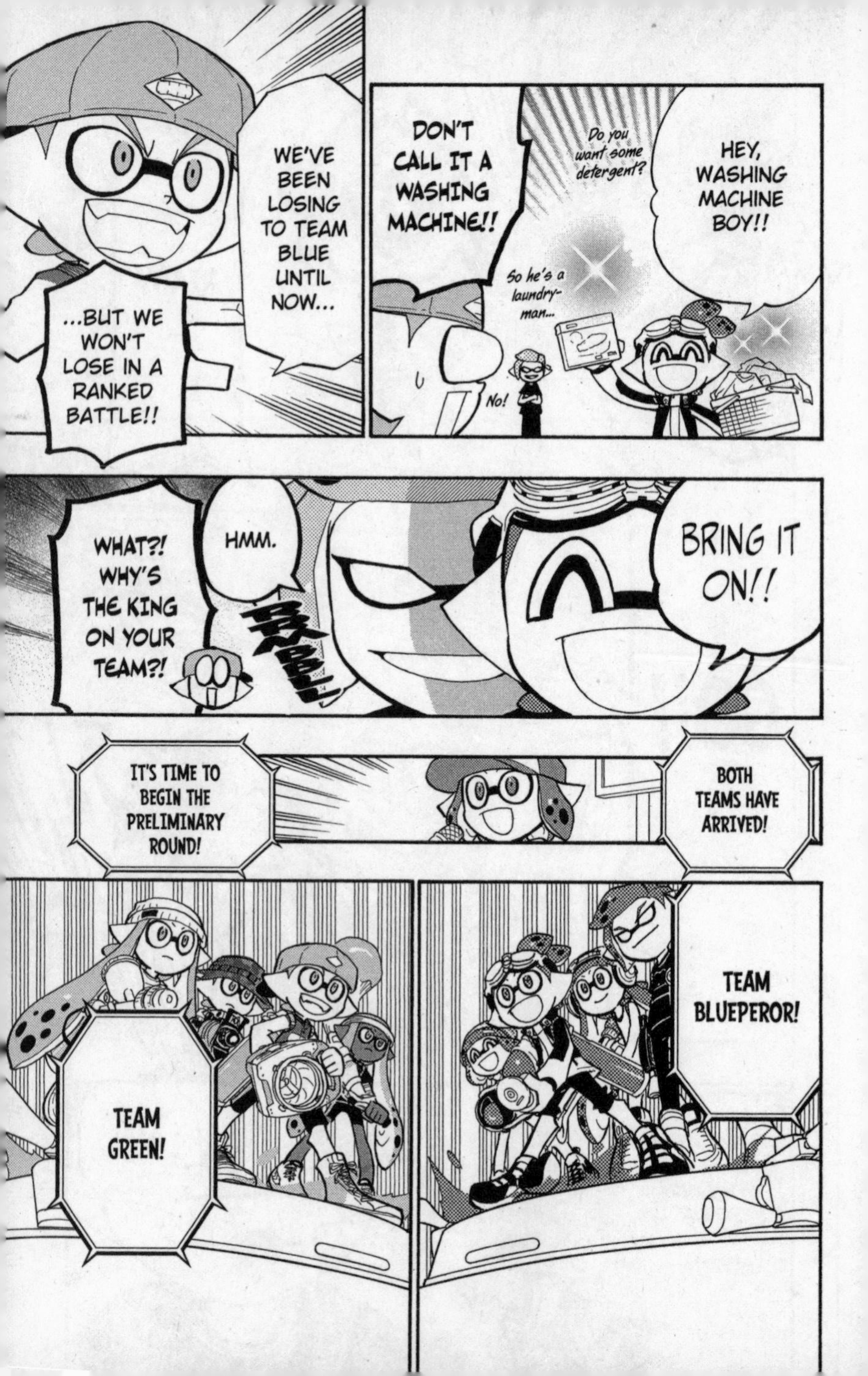

HEY, WASHING MACHINE BOY!!
Do you want some detergent?
DON'T CALL IT A WASHING MACHINE!!
So he's a laundryman...
No!
WE'VE BEEN LOSING TO TEAM BLUE UNTIL NOW...
...BUT WE WON'T LOSE IN A RANKED BATTLE!!
BRING IT ON!!
HMM.
WHAT?! WHY'S THE KING ON YOUR TEAM?!
BOTH TEAMS HAVE ARRIVED!
IT'S TIME TO BEGIN THE PRELIMINARY ROUND!
TEAM BLUEPEROR!
TEAM GREEN!

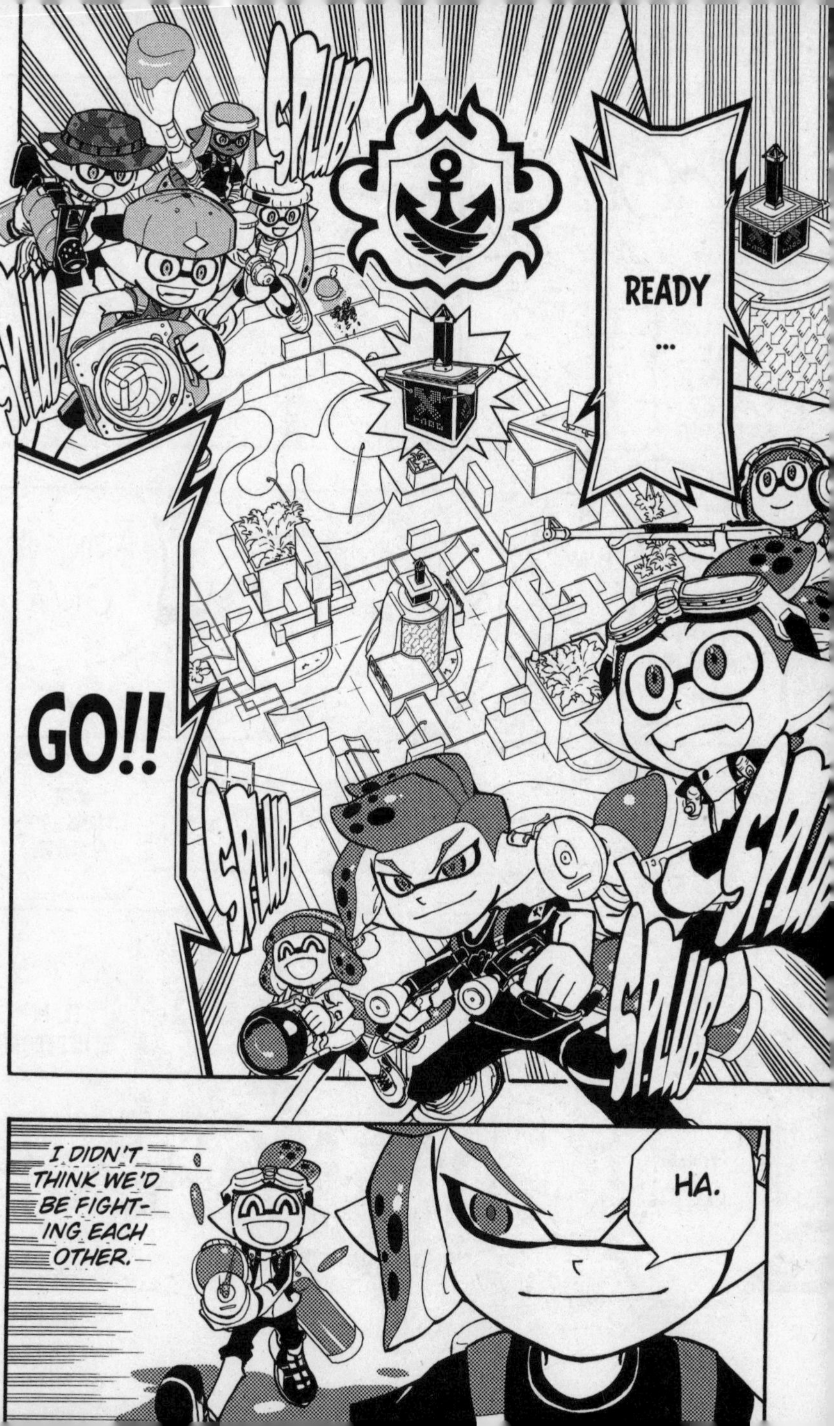
SPLUB
READY ...
SPLUB
GO!!
SPLUB
SPLUB
SPLUB
HA.
I DIDN'T THINK WE'D BE FIGHTING EACH OTHER.

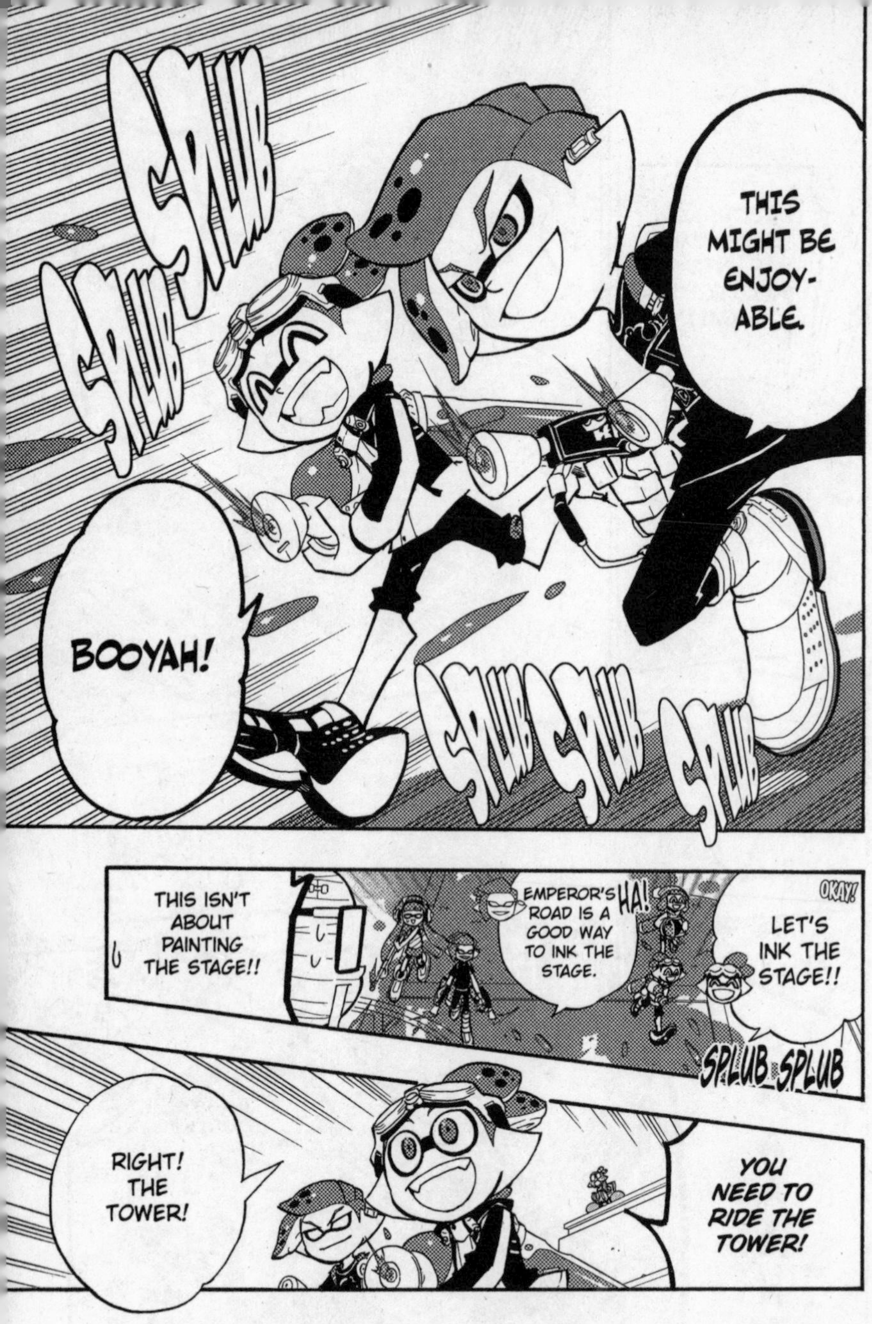
THIS MIGHT BE ENJOY-ABLE.
SPLUB SPLUB
SPLUB
BOOYAH!
SPLUB SPLUB
SPLUB
OKAY!
LET'S INK THE STAGE!!
HA!
EMPEROR'S ROAD IS A GOOD WAY TO INK THE STAGE.
THIS ISN'T ABOUT PAINTING THE STAGE!!
SPLUB SPLUB
YOU NEED TO RIDE THE TOWER!
RIGHT! THE TOWER!

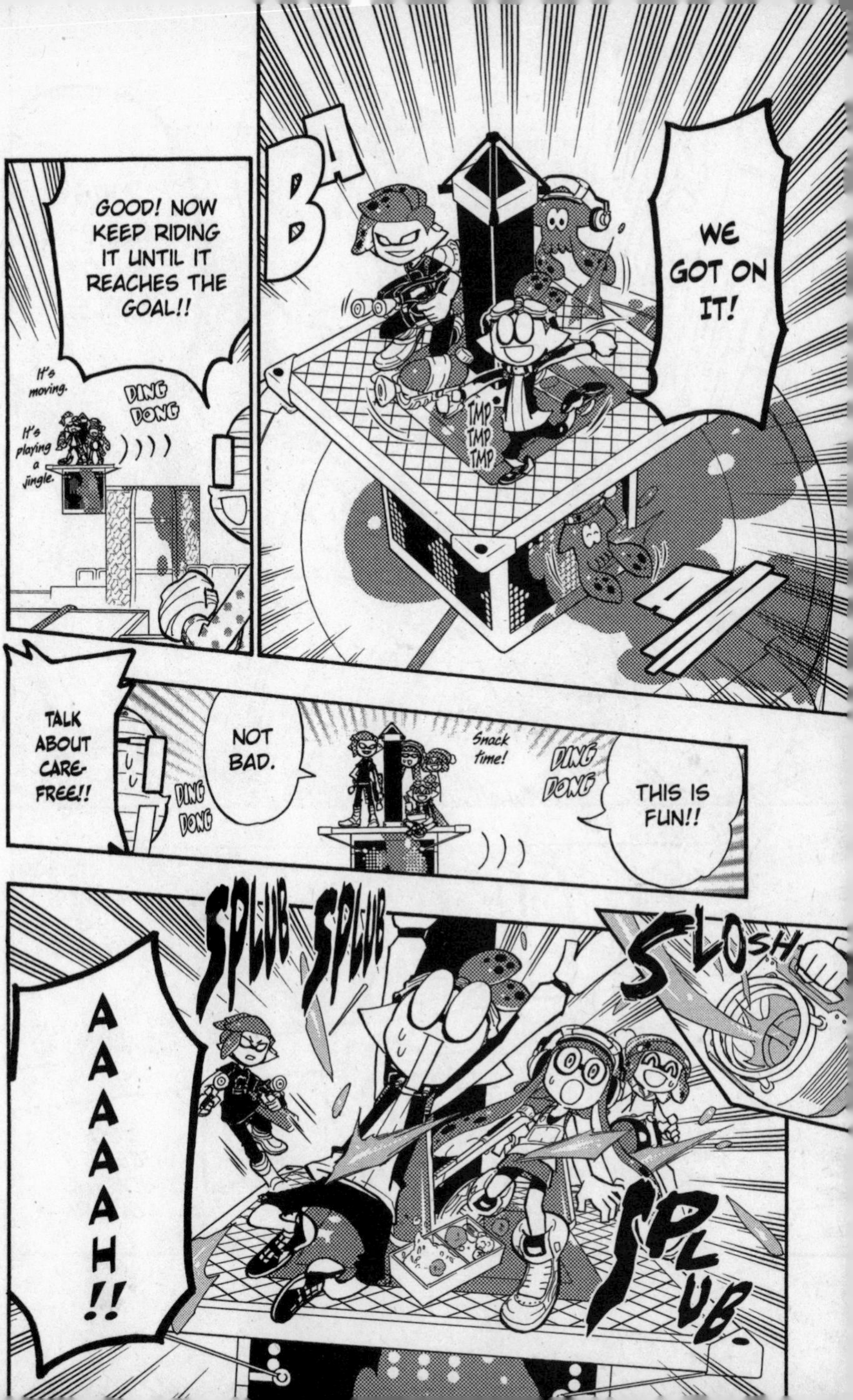
WE GOT ON IT!
BA
TMP TMP TMP
A
GOOD! NOW KEEP RIDING IT UNTIL IT REACHES THE GOAL!!
It's moving.
DING DONG
It's playing a jingle.
THIS IS FUN!!
DING DONG
Snack time!
NOT BAD.
DING DONG
TALK ABOUT CARE-FREE!!
SLOSH
SPLUB SPLUB
AAAAAH!!
SPLUB

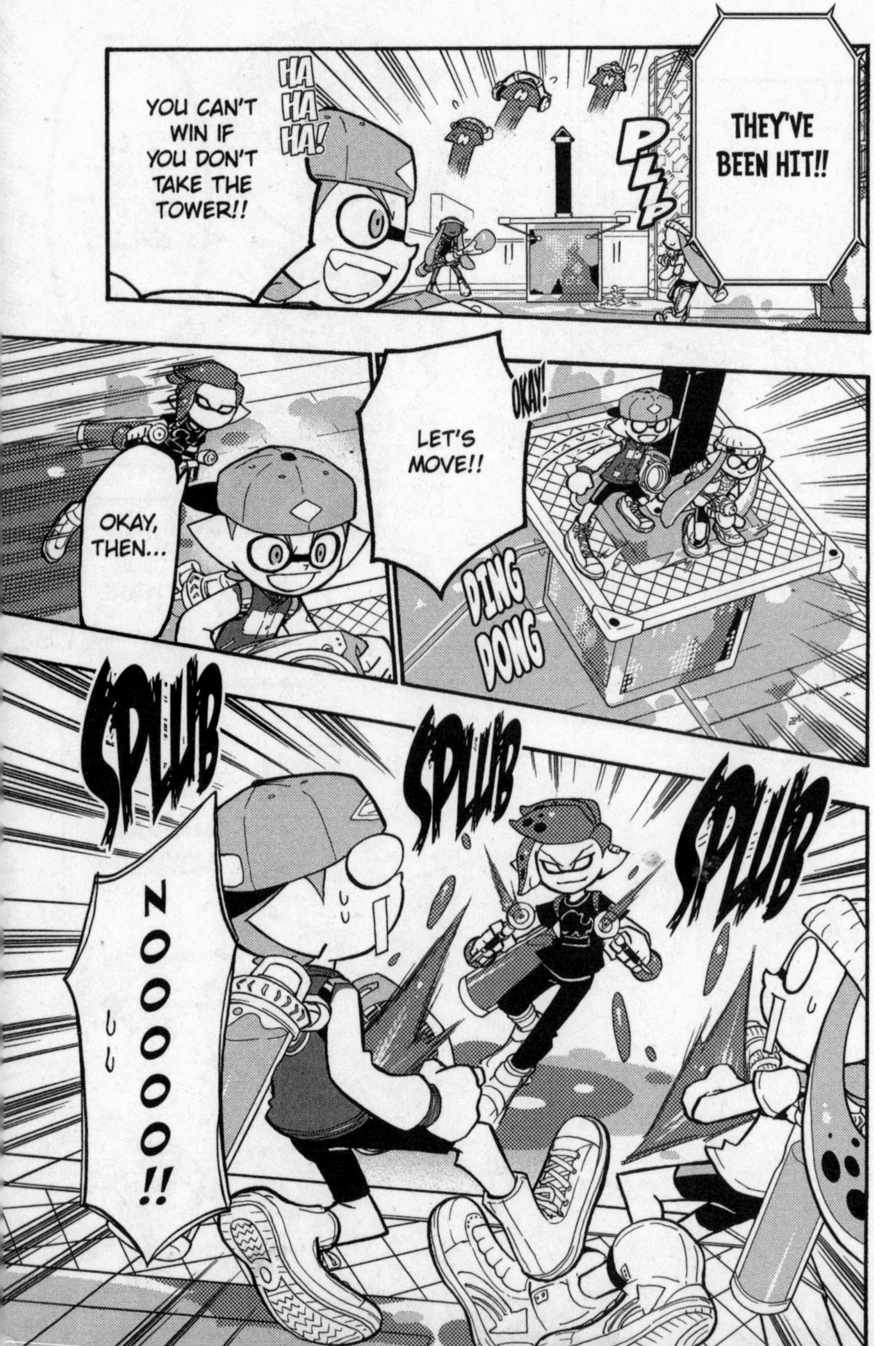
THEY'VE BEEN HIT!!
PLIP
HA HA HA!
YOU CAN'T WIN IF YOU DON'T TAKE THE TOWER!!
OKAY!
LET'S MOVE!!
DING DONG
OKAY, THEN...
SPLUB
SPLUB
SPLUB
NOOOOOO!!

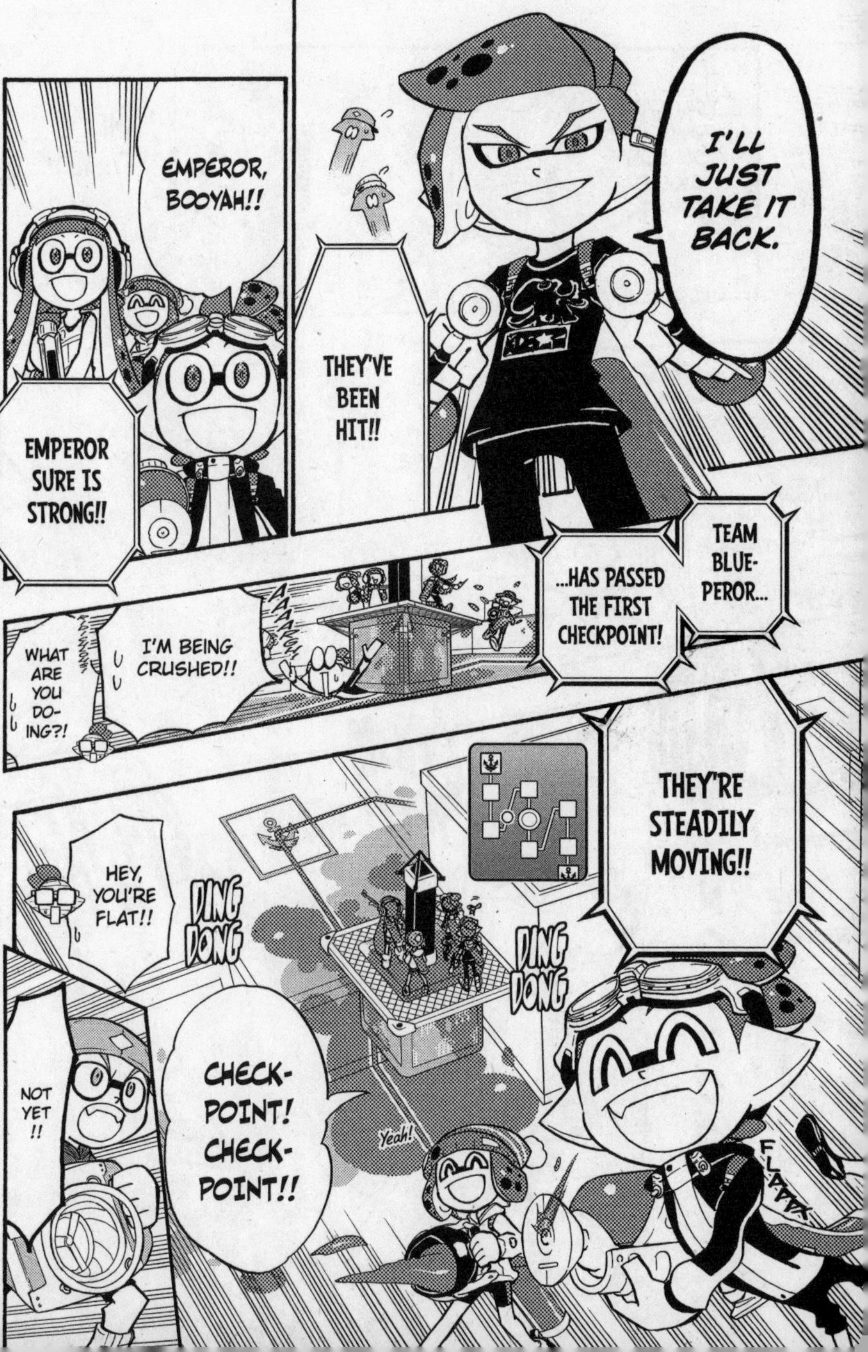
I'LL JUST TAKE IT BACK.
THEY'VE BEEN HIT!!
EMPEROR, BOOYAH!!
EMPEROR SURE IS STRONG!!
TEAM BLUE-PEROR...
...HAS PASSED THE FIRST CHECKPOINT!
I'M BEING CRUSHED!!
WHAT ARE YOU DO-ING?!
THEY'RE STEADILY MOVING!!
DING DONG
DING DONG
HEY, YOU'RE FLAT!!
Yeah!
CHECK-POINT! CHECK-POINT!!
NOT YET!!

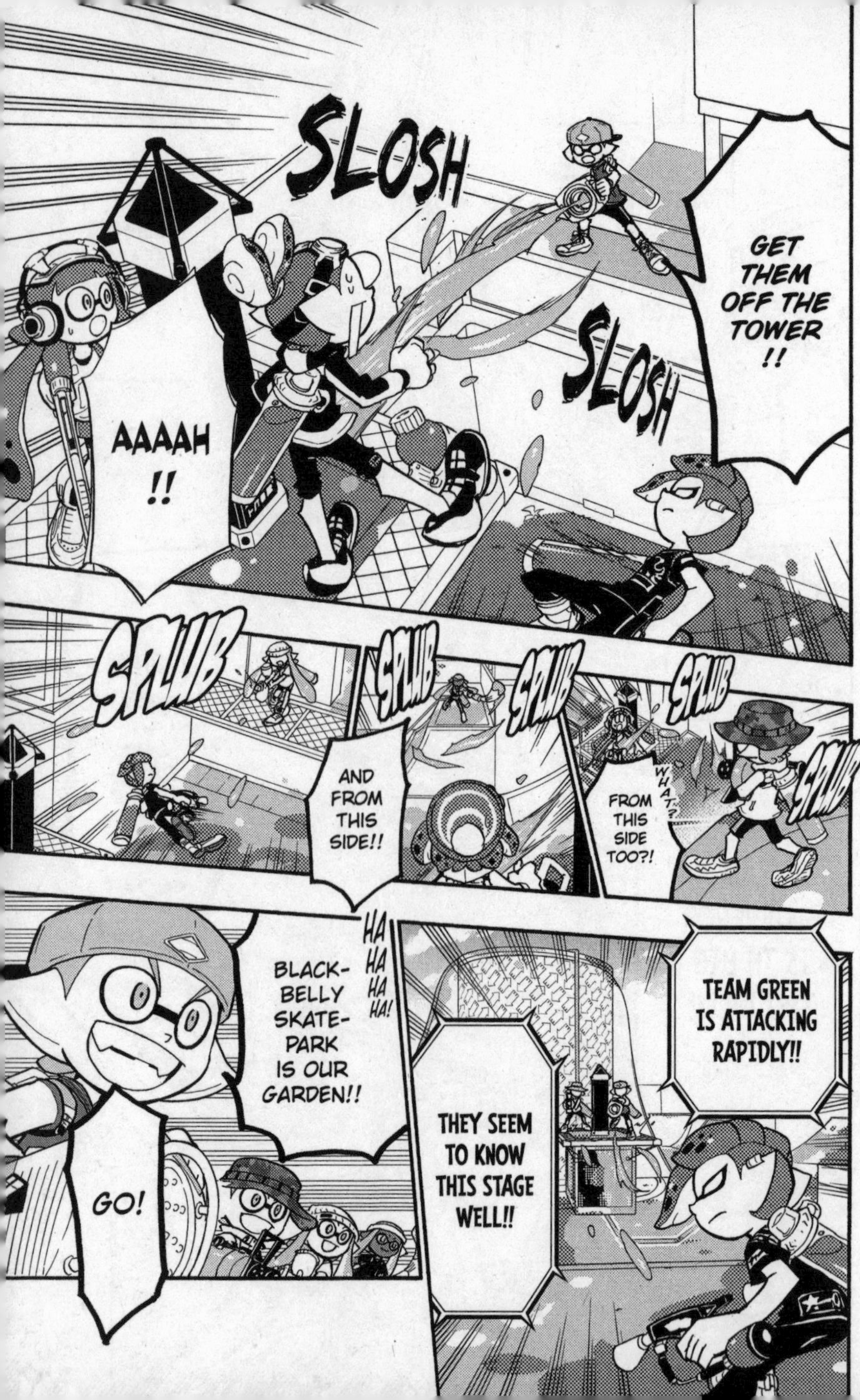
SLOSH
GET THEM OFF THE TOWER!!
SLOSH
AAAAH!!
SPLUB
SPLUB
WHAT?
FROM THIS SIDE TOO?!
SPLUB
SPLUB
AND FROM THIS SIDE!!
SPLUB
TEAM GREEN IS ATTACKING RAPIDLY!!
THEY SEEM TO KNOW THIS STAGE WELL!!
HA HA HA HA HA!
BLACK-BELLY SKATE-PARK IS OUR GARDEN!!
GO!

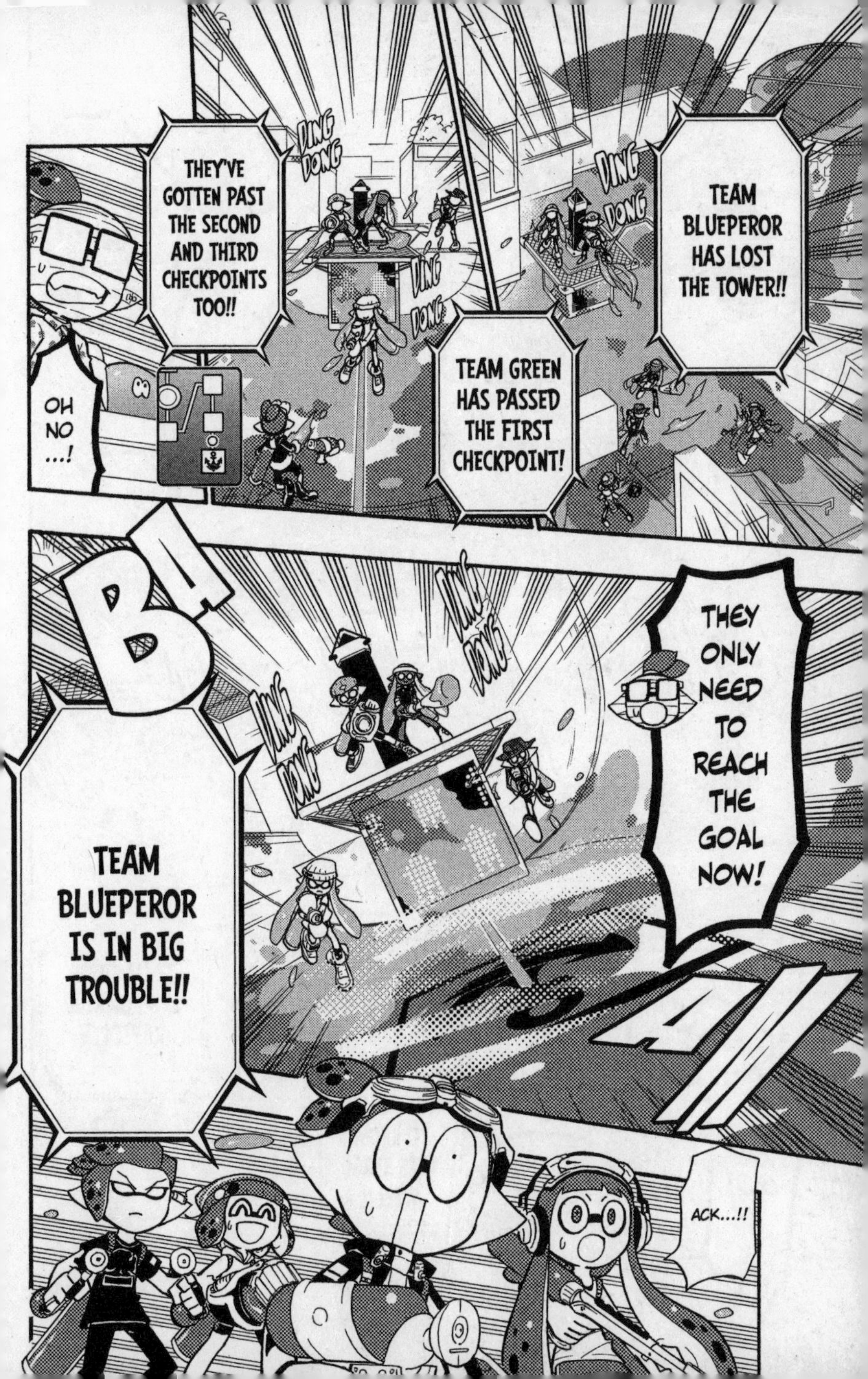
DING DONG
TEAM BLUEPEROR HAS LOST THE TOWER!!
DING DONG
TEAM GREEN HAS PASSED THE FIRST CHECKPOINT!
DING DONG
DING DONG
THEY'VE GOTTEN PAST THE SECOND AND THIRD CHECKPOINTS TOO!!
OH NO ...!
THEY ONLY NEED TO REACH THE GOAL NOW!
DING DONG
DING DONG
BA
TEAM BLUEPEROR IS IN BIG TROUBLE!!
ACK...!!

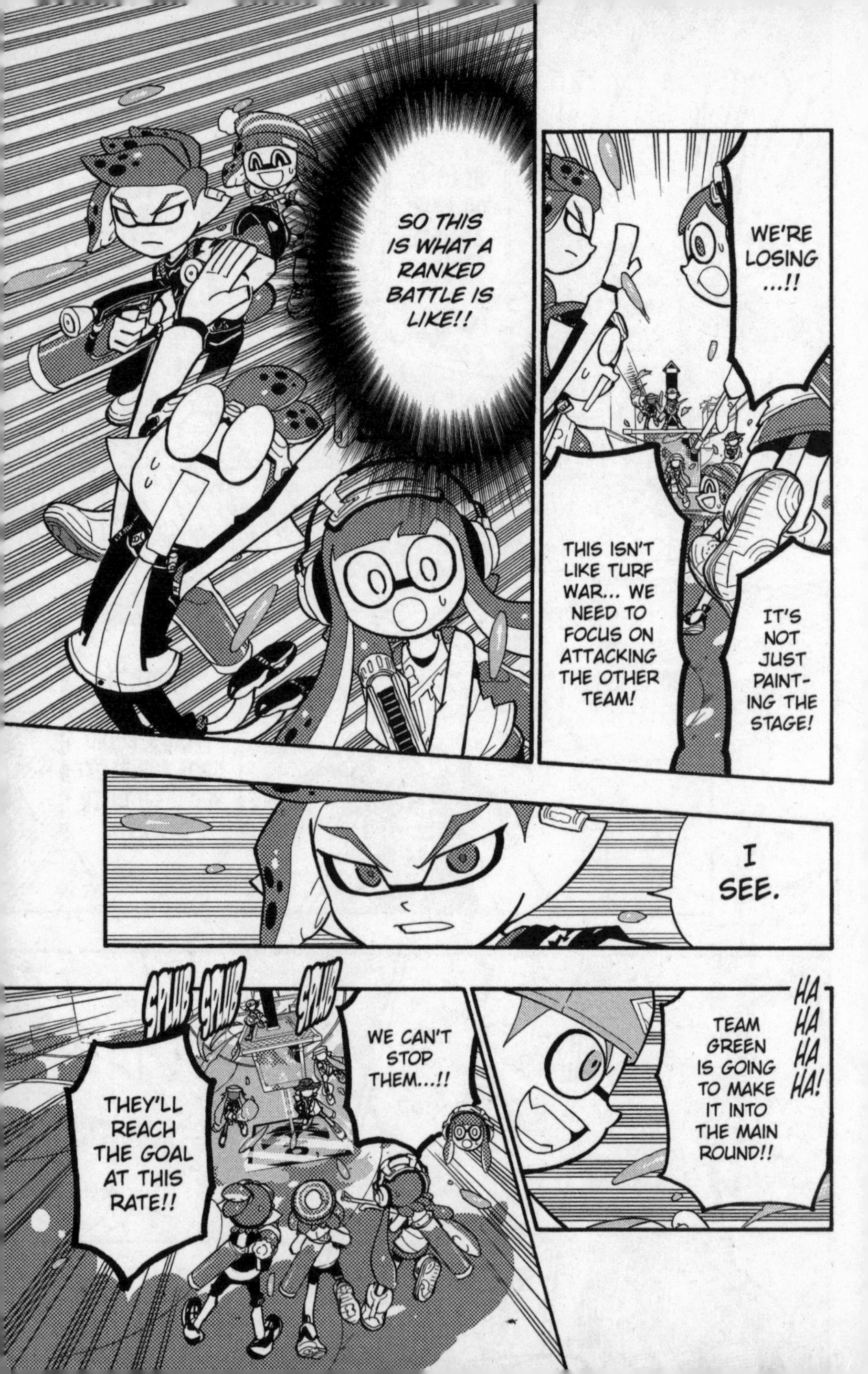
WE'RE LOSING ...!!
THIS ISN'T LIKE TURF WAR... WE NEED TO FOCUS ON ATTACKING THE OTHER TEAM!
IT'S NOT JUST PAINT-ING THE STAGE!
SO THIS IS WHAT A RANKED BATTLE IS LIKE!!
I SEE.
HA HA HA HA!
TEAM GREEN IS GOING TO MAKE IT INTO THE MAIN ROUND!!
SPLUB SPLUB SPLUB
WE CAN'T STOP THEM...!!
THEY'LL REACH THE GOAL AT THIS RATE!!

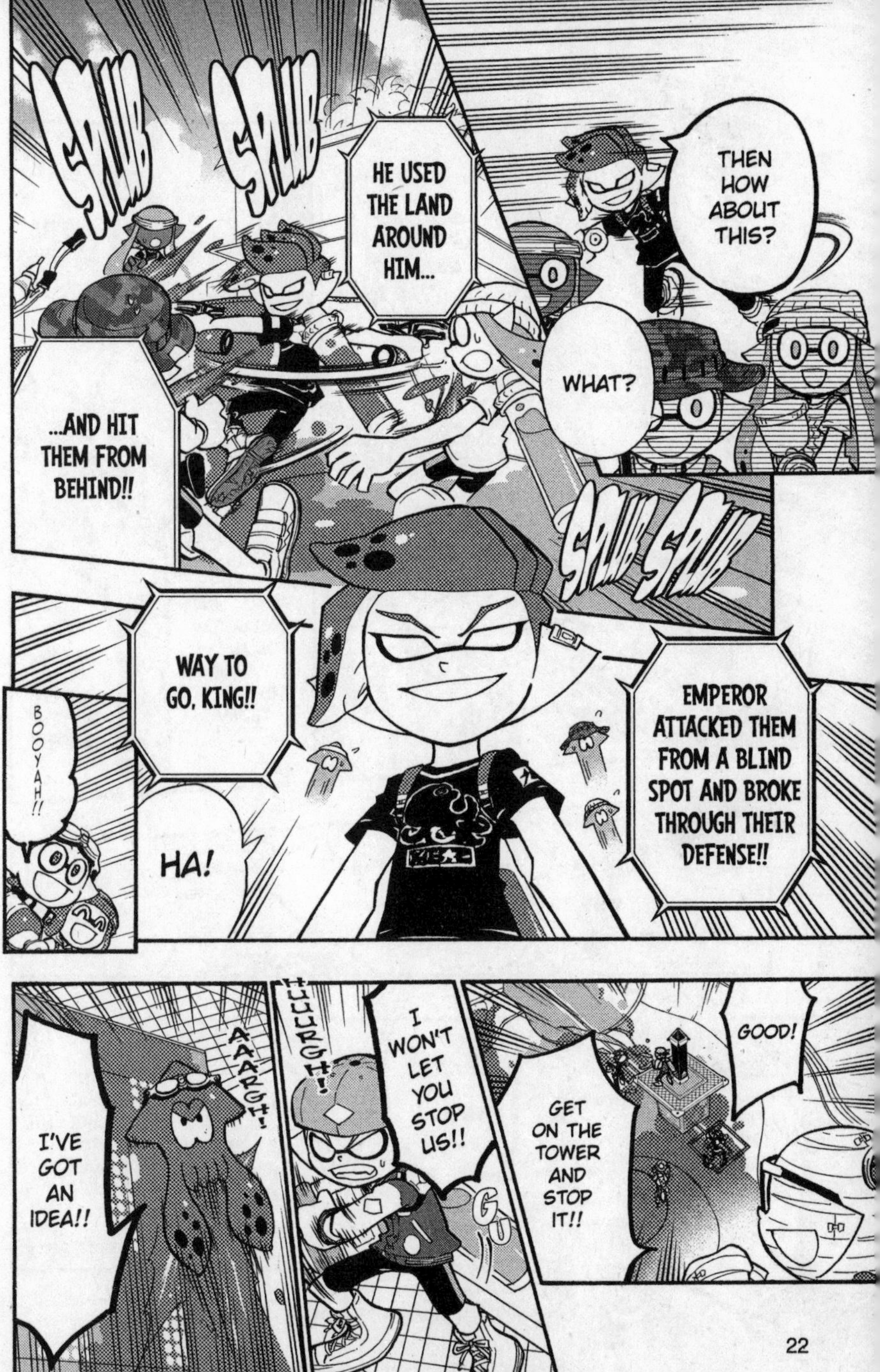
THEN HOW ABOUT THIS?
WHAT?
SPLUB
SPLUB
HE USED THE LAND AROUND HIM...
...AND HIT THEM FROM BEHIND!!
SPLUB SPLUB
EMPEROR ATTACKED THEM FROM A BLIND SPOT AND BROKE THROUGH THEIR DEFENSE!!
WAY TO GO, KING!!
HA!
BOOYAH!!
GOOD!
GET ON THE TOWER AND STOP IT!!
I WON'T LET YOU STOP US!!
HUUURGH!
GU
AAAARGH!
I'VE GOT AN IDEA!!

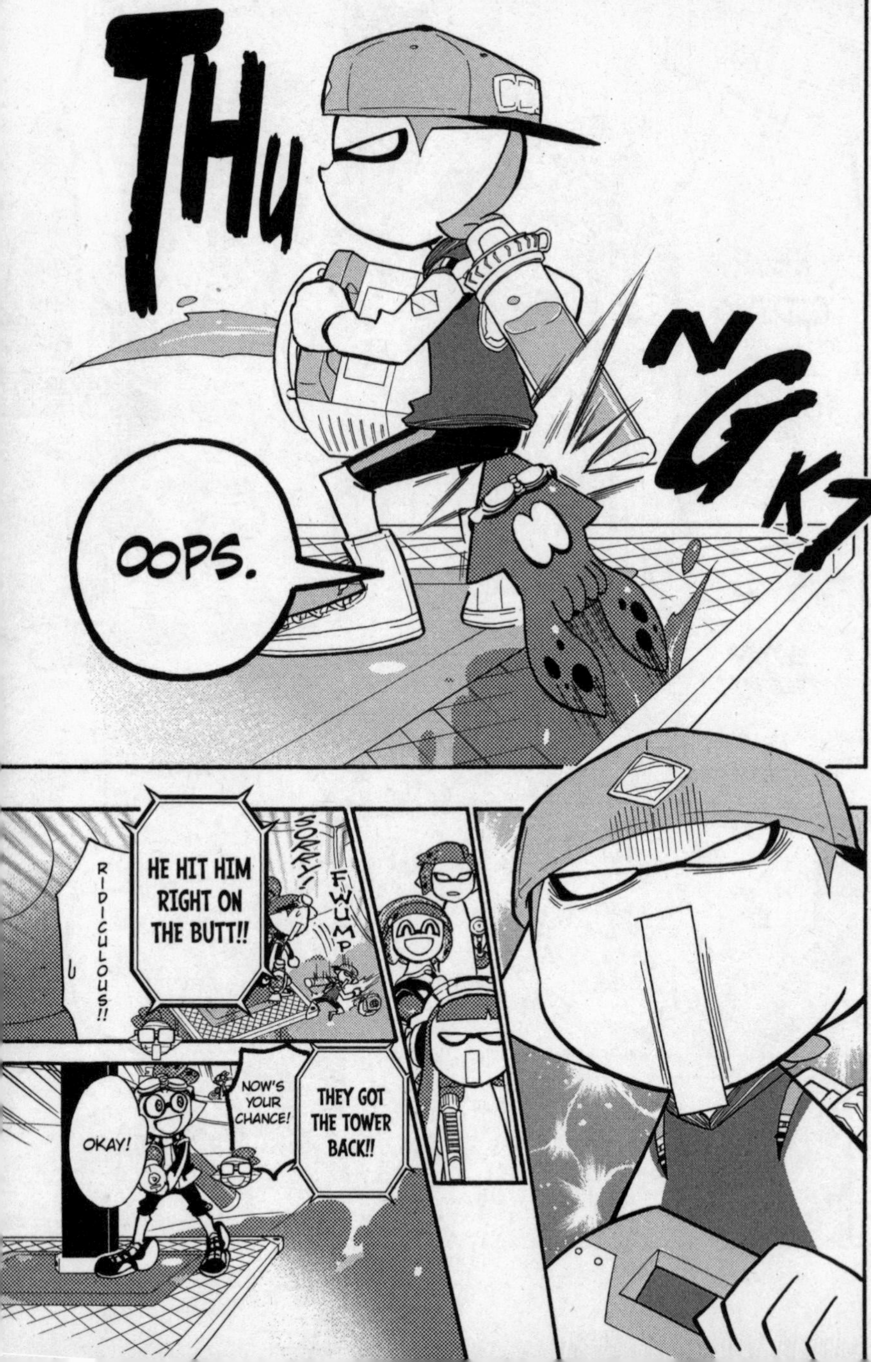
THUNGK
OOPS.
SORRY!
FWUMP
HE HIT HIM RIGHT ON THE BUTT!!
RIDICULOUS!!
THEY GOT THE TOWER BACK!!
NOW'S YOUR CHANCE!
OKAY!

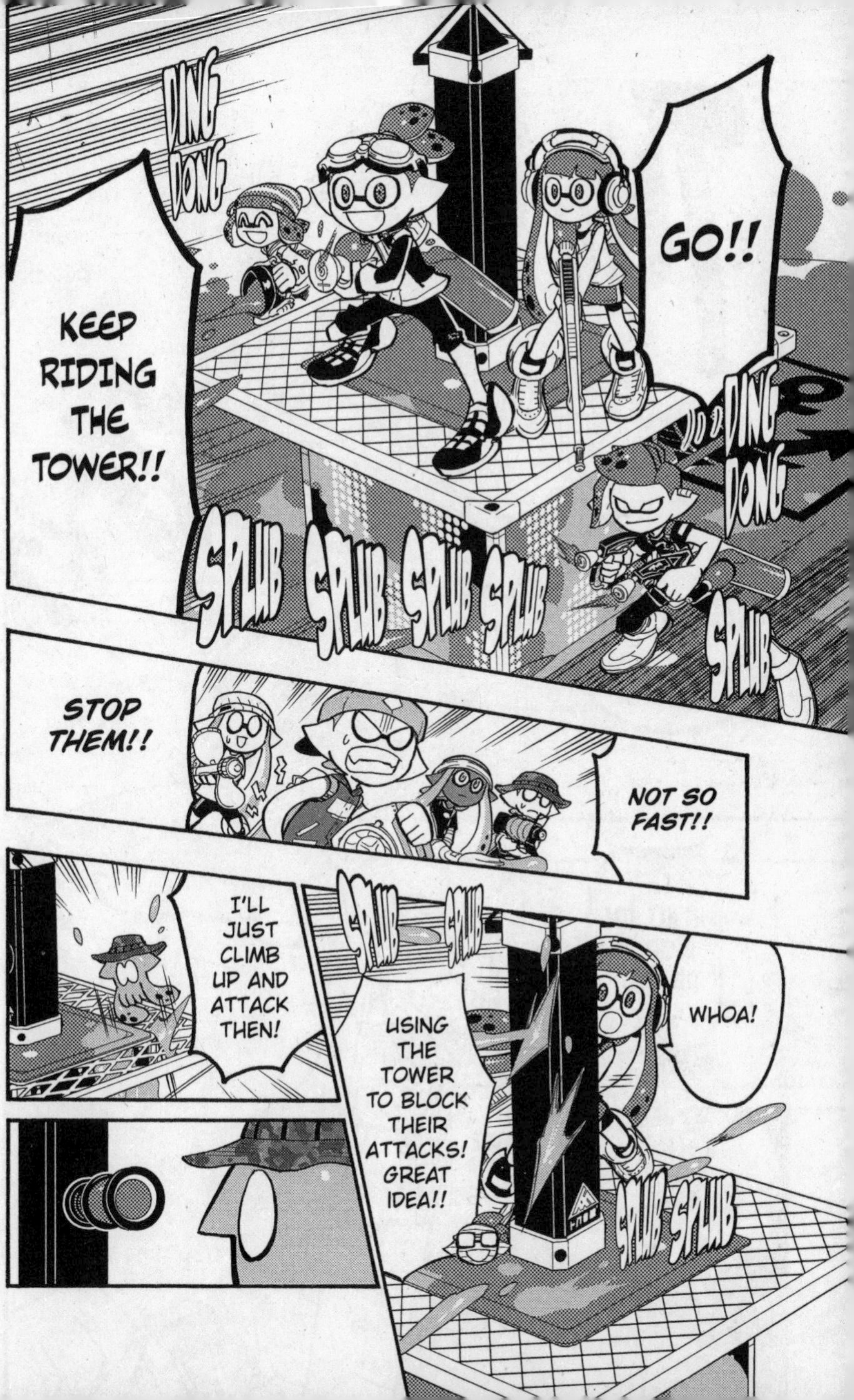
GO!!
DING DONG
DING DONG
KEEP RIDING THE TOWER!!
SPLUB SPLUB SPLUB SPLUB
SPLUB
NOT SO FAST!!
STOP THEM!!
WHOA!
SPLUB SPLUB
SPLUB SPLUB
USING THE TOWER TO BLOCK THEIR ATTACKS! GREAT IDEA!!
I'LL JUST CLIMB UP AND ATTACK THEN!

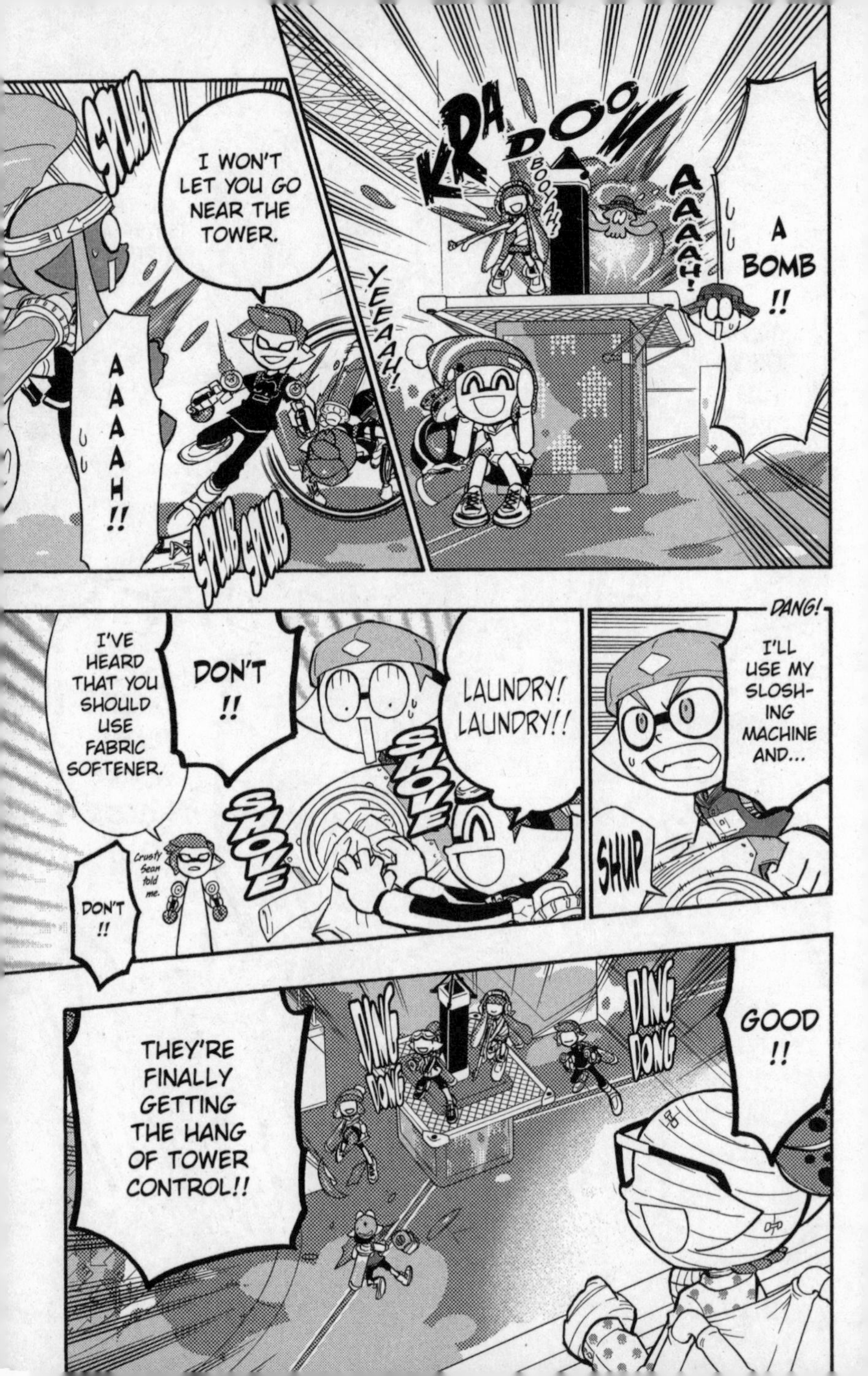
KRADOOM
BOOYAH!
AAAAAH!
A BOMB !!
YEEAAAH!
SPLUB
I WON'T LET YOU GO NEAR THE TOWER.
AAAAAH!!
SPLUB SPLUB
DANG!
I'LL USE MY SLOSH-ING MACHINE AND...
SHUP
LAUNDRY! LAUNDRY!!
SHOVE
SHOVE
DON'T !!
I'VE HEARD THAT YOU SHOULD USE FABRIC SOFTENER.
Crusty Sean told me.
DON'T !!
GOOD !!
DING DONG
DING DONG
THEY'RE FINALLY GETTING THE HANG OF TOWER CONTROL!!

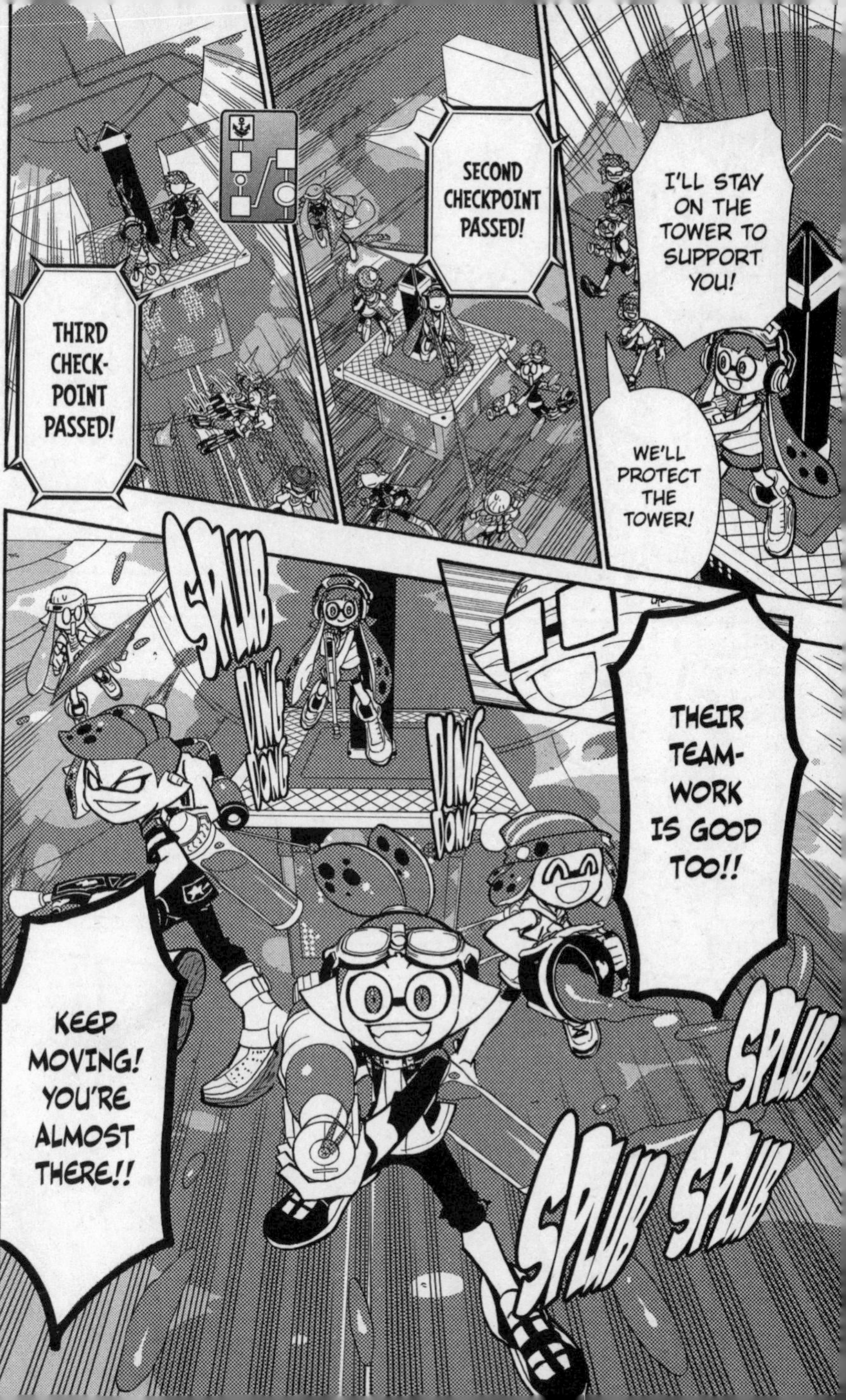
I'LL STAY ON THE TOWER TO SUPPORT YOU!
WE'LL PROTECT THE TOWER!
SECOND CHECKPOINT PASSED!
THIRD CHECK-POINT PASSED!
THEIR TEAM-WORK IS GOOD TOO!!
SPLUB
SPLUB SPLUB
DING DONG
DING DONG
SPLUB
KEEP MOVING! YOU'RE ALMOST THERE!!

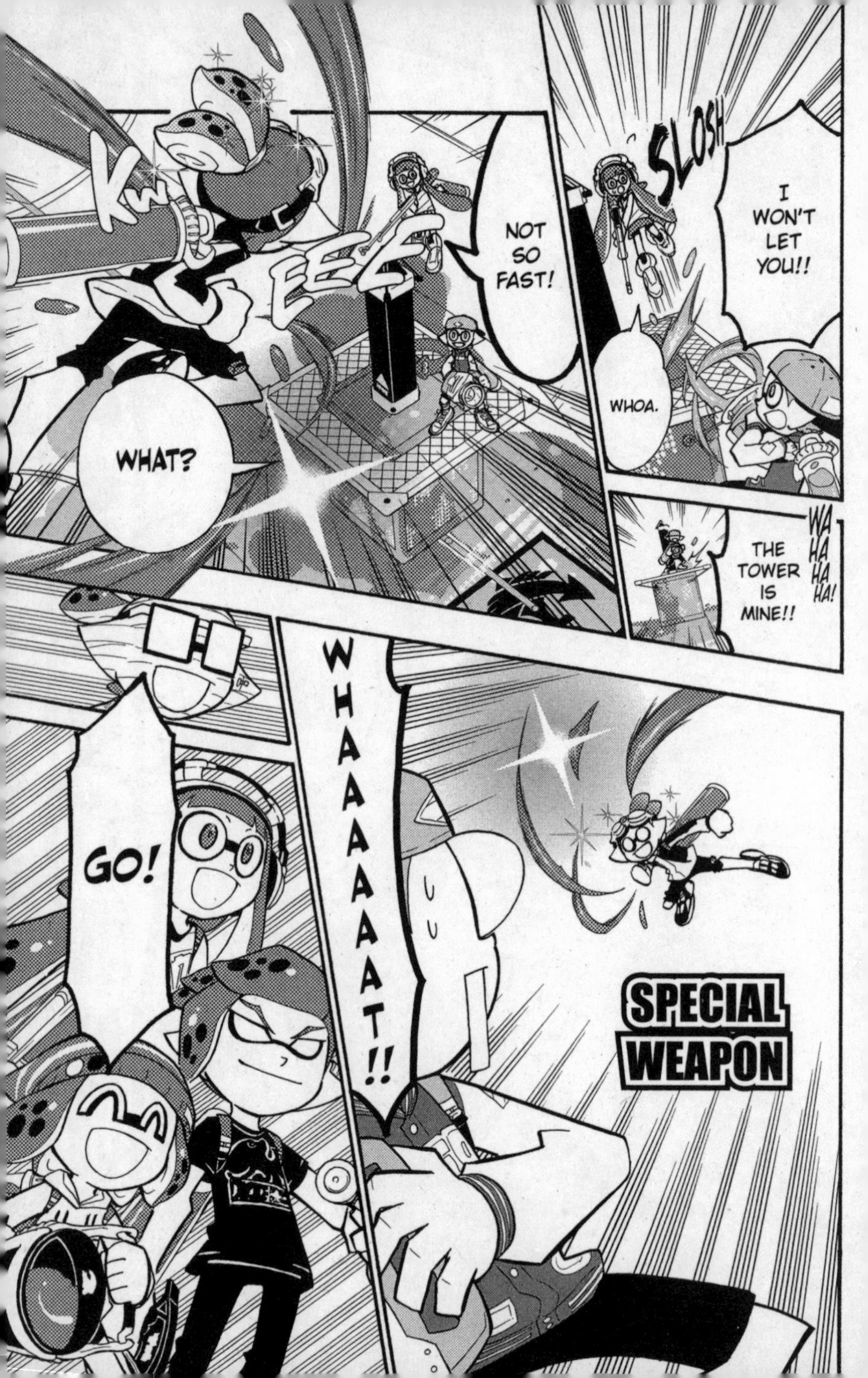
SLOSH
I WON'T LET YOU!!
WHOA.
THE TOWER IS MINE!!
WA HA HA HA!
KWEEE
NOT SO FAST!
WHAT?
WHAAAAAAAT!!
SPECIAL WEAPON
GO!

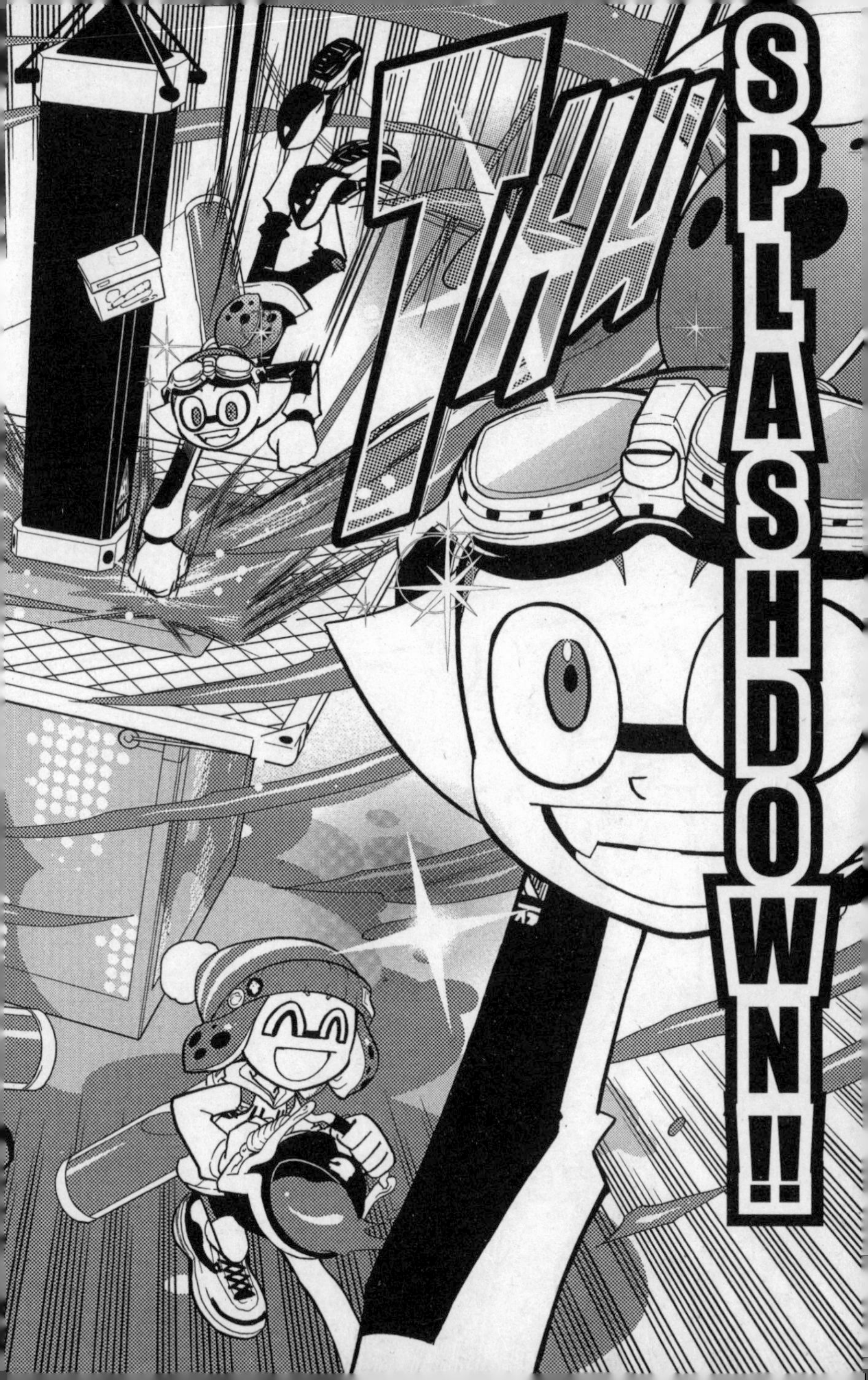
SPLASHDOWN!!

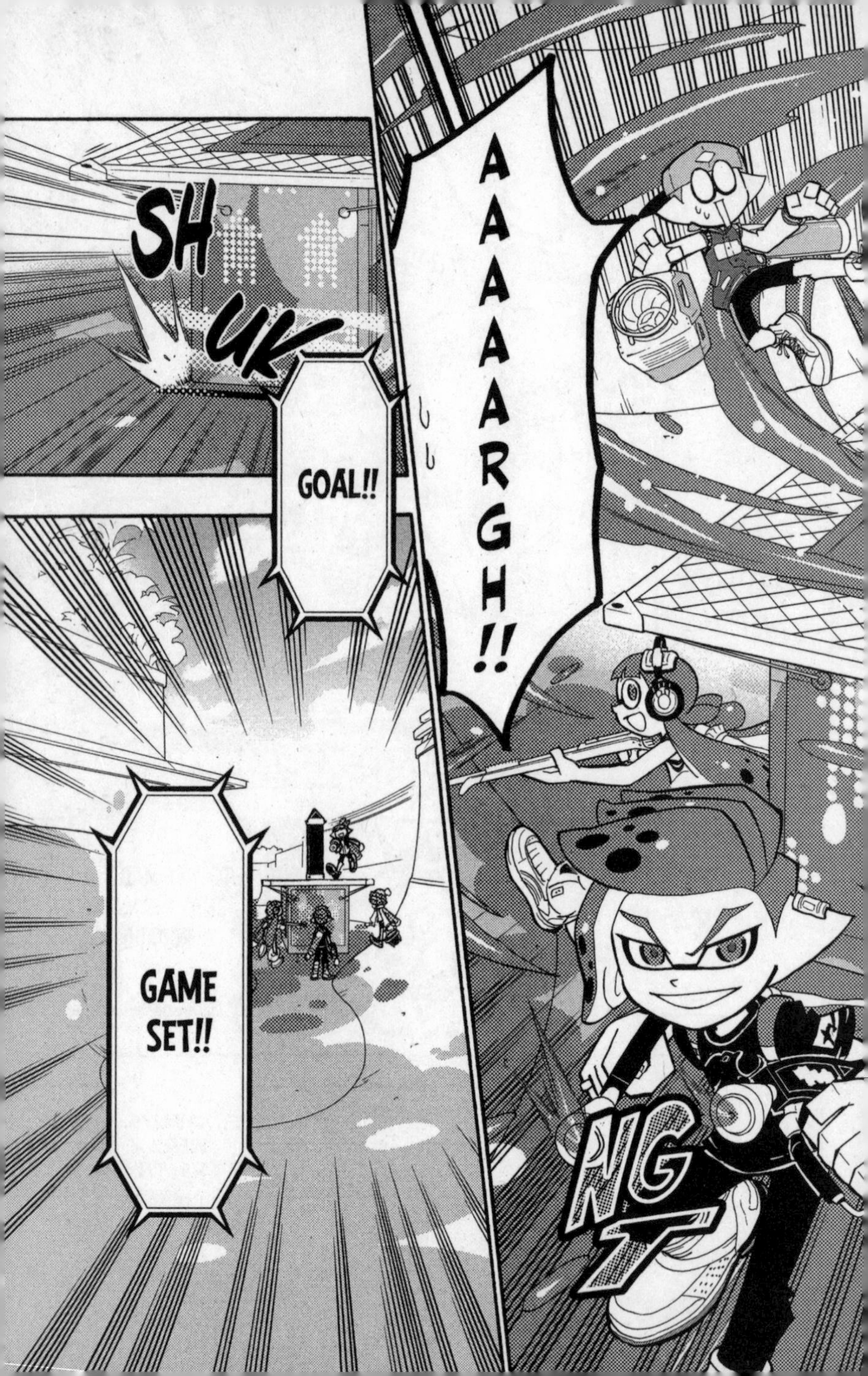
AAAAARGH!!
NG
SH UK
GOAL!!
GAME SET!!

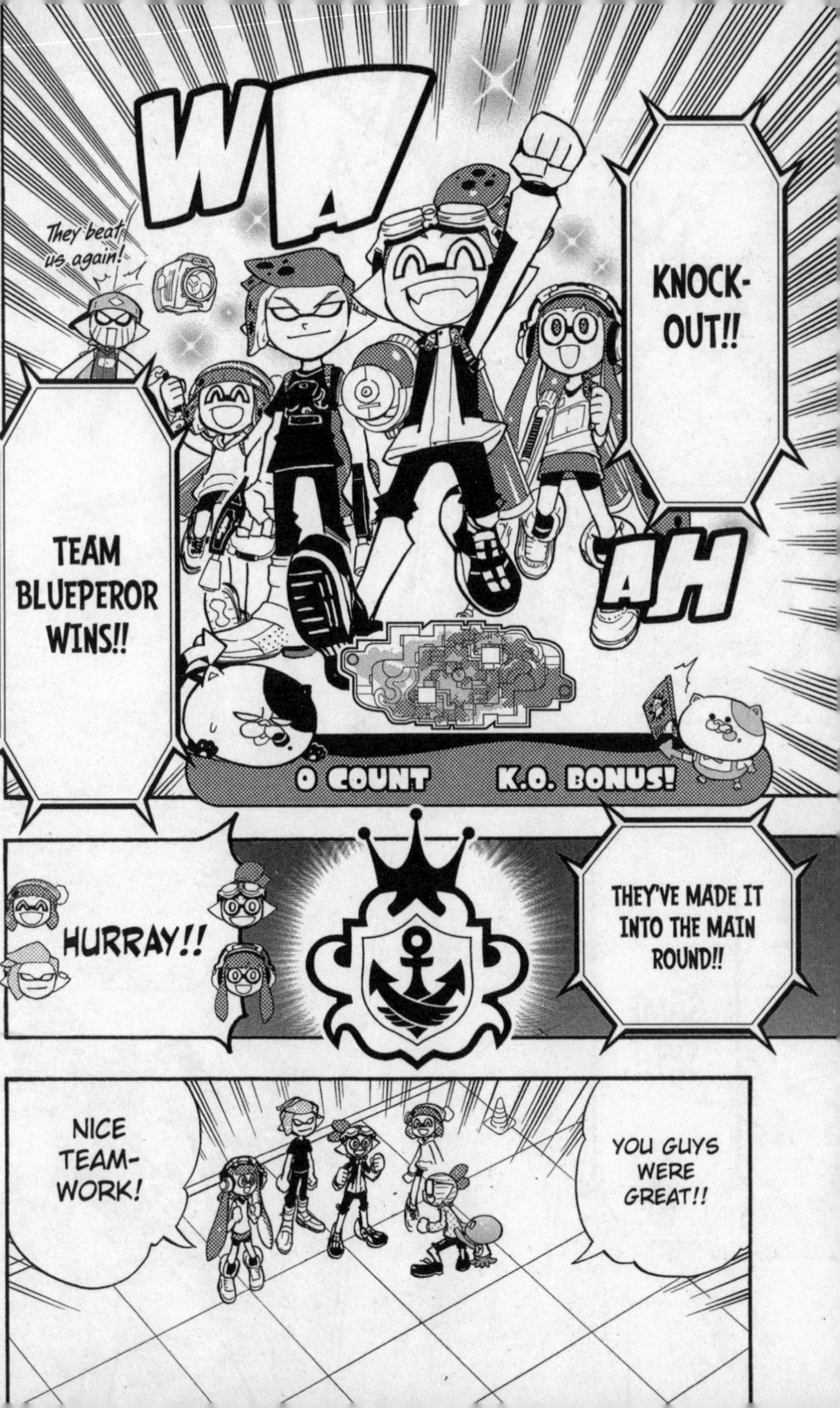
KNOCK-OUT!!
WAAH
They beat us again!
TEAM BLUEPEROR WINS!!
0 COUNT K.O. BONUS!
THEY'VE MADE IT INTO THE MAIN ROUND!!
HURRAY!!
YOU GUYS WERE GREAT!!
NICE TEAM-WORK!

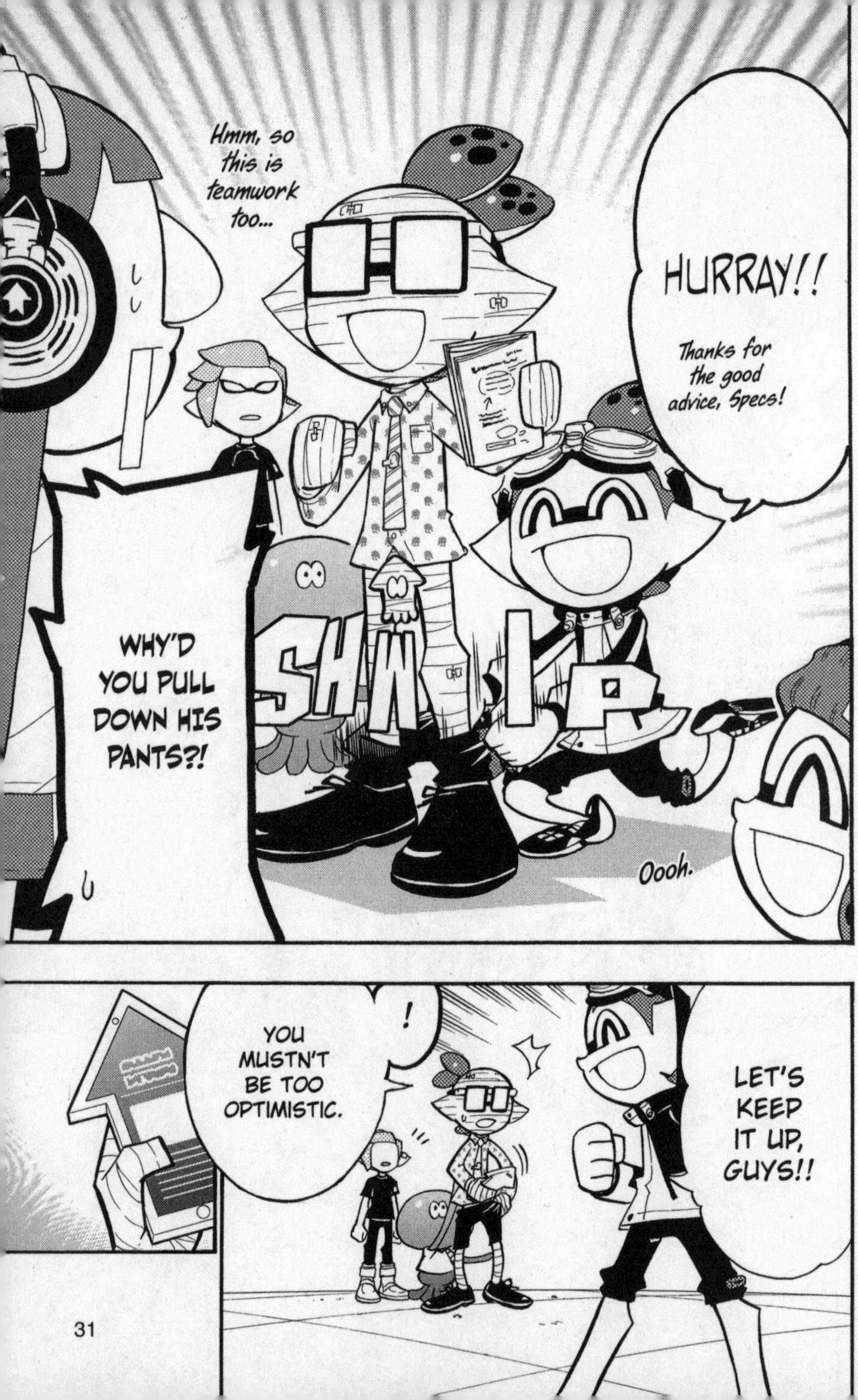
HURRAY!!
Thanks for the good advice, Specs!
Hmm, so this is teamwork too...
SHWIP
WHY'D YOU PULL DOWN HIS PANTS?!
Oooh.
LET'S KEEP IT UP, GUYS!!
!
YOU MUSTN'T BE TOO OPTIMISTIC.

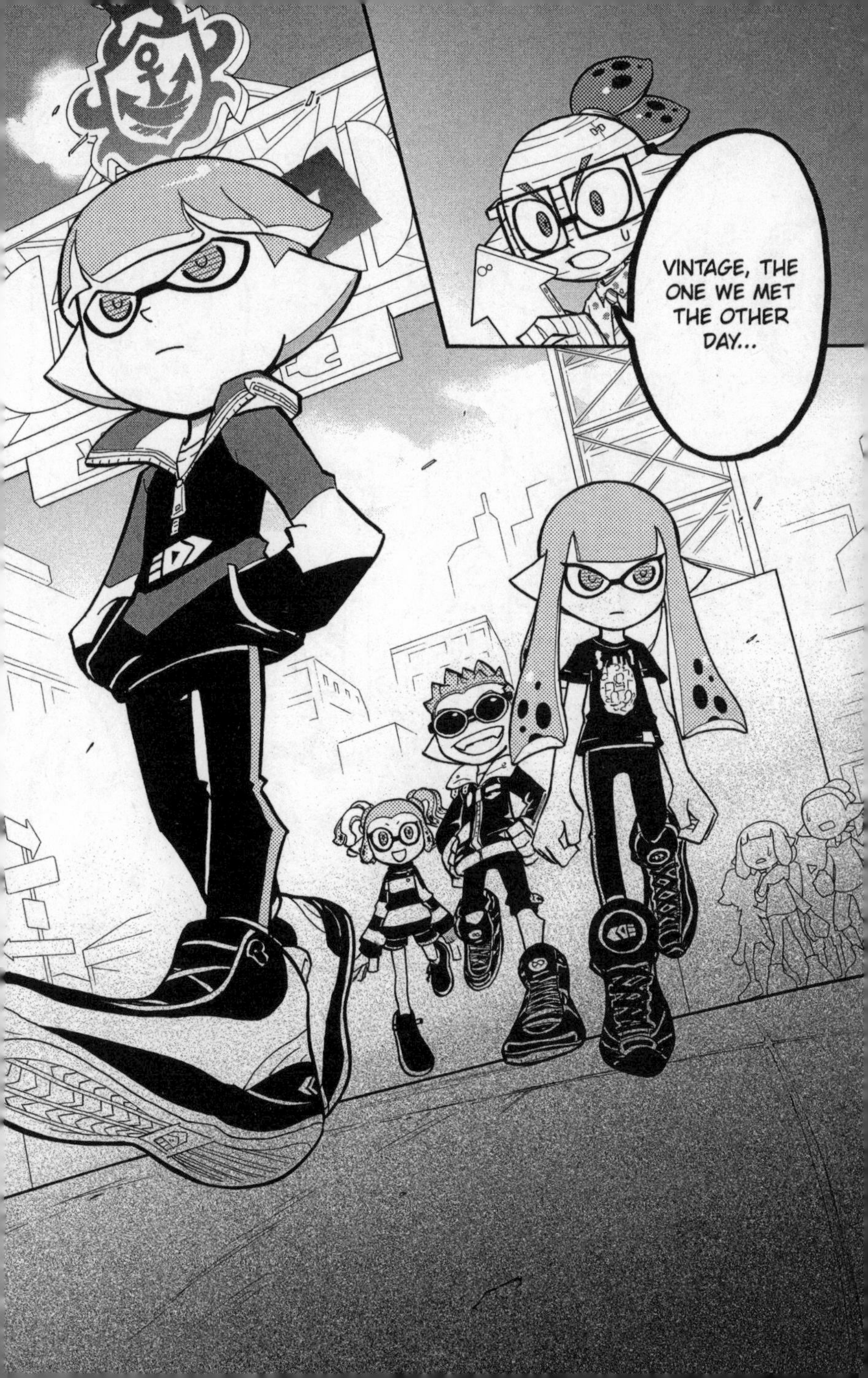
VINTAGE, THE ONE WE MET THE OTHER DAY...

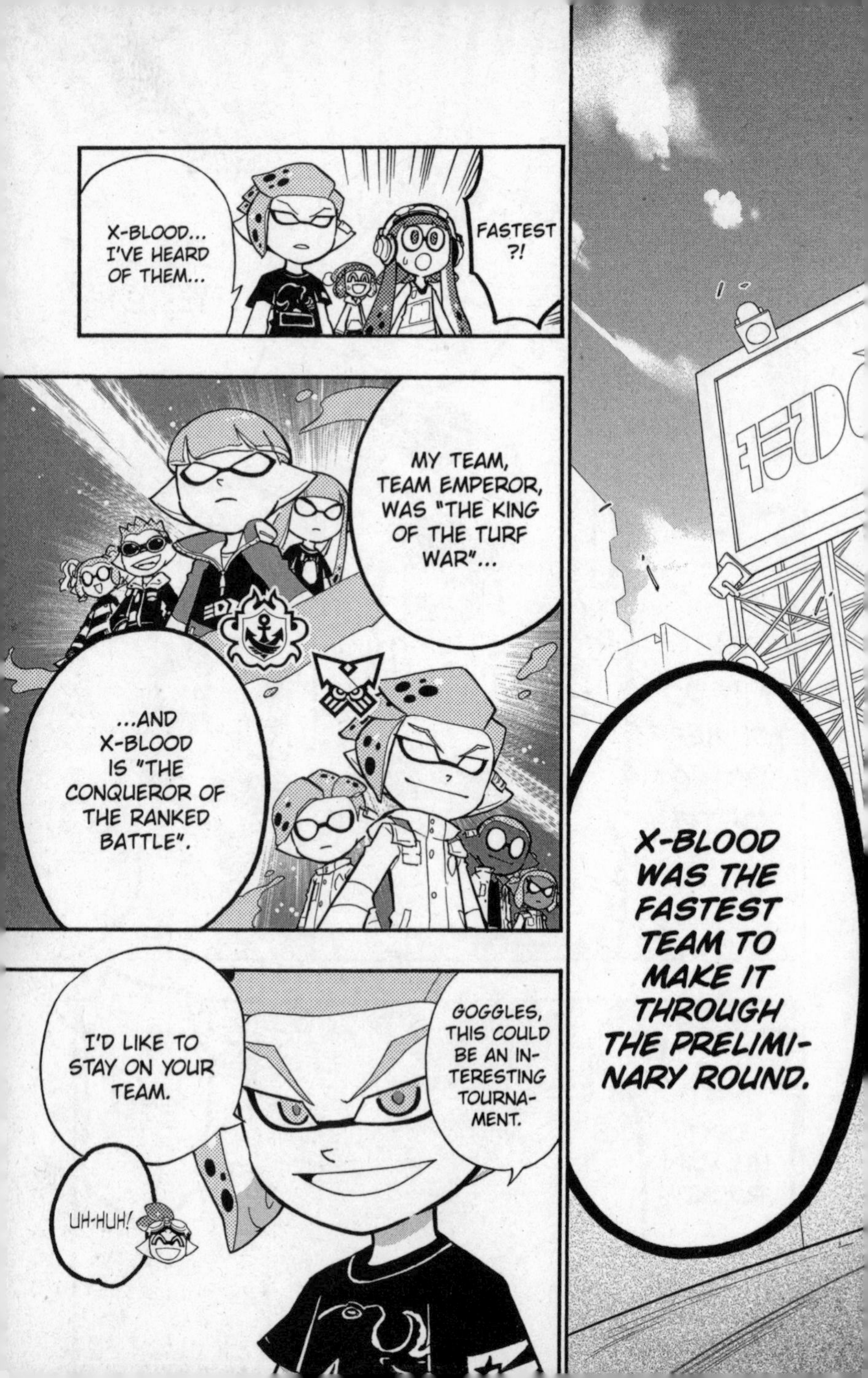
X-BLOOD WAS THE FASTEST TEAM TO MAKE IT THROUGH THE PRELIMI-NARY ROUND.
FASTEST ?!
X-BLOOD... I'VE HEARD OF THEM...
MY TEAM, TEAM EMPEROR, WAS "THE KING OF THE TURF WAR"...
...AND X-BLOOD IS "THE CONQUEROR OF THE RANKED BATTLE".
GOGGLES, THIS COULD BE AN IN-TERESTING TOURNA-MENT.
I'D LIKE TO STAY ON YOUR TEAM.
UH-HUH!

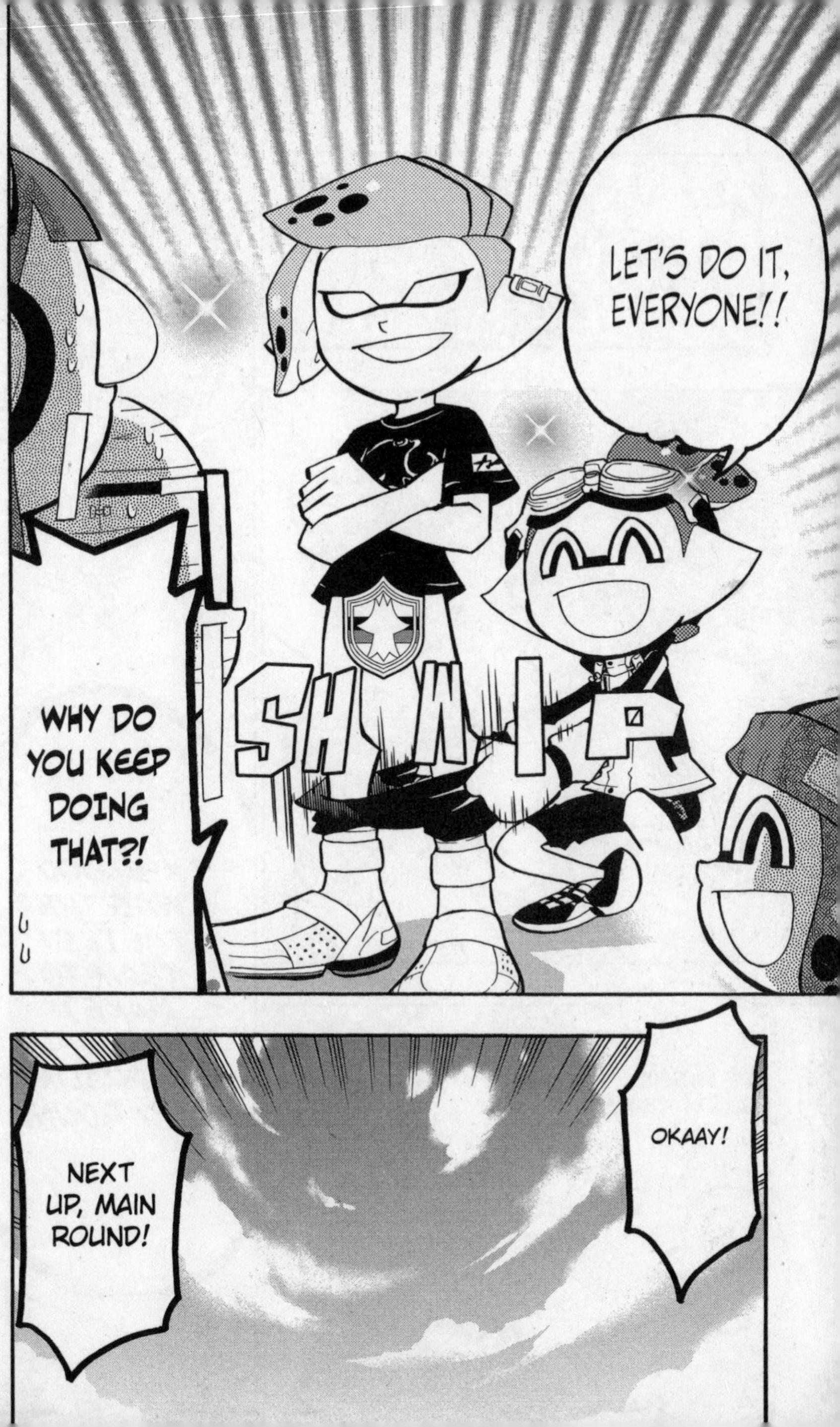
LET'S DO IT, EVERYONE!!
SHWIP
WHY DO YOU KEEP DOING THAT?!
OKAAY!
NEXT UP, MAIN ROUND!

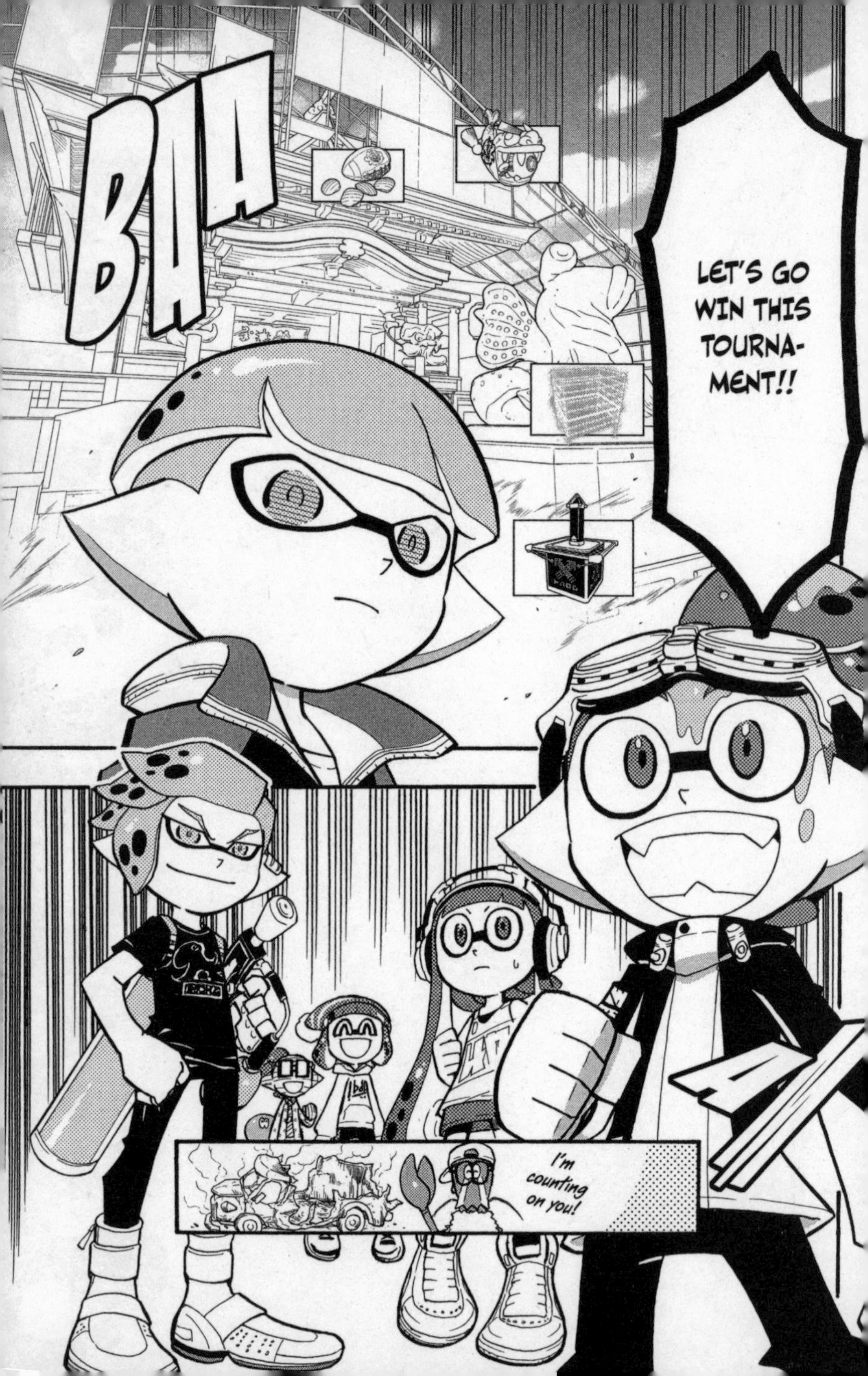
LET'S GO WIN THIS TOURNA-MENT!!
BAA
I'm counting on you!

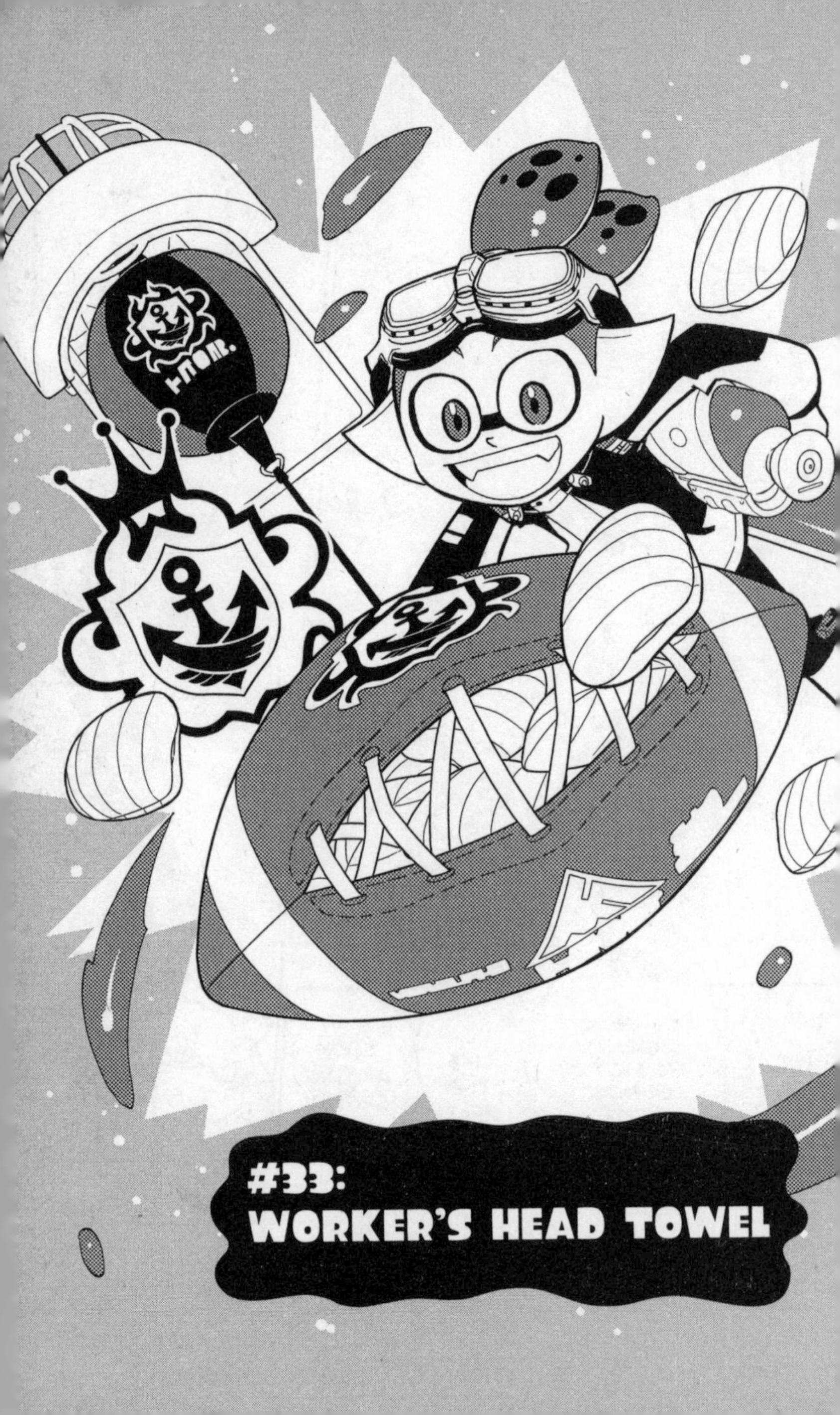

#33: WORKER'S HEAD TOWEL

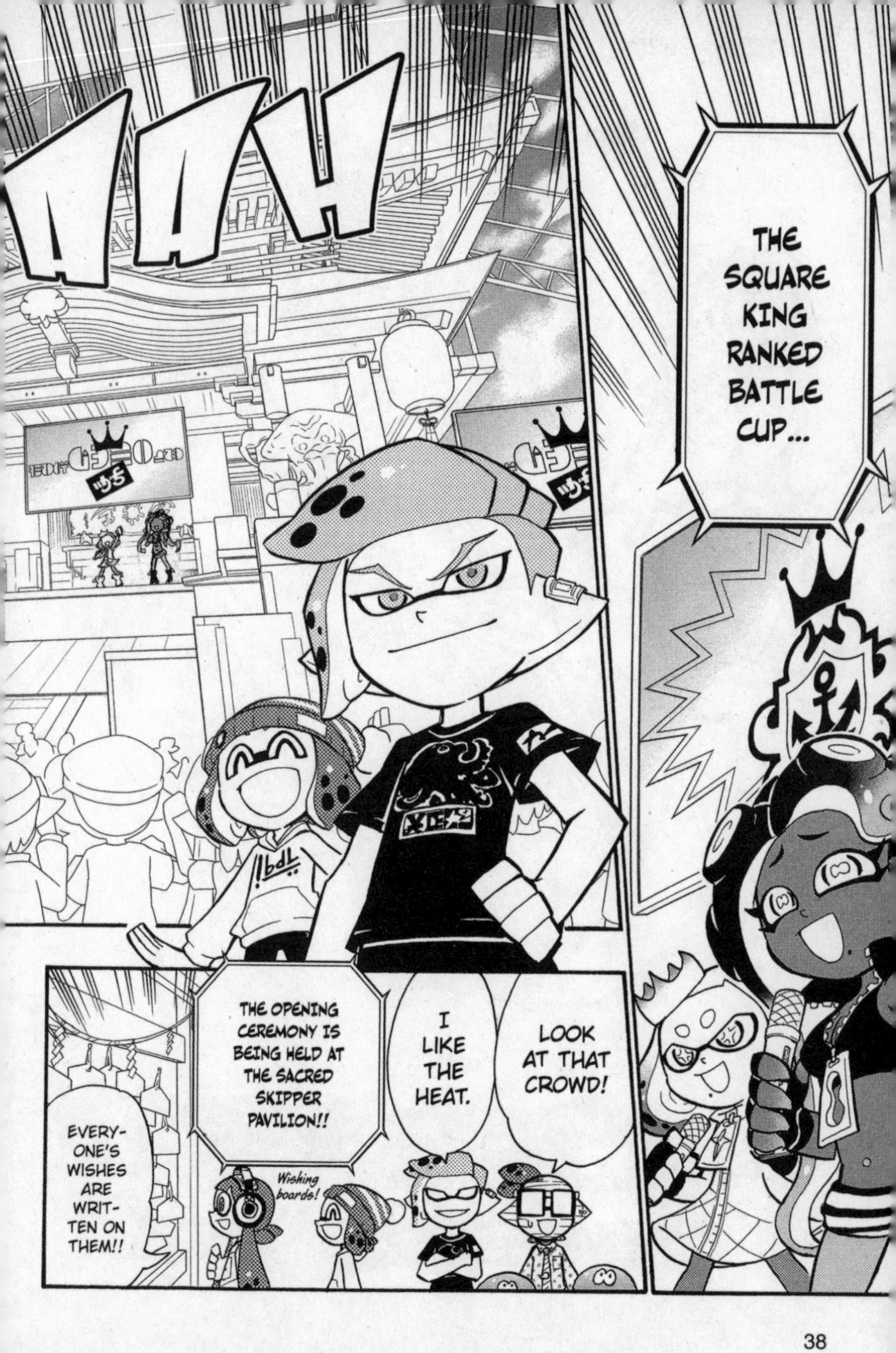
THE SQUARE KING RANKED BATTLE CUP...
WAAH
LOOK AT THAT CROWD!
I LIKE THE HEAT.
THE OPENING CEREMONY IS BEING HELD AT THE SACRED SKIPPER PAVILION!!
Wishing boards!
EVERY-ONE'S WISHES ARE WRIT-TEN ON THEM!!

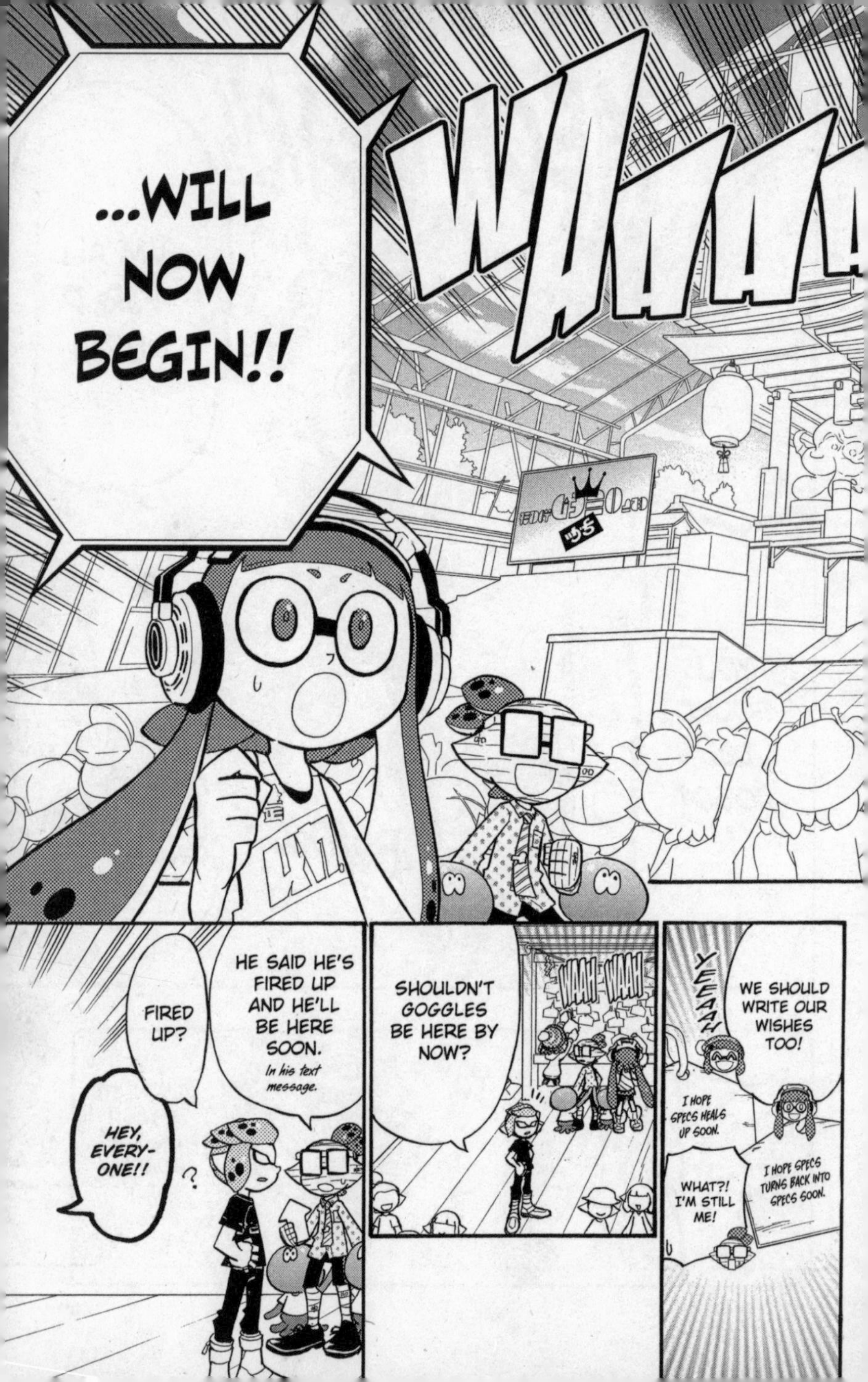
...WILL NOW BEGIN!!
WAAAA
YEEAAAH
WE SHOULD WRITE OUR WISHES TOO!
I HOPE SPECS HEALS UP SOON.
I HOPE SPECS TURNS BACK INTO SPECS SOON.
WHAT?! I'M STILL ME!
WAAH WAAH
SHOULDN'T GOGGLES BE HERE BY NOW?
HE SAID HE'S FIRED UP AND HE'LL BE HERE SOON.
In his text message.
FIRED UP?
HEY, EVERY-ONE!!

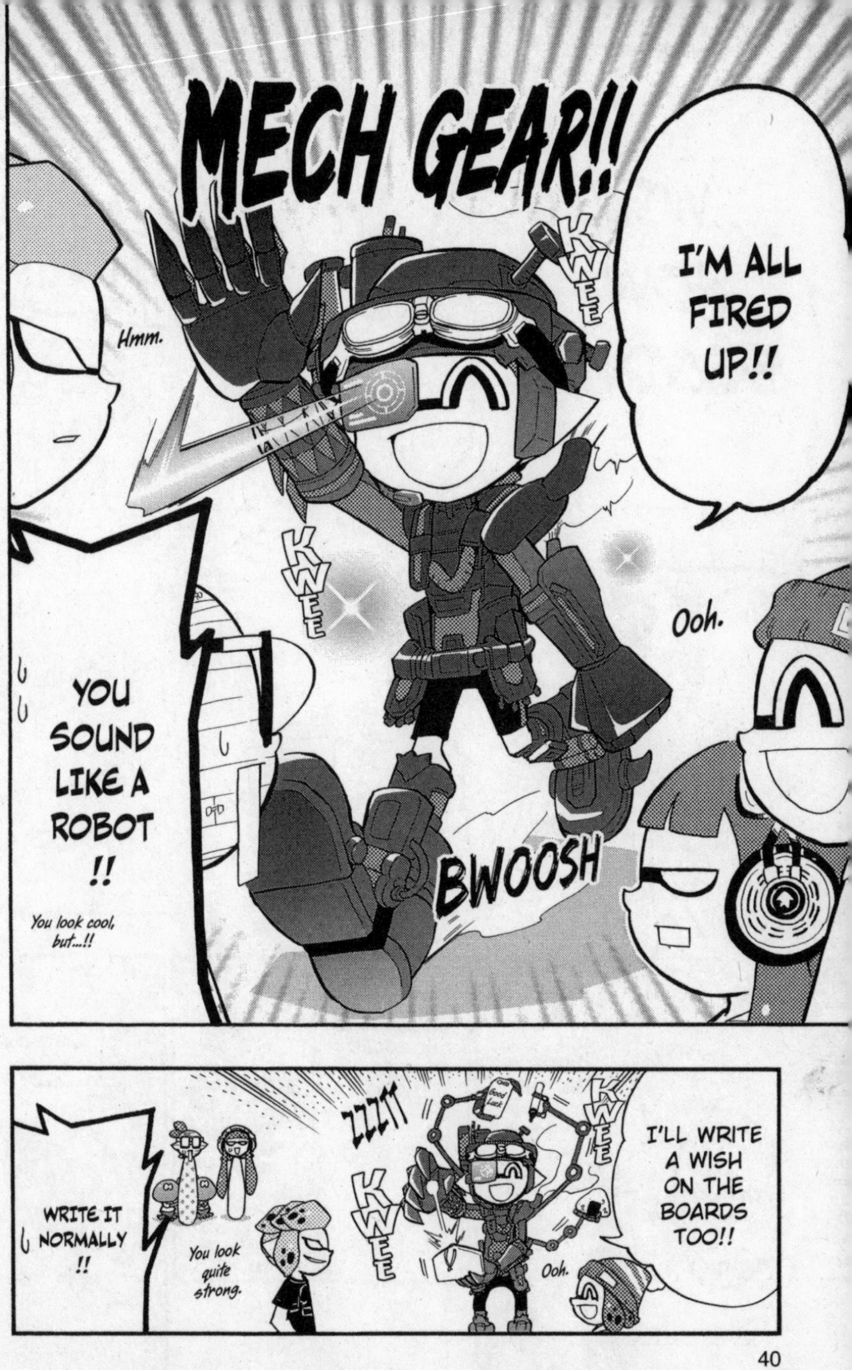
MECH GEAR!!
I'M ALL FIRED UP!!
KWEE
KWEE
Hmm.
Ooh.
BWOOSH
YOU SOUND LIKE A ROBOT!!
You look cool, but...!!
I'LL WRITE A WISH ON THE BOARDS TOO!!
KWEE
Good Luck
ZZZTT
KWEE
Ooh.
You look quite strong.
WRITE IT NORMALLY!!

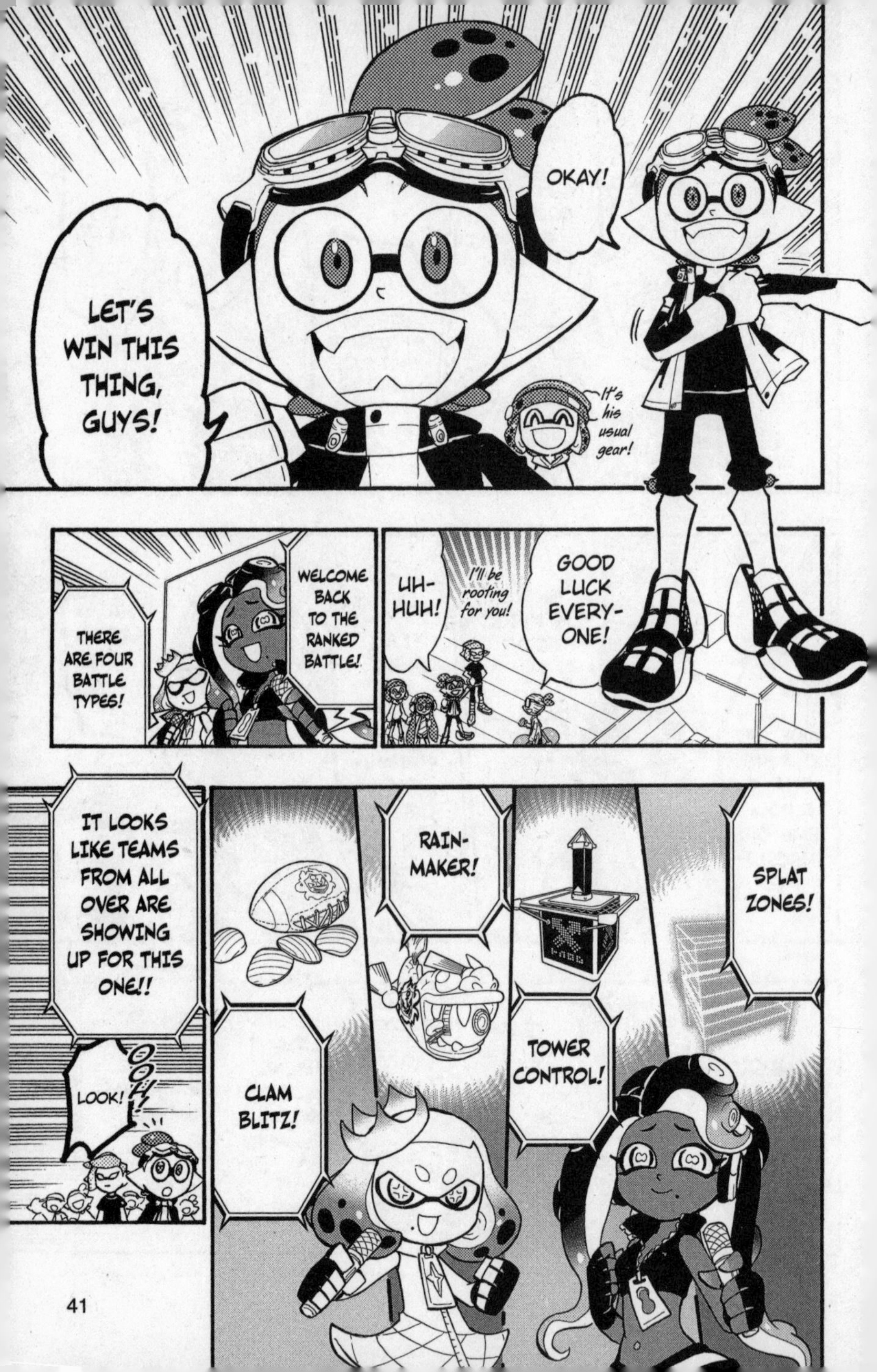
OKAY!
LET'S WIN THIS THING, GUYS!
It's his usual gear!
GOOD LUCK EVERY-ONE!
I'll be rooting for you!
UH-HUH!
WELCOME BACK TO THE RANKED BATTLE!
THERE ARE FOUR BATTLE TYPES!
SPLAT ZONES!
RAIN-MAKER!
TOWER CONTROL!
CLAM BLITZ!
IT LOOKS LIKE TEAMS FROM ALL OVER ARE SHOWING UP FOR THIS ONE!!
OOOH!!
LOOK!

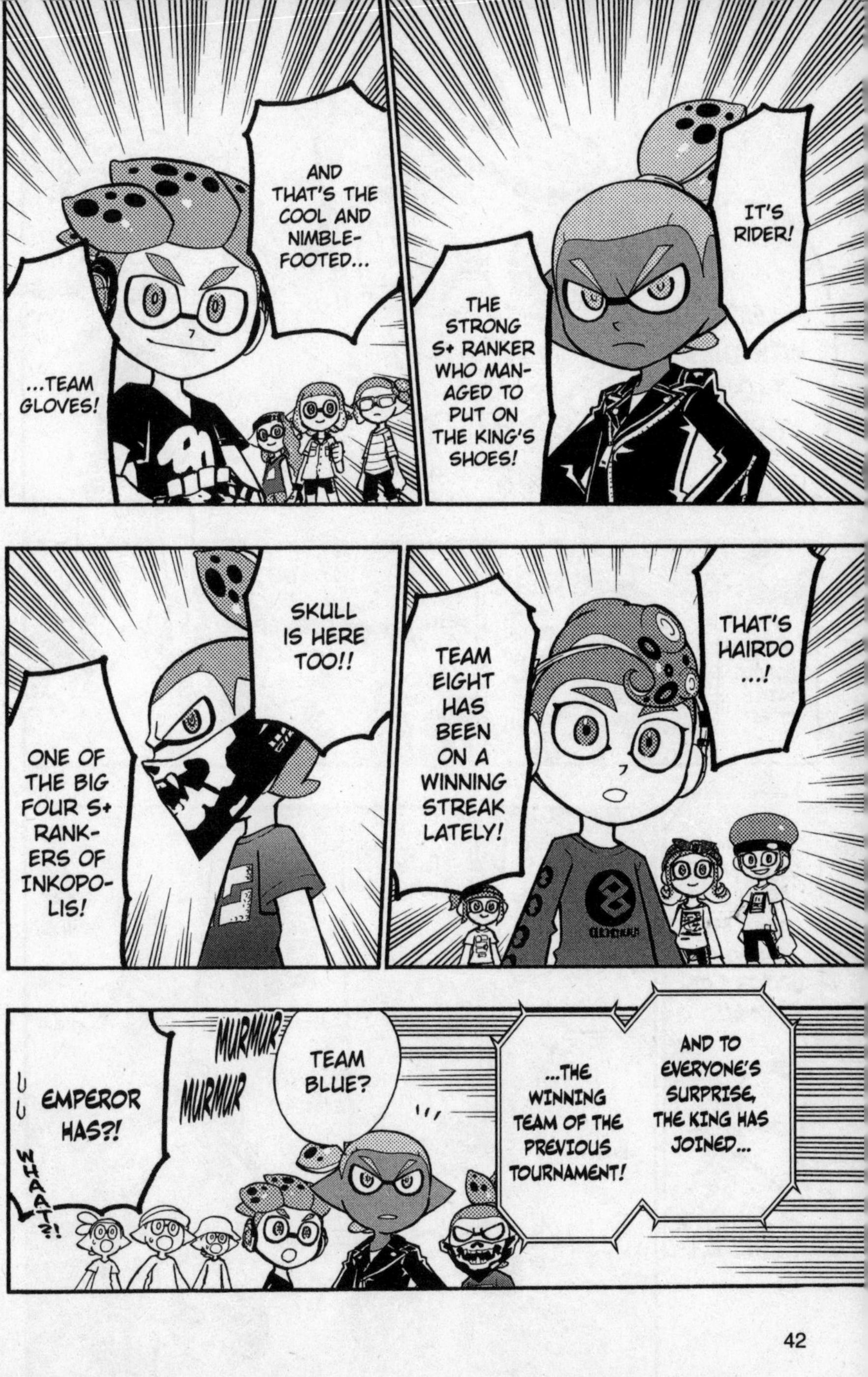
IT'S RIDER!
THE STRONG S+ RANKER WHO MAN-AGED TO PUT ON THE KING'S SHOES!
AND THAT'S THE COOL AND NIMBLE-FOOTED...
...TEAM GLOVES!
THAT'S HAIRDO ...!
TEAM EIGHT HAS BEEN ON A WINNING STREAK LATELY!
SKULL IS HERE TOO!!
ONE OF THE BIG FOUR S+ RANK-ERS OF INKOPO-LIS!
AND TO EVERYONE'S SURPRISE, THE KING HAS JOINED...
...THE WINNING TEAM OF THE PREVIOUS TOURNAMENT!
TEAM BLUE?
MURMUR
MURMUR
EMPEROR HAS?!
WHAAAT?!

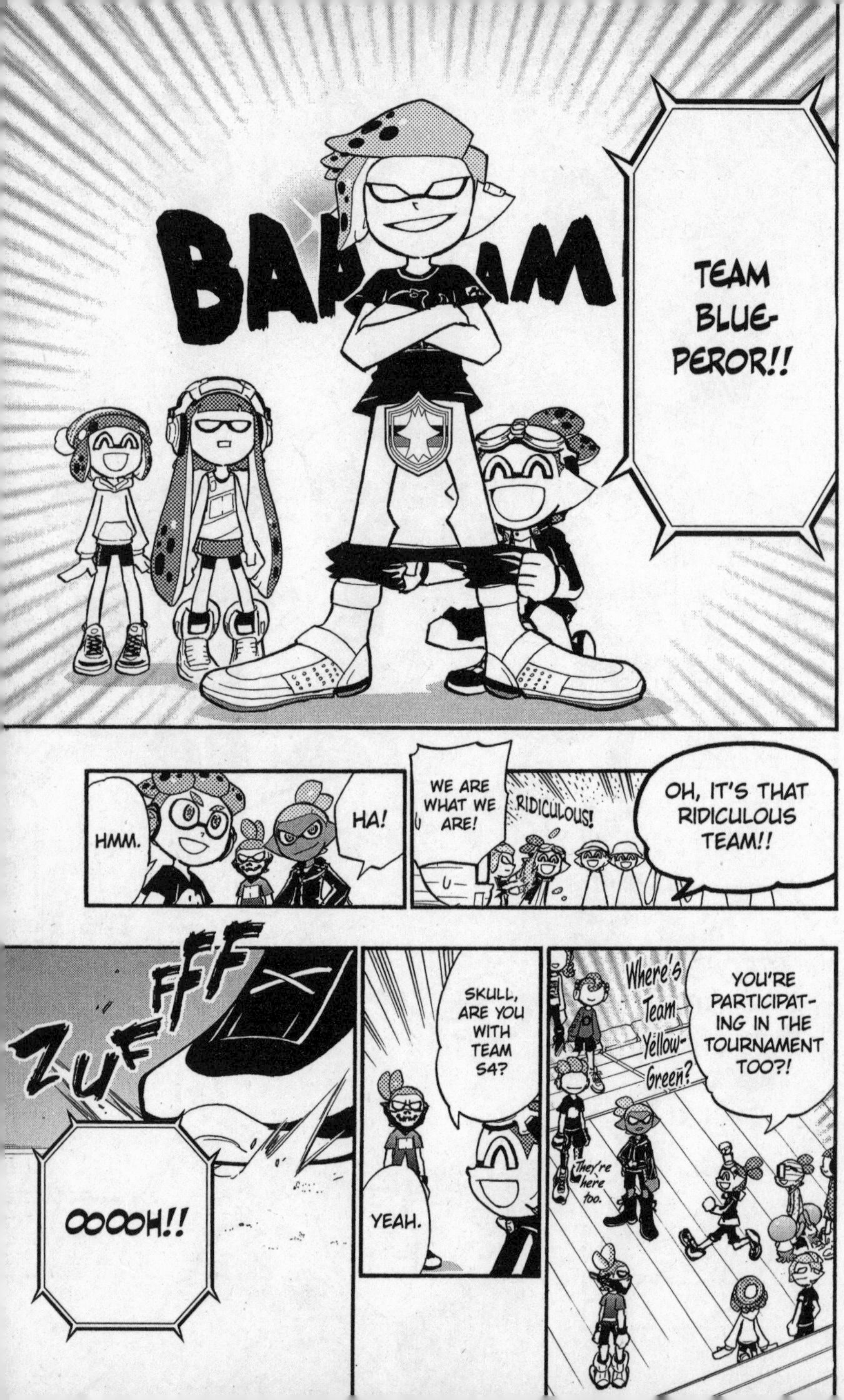
TEAM BLUE-PEROR!!
OH, IT'S THAT RIDICULOUS TEAM!!
RIDICULOUS!
WE ARE WHAT WE ARE!
HA!
HMM.
YOU'RE PARTICIPATING IN THE TOURNAMENT TOO?!
Where's Team Yellow-Green?
They're here too.
SKULL, ARE YOU WITH TEAM S4?
YEAH.
ZUFFFF
OOOOH!!

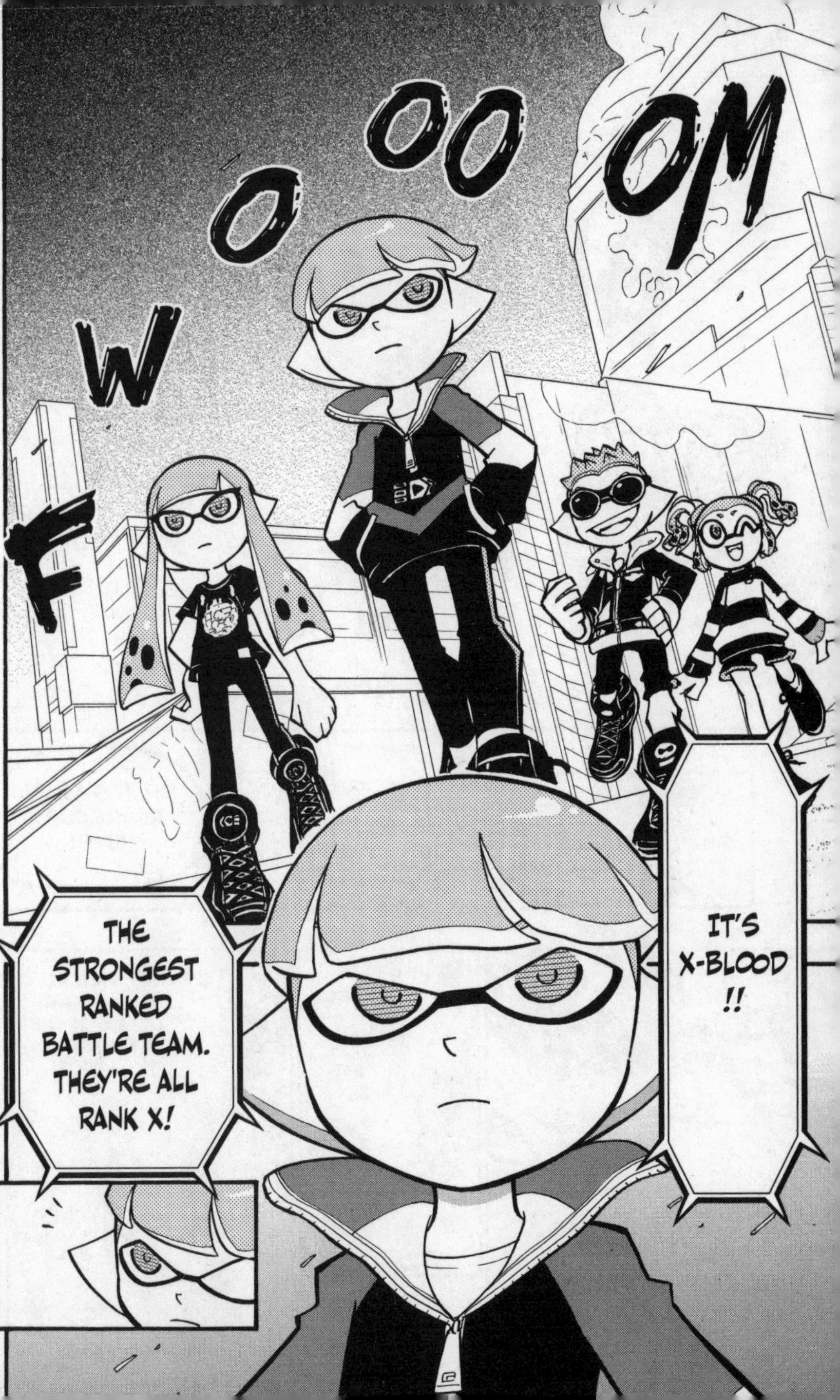
FWOOOOM
IT'S X-BLOOD !!
THE STRONGEST RANKED BATTLE TEAM. THEY'RE ALL RANK X!

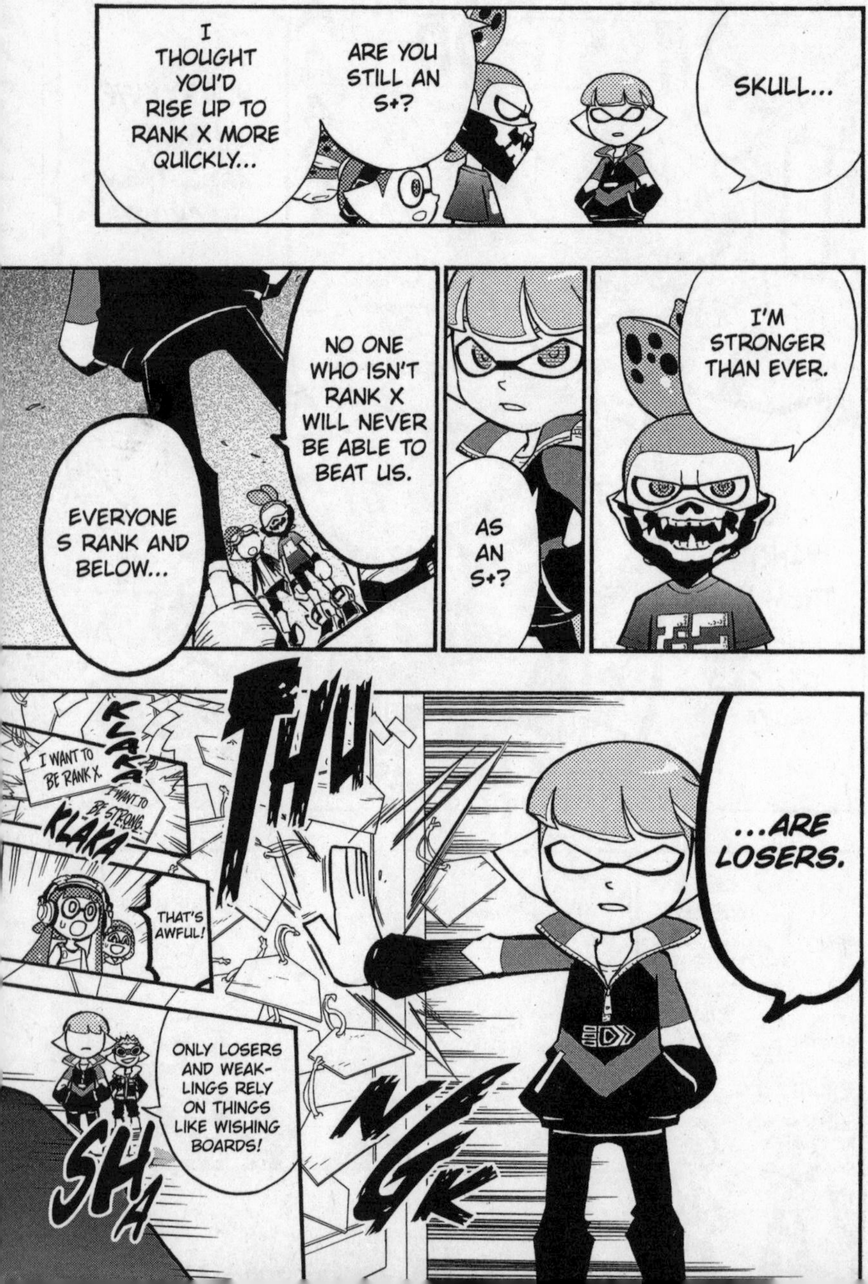
SKULL...
ARE YOU STILL AN S+?
I THOUGHT YOU'D RISE UP TO RANK X MORE QUICKLY...
I'M STRONGER THAN EVER.
AS AN S+?
NO ONE WHO ISN'T RANK X WILL NEVER BE ABLE TO BEAT US.
EVERYONE S RANK AND BELOW...
...ARE LOSERS.
THU
KLAKA
I WANT TO BE RANK X.
I WANT TO BE STRONG.
KLAKA
THAT'S AWFUL!
ONLY LOSERS AND WEAK-LINGS RELY ON THINGS LIKE WISHING BOARDS!
NK
SHA

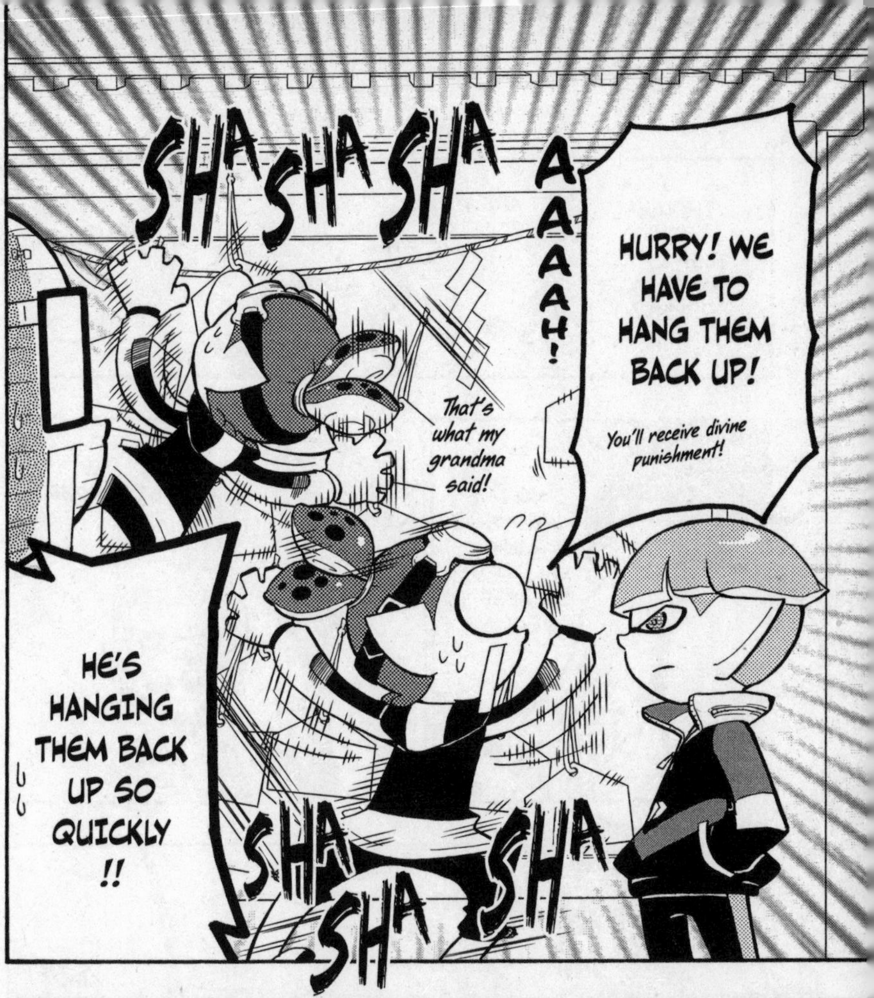
HURRY! WE HAVE TO HANG THEM BACK UP!
You'll receive divine punishment!
AAAAH!
SHA SHA SHA
That's what my grandma said!
HE'S HANGING THEM BACK UP SO QUICKLY !!
SHA SHA SHA SHA
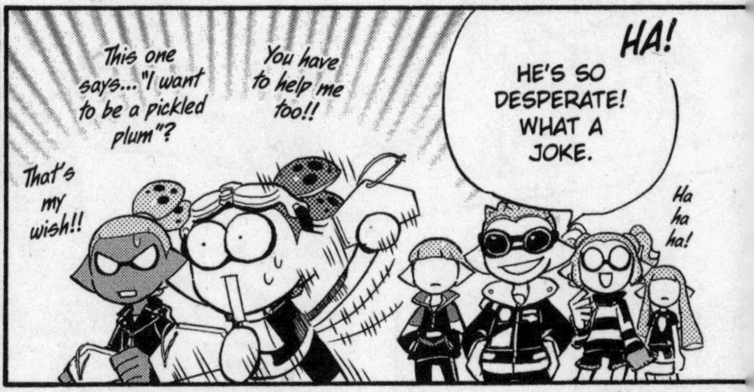
HA!
HE'S SO DESPERATE! WHAT A JOKE.
Ha ha ha!
You have to help me too!!
This one says... "I want to be a pickled plum"?
That's my wish!!
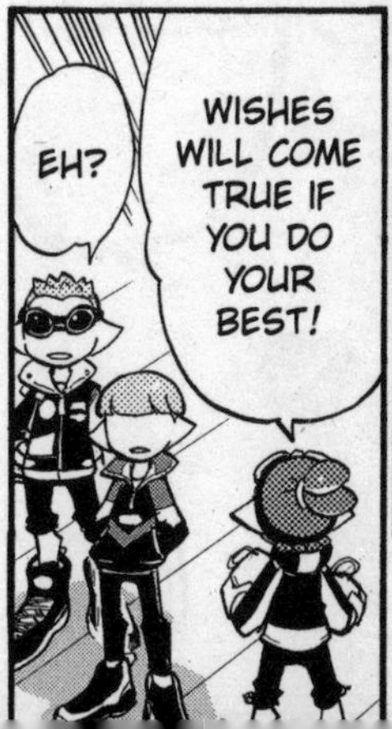
WISHES WILL COME TRUE IF YOU DO YOUR BEST!
EH?

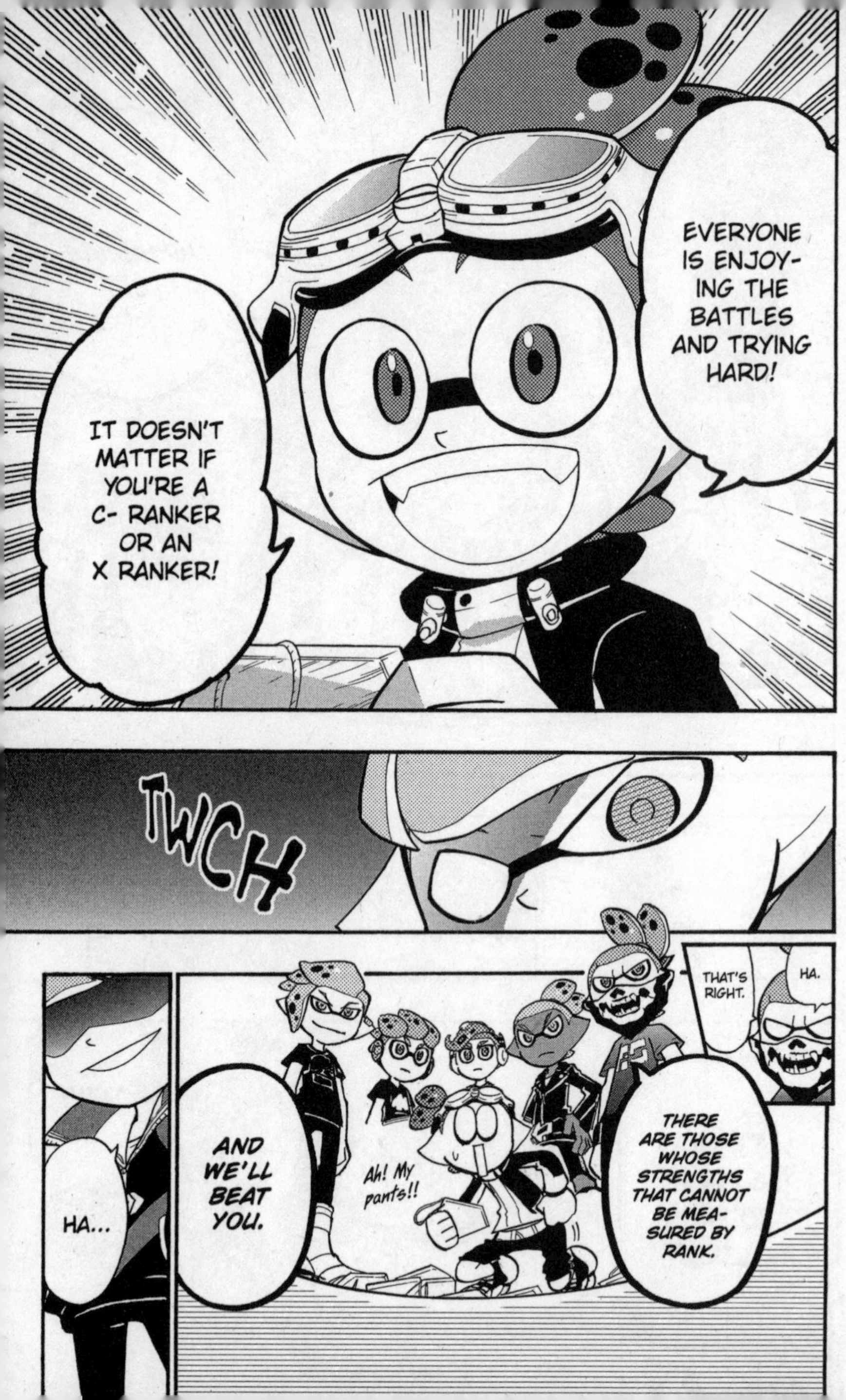
EVERYONE IS ENJOYING THE BATTLES AND TRYING HARD!
IT DOESN'T MATTER IF YOU'RE A C- RANKER OR AN X RANKER!
TWCH
HA.
THAT'S RIGHT.
THERE ARE THOSE WHOSE STRENGTHS THAT CANNOT BE MEASURED BY RANK.
Ah! My pants!!
AND WE'LL BEAT YOU.
HA...

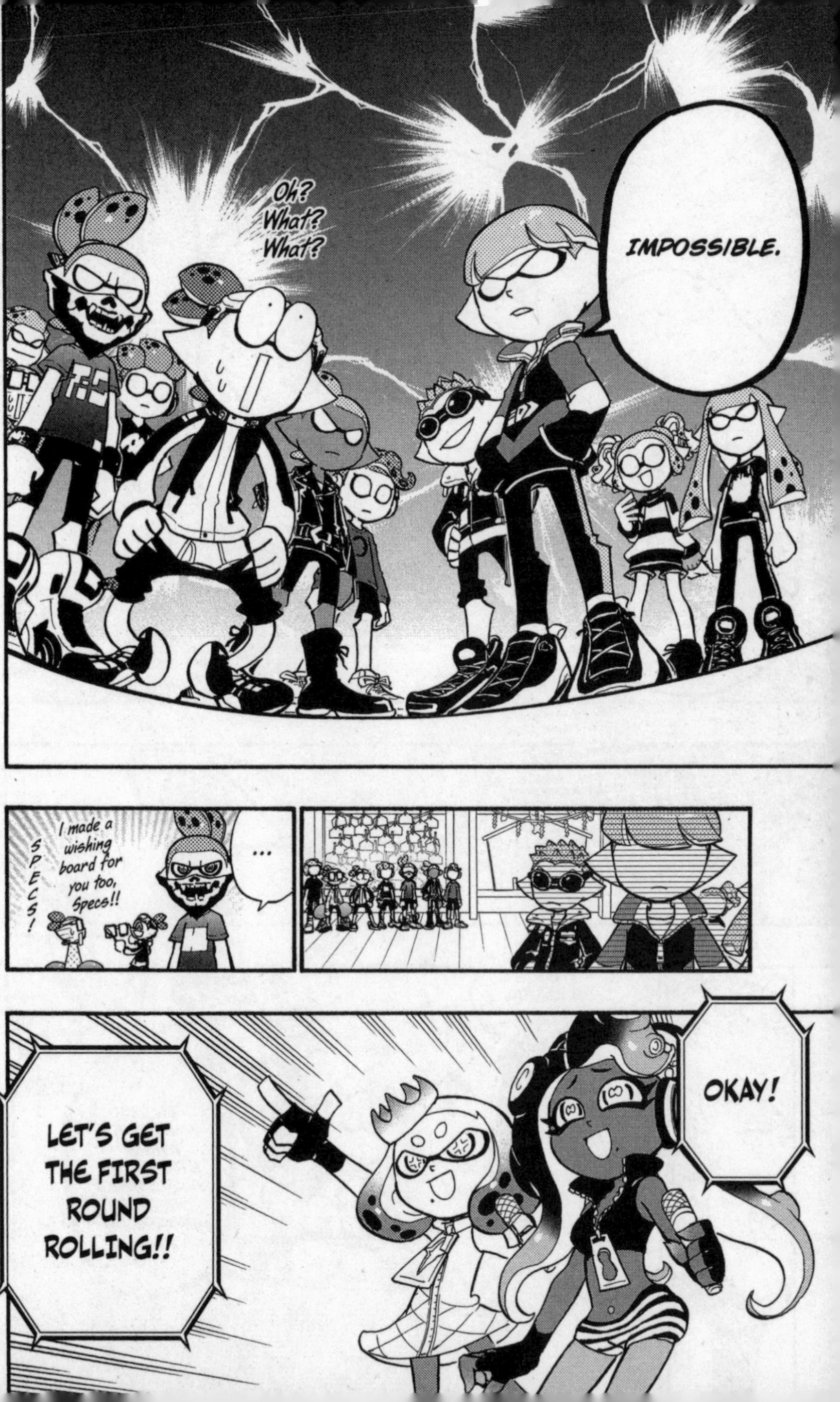
IMPOSSIBLE.
Oh? What? What?
...
I made a wishing board for you too, Specs!!
SPECS!
OKAY!
LET'S GET THE FIRST ROUND ROLLING!!

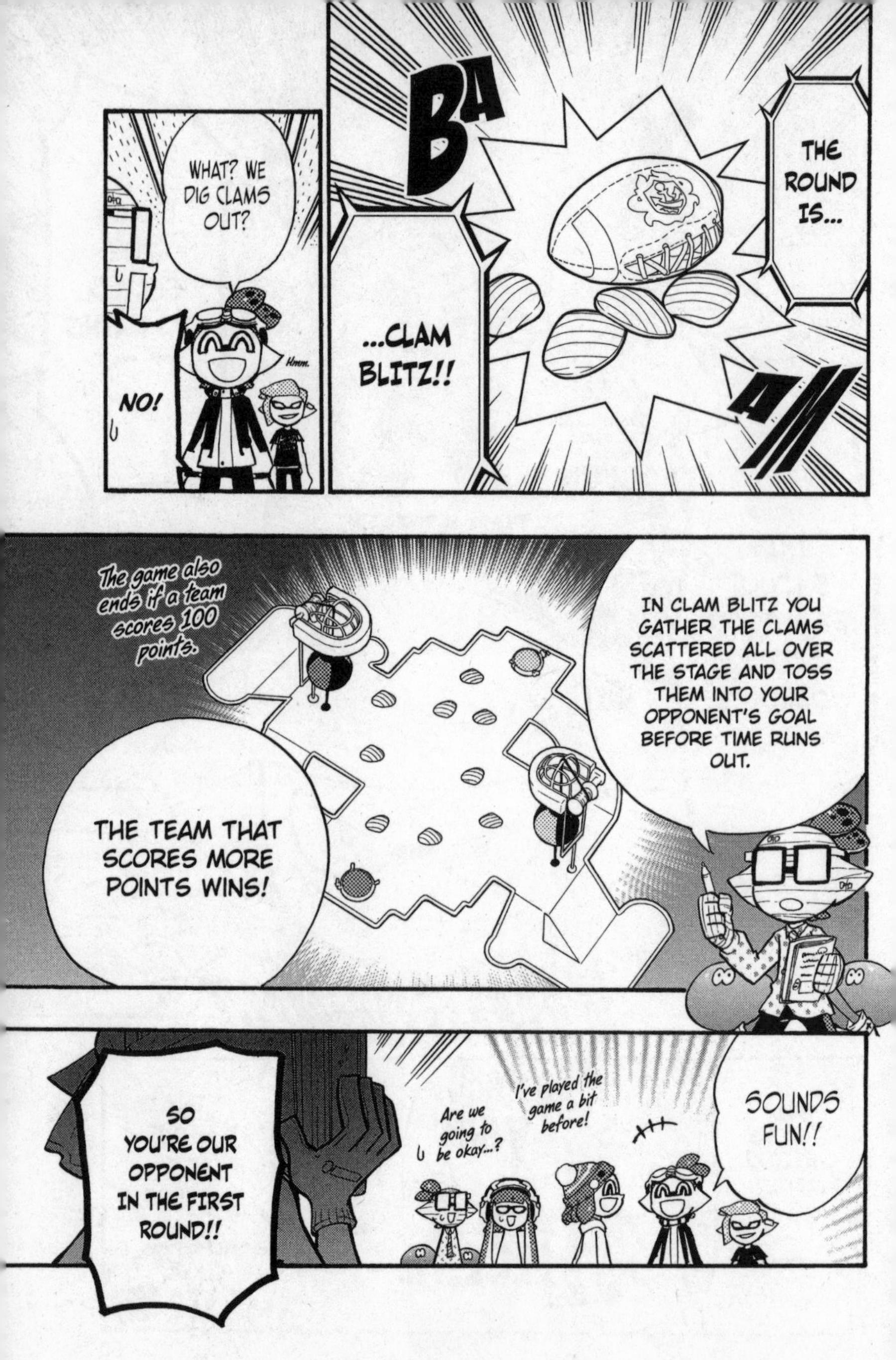
THE ROUND IS...
BAM
...CLAM BLITZ!!
WHAT? WE DIG CLAMS OUT?
NO!
Hmm.
IN CLAM BLITZ YOU GATHER THE CLAMS SCATTERED ALL OVER THE STAGE AND TOSS THEM INTO YOUR OPPONENT'S GOAL BEFORE TIME RUNS OUT.
The game also ends if a team scores 100 points.
THE TEAM THAT SCORES MORE POINTS WINS!
SOUNDS FUN!!
I've played the game a bit before!
Are we going to be okay...?
SO YOU'RE OUR OPPONENT IN THE FIRST ROUND!!

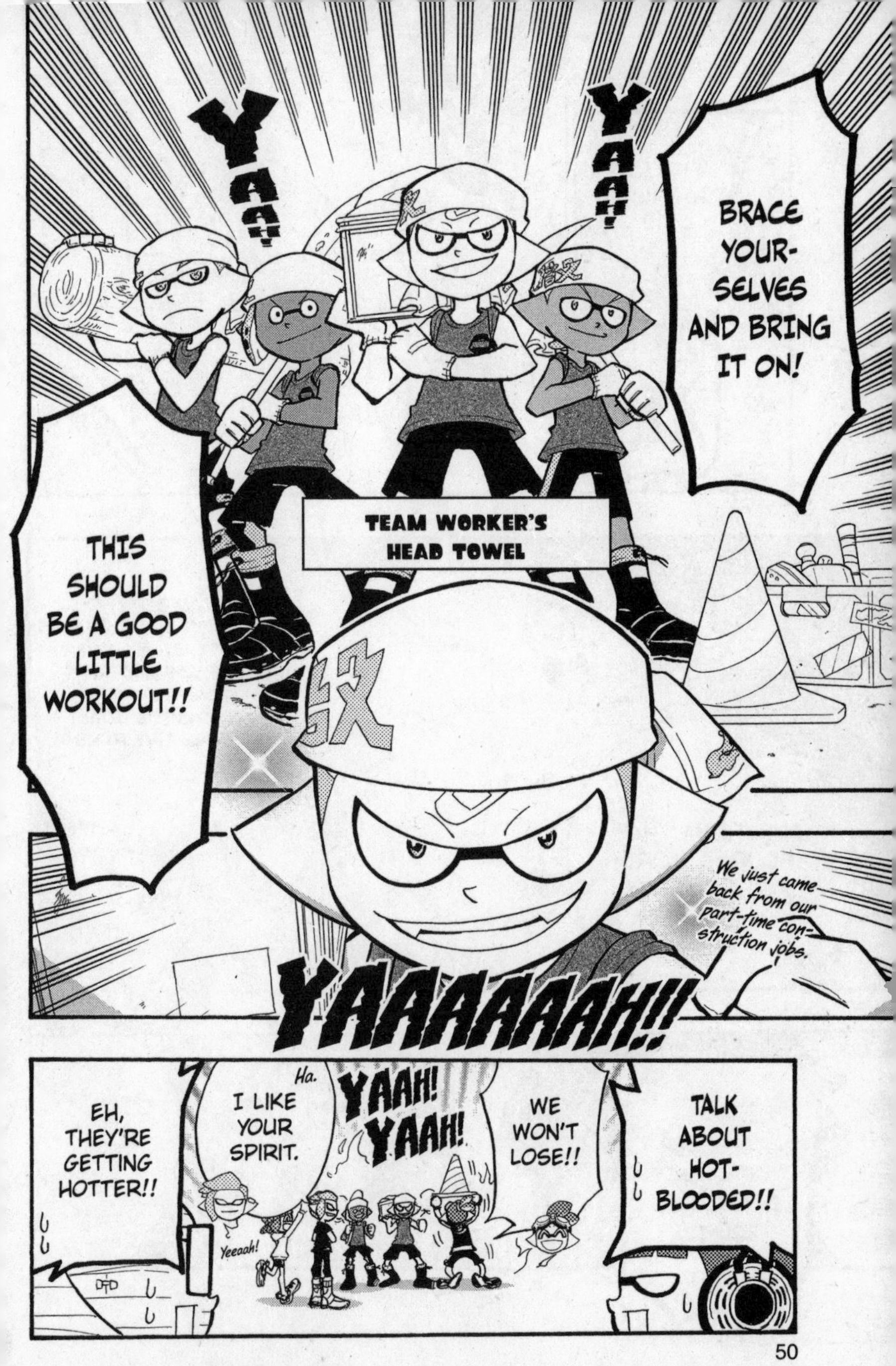
YAAH!
BRACE YOURSELVES AND BRING IT ON!
YAAH!
TEAM WORKER'S HEAD TOWEL
THIS SHOULD BE A GOOD LITTLE WORKOUT!!
We just came back from our part-time construction jobs.
YAAAAAAH!!
TALK ABOUT HOT-BLOODED!!
WE WON'T LOSE!!
YAAH! YAAH!
Ha. I LIKE YOUR SPIRIT.
Yeeaah!
EH, THEY'RE GETTING HOTTER!!

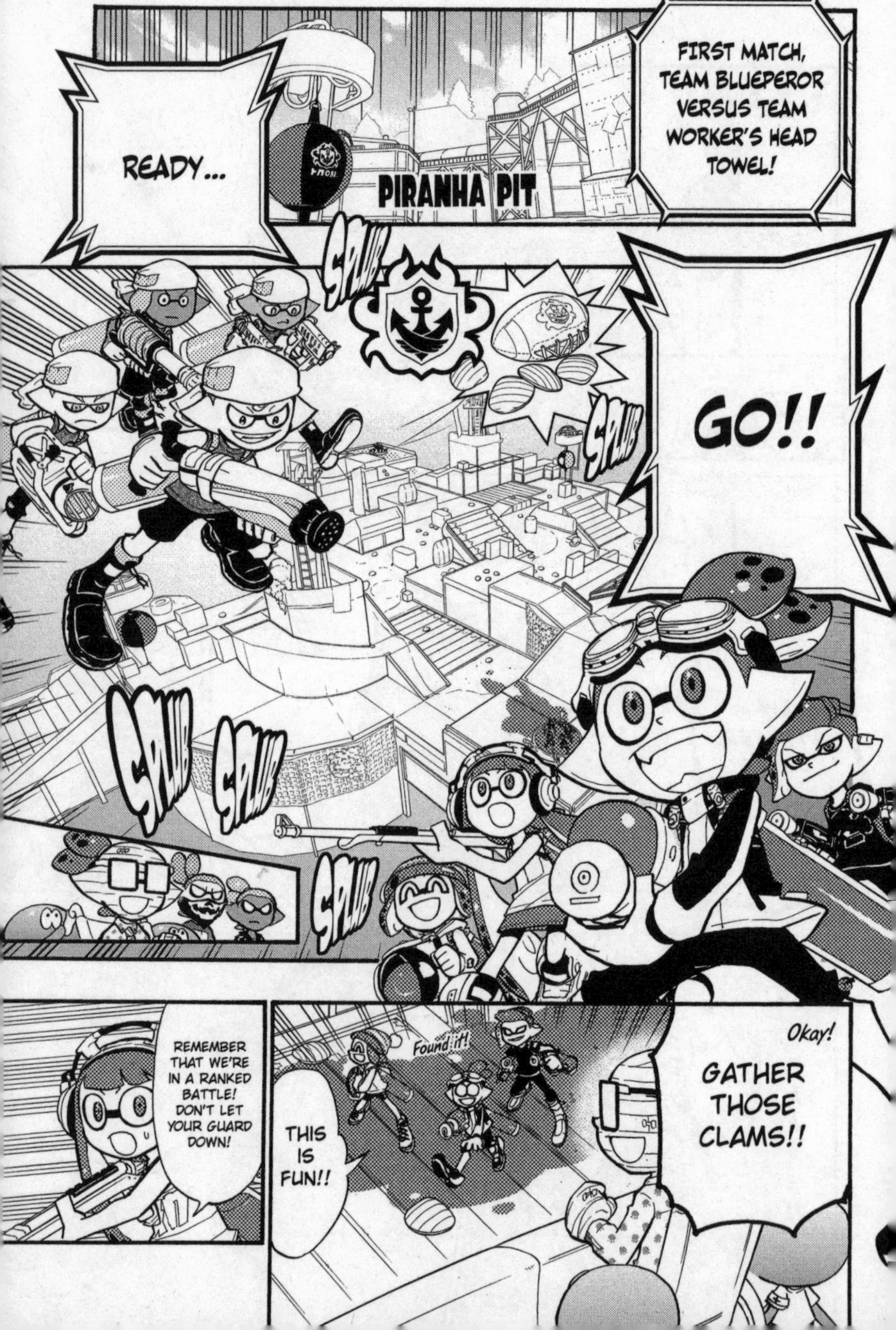
FIRST MATCH, TEAM BLUEPEROR VERSUS TEAM WORKER'S HEAD TOWEL!
READY...
PIRANHA PIT
GO!!
SPLUB
SPLUB
SPLUB
SPLUB
SPLUB
Okay!
GATHER THOSE CLAMS!!
Found it!
THIS IS FUN!!
REMEMBER THAT WE'RE IN A RANKED BATTLE! DON'T LET YOUR GUARD DOWN!

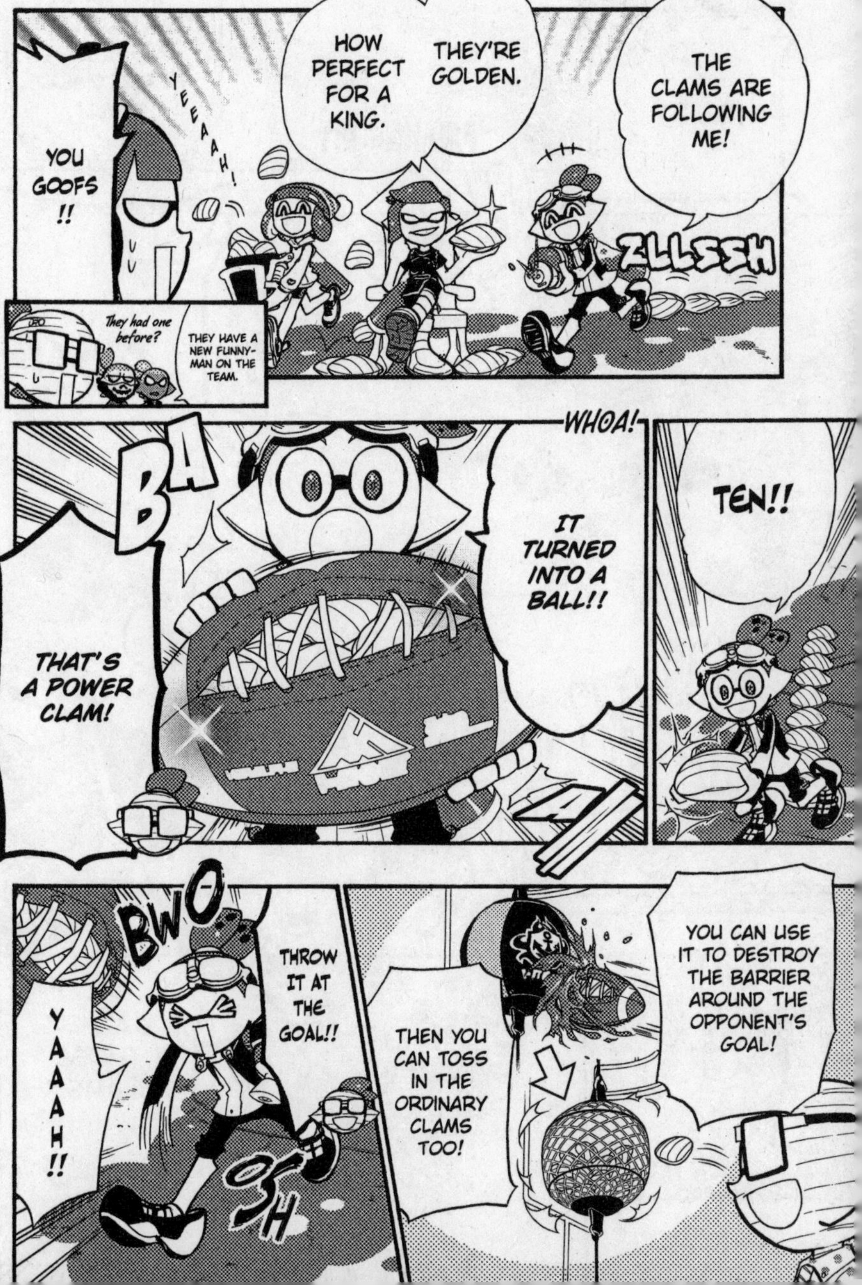
THE CLAMS ARE FOLLOWING ME!
ZLLSSH
THEY'RE GOLDEN.
HOW PERFECT FOR A KING.
YEEAAH!
YOU GOOFS!!
THEY HAVE A NEW FUNNY-MAN ON THE TEAM.
They had one before?
TEN!!
WHOA!
IT TURNED INTO A BALL!!
BA
THAT'S A POWER CLAM!
YOU CAN USE IT TO DESTROY THE BARRIER AROUND THE OPPONENT'S GOAL!
THEN YOU CAN TOSS IN THE ORDINARY CLAMS TOO!
BWO
THROW IT AT THE GOAL!!
YAAAAH!!

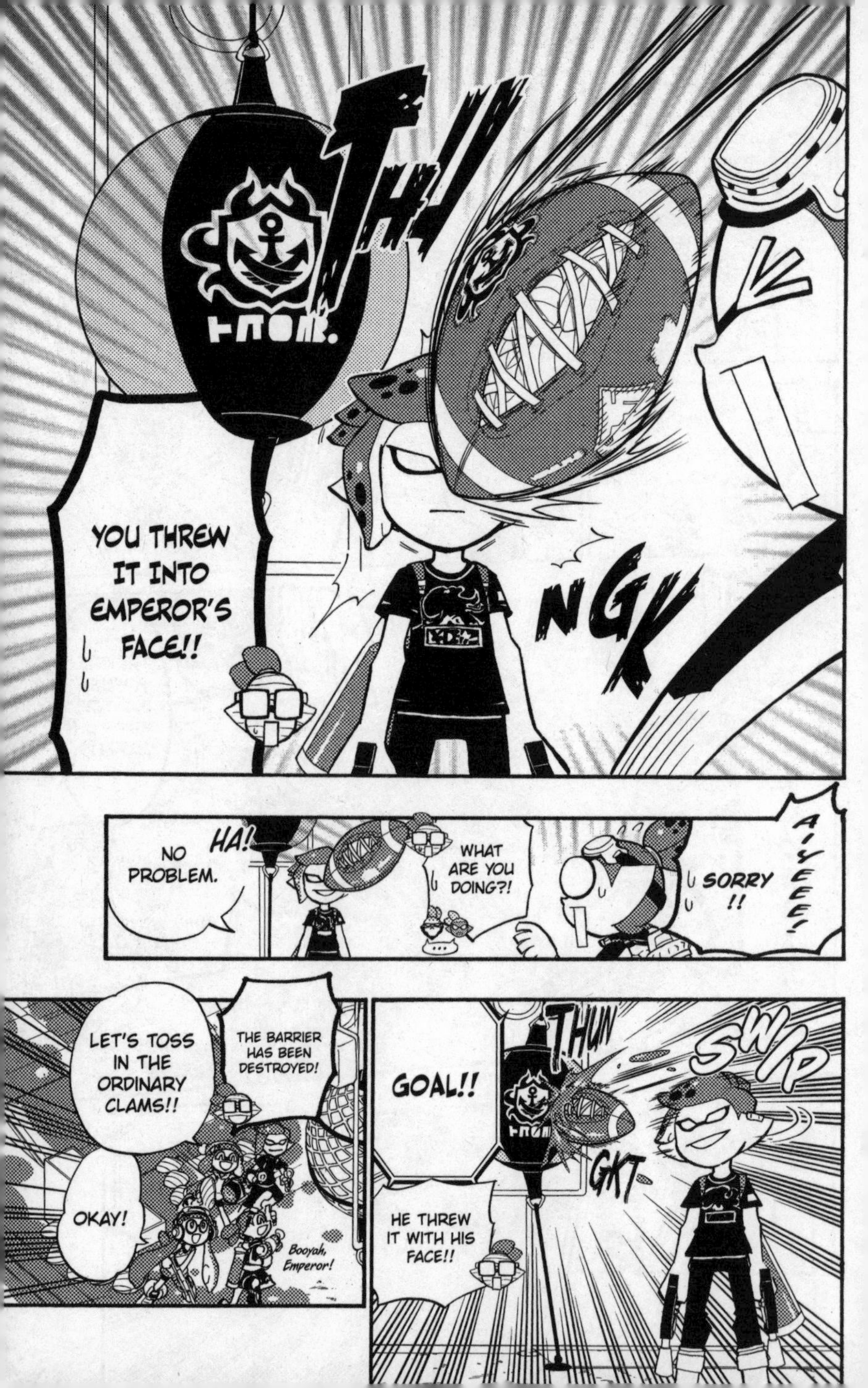
YOU THREW IT INTO EMPEROR'S FACE!!
NGK
AIYEEEE!
SORRY!!
WHAT ARE YOU DOING?!
HA!
NO PROBLEM.
SWIP
THUN
GOAL!!
GKT
HE THREW IT WITH HIS FACE!!
THE BARRIER HAS BEEN DESTROYED!
LET'S TOSS IN THE ORDINARY CLAMS!!
OKAY!
Booyah, Emperor!

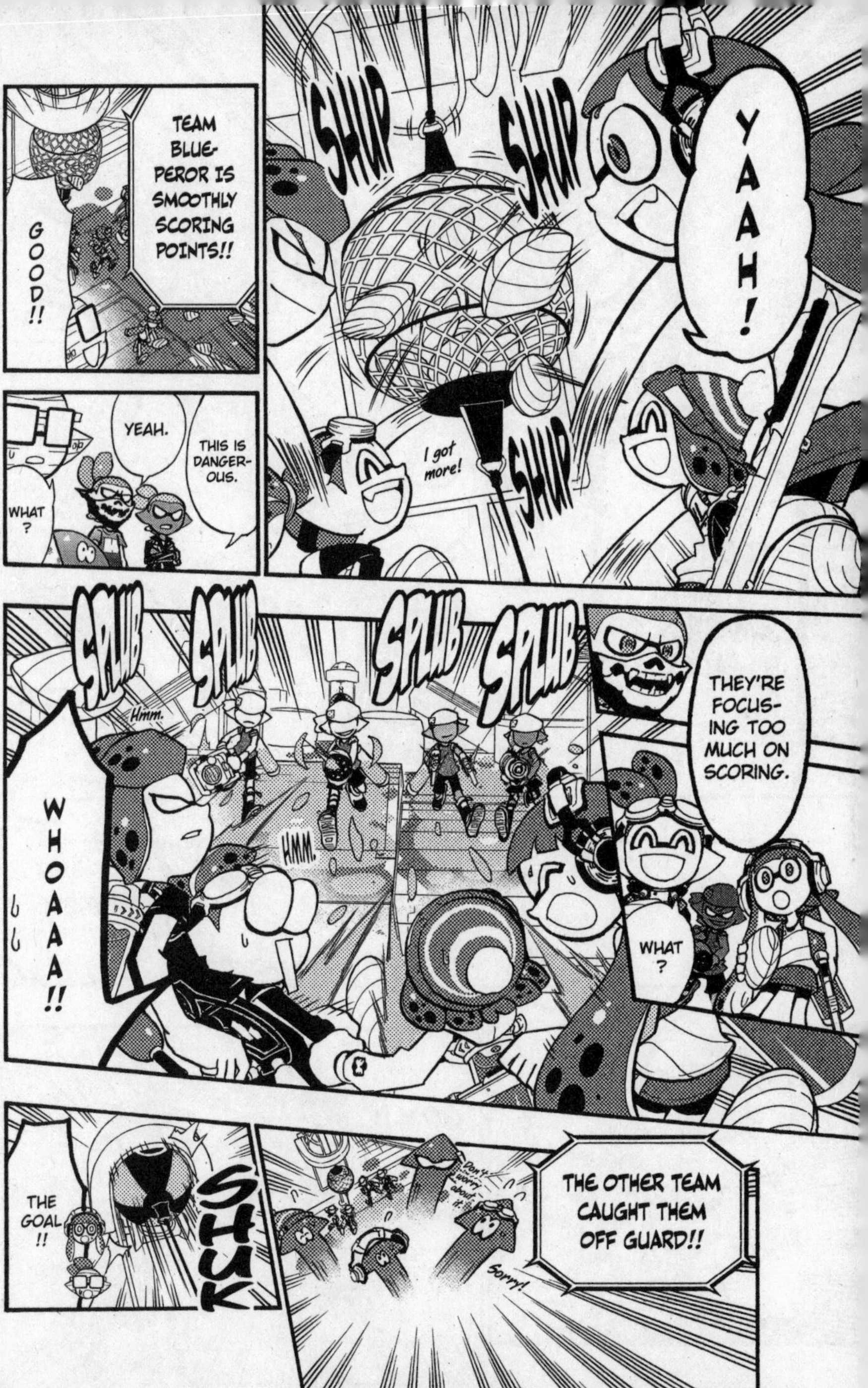
YAAH!
SHUP
SHUP
I got more!
SHUP
TEAM BLUE-PEROR IS SMOOTHLY SCORING POINTS!!
GOOD!!
THIS IS DANGEROUS.
YEAH.
WHAT?
SPLUB
SPLUB
SPLUB
SPLUB
THEY'RE FOCUSING TOO MUCH ON SCORING.
WHAT?
Hmm.
HMM.
WHOAAAA!!
THE OTHER TEAM CAUGHT THEM OFF GUARD!!
Don't worry about it.
Sorry!
SHUK
THE GOAL!!

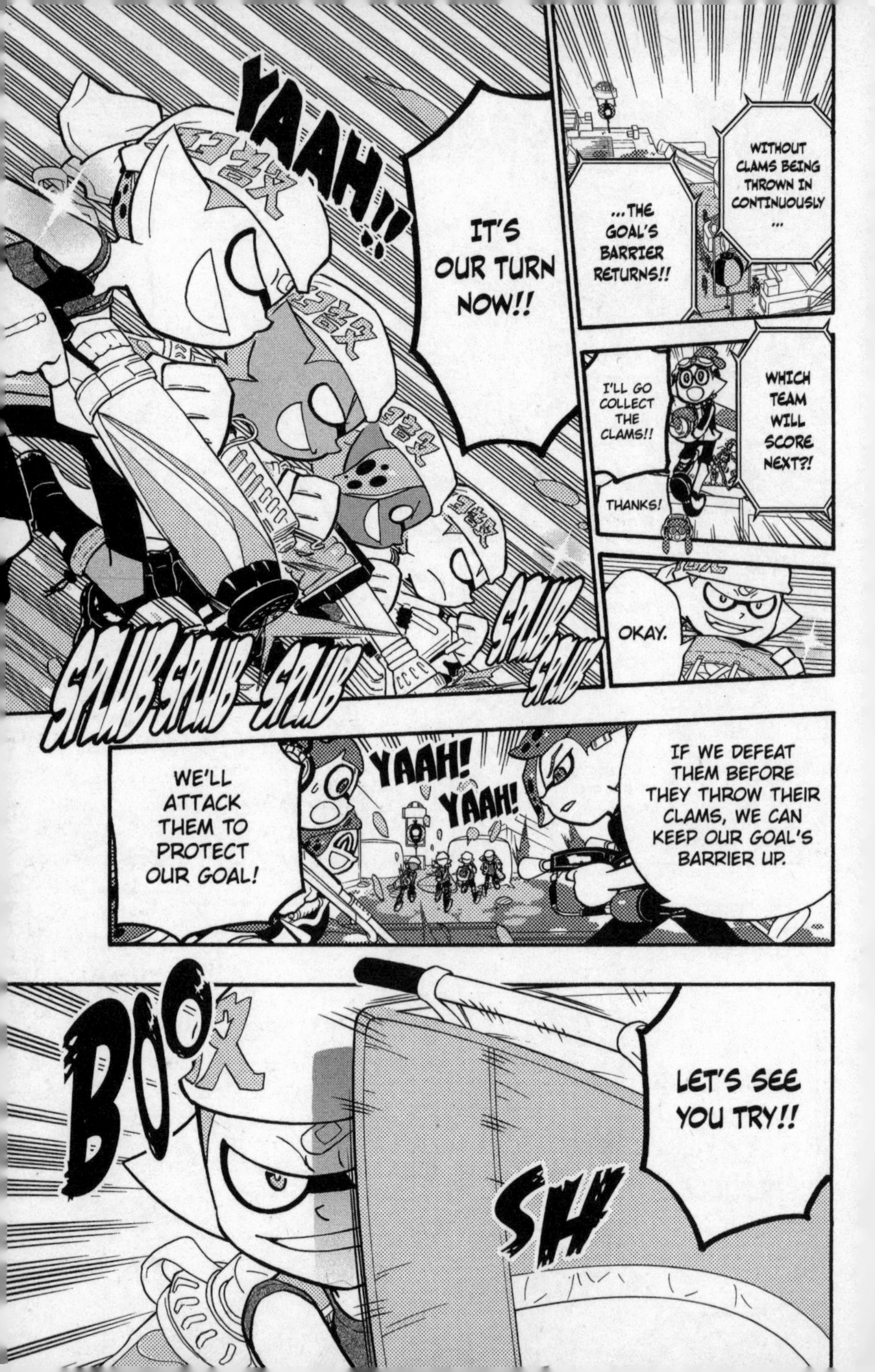

WITHOUT CLAMS BEING THROWN IN CONTINUOUSLY...
...THE GOAL'S BARRIER RETURNS!!
WHICH TEAM WILL SCORE NEXT?!
I'LL GO COLLECT THE CLAMS!!
THANKS!
OKAY.
YAAAH!!
IT'S OUR TURN NOW!!
SPLUB SPLUB
SPLUB SPLUB SPLUB
IF WE DEFEAT THEM BEFORE THEY THROW THEIR CLAMS, WE CAN KEEP OUR GOAL'S BARRIER UP.
YAAH!
YAAH!
WE'LL ATTACK THEM TO PROTECT OUR GOAL!
LET'S SEE YOU TRY!!
BOOOM
SH

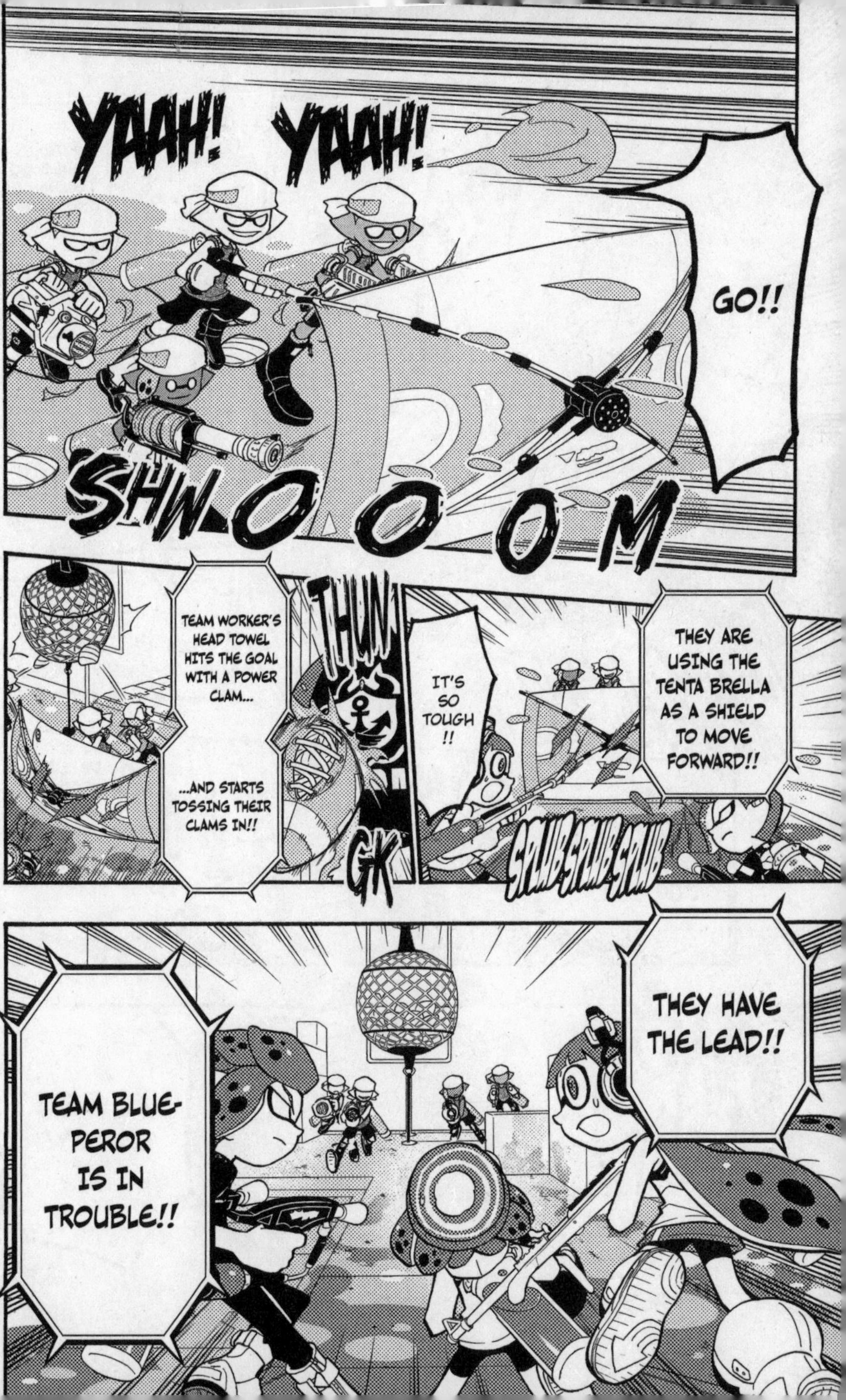
GO!!
YAAH! YAAH!
SHW-O-O-O-M
THEY ARE USING THE TENTA BRELLA AS A SHIELD TO MOVE FORWARD!!
IT'S SO TOUGH!!
SPLUB SPLUB SPLUB
THUN
GK
TEAM WORKER'S HEAD TOWEL HITS THE GOAL WITH A POWER CLAM...
...AND STARTS TOSSING THEIR CLAMS IN!!
THEY HAVE THE LEAD!!
TEAM BLUE-PEROR IS IN TROUBLE!!

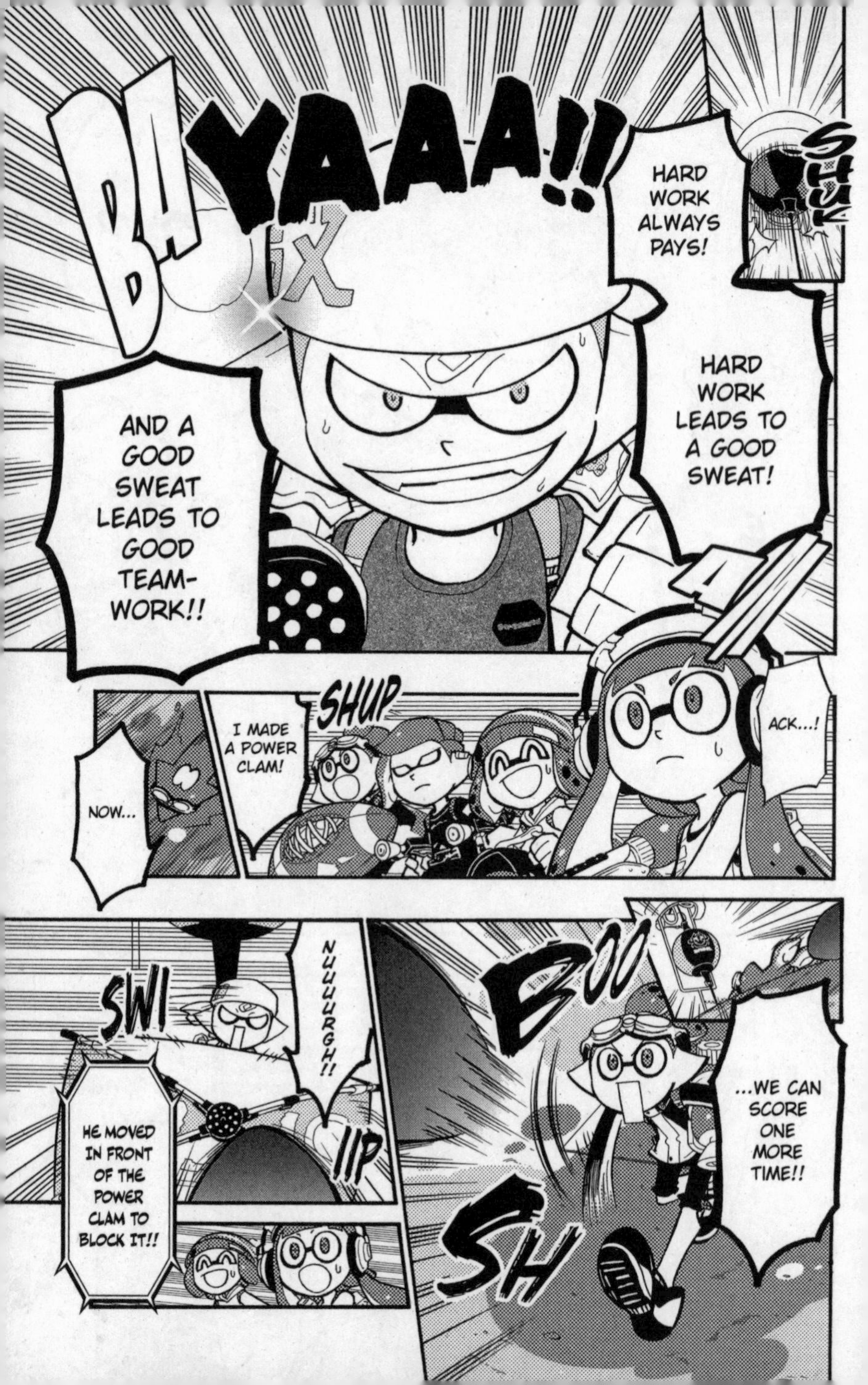

SHUK
HARD WORK ALWAYS PAYS!
BAYAAA!!
HARD WORK LEADS TO A GOOD SWEAT!
AND A GOOD SWEAT LEADS TO GOOD TEAM-WORK!!
ACK...!
SHUP
I MADE A POWER CLAM!
NOW...
BOOO
...WE CAN SCORE ONE MORE TIME!!
SH
NUUUURGH!!
SWI
IIP
HE MOVED IN FRONT OF THE POWER CLAM TO BLOCK IT!!

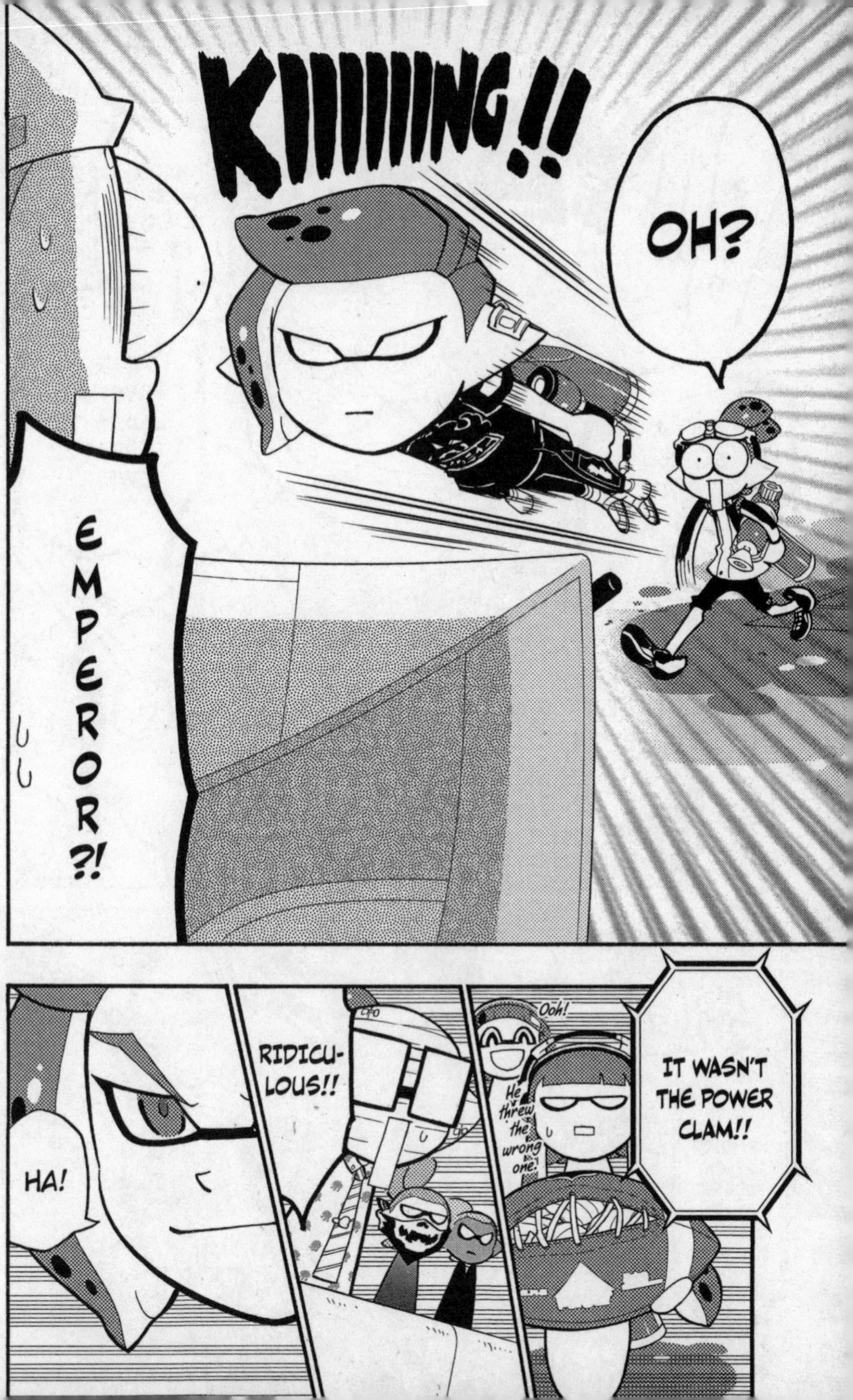
KIIIIIIING!!
OH?
EMPEROR?!
IT WASN'T THE POWER CLAM!!
Ooh!
He threw the wrong one.
RIDICU-LOUS!!
HA!

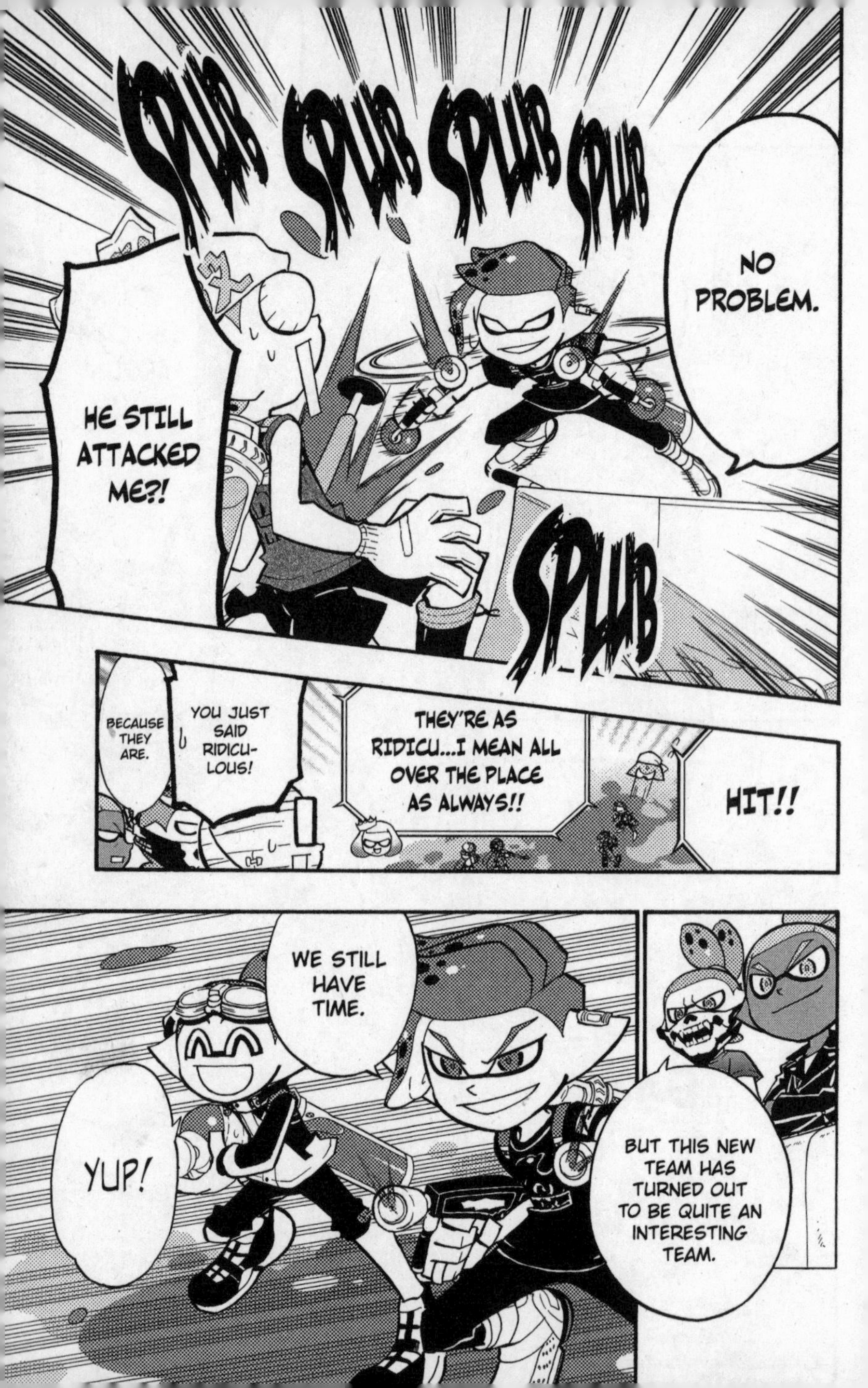
SPLUB SPLUB SPLUB SPLUB
NO PROBLEM.
HE STILL ATTACKED ME?!
SPLUB
HIT!!
THEY'RE AS RIDICU...I MEAN ALL OVER THE PLACE AS ALWAYS!!
YOU JUST SAID RIDICU-LOUS!
BECAUSE THEY ARE.
BUT THIS NEW TEAM HAS TURNED OUT TO BE QUITE AN INTERESTING TEAM.
WE STILL HAVE TIME.
YUP!

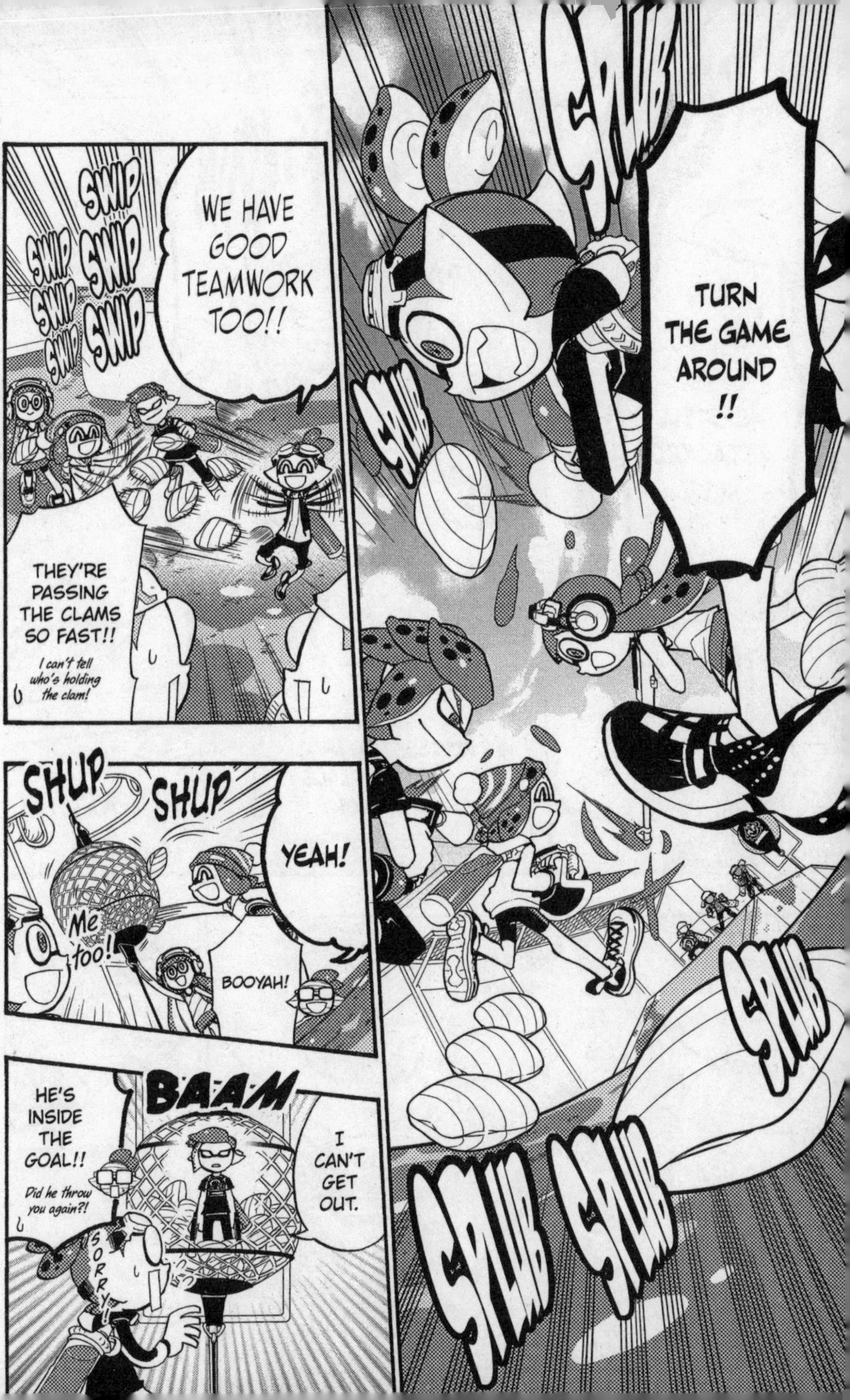
SPLUB
TURN THE GAME AROUND!!
SPLUB
SPLUB
SPLUB SPLUB
WE HAVE GOOD TEAMWORK TOO!!
SWIP SWIP SWIP SWIP
SWIP SWIP SWIP
THEY'RE PASSING THE CLAMS SO FAST!!
I can't tell who's holding the clam!
YEAH!
SHUP SHUP
BOOYAH!
Me too!
BAAM
I CAN'T GET OUT.
HE'S INSIDE THE GOAL!!
Did he throw you again?!
SORRY!

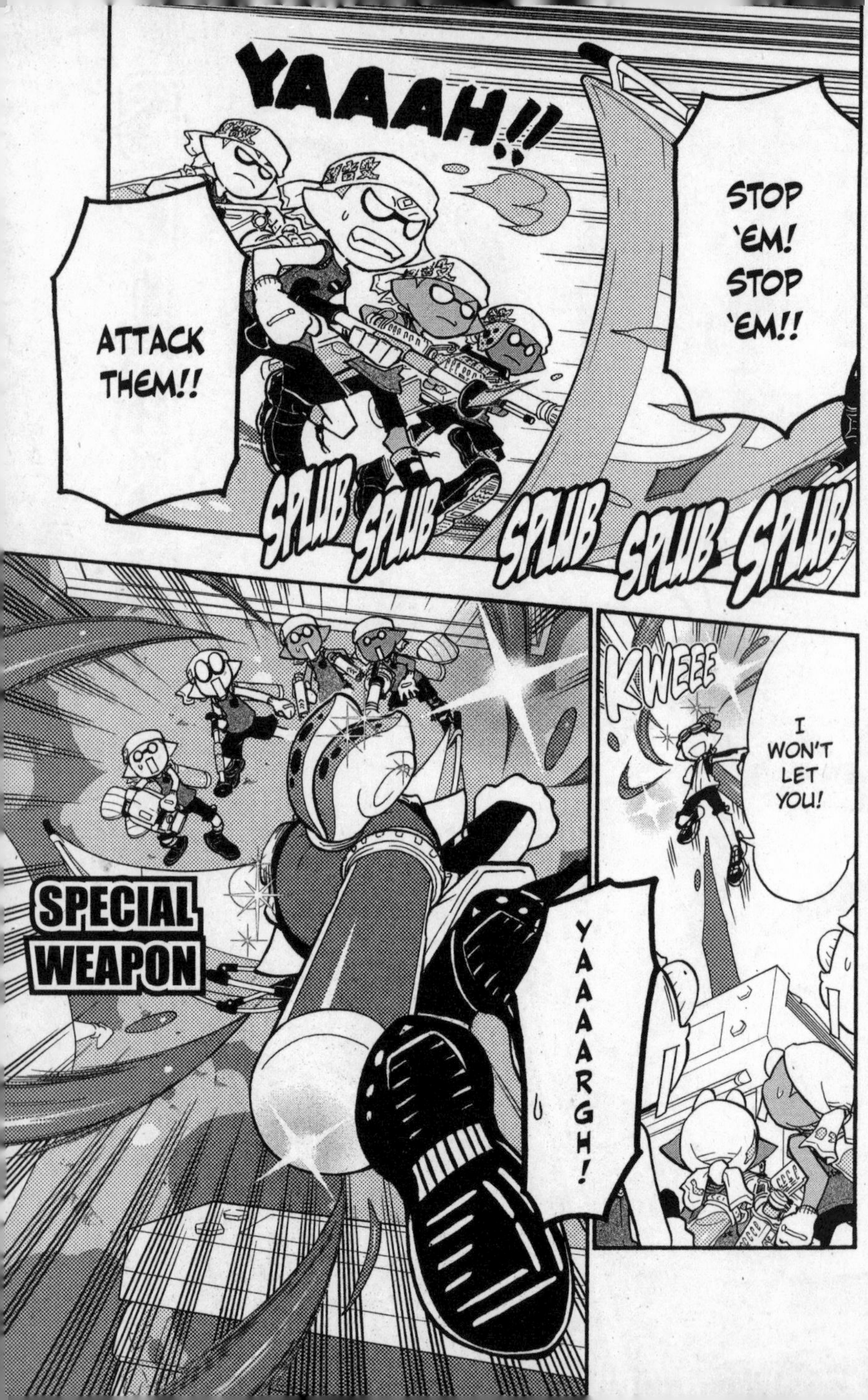
STOP 'EM! STOP 'EM!!
YAAAH!!
ATTACK THEM!!
SPLUB SPLUB SPLUB SPLUB SPLUB
KWEEE
I WON'T LET YOU!
YAAAARGH!
SPECIAL WEAPON

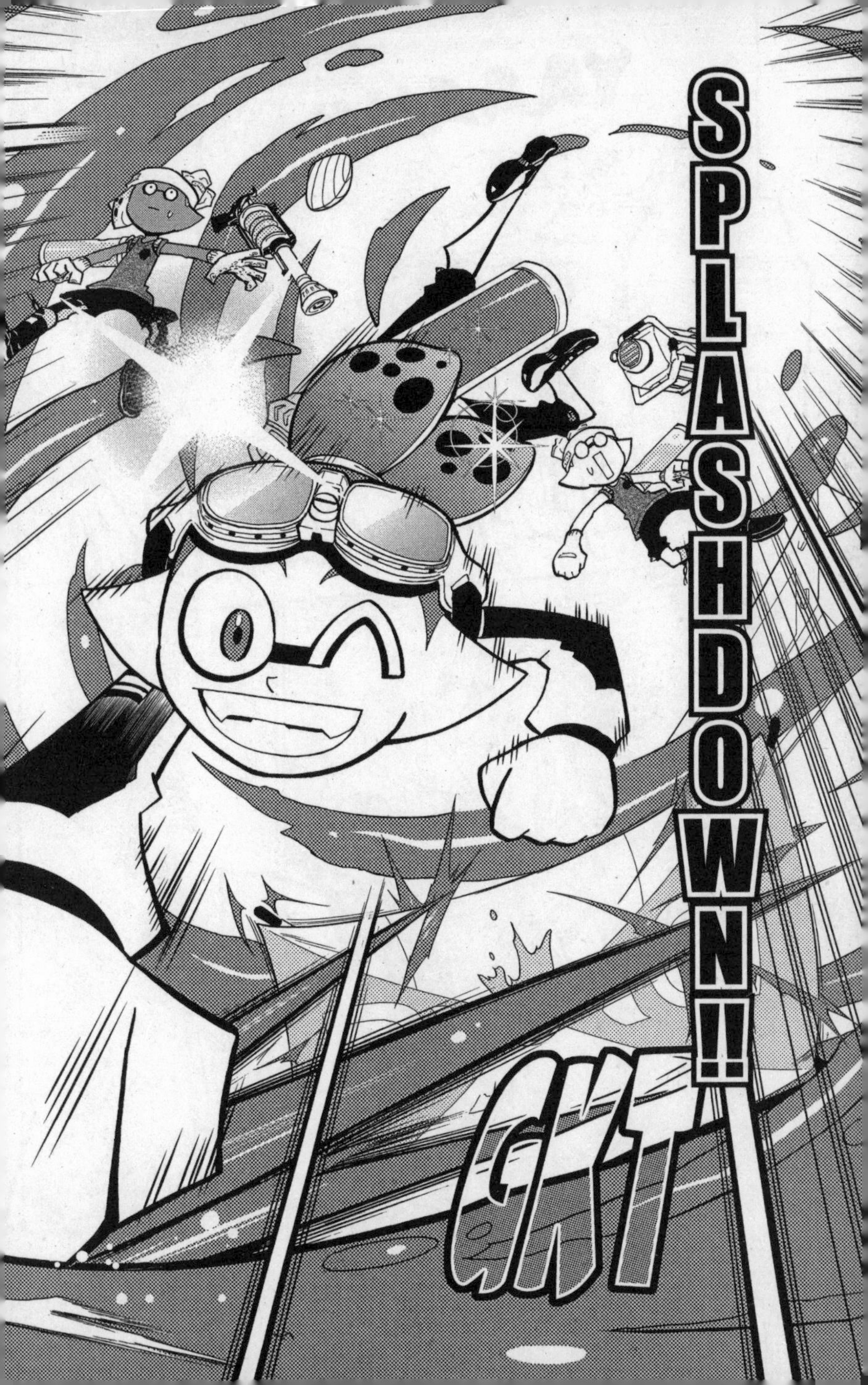
SPLASHDOWN!!
GKT

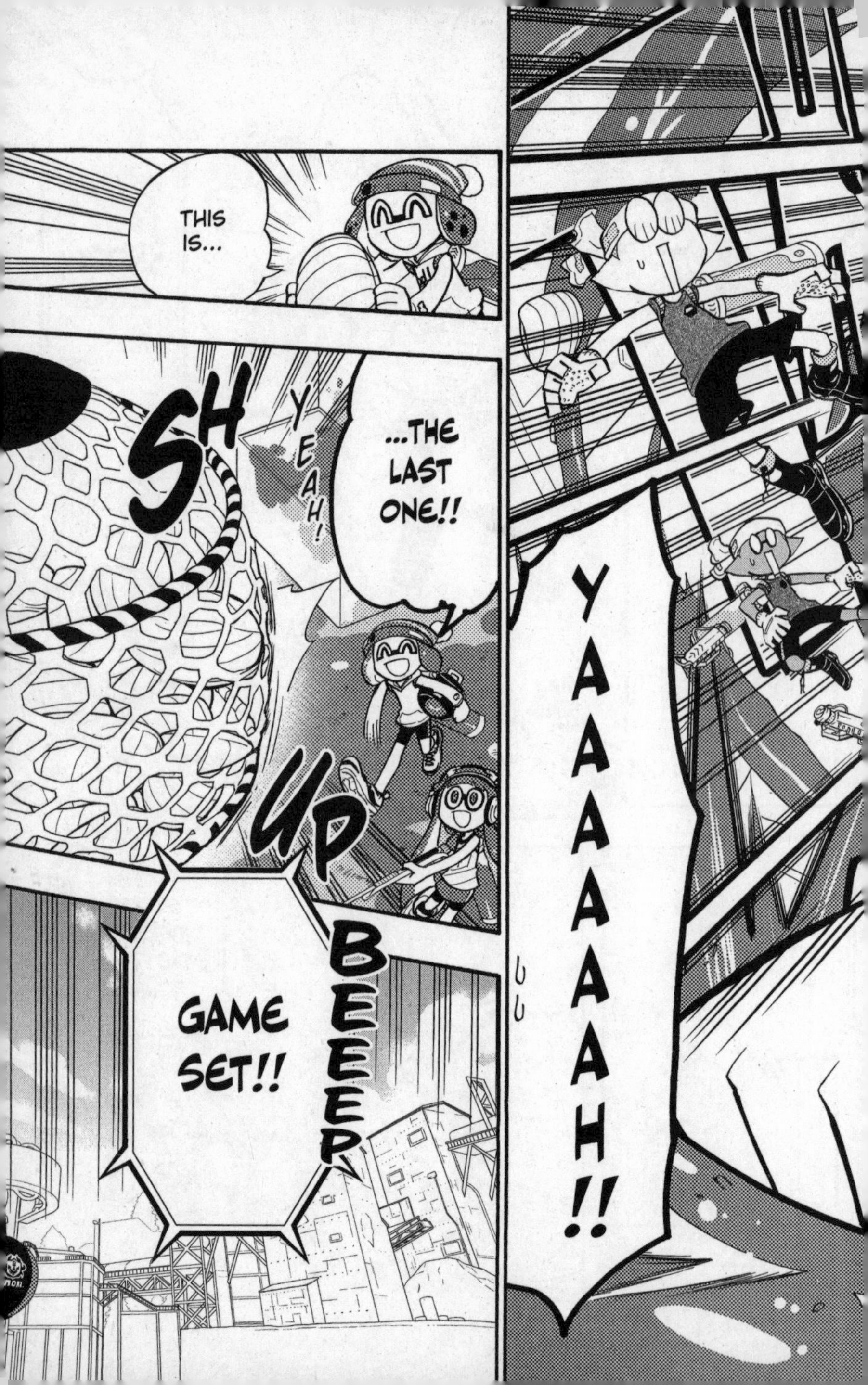
YAAAAAAH!!
THIS IS...
YEAH!
...THE LAST ONE!!
SHUP
GAME SET!!
BEEEEP

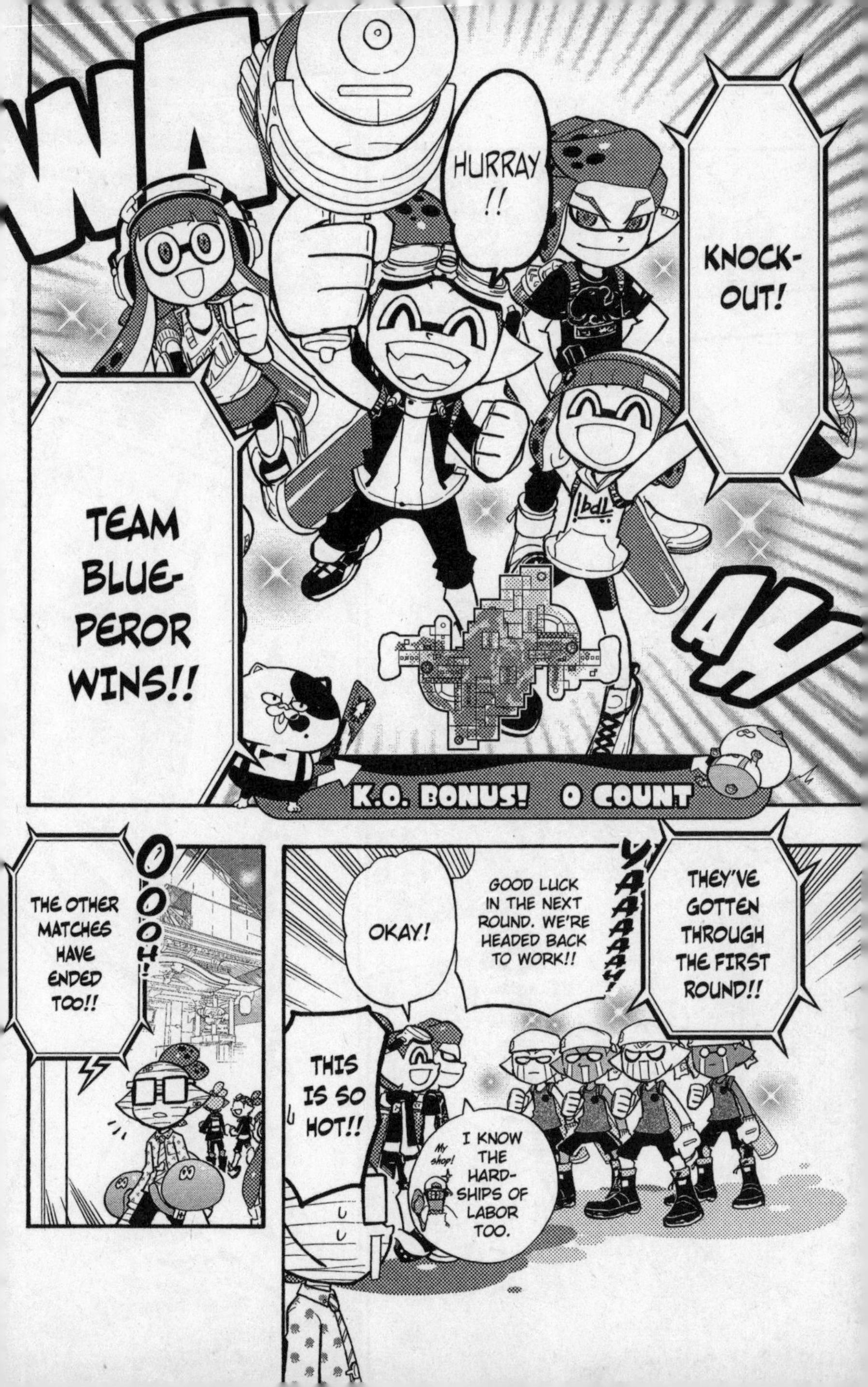

KNOCK-OUT!
HURRAY!!
WA
TEAM BLUE-PEROR WINS!!
AH
K.O. BONUS! 0 COUNT
THEY'VE GOTTEN THROUGH THE FIRST ROUND!!
YAAAAAAH!
GOOD LUCK IN THE NEXT ROUND. WE'RE HEADED BACK TO WORK!!
OKAY!
THIS IS SO HOT!!
I KNOW THE HARD-SHIPS OF LABOR TOO.
My shop!
OOOOH!
THE OTHER MATCHES HAVE ENDED TOO!!

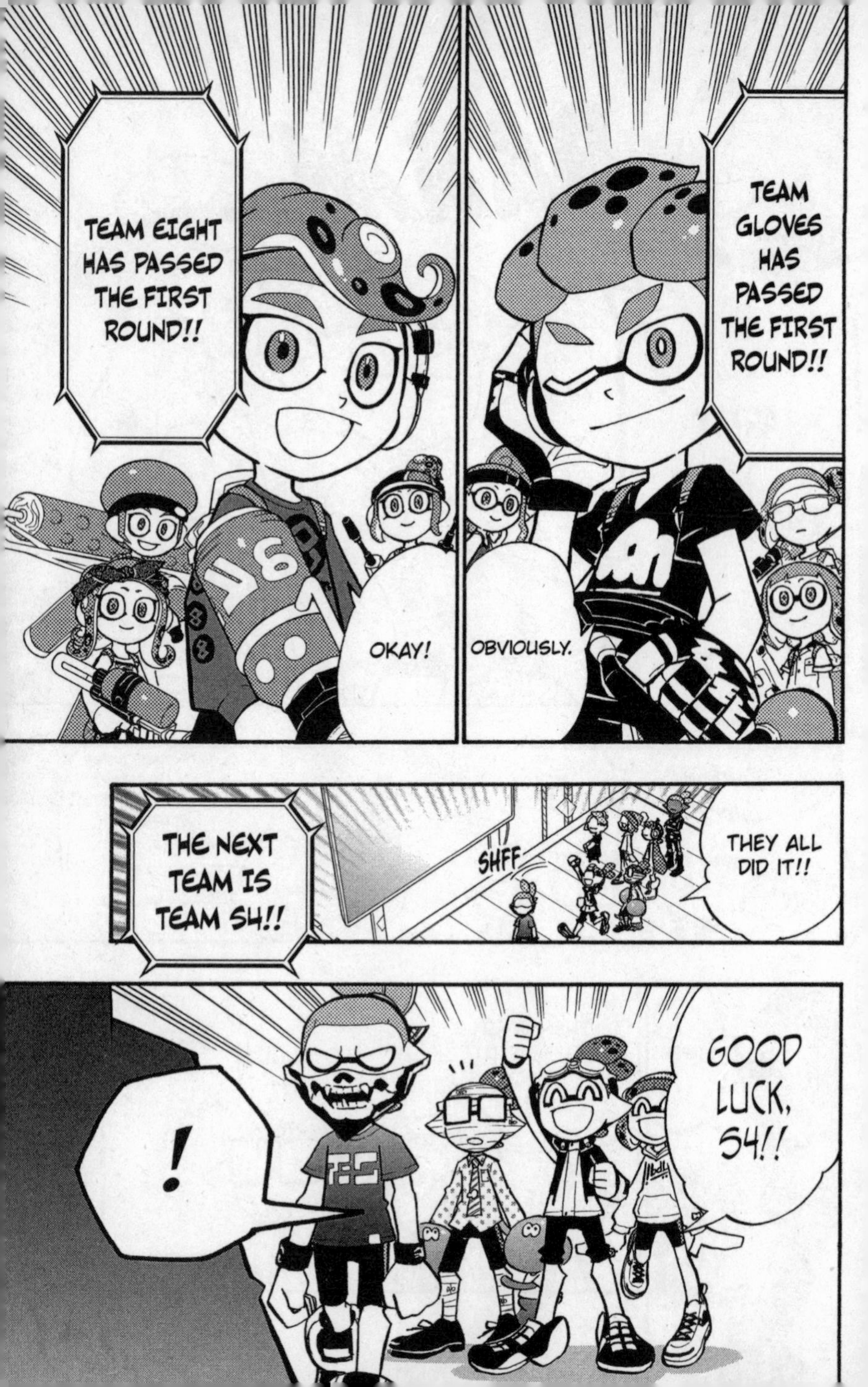
TEAM GLOVES HAS PASSED THE FIRST ROUND!!
OBVIOUSLY.
TEAM EIGHT HAS PASSED THE FIRST ROUND!!
OKAY!
THEY ALL DID IT!!
SHFF
THE NEXT TEAM IS TEAM 54!!
GOOD LUCK, 54!!
!

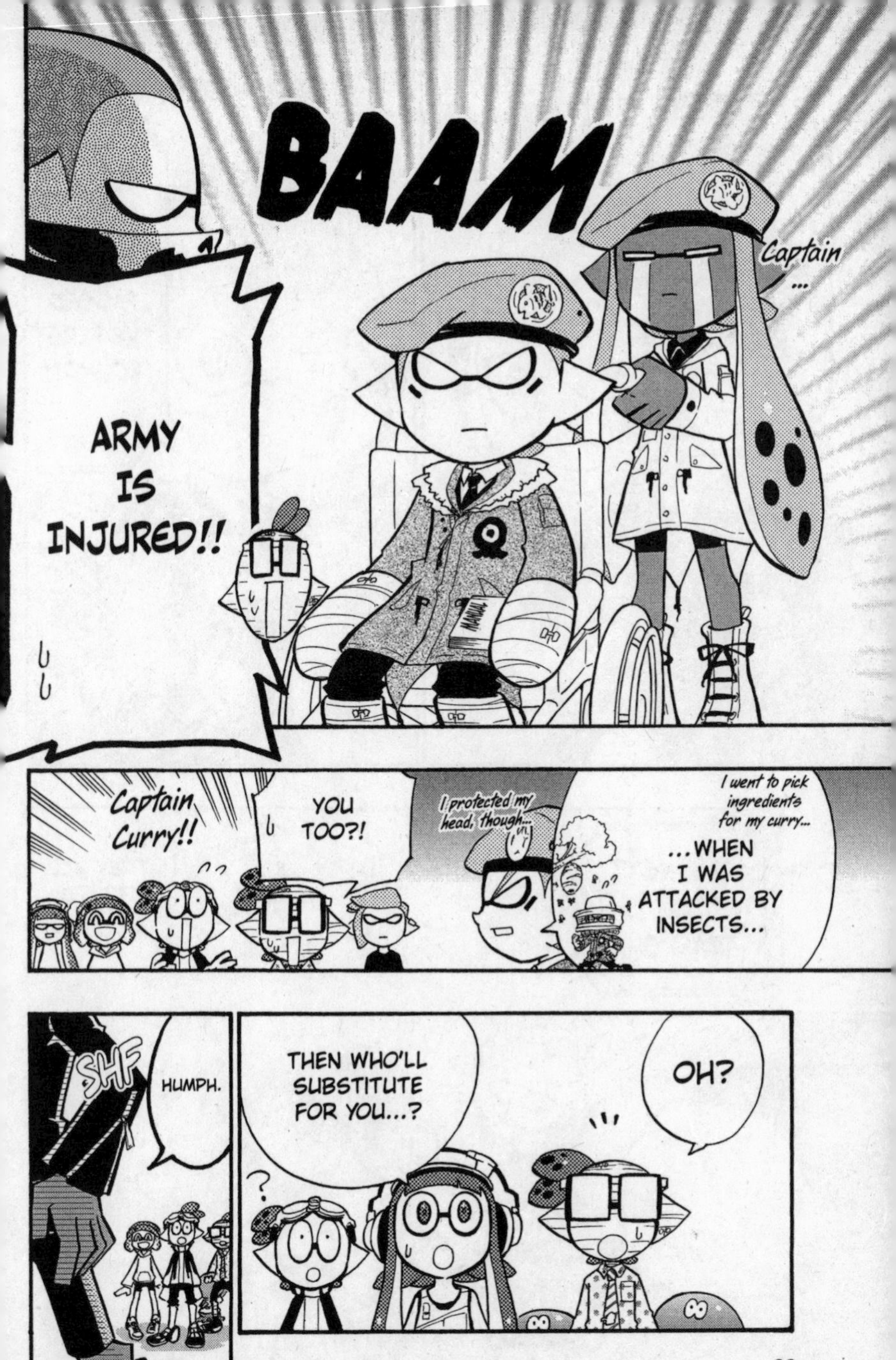
BAAM
Captain ...
ARMY IS INJURED!!
I went to pick ingredients for my curry...
...WHEN I WAS ATTACKED BY INSECTS...
I protected my head, though...
YOU TOO?!
Captain Curry!!
OH?
THEN WHO'LL SUBSTITUTE FOR YOU...?
SHF
HUMPH.

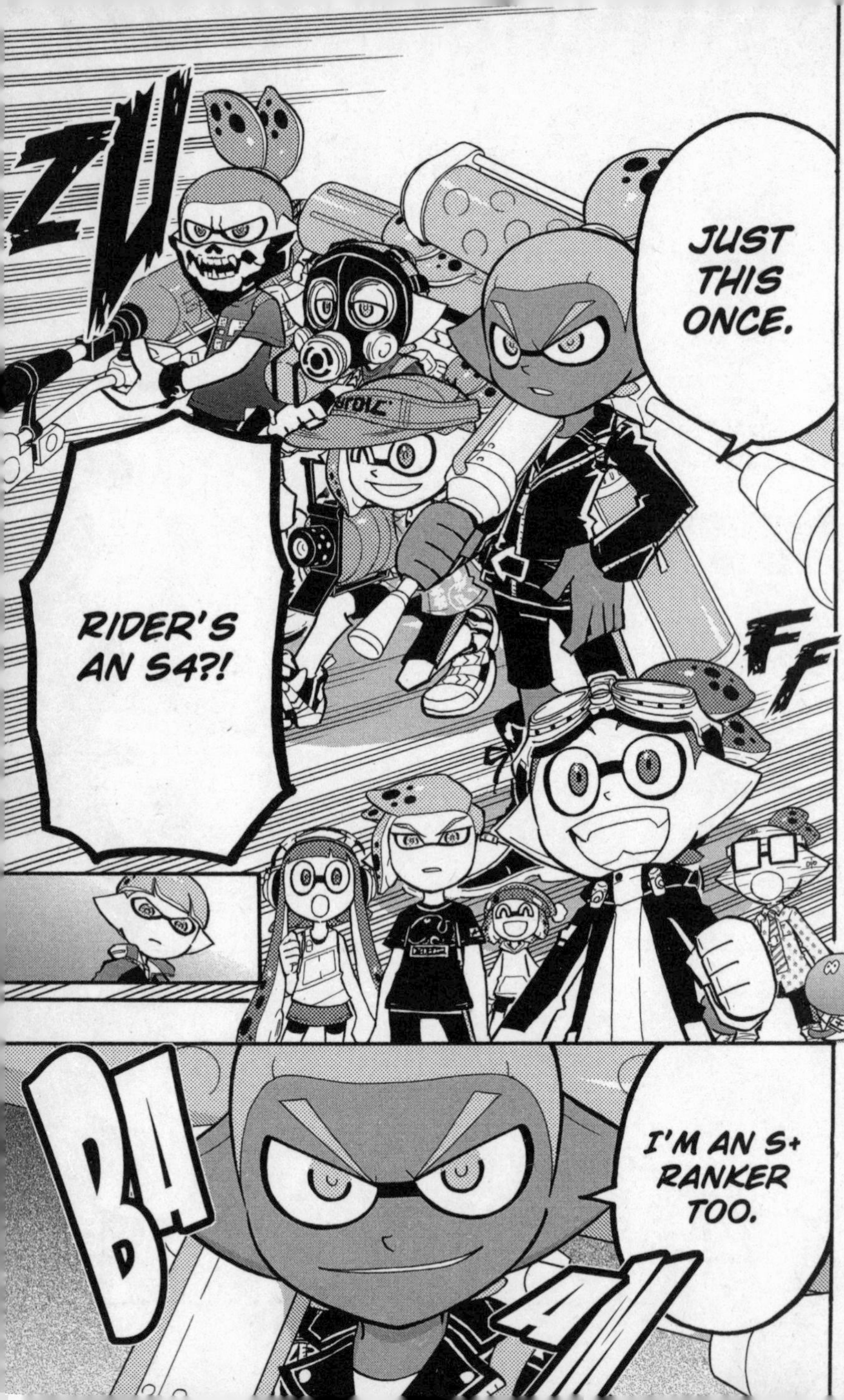
JUST THIS ONCE.
ZU
FF
RIDER'S AN S4?!
I'M AN S+ RANKER TOO.
BA

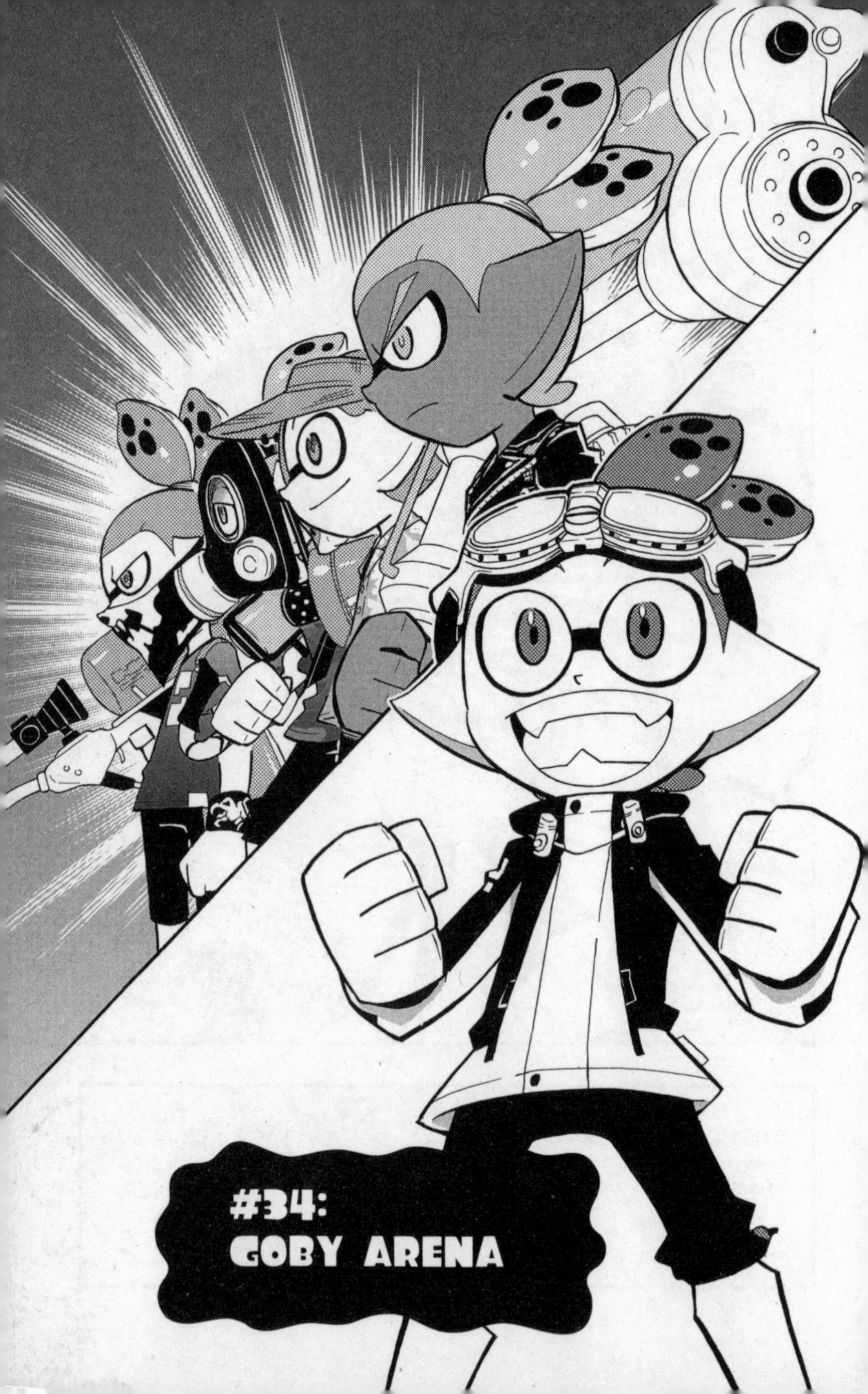
#34:
GOBY ARENA

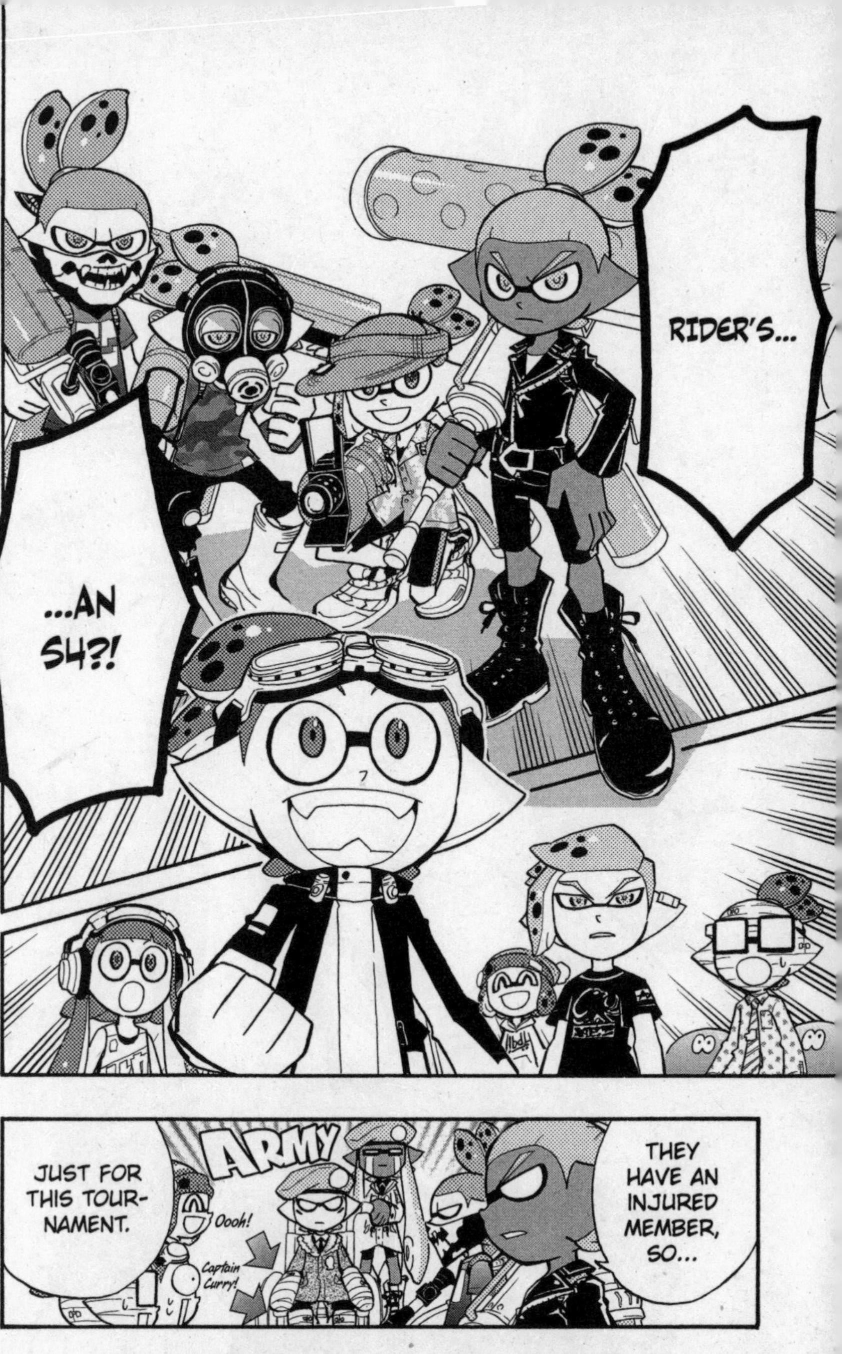
RIDER'S...
...AN S4?!
THEY HAVE AN INJURED MEMBER, SO...
ARMY
JUST FOR THIS TOUR-NAMENT.
Oooh!
Captain Curry!

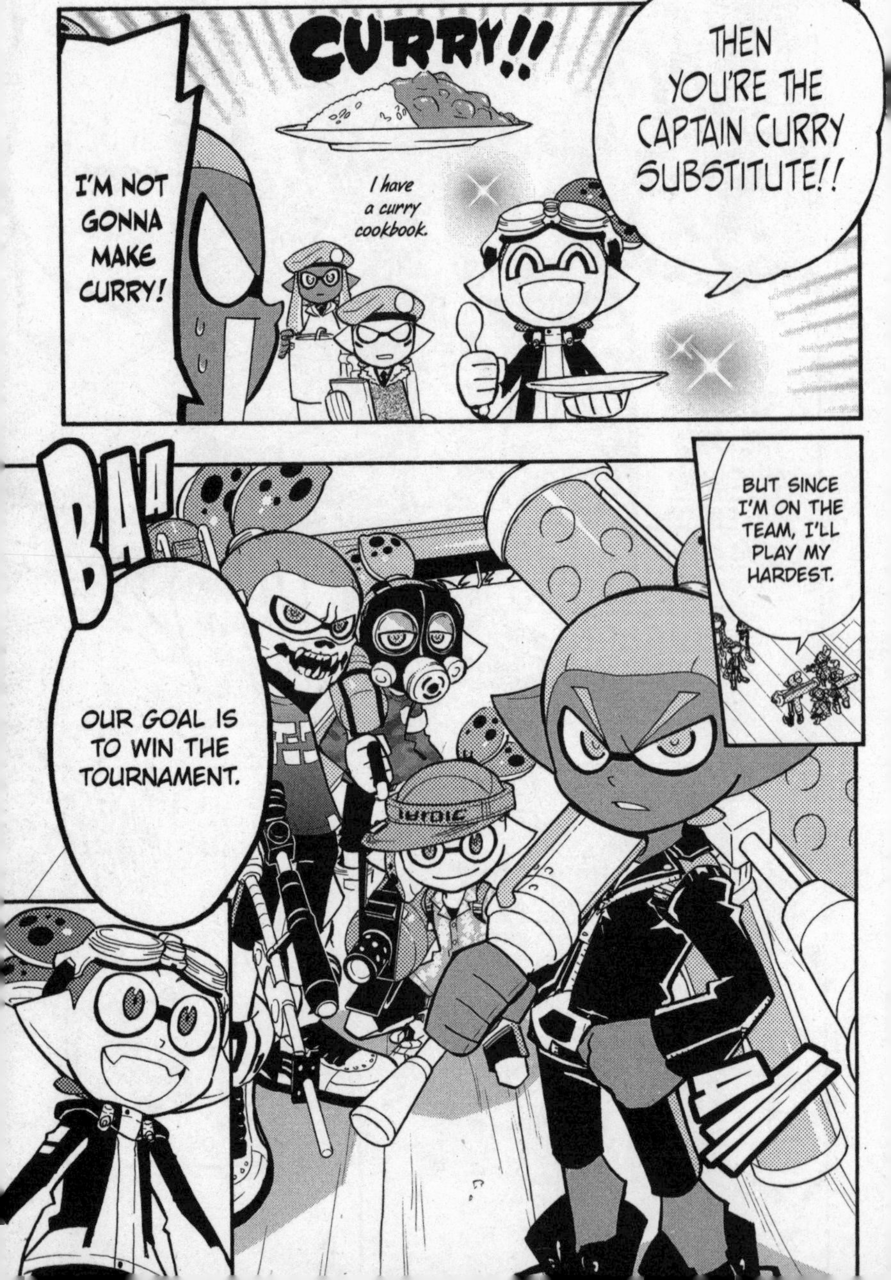
THEN YOU'RE THE CAPTAIN CURRY SUBSTITUTE!!
CURRY!!
I have a curry cookbook.
I'M NOT GONNA MAKE CURRY!
BUT SINCE I'M ON THE TEAM, I'LL PLAY MY HARDEST.
BA
OUR GOAL IS TO WIN THE TOURNAMENT.

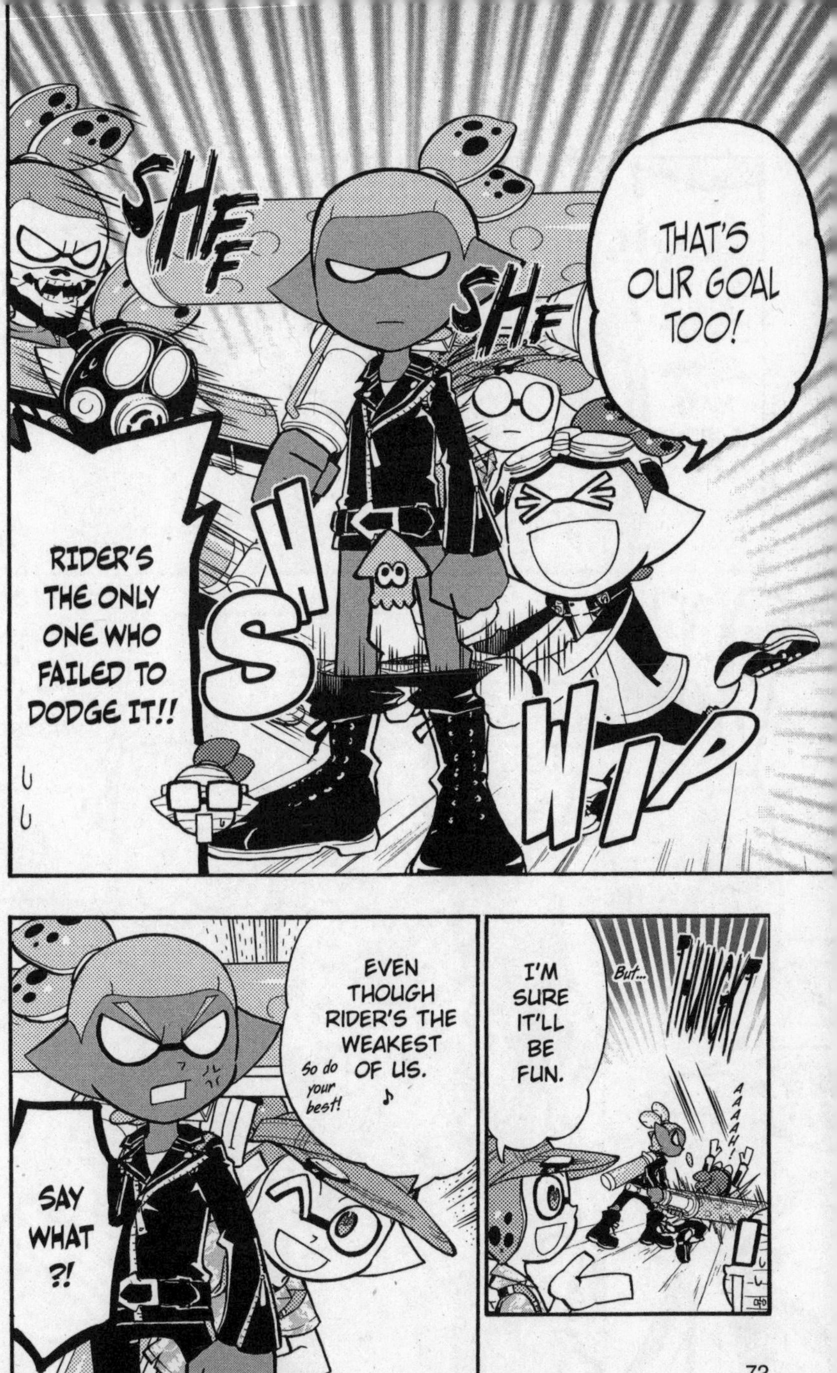
THAT'S OUR GOAL TOO!
SHF
SHF
RIDER'S THE ONLY ONE WHO FAILED TO DODGE IT!!
WHIP
I'M SURE IT'LL BE FUN.
But...
THUNCK
AAAAH!
EVEN THOUGH RIDER'S THE WEAKEST OF US.
So do your best! ♪
SAY WHAT?!

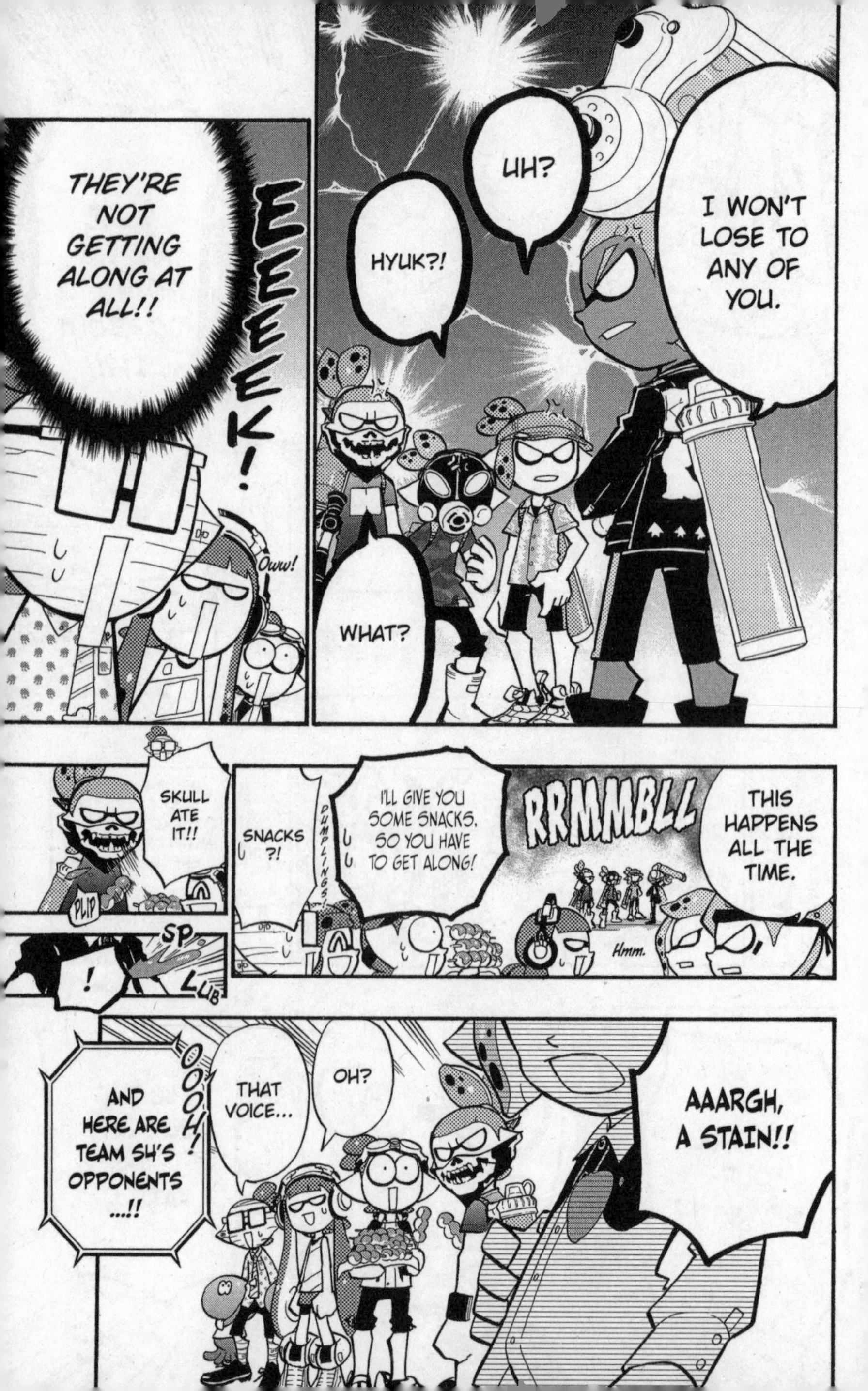
I WON'T LOSE TO ANY OF YOU.
UH?
HYUK?!
WHAT?
EEEEEK!
THEY'RE NOT GETTING ALONG AT ALL!!
Oww!
THIS HAPPENS ALL THE TIME.
RRMMBLL
Hmm.
I'LL GIVE YOU SOME SNACKS, SO YOU HAVE TO GET ALONG!
DUMPLINGS!
SNACKS?!
SKULL ATE IT!!
PLIP
SPLUB
!
AAARGH, A STAIN!!
OH?
THAT VOICE...
OOOOH!
AND HERE ARE TEAM S4'S OPPONENTS...!!

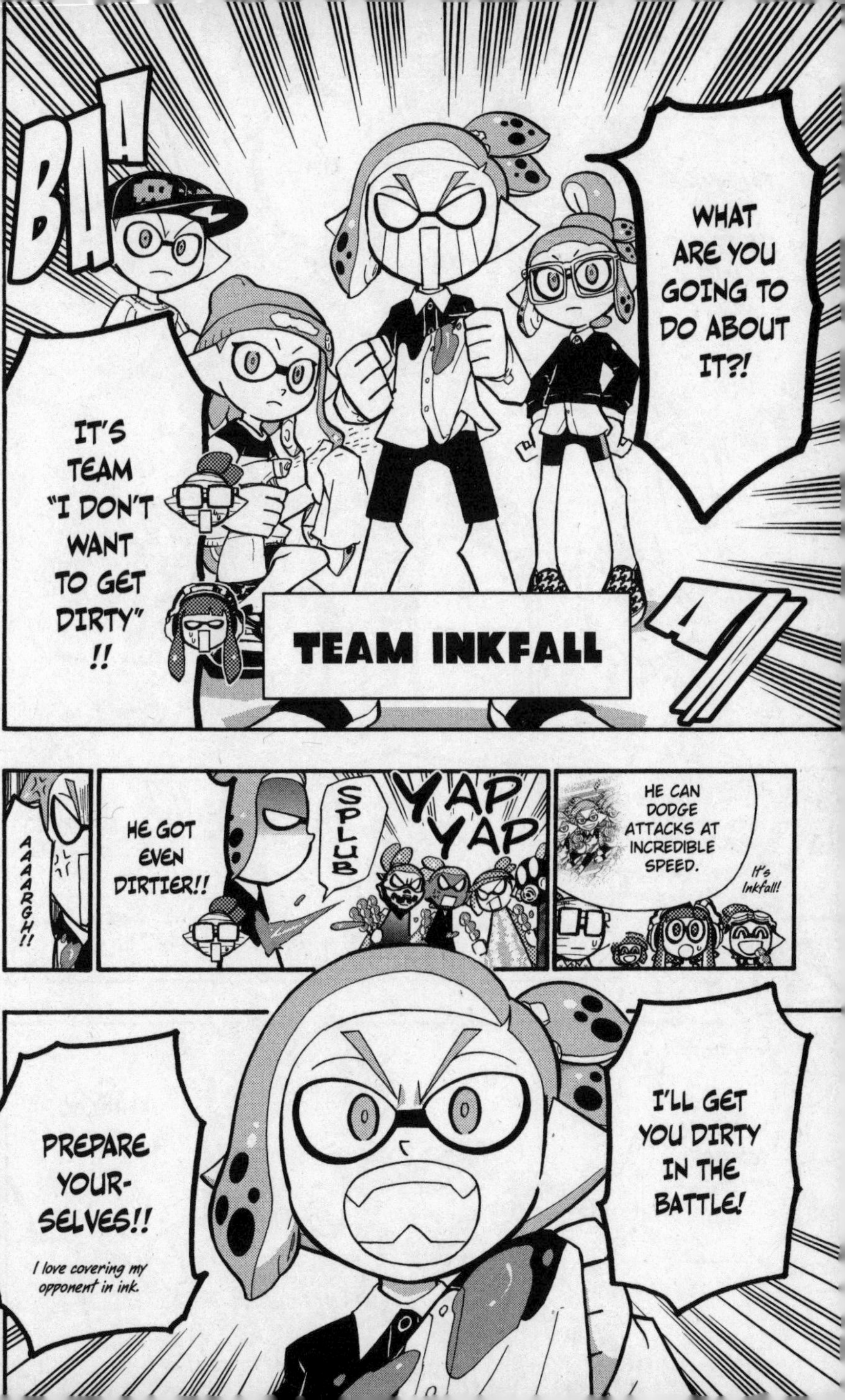
WHAT ARE YOU GOING TO DO ABOUT IT?!
TEAM INKFALL
BAA!
IT'S TEAM "I DON'T WANT TO GET DIRTY"!!
HE CAN DODGE ATTACKS AT INCREDIBLE SPEED.
It's Inkfall!
YAP YAP
SPLUB
HE GOT EVEN DIRTIER!!
AAAARGH!!
I'LL GET YOU DIRTY IN THE BATTLE!
PREPARE YOUR-SELVES!!
I love covering my opponent in ink.

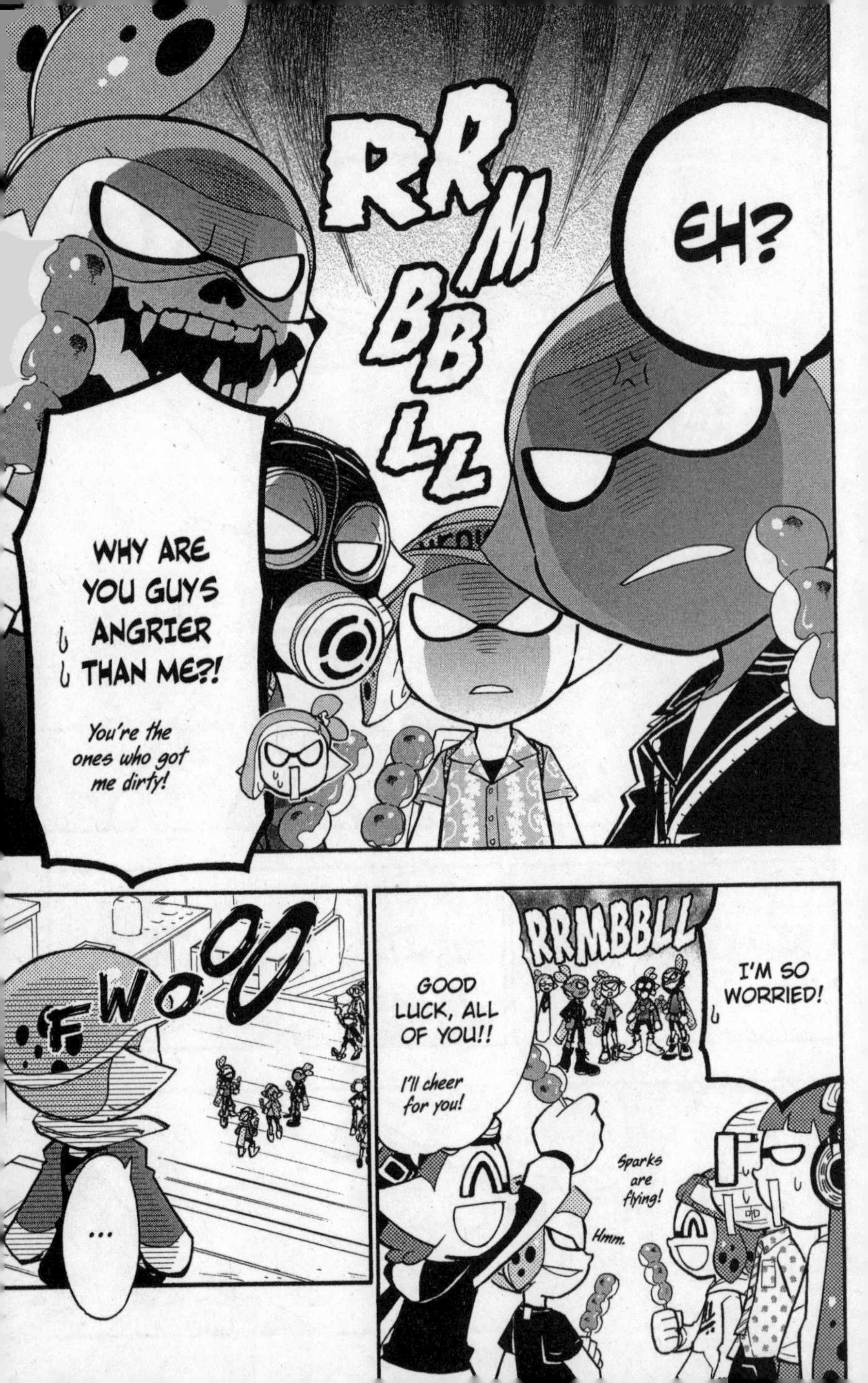
EH?
RRMBBLL
WHY ARE YOU GUYS ANGRIER THAN ME?!
You're the ones who got me dirty!
I'M SO WORRIED!
RRMBBLL
GOOD LUCK, ALL OF YOU!!
I'll cheer for you!
Sparks are flying!
Hmm.
FWOOO
...

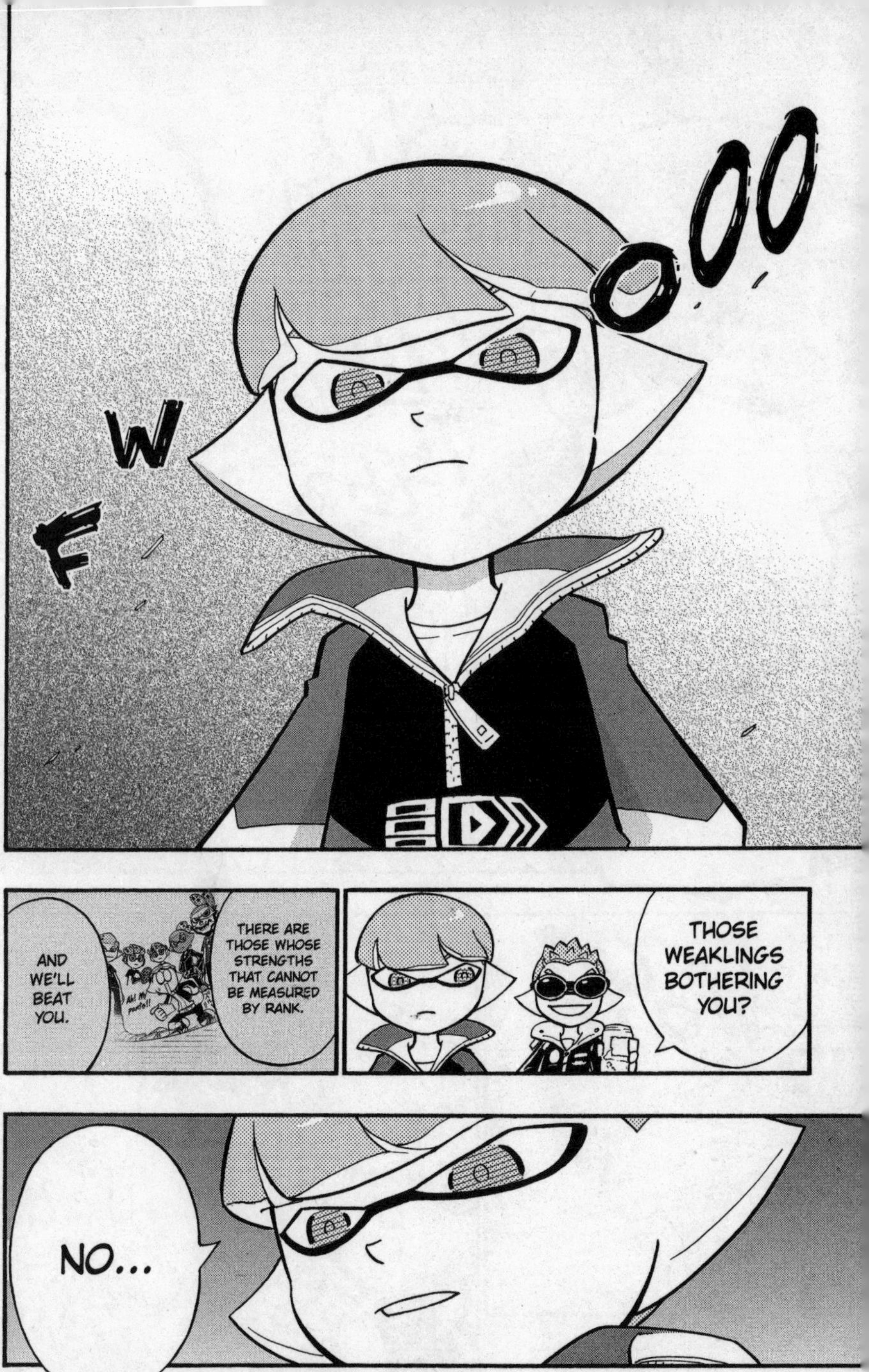
FWOOO
THOSE WEAKLINGS BOTHERING YOU?
THERE ARE THOSE WHOSE STRENGTHS THAT CANNOT BE MEASURED BY RANK.
AND WE'LL BEAT YOU.
NO...

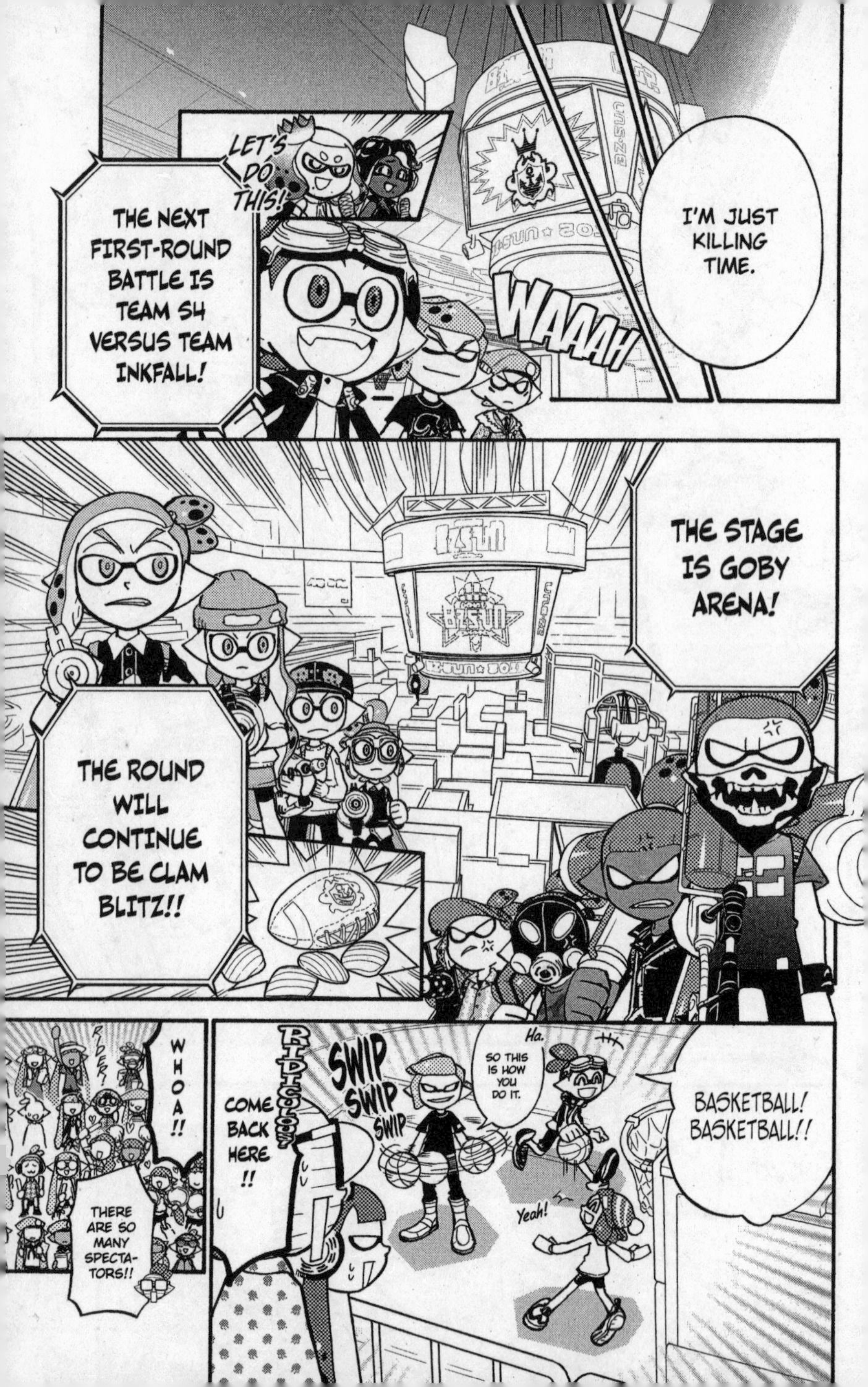
I'M JUST KILLING TIME.
LET'S DO THIS!
WAAAH
THE NEXT FIRST-ROUND BATTLE IS TEAM S4 VERSUS TEAM INKFALL!
THE STAGE IS GOBY ARENA!
THE ROUND WILL CONTINUE TO BE CLAM BLITZ!!
BASKETBALL! BASKETBALL!!
Ha.
SO THIS IS HOW YOU DO IT.
SWIP SWIP SWIP
RIDICOLO
COME BACK HERE!!
Yeah!
WHOA!!
RIDER!
THERE ARE SO MANY SPECTATORS!!

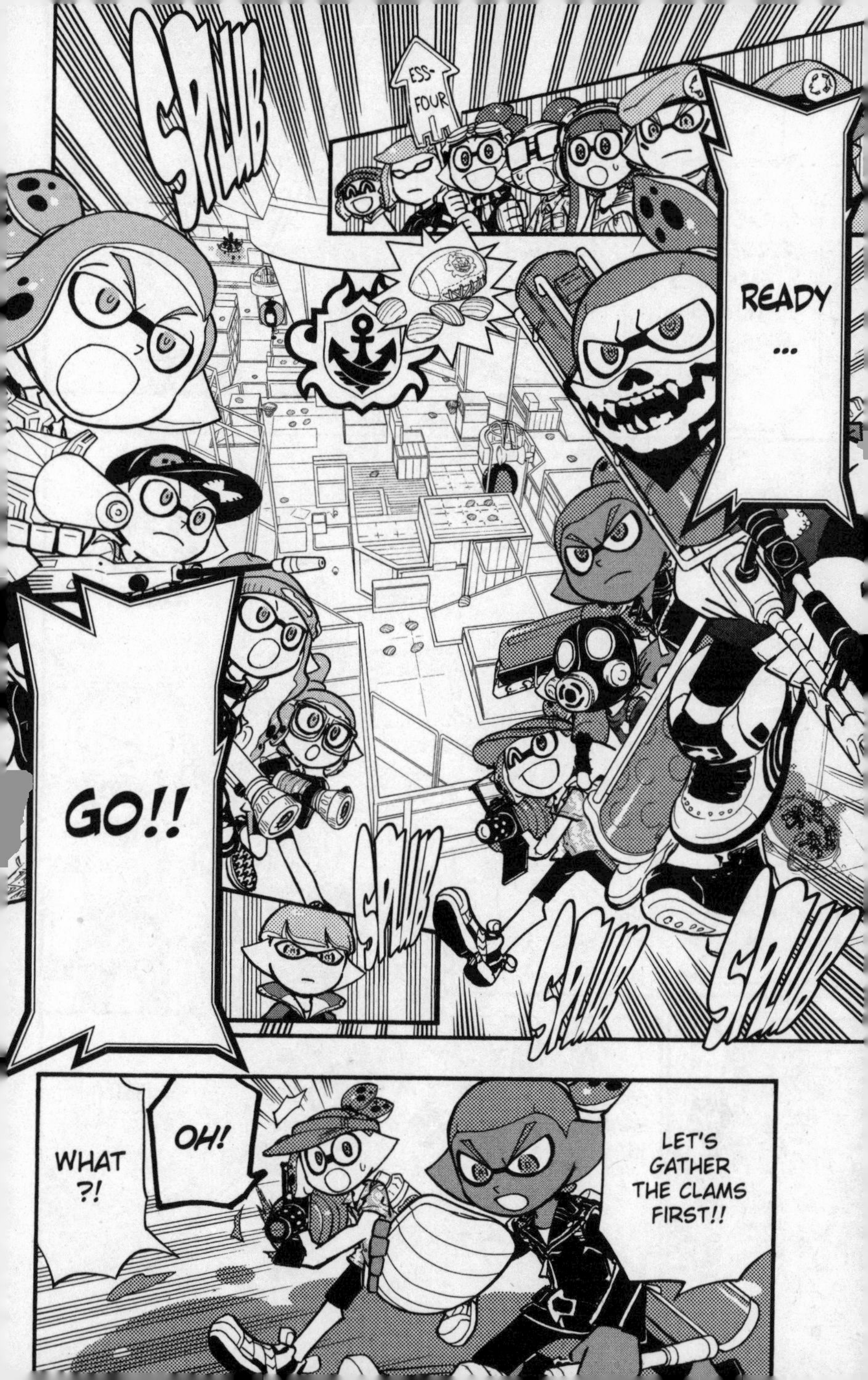
ESS-FOUR
READY ...
SPLUB
GO!!
LET'S GATHER THE CLAMS FIRST!!
OH!
WHAT ?!

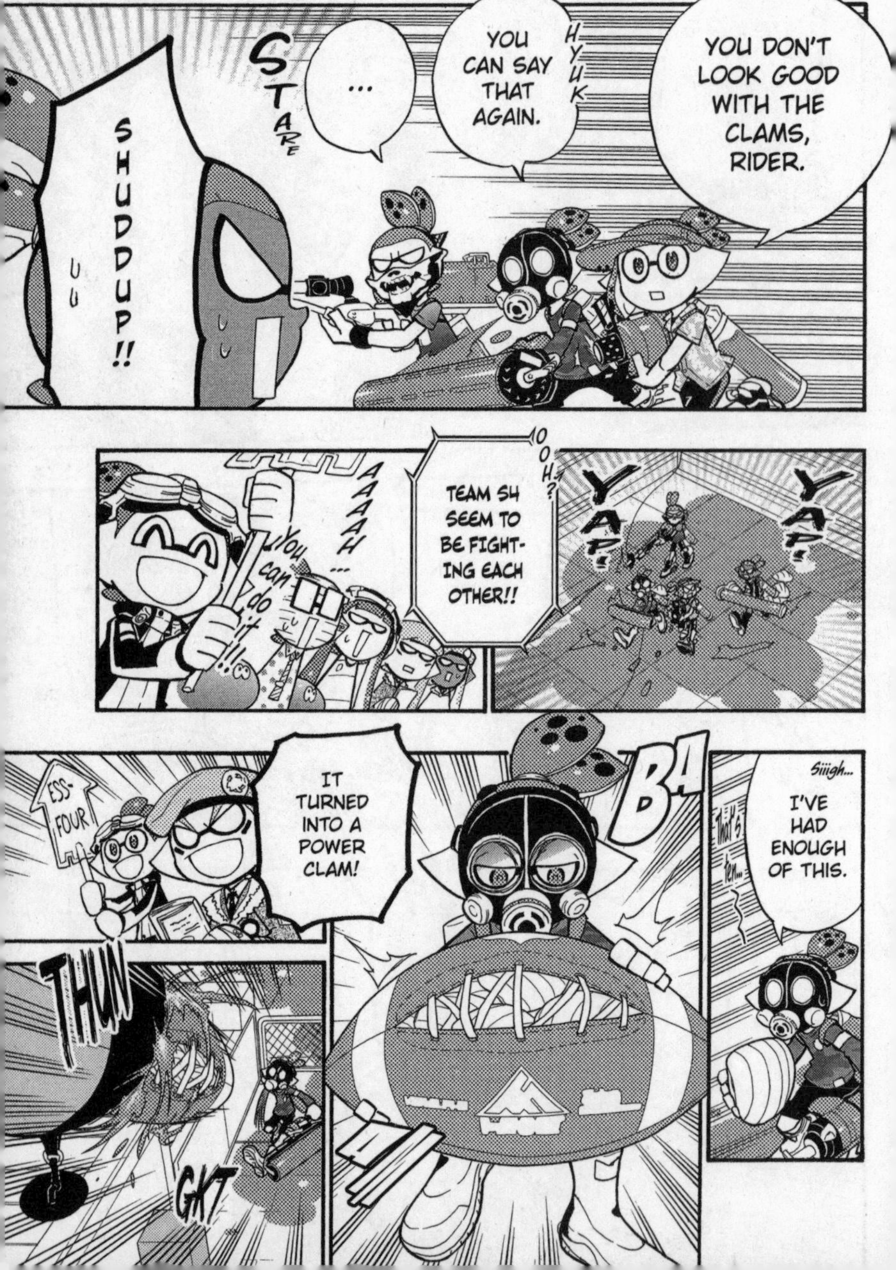
YOU DON'T LOOK GOOD WITH THE CLAMS, RIDER.
HYUK
YOU CAN SAY THAT AGAIN.
...
STARE
SHUDDUP!!
YAP
YAP
OOH?
TEAM S4 SEEM TO BE FIGHTING EACH OTHER!!
AAAAH...
You can do it!!!
Siiigh...
I'VE HAD ENOUGH OF THIS.
That's ten...
BA
IT TURNED INTO A POWER CLAM!
ESS-FOUR
THUN
GKT

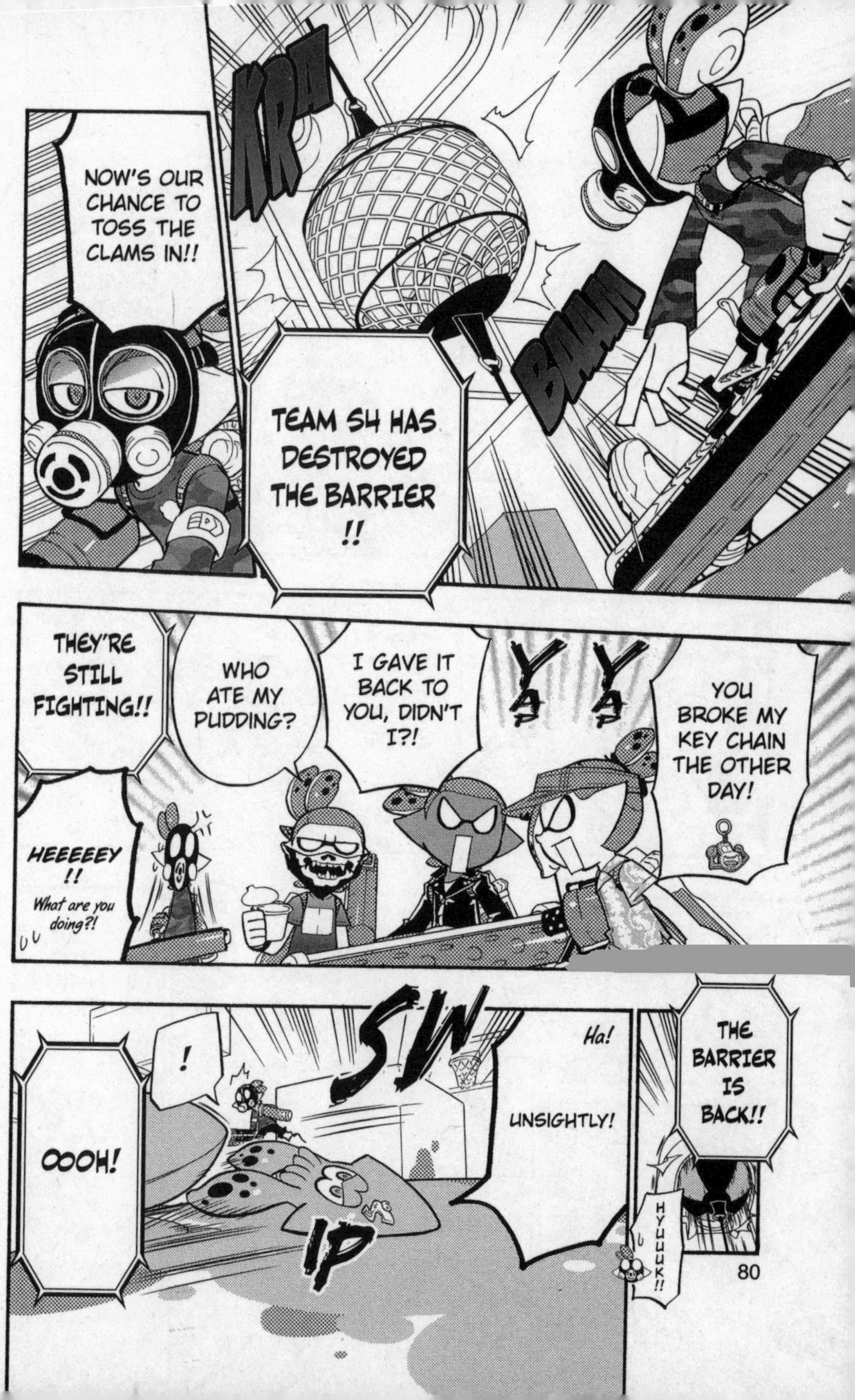
KRA
BAAM
TEAM S4 HAS DESTROYED THE BARRIER!!
NOW'S OUR CHANCE TO TOSS THE CLAMS IN!!
YOU BROKE MY KEY CHAIN THE OTHER DAY!
I GAVE IT BACK TO YOU, DIDN'T I?!
WHO ATE MY PUDDING?
THEY'RE STILL FIGHTING!!
HEEEEEY!!
What are you doing?!
THE BARRIER IS BACK!!
HYUUUK!!
SW
IP
Ha!
UNSIGHTLY!
!
OOOH!

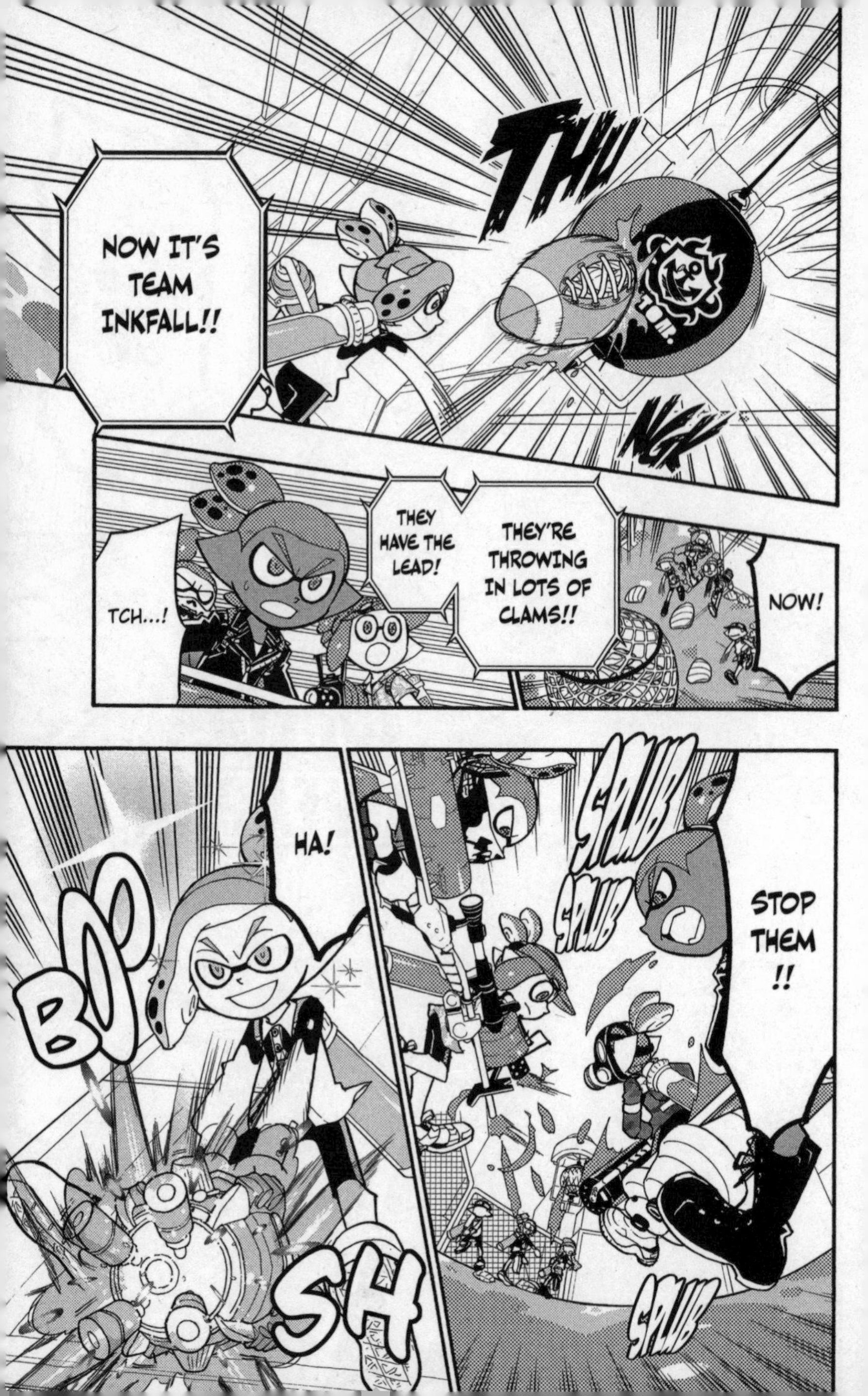
NOW IT'S TEAM INKFALL!!
NGH
NOW!
THEY'RE THROWING IN LOTS OF CLAMS!!
THEY HAVE THE LEAD!
TCH...!
STOP THEM!!
HA!
BOOSH

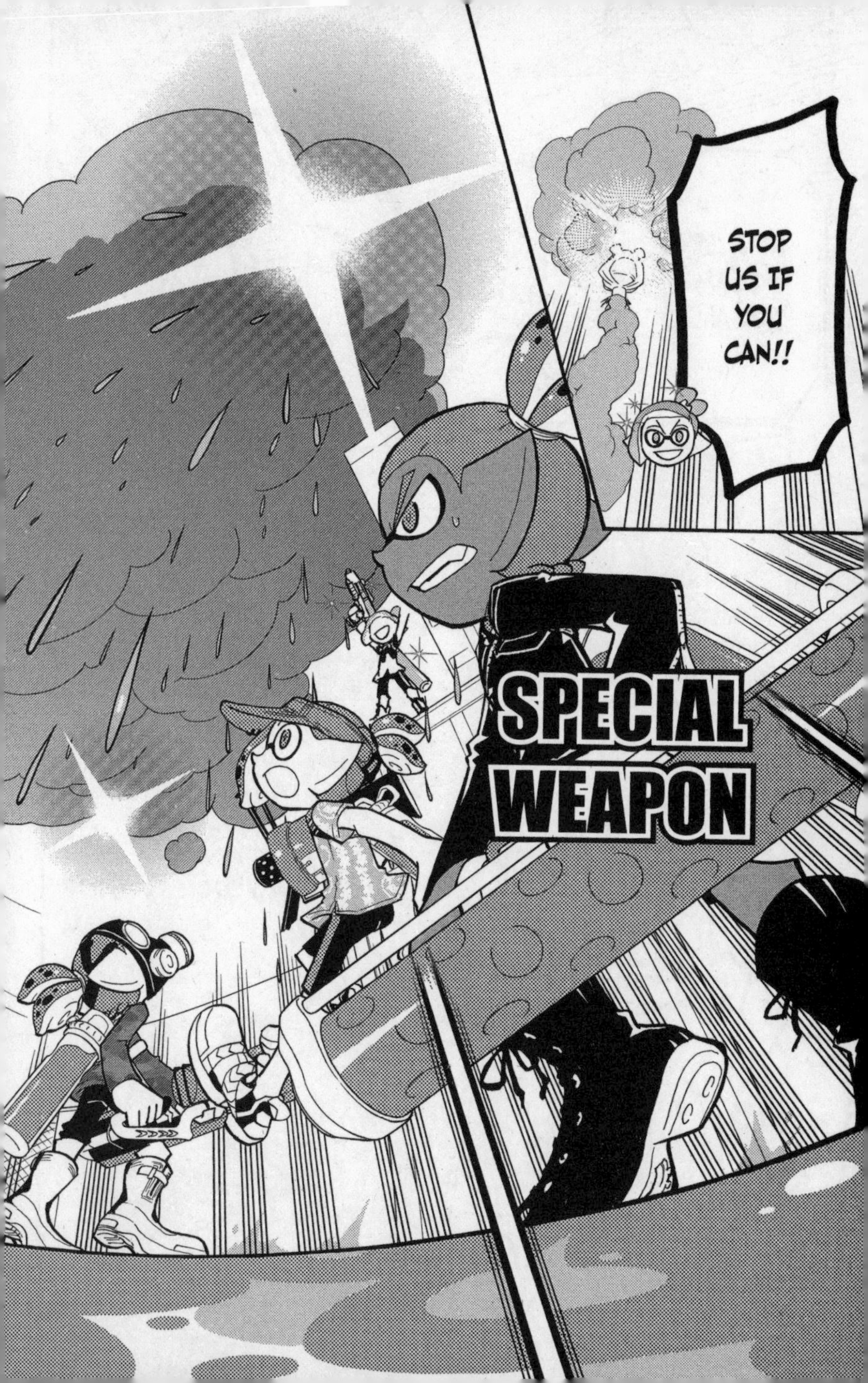
STOP US IF YOU CAN!!
SPECIAL WEAPON

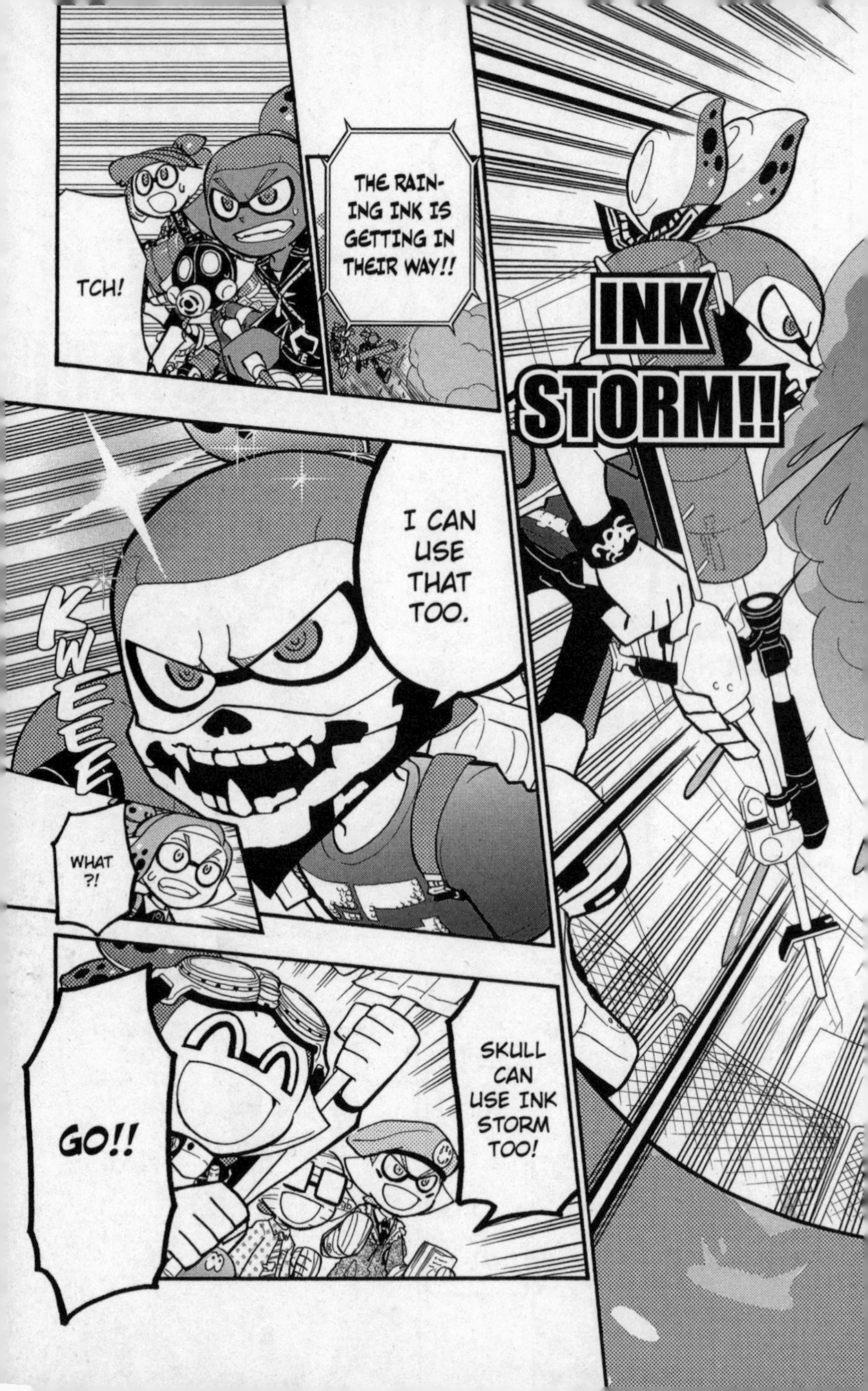
INK STORM!!
THE RAIN-ING INK IS GETTING IN THEIR WAY!!
TCH!
I CAN USE THAT TOO.
KWEEE
WHAT?!
SKULL CAN USE INK STORM TOO!
GO!!

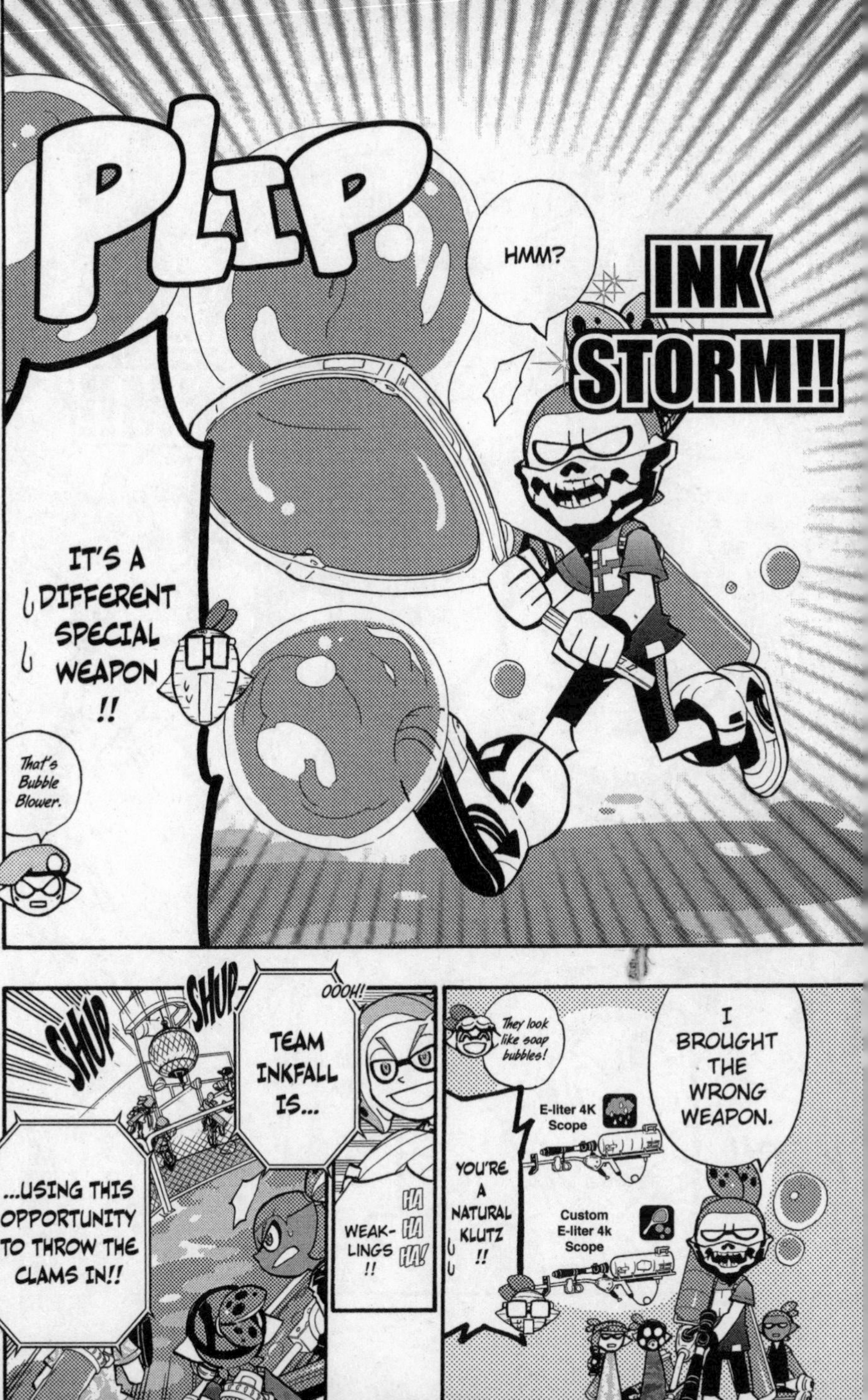
PLIP
HMM?
INK STORM!!
IT'S A DIFFERENT SPECIAL WEAPON!!
That's Bubble Blower.
I BROUGHT THE WRONG WEAPON.
They look like soap bubbles!
E-liter 4K Scope
Custom E-liter 4k Scope
YOU'RE A NATURAL KLUTZ!!
OOOH!
TEAM INKFALL IS...
HA HA HA!
WEAK-LINGS!!
SHUP
SHUP
...USING THIS OPPORTUNITY TO THROW THE CLAMS IN!!

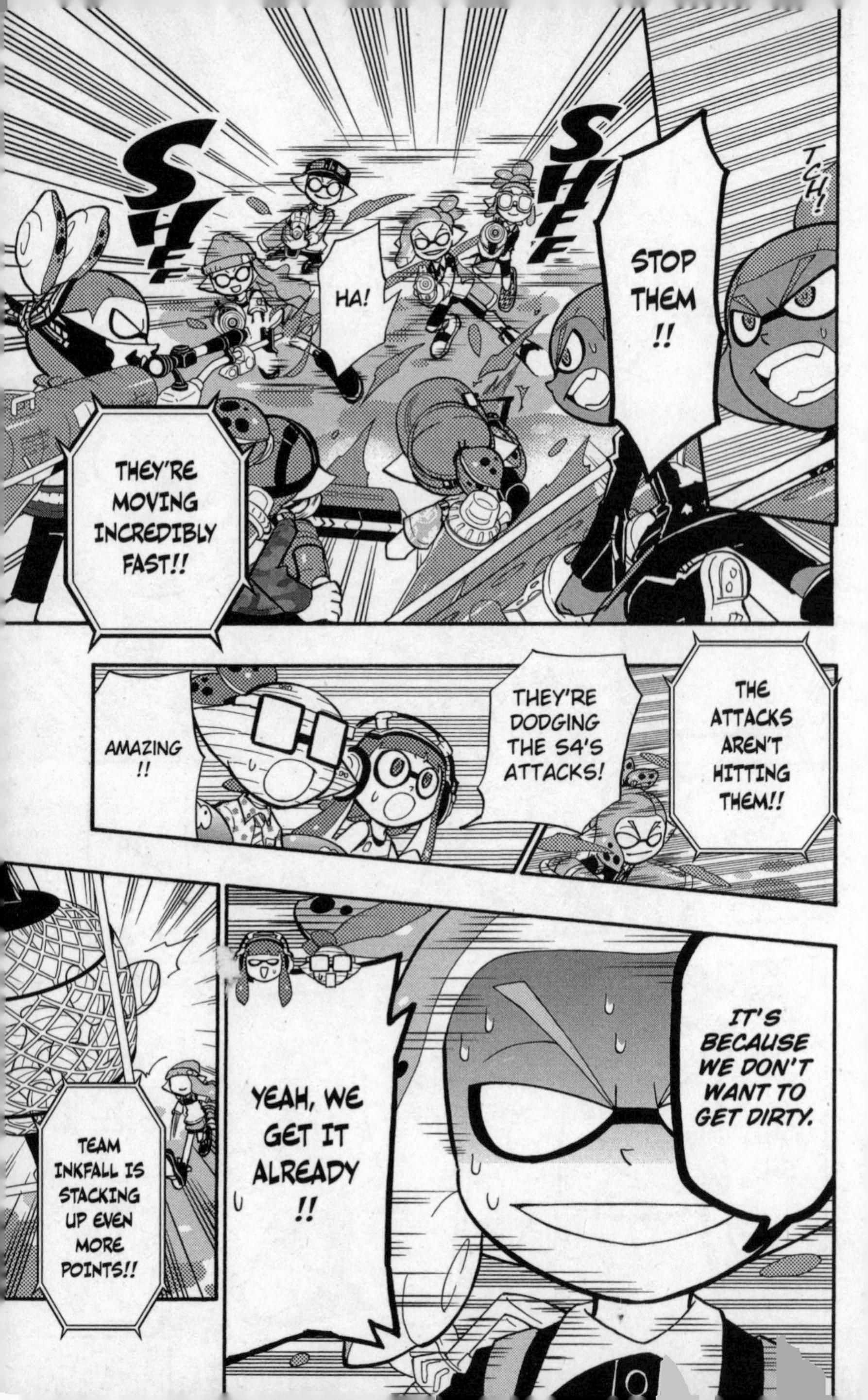
T'CH!
STOP THEM!!
SHFF
HA!
SHFF
THEY'RE MOVING INCREDIBLY FAST!!
THE ATTACKS AREN'T HITTING THEM!!
THEY'RE DODGING THE S4'S ATTACKS!
AMAZING!!
IT'S BECAUSE WE DON'T WANT TO GET DIRTY.
YEAH, WE GET IT ALREADY!!
TEAM INKFALL IS STACKING UP EVEN MORE POINTS!!

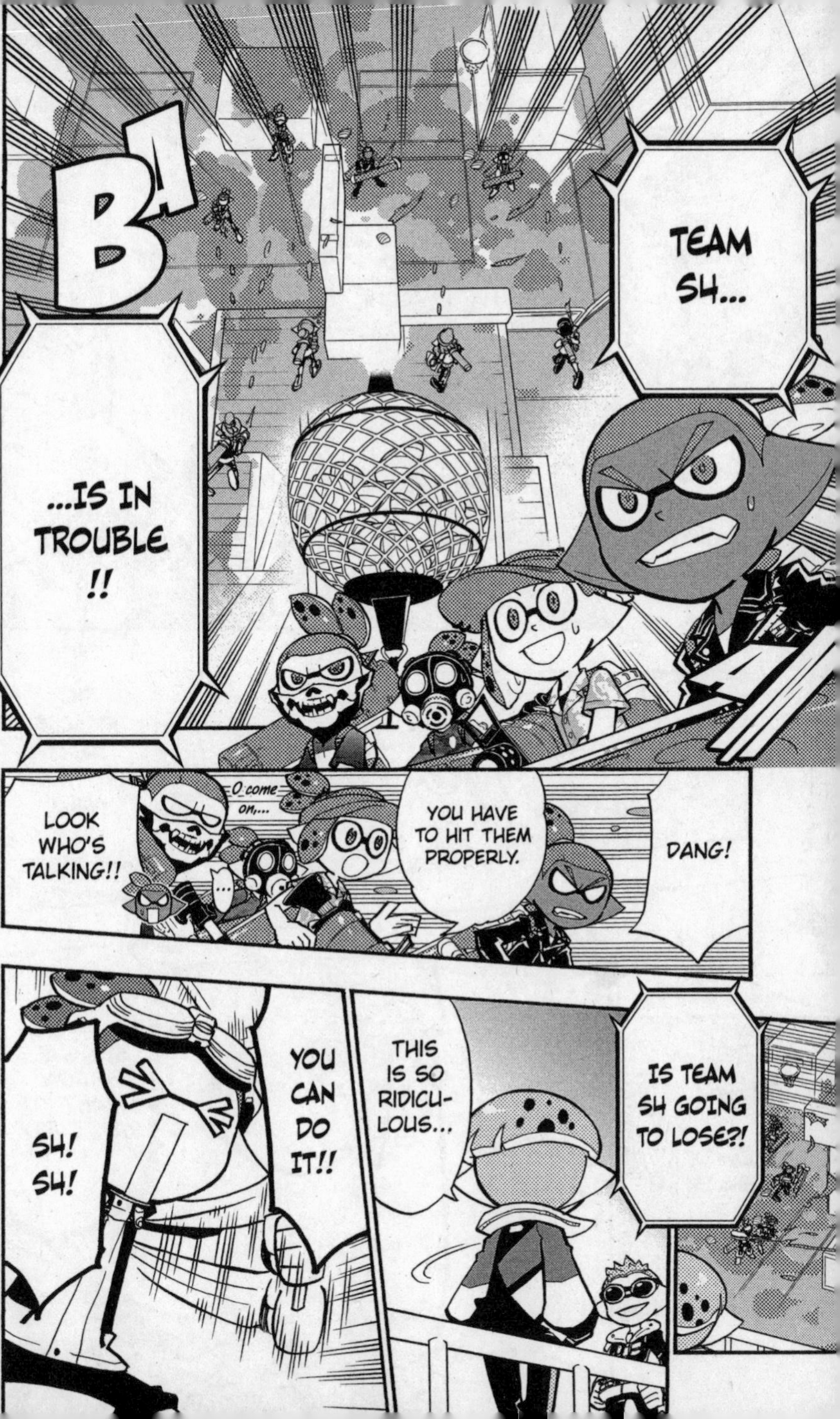
TEAM S4...
BA
...IS IN TROUBLE !!
DANG!
YOU HAVE TO HIT THEM PROPERLY.
O_come on,...
LOOK WHO'S TALKING!!
...
IS TEAM S4 GOING TO LOSE?!
THIS IS SO RIDICULOUS...
YOU CAN DO IT!!
S4! S4!

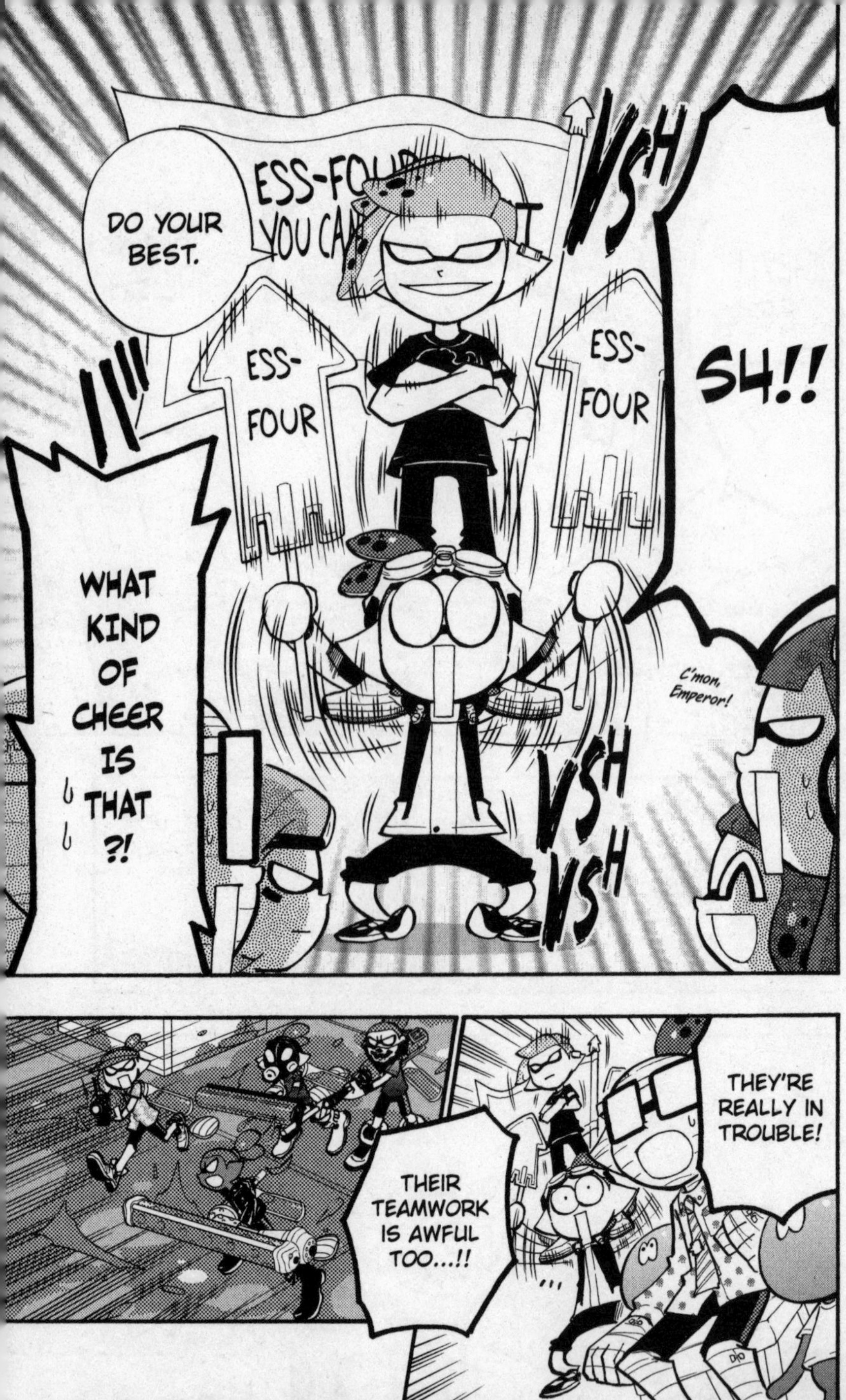
VSH
S4!!
ESS-FOU
YOU CA
ESS-
FOUR
ESS-
FOUR
DO YOUR BEST.
C'mon, Emperor!
VSH
VSH
WHAT KIND OF CHEER IS THAT?!
THEY'RE REALLY IN TROUBLE!
THEIR TEAMWORK IS AWFUL TOO...!!
...

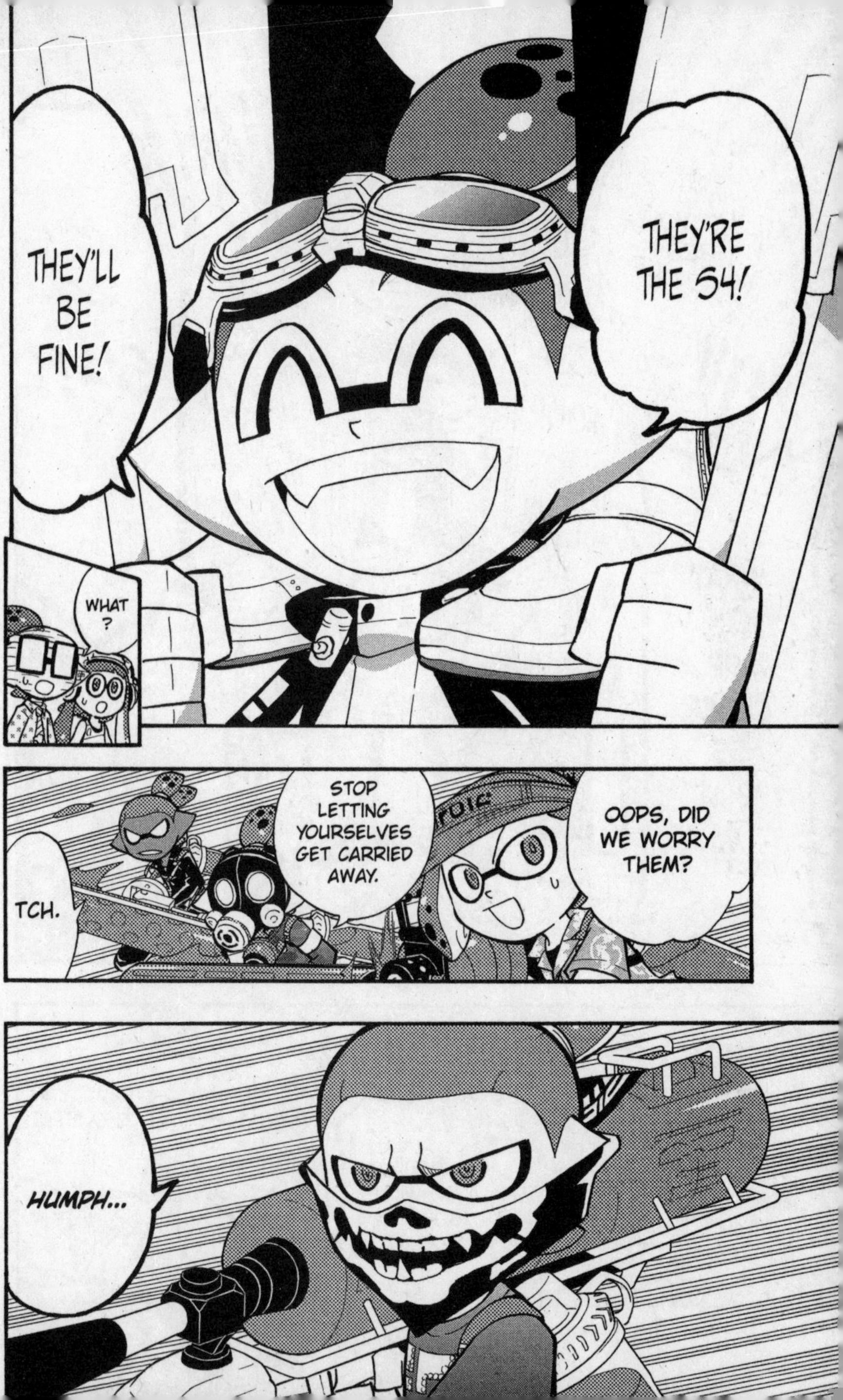
THEY'RE THE S4!
THEY'LL BE FINE!
WHAT?
OOPS, DID WE WORRY THEM?
STOP LETTING YOURSELVES GET CARRIED AWAY.
TCH.
HUMPH...

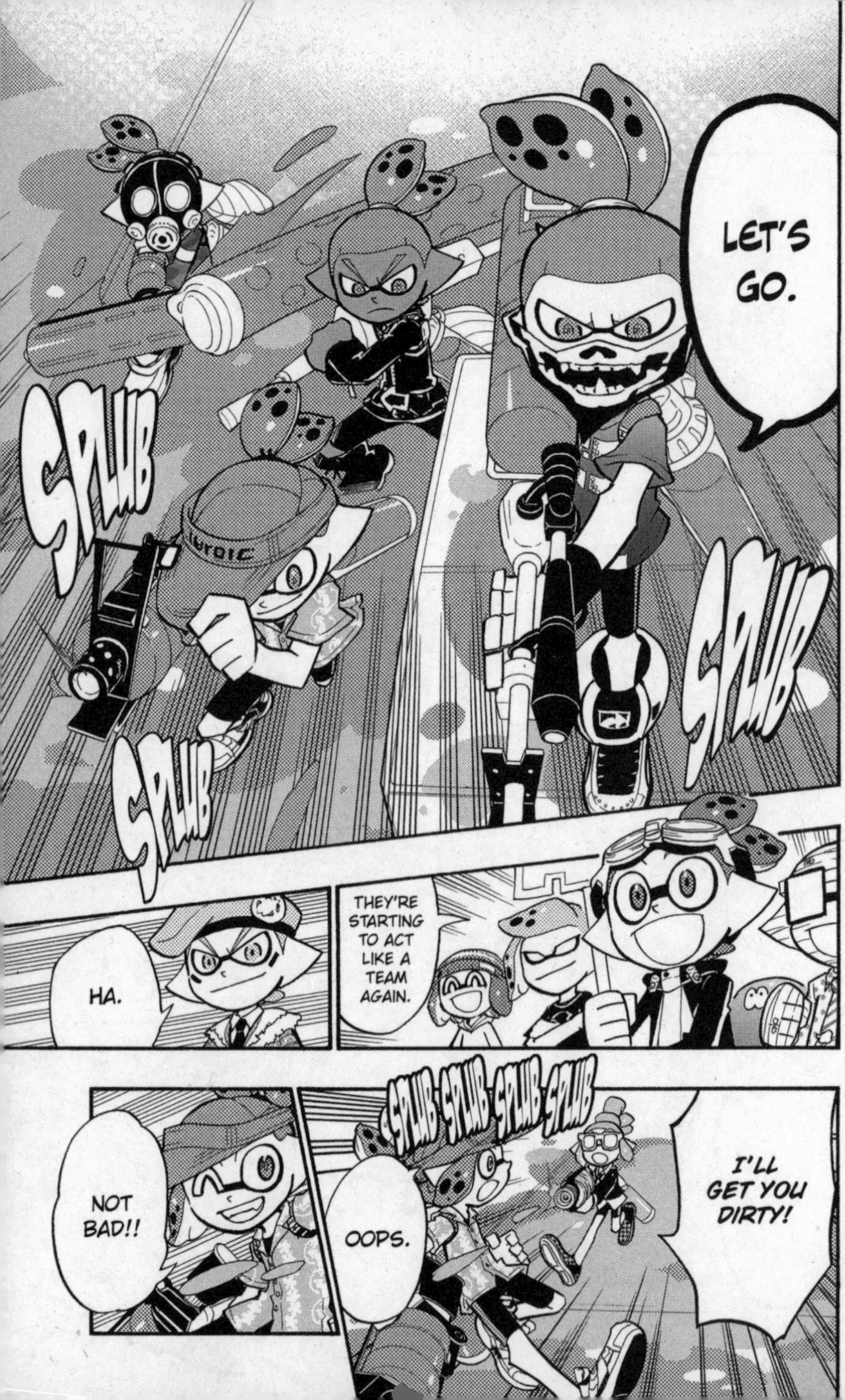
LET'S GO.
SPLUB
SPLUB
SPLUB
THEY'RE STARTING TO ACT LIKE A TEAM AGAIN.
HA.
SPLUB SPLUB SPLUB SPLUB
I'LL GET YOU DIRTY!
OOPS.
NOT BAD!!

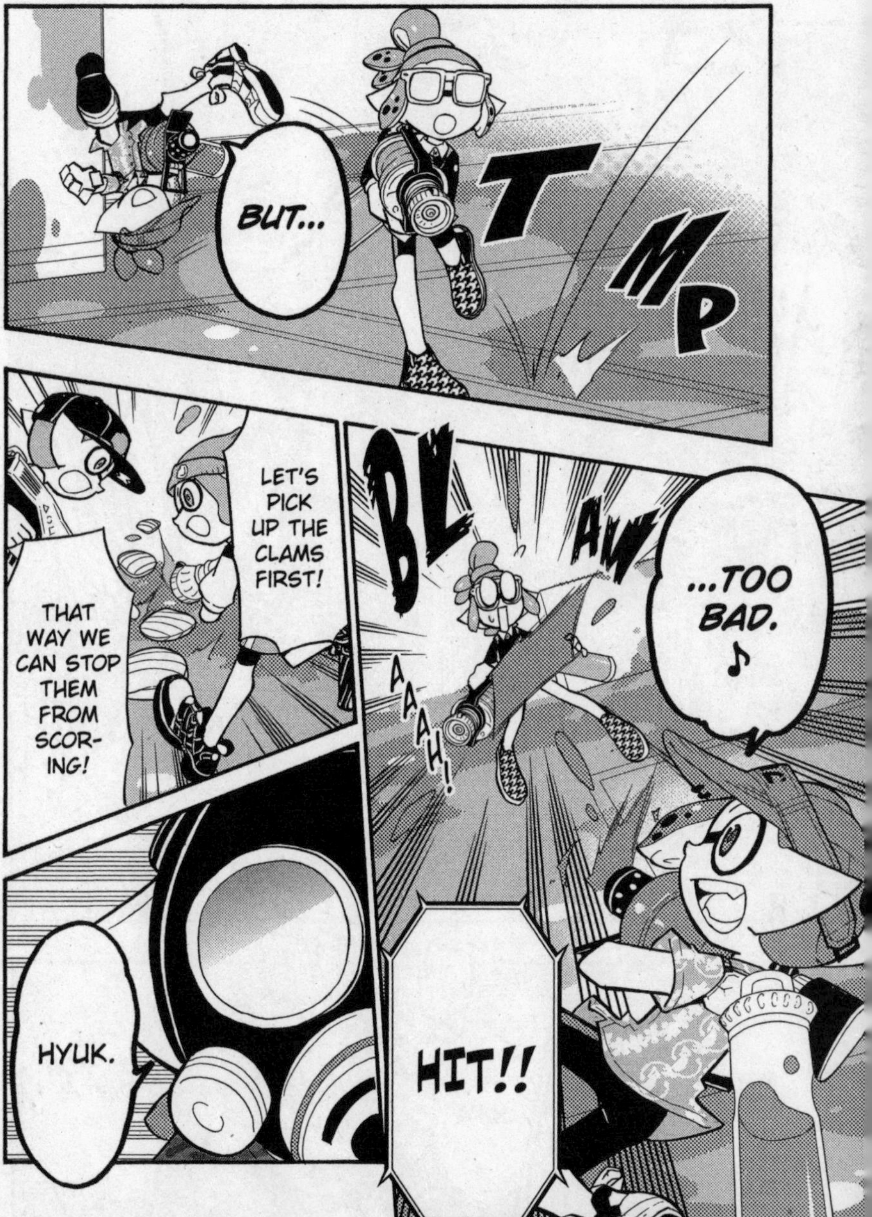
BUT...
TMP
BLAM
AAAAH!
...TOO BAD. ♪
LET'S PICK UP THE CLAMS FIRST!
THAT WAY WE CAN STOP THEM FROM SCOR-ING!
HIT!!
HYUK.

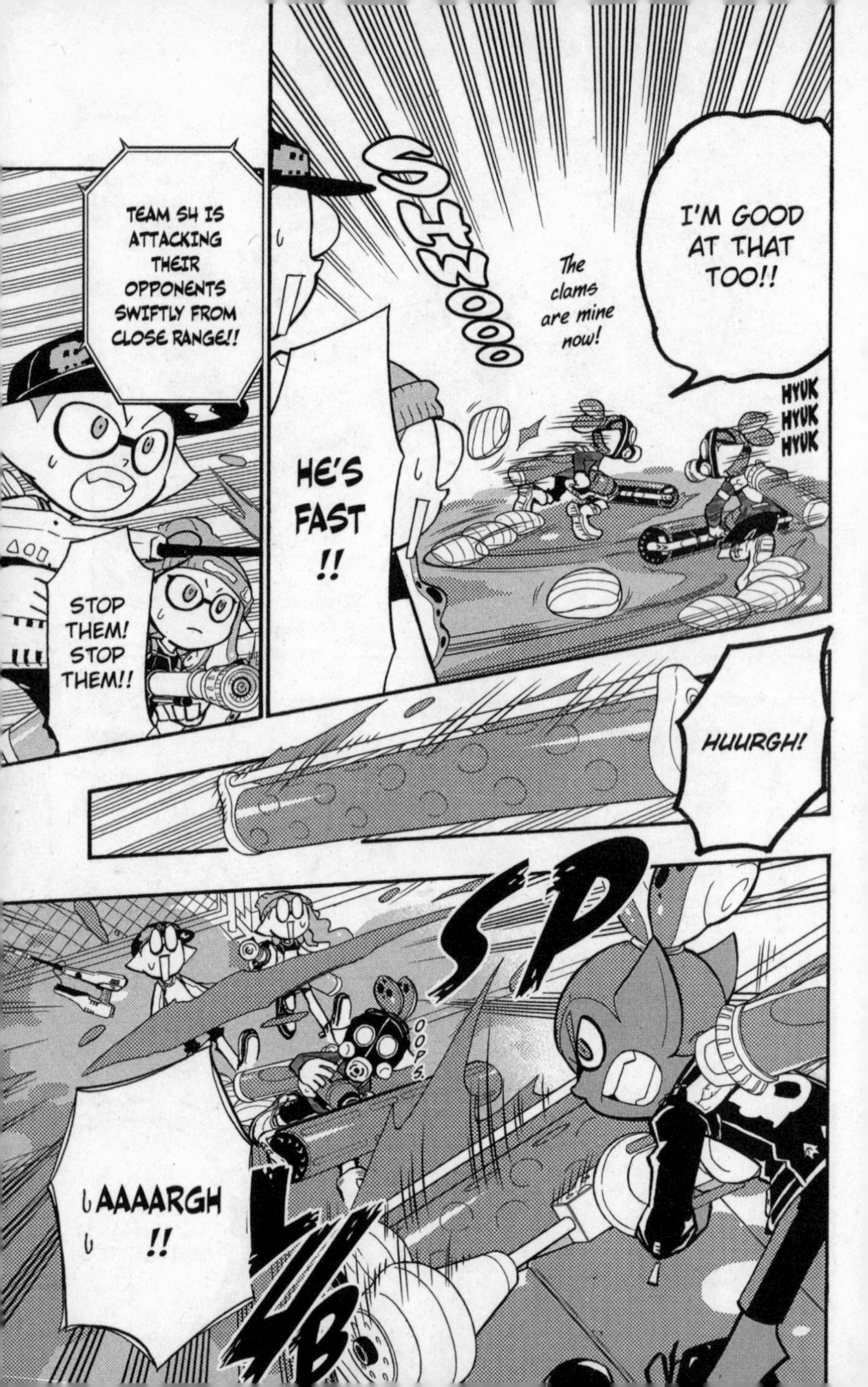
I'M GOOD AT THAT TOO!!
HYUK HYUK HYUK
The clams are mine now!
SHWOOOO
HE'S FAST !!
TEAM S4 IS ATTACKING THEIR OPPONENTS SWIFTLY FROM CLOSE RANGE!!
STOP THEM! STOP THEM!!
HUURGH!
SP
OOPS.
AAAARGH !!

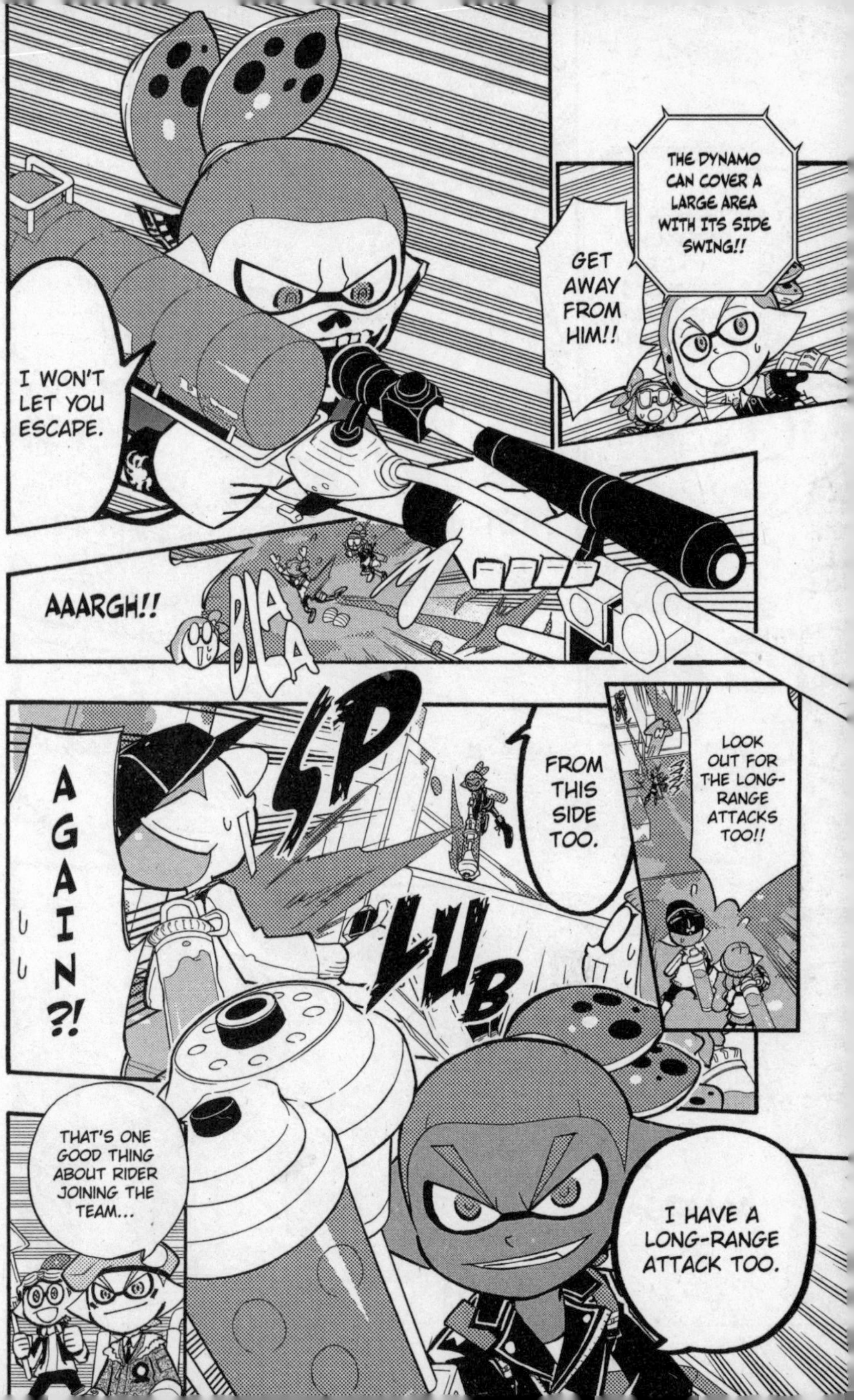
THE DYNAMO CAN COVER A LARGE AREA WITH ITS SIDE SWING!!
GET AWAY FROM HIM!!
I WON'T LET YOU ESCAPE.
BLAM
AAARGH!!
LOOK OUT FOR THE LONG-RANGE ATTACKS TOO!!
FROM THIS SIDE TOO.
SPLUB
AGAIN?!
THAT'S ONE GOOD THING ABOUT RIDER JOINING THE TEAM...
I HAVE A LONG-RANGE ATTACK TOO.

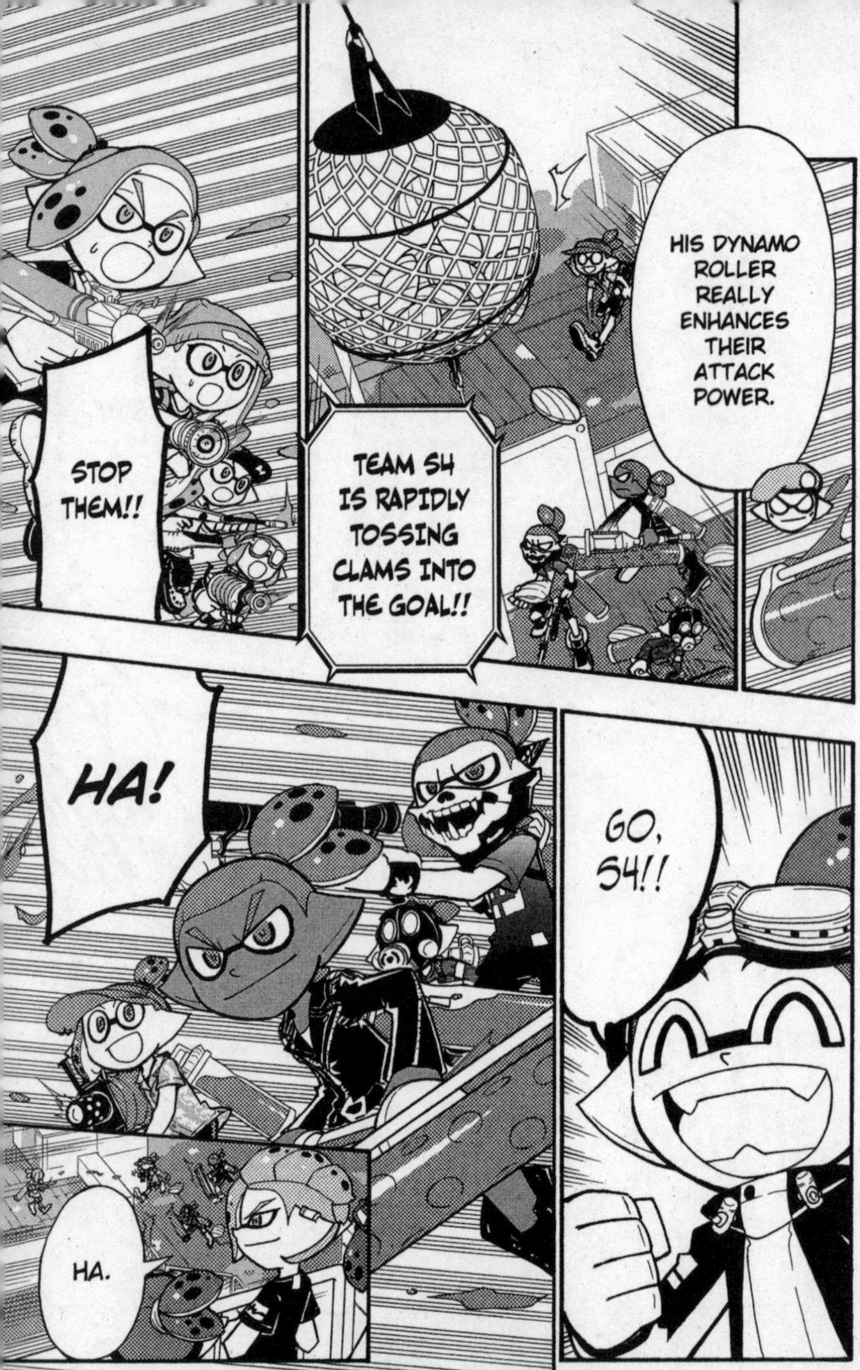
HIS DYNAMO ROLLER REALLY ENHANCES THEIR ATTACK POWER.
TEAM S4 IS RAPIDLY TOSSING CLAMS INTO THE GOAL!!
STOP THEM!!
GO, S4!!
HA!
HA.

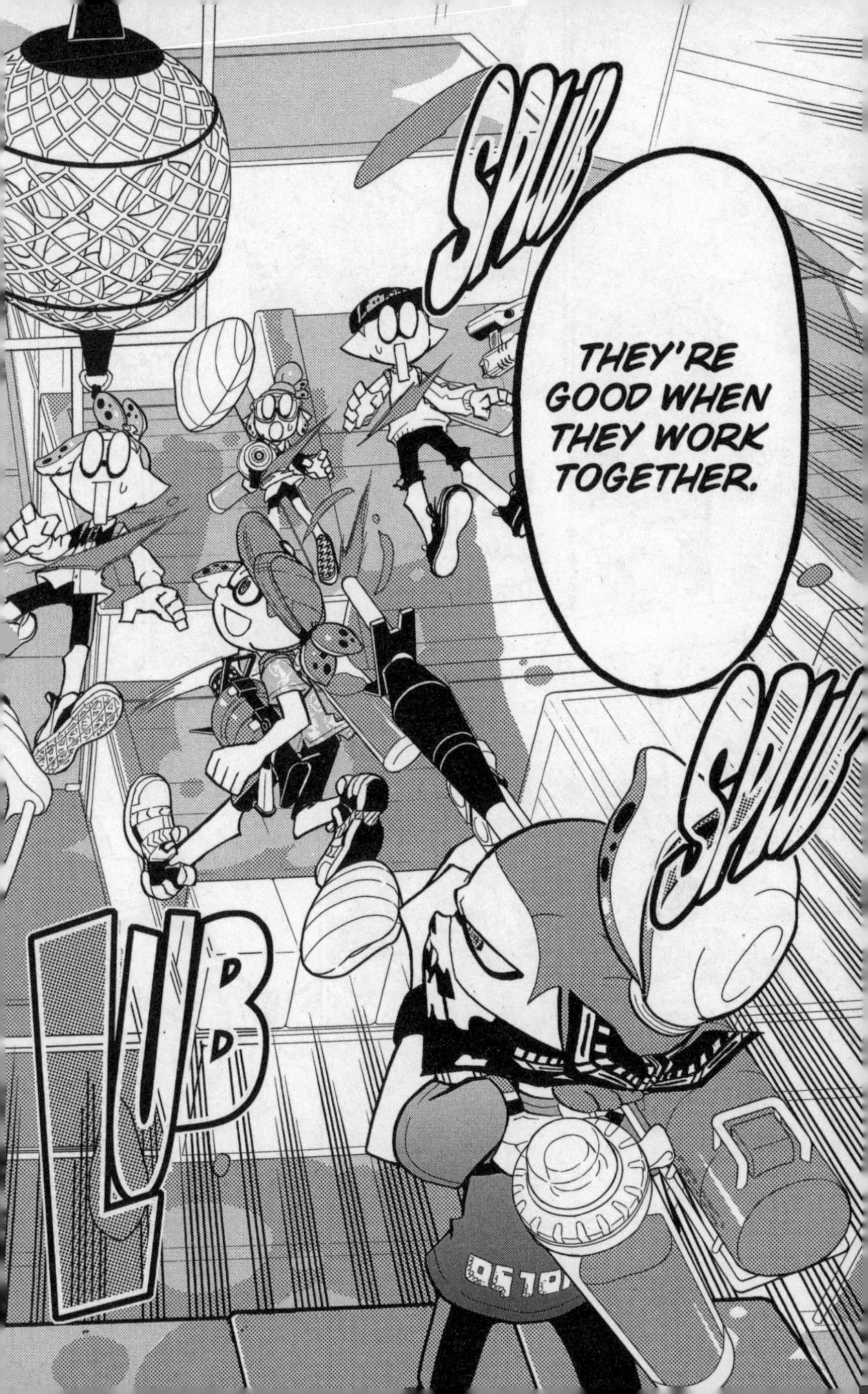
THEY'RE GOOD WHEN THEY WORK TOGETHER.

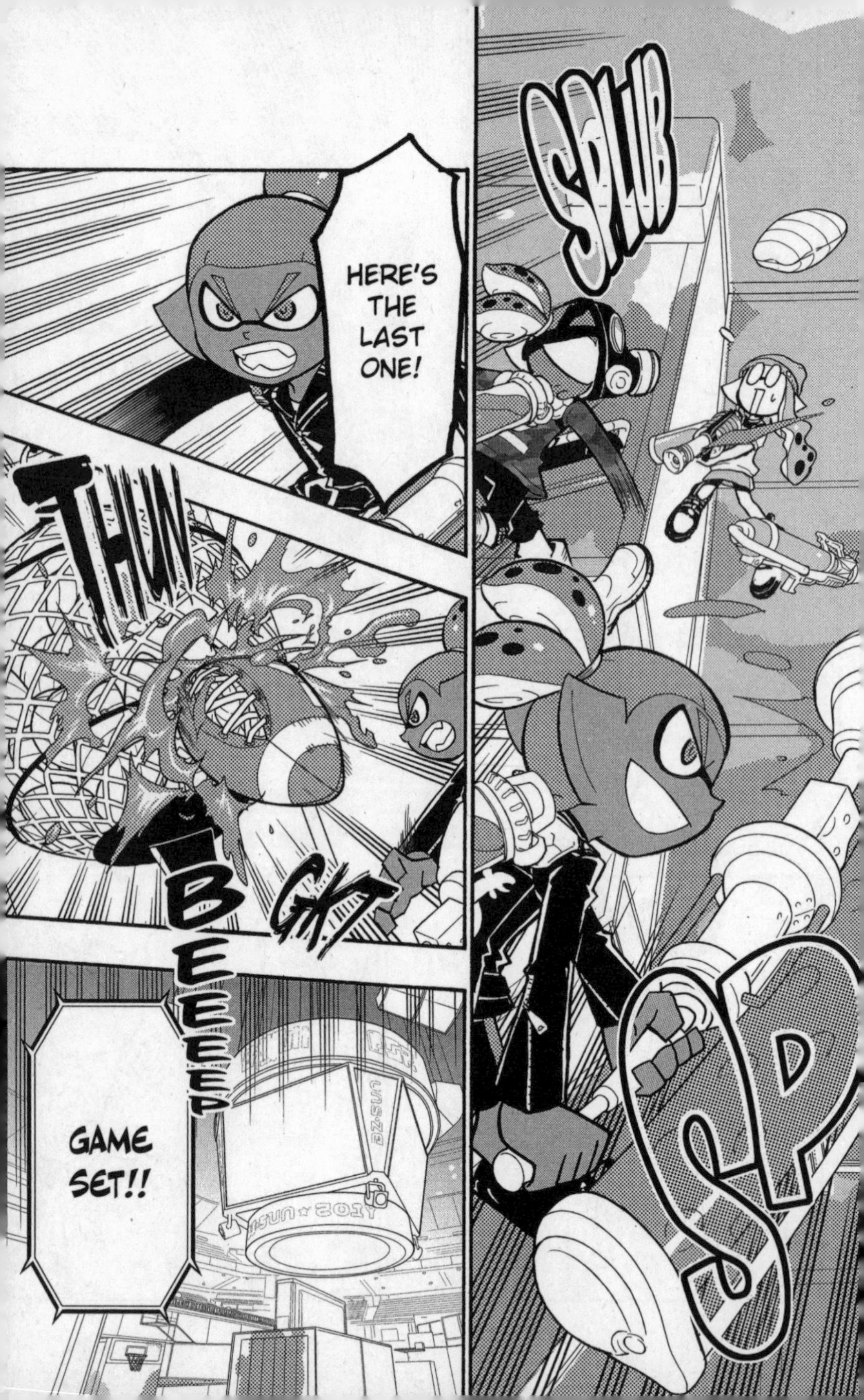
SPLUB
SP
HERE'S THE LAST ONE!
THUN
GKT
BEEEEP
GAME SET!!

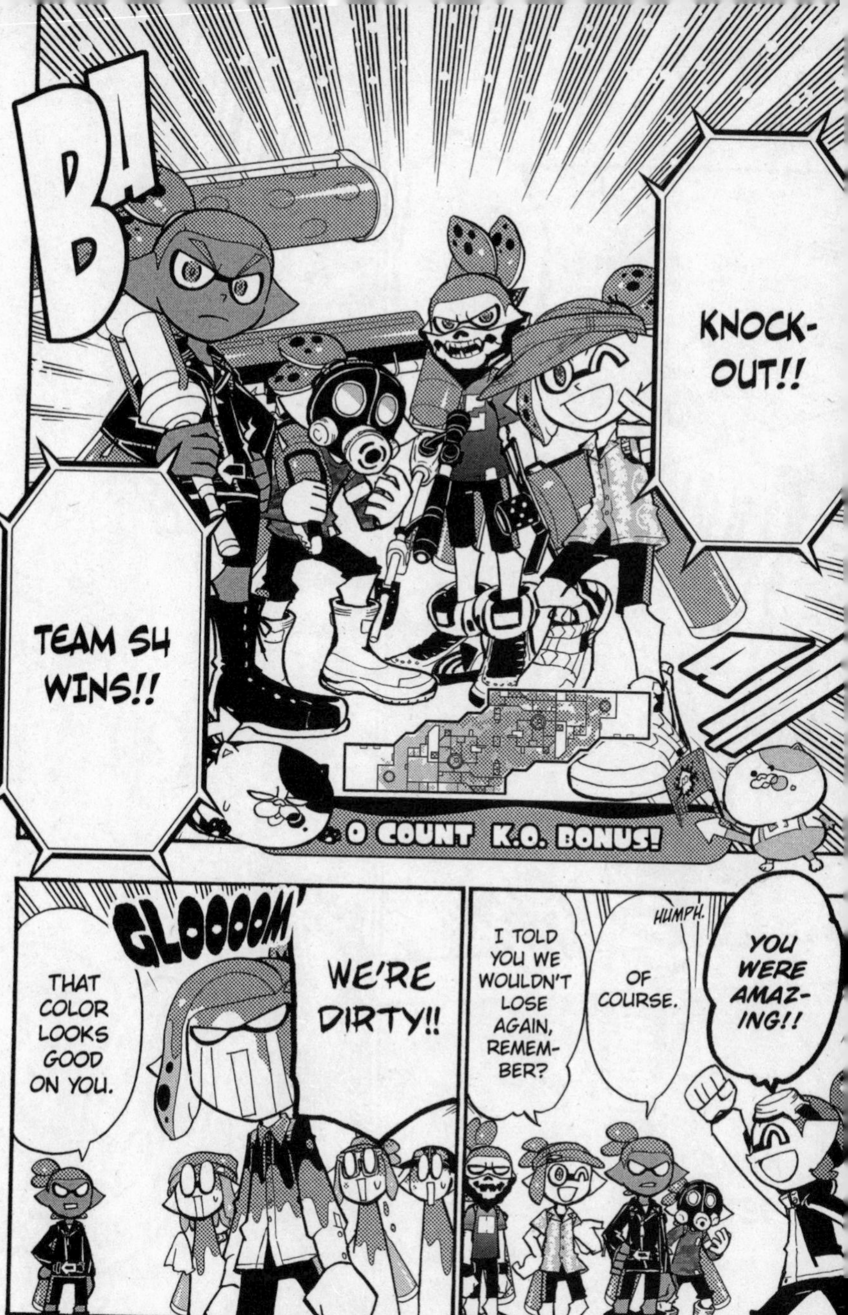
KNOCK-OUT!!
BA
TEAM 54 WINS!!
0 COUNT K.O. BONUS!
YOU WERE AMAZ-ING!!
HUMPH.
OF COURSE.
I TOLD YOU WE WOULDN'T LOSE AGAIN, REMEMBER?
GLOOOOM
WE'RE DIRTY!!
THAT COLOR LOOKS GOOD ON YOU.

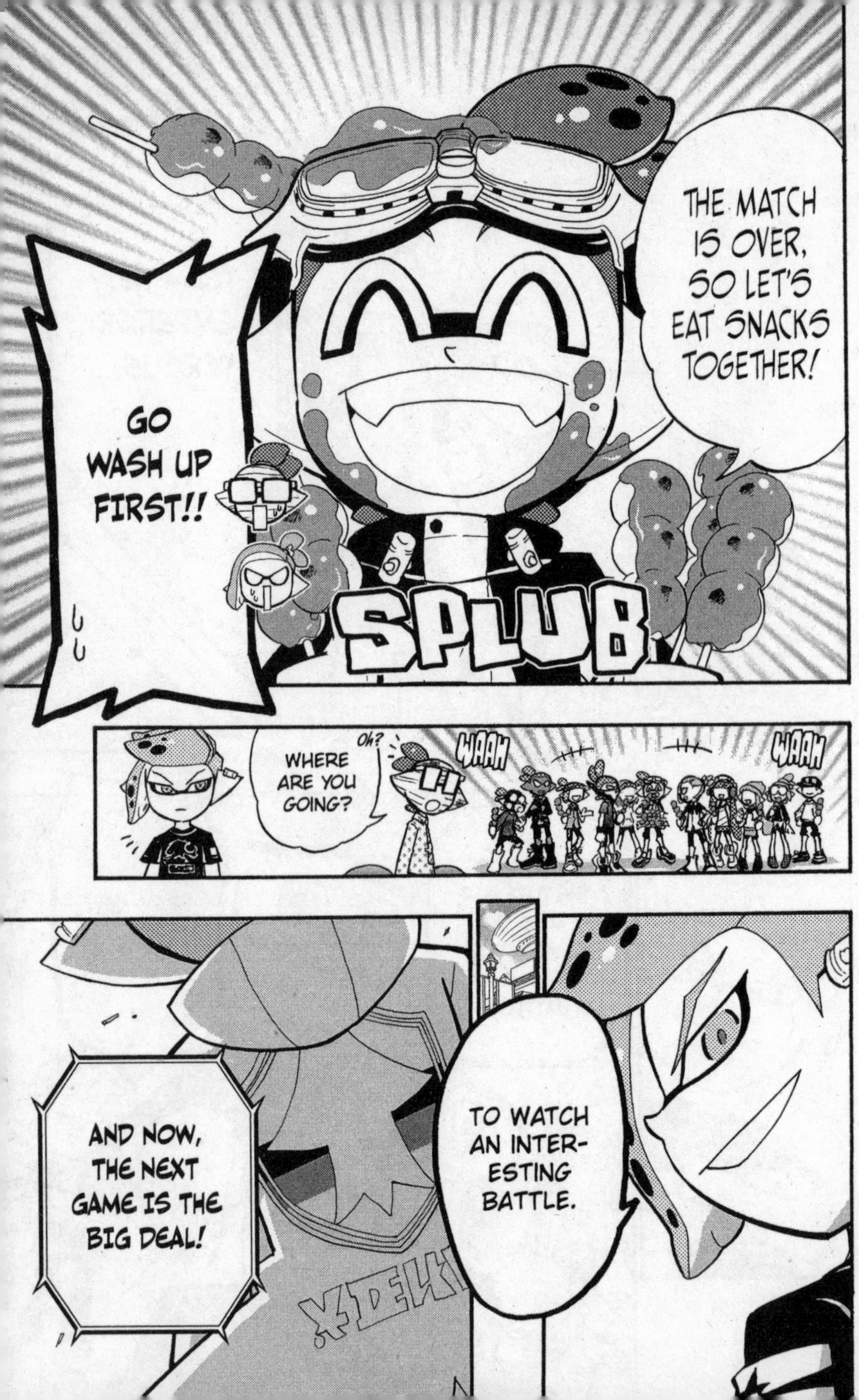
THE MATCH IS OVER, SO LET'S EAT SNACKS TOGETHER!
SPLUB
GO WASH UP FIRST!!
WAAH
WAAH
Oh?
WHERE ARE YOU GOING?
TO WATCH AN INTER-ESTING BATTLE.
AND NOW, THE NEXT GAME IS THE BIG DEAL!

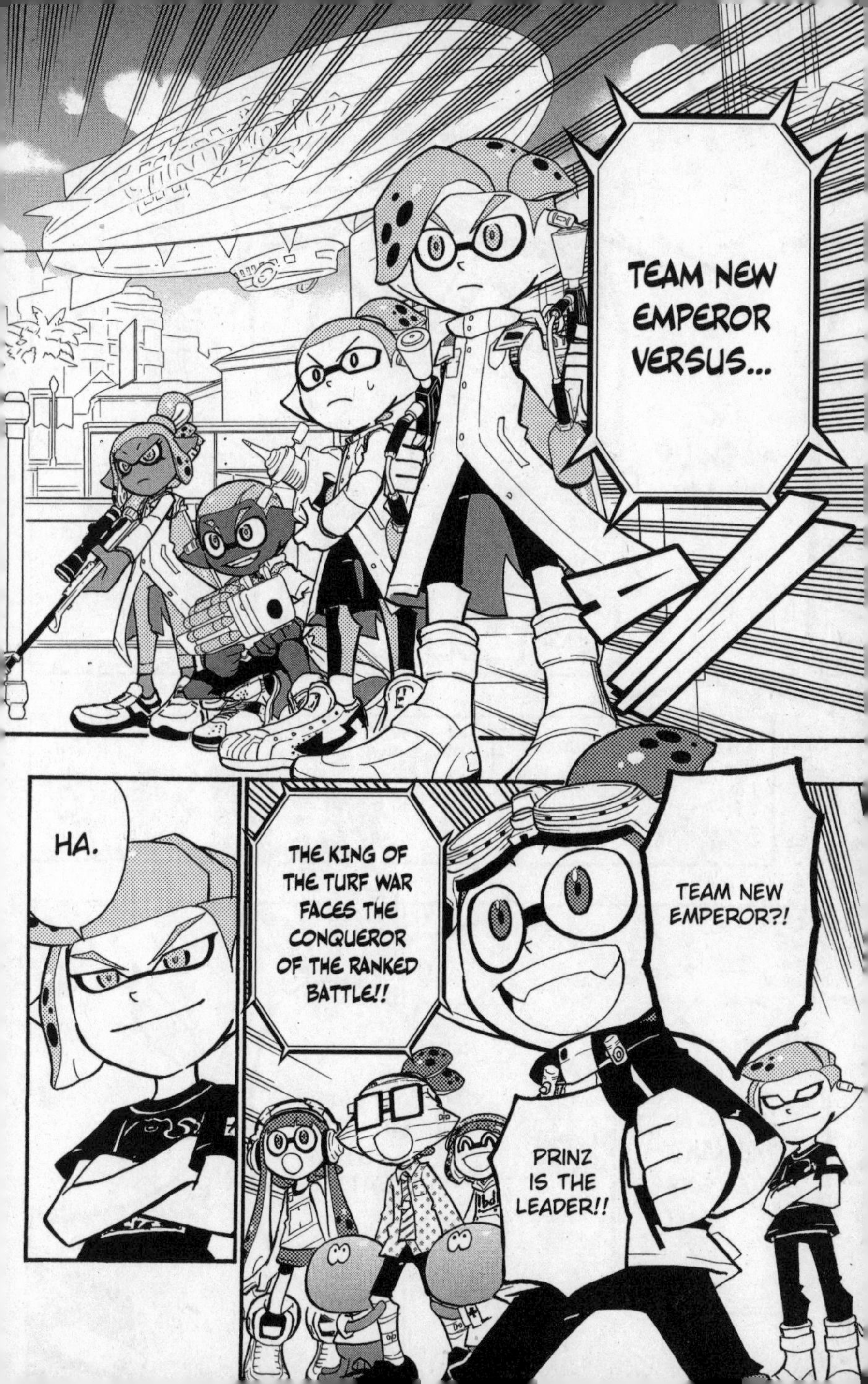
TEAM NEW EMPEROR VERSUS...
TEAM NEW EMPEROR?!
THE KING OF THE TURF WAR FACES THE CONQUEROR OF THE RANKED BATTLE!!
PRINZ IS THE LEADER!!
HA.

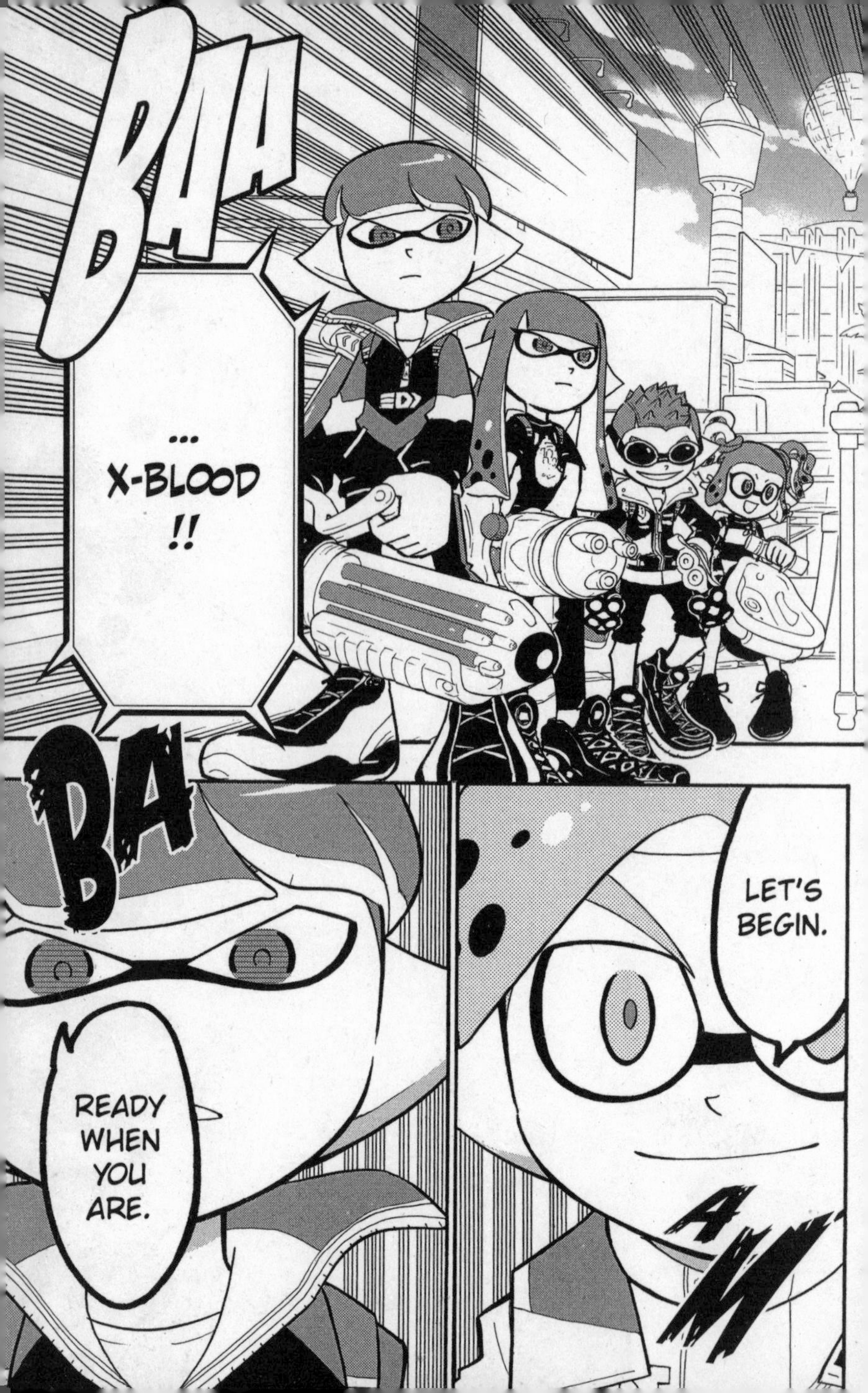
BAA
... X-BLOOD !!
LET'S BEGIN.
BA
READY WHEN YOU ARE.

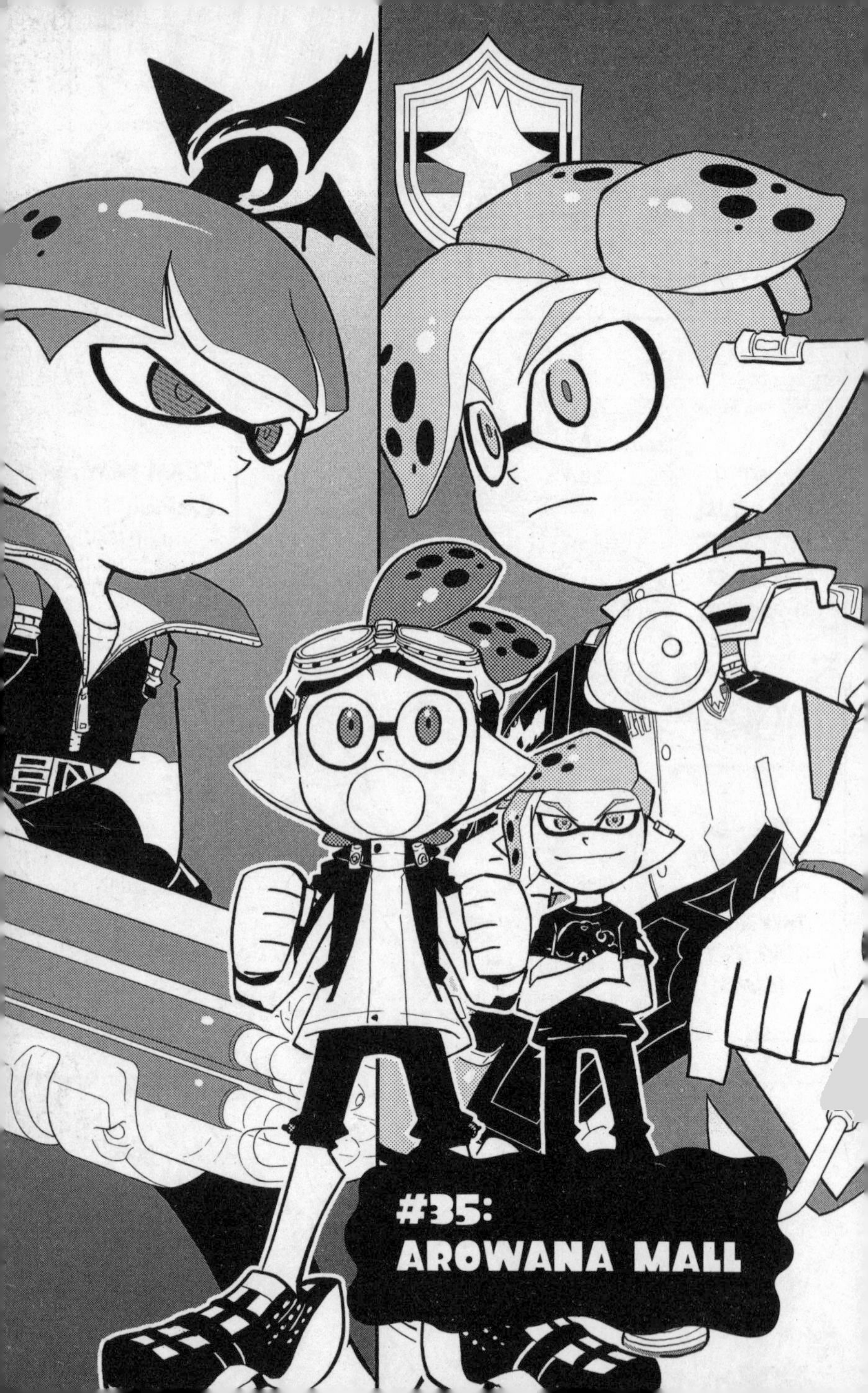
#35:
AROWANA MALL

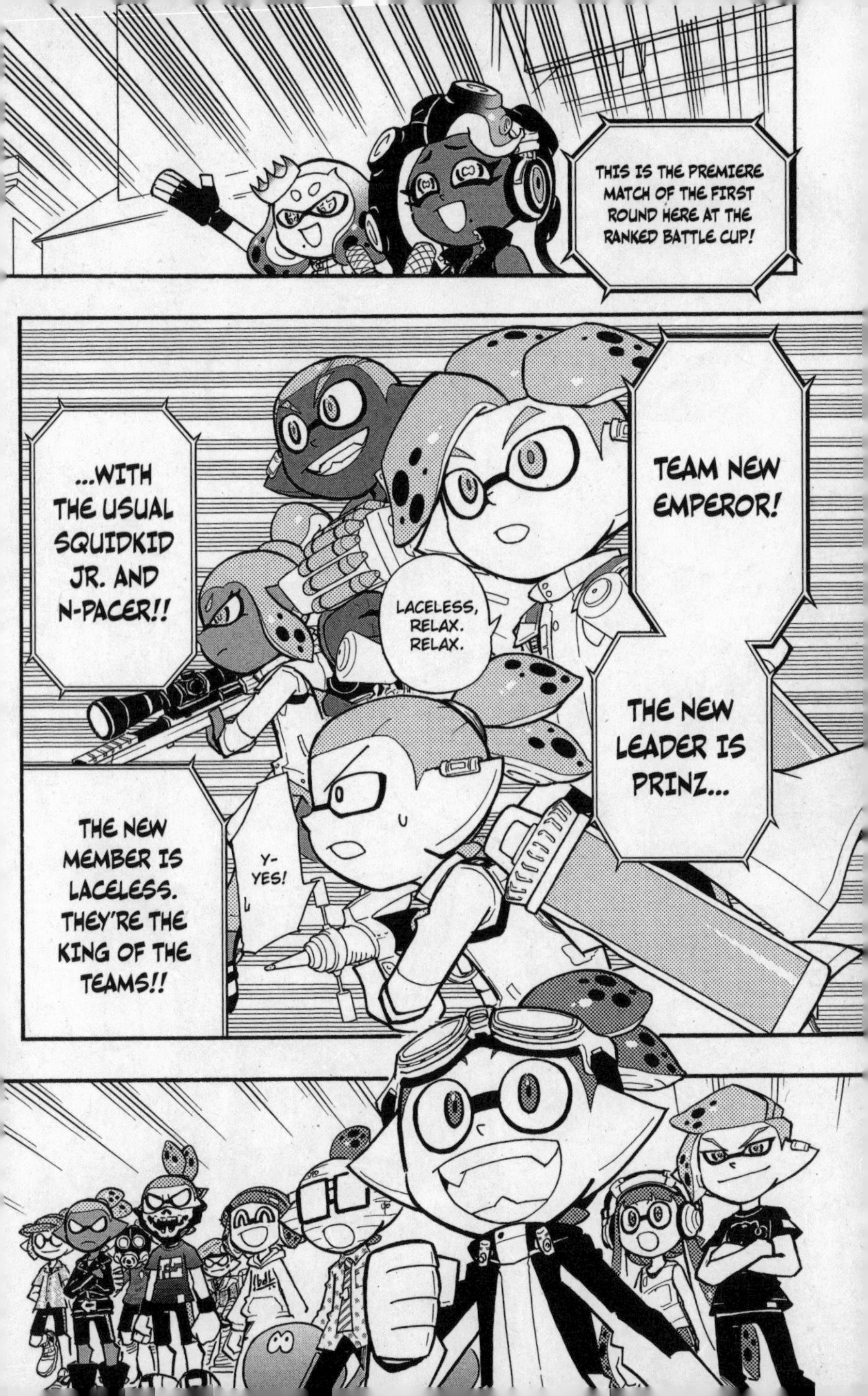
THIS IS THE PREMIERE MATCH OF THE FIRST ROUND HERE AT THE RANKED BATTLE CUP!
TEAM NEW EMPEROR!
THE NEW LEADER IS PRINZ...
...WITH THE USUAL SQUIDKID JR. AND N-PACER!!
LACELESS, RELAX. RELAX.
THE NEW MEMBER IS LACELESS. THEY'RE THE KING OF THE TEAMS!!
Y- YES!

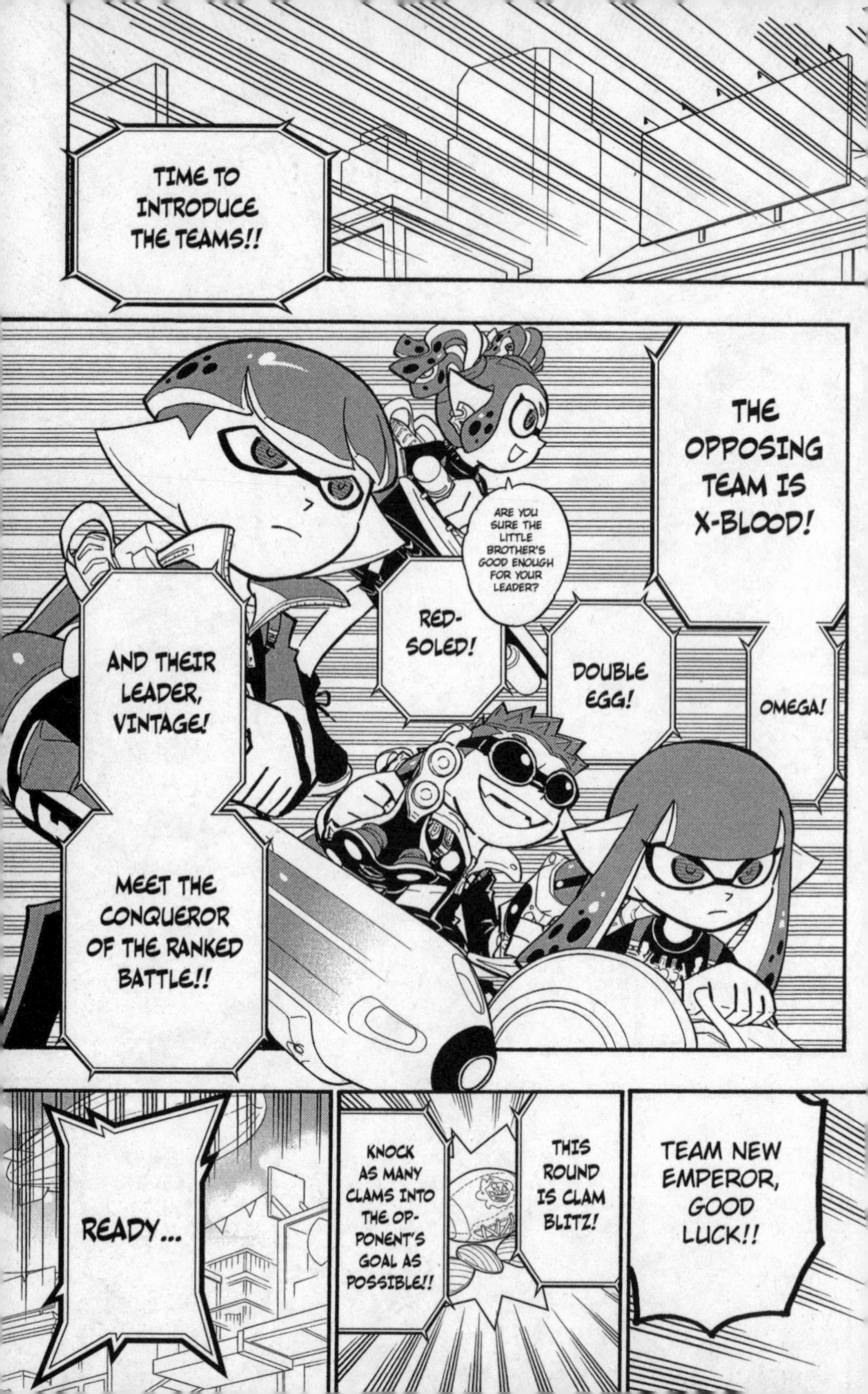
TIME TO INTRODUCE THE TEAMS!!
THE OPPOSING TEAM IS X-BLOOD!
OMEGA!
DOUBLE EGG!
RED-SOLED!
ARE YOU SURE THE LITTLE BROTHER'S GOOD ENOUGH FOR YOUR LEADER?
AND THEIR LEADER, VINTAGE!
MEET THE CONQUEROR OF THE RANKED BATTLE!!
TEAM NEW EMPEROR, GOOD LUCK!!
THIS ROUND IS CLAM BLITZ!
KNOCK AS MANY CLAMS INTO THE OP-PONENT'S GOAL AS POSSIBLE!!
READY...

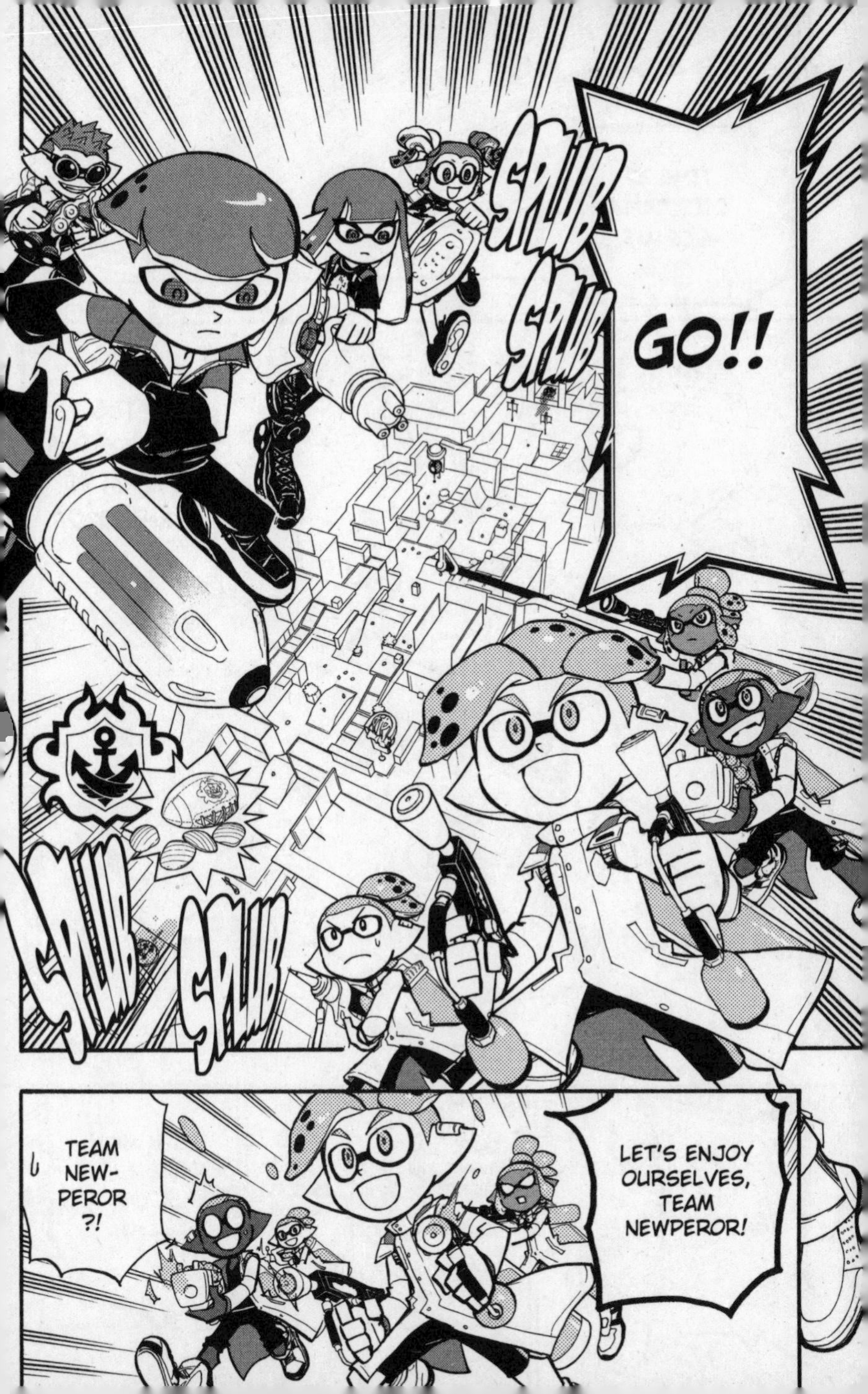
GO!!
SPLUB
SPLUB
SPLUB
SPLUB
SPLUB
LET'S ENJOY OURSELVES, TEAM NEWPEROR!
TEAM NEW-PEROR ?!

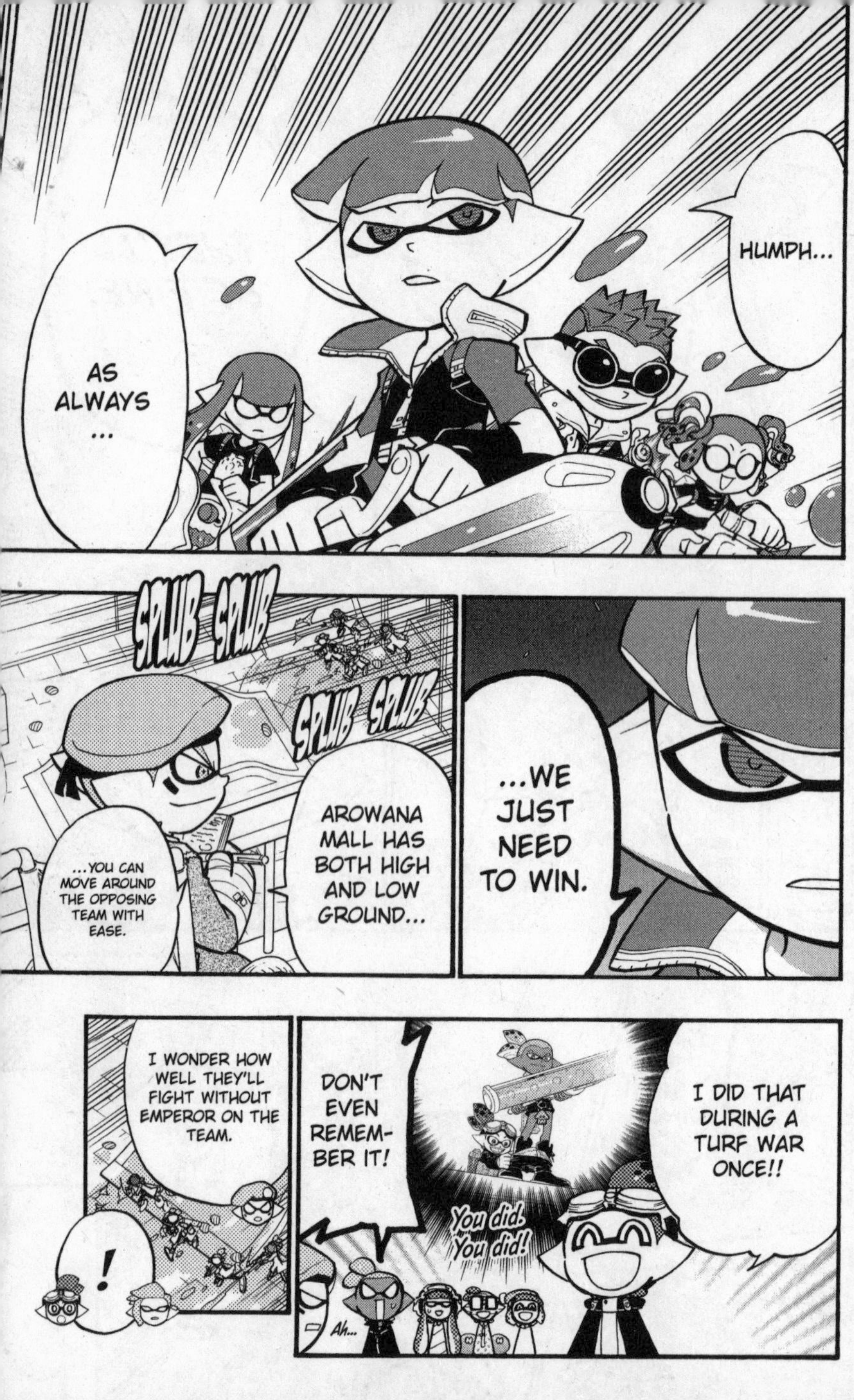
HUMPH...
AS ALWAYS ...
...WE JUST NEED TO WIN.
SPLUB SPLUB
SPLUB SPLUB
AROWANA MALL HAS BOTH HIGH AND LOW GROUND...
...YOU CAN MOVE AROUND THE OPPOSING TEAM WITH EASE.
I DID THAT DURING A TURF WAR ONCE!!
You did. You did!
DON'T EVEN REMEM-BER IT!
Ah...
I WONDER HOW WELL THEY'LL FIGHT WITHOUT EMPEROR ON THE TEAM.
!

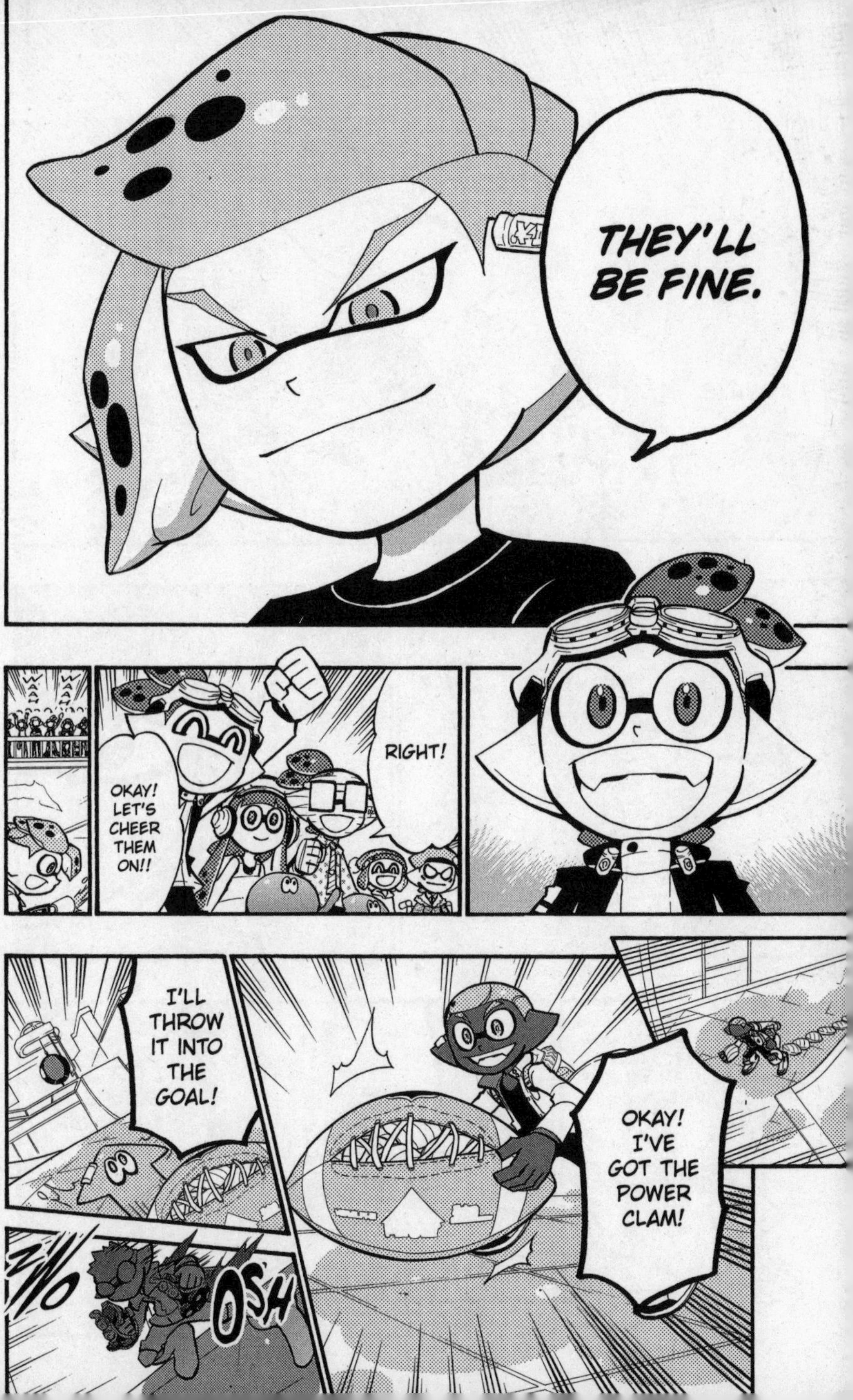
THEY'LL BE FINE.
RIGHT!
OKAY! LET'S CHEER THEM ON!!
WAAH
WAAH
OKAY! I'VE GOT THE POWER CLAM!
I'LL THROW IT INTO THE GOAL!
ZWOOSH

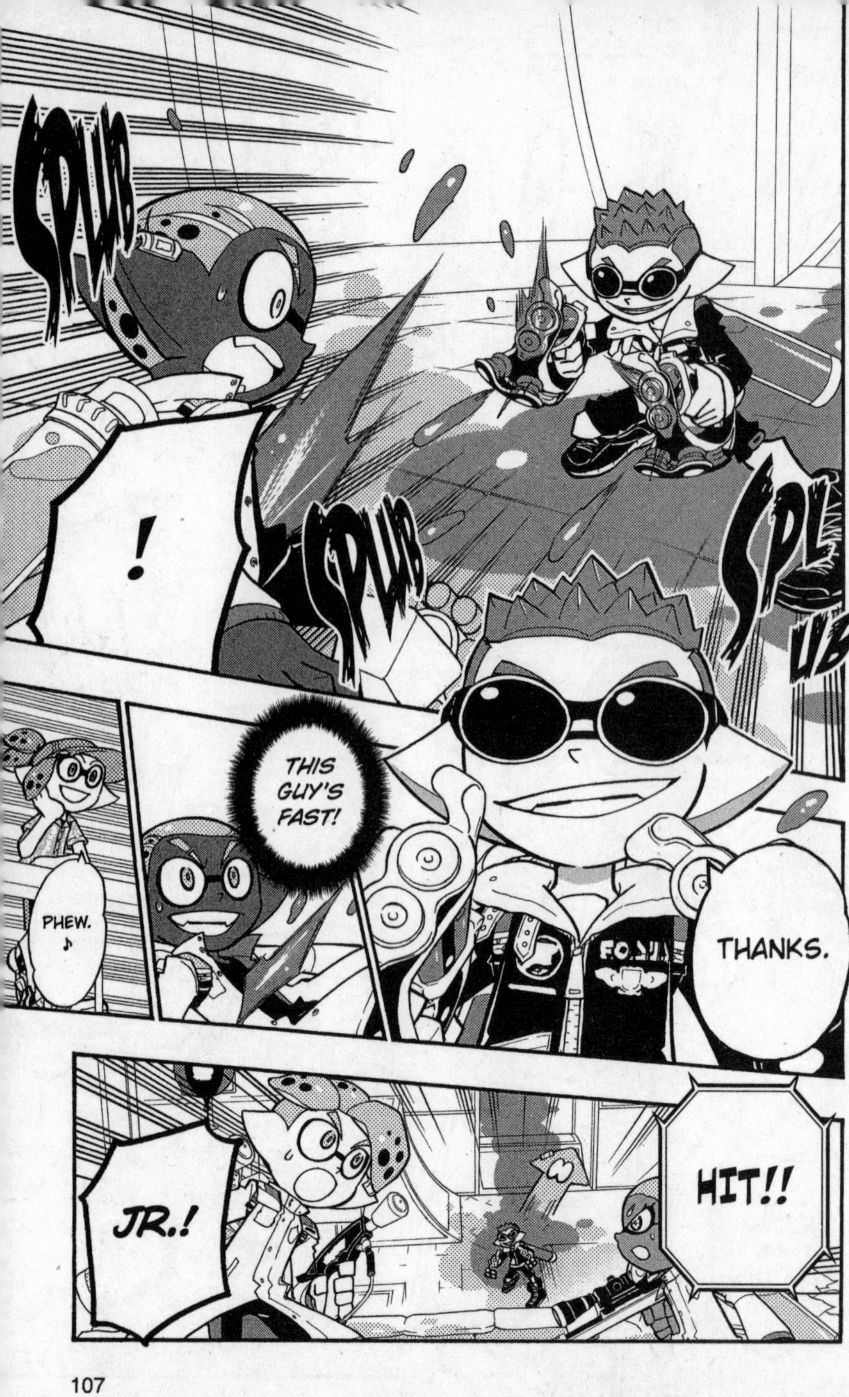
SPLUB
SPLUB
SPLUB
!
THANKS.
THIS GUY'S FAST!
PHEW. ♪
HIT!!
JR.!

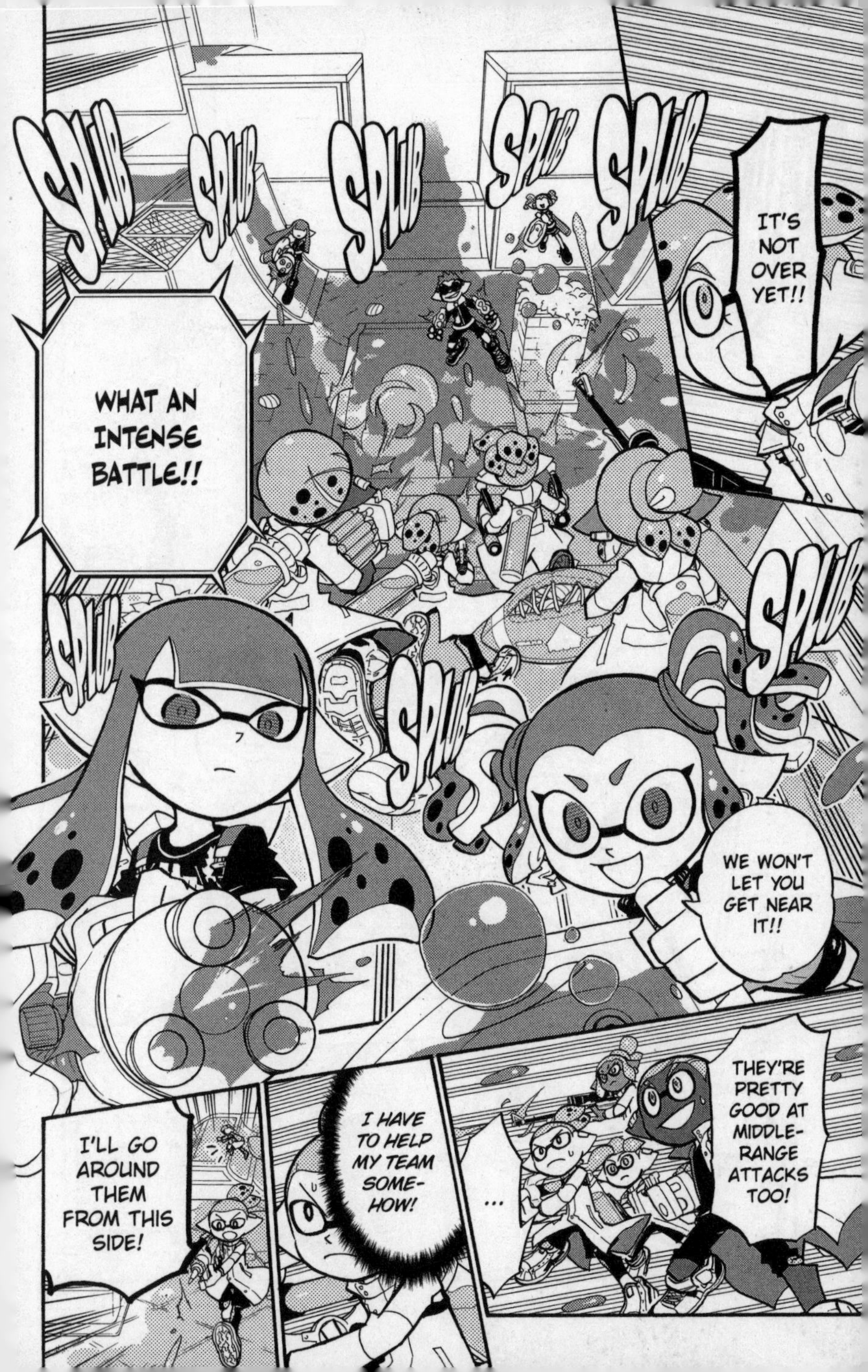
IT'S NOT OVER YET!!
SPLUB
SPLUB
SPLUB
SPLUB
SPLUB
WHAT AN INTENSE BATTLE!!
SPLUB
SPLUB
SPLUB
WE WON'T LET YOU GET NEAR IT!!
THEY'RE PRETTY GOOD AT MIDDLE-RANGE ATTACKS TOO!
...
I HAVE TO HELP MY TEAM SOME-HOW!
I'LL GO AROUND THEM FROM THIS SIDE!

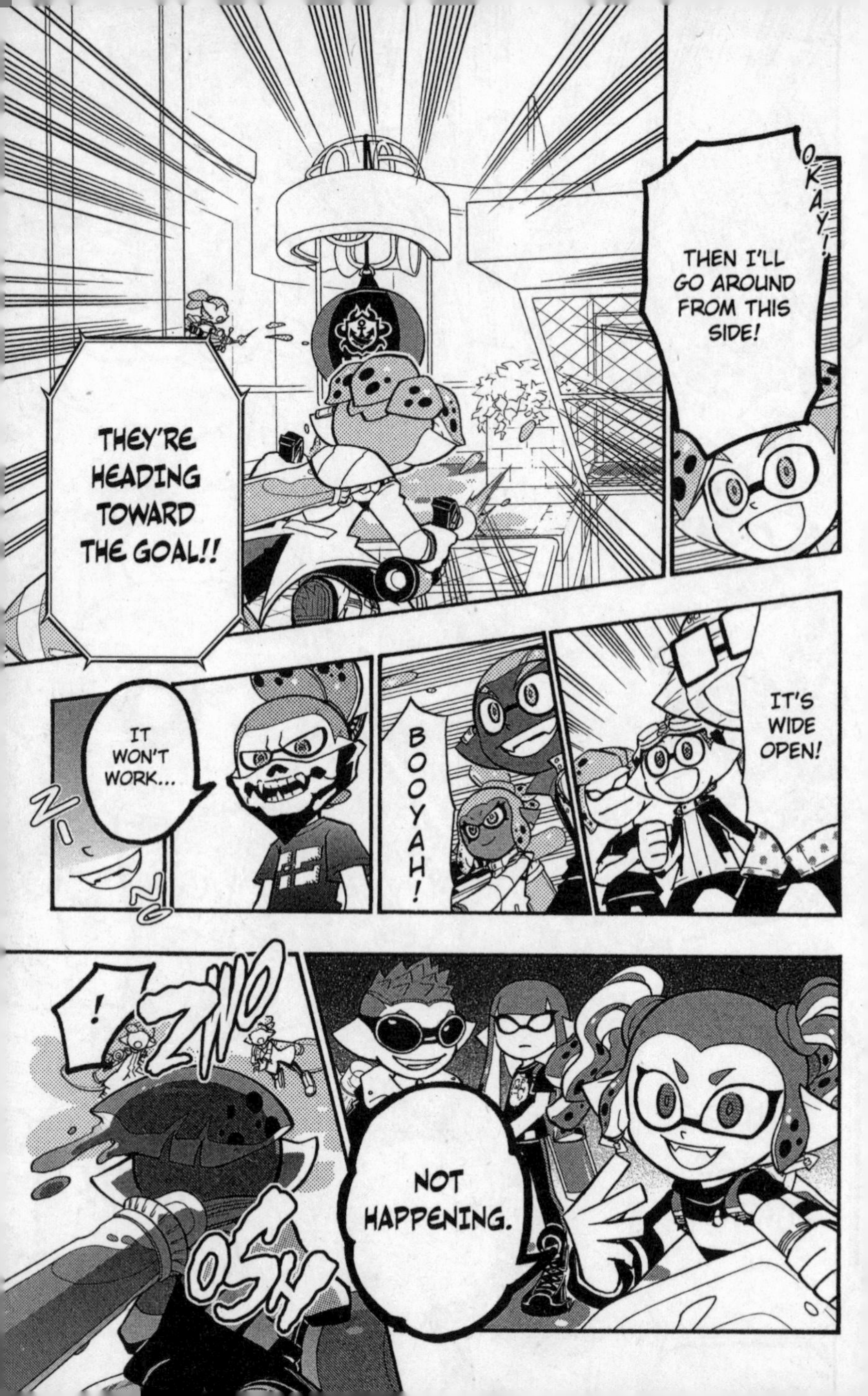
OKAY!
THEN I'LL GO AROUND FROM THIS SIDE!
THEY'RE HEADING TOWARD THE GOAL!!
IT'S WIDE OPEN!
BOOYAH!
IT WON'T WORK...
NOT HAPPENING.
!
ZWO
OSH

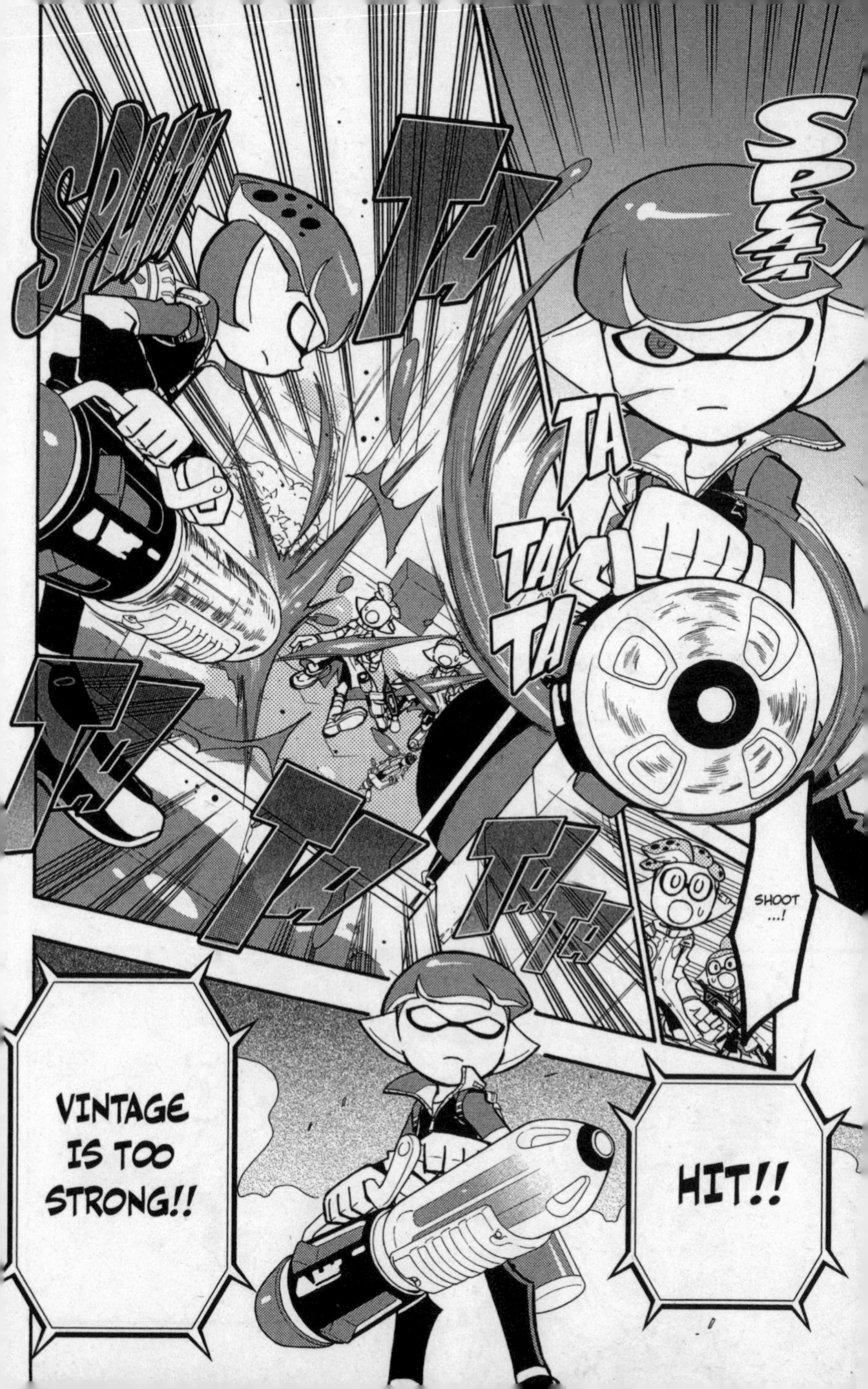

TA
TA
TA
TA
TA
TA
SHOOT ...!
HIT!!
VINTAGE IS TOO STRONG!!

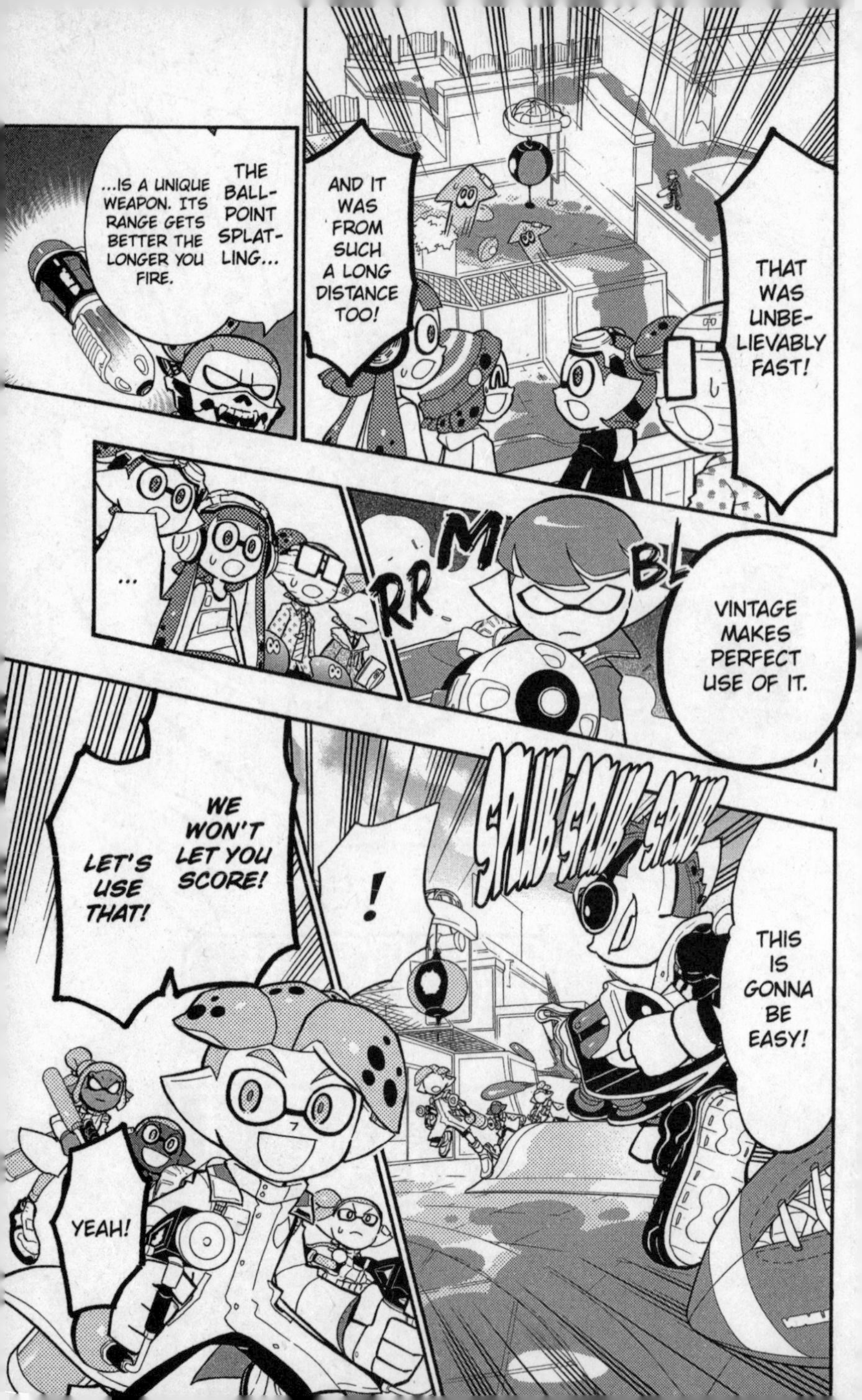
THAT WAS UNBELIEVABLY FAST!
AND IT WAS FROM SUCH A LONG DISTANCE TOO!
THE BALLPOINT SPLATLING...
...IS A UNIQUE WEAPON. ITS RANGE GETS BETTER THE LONGER YOU FIRE.
RRMBL
VINTAGE MAKES PERFECT USE OF IT.
...
THIS IS GONNA BE EASY!
!
WE WON'T LET YOU SCORE!
LET'S USE THAT!
YEAH!

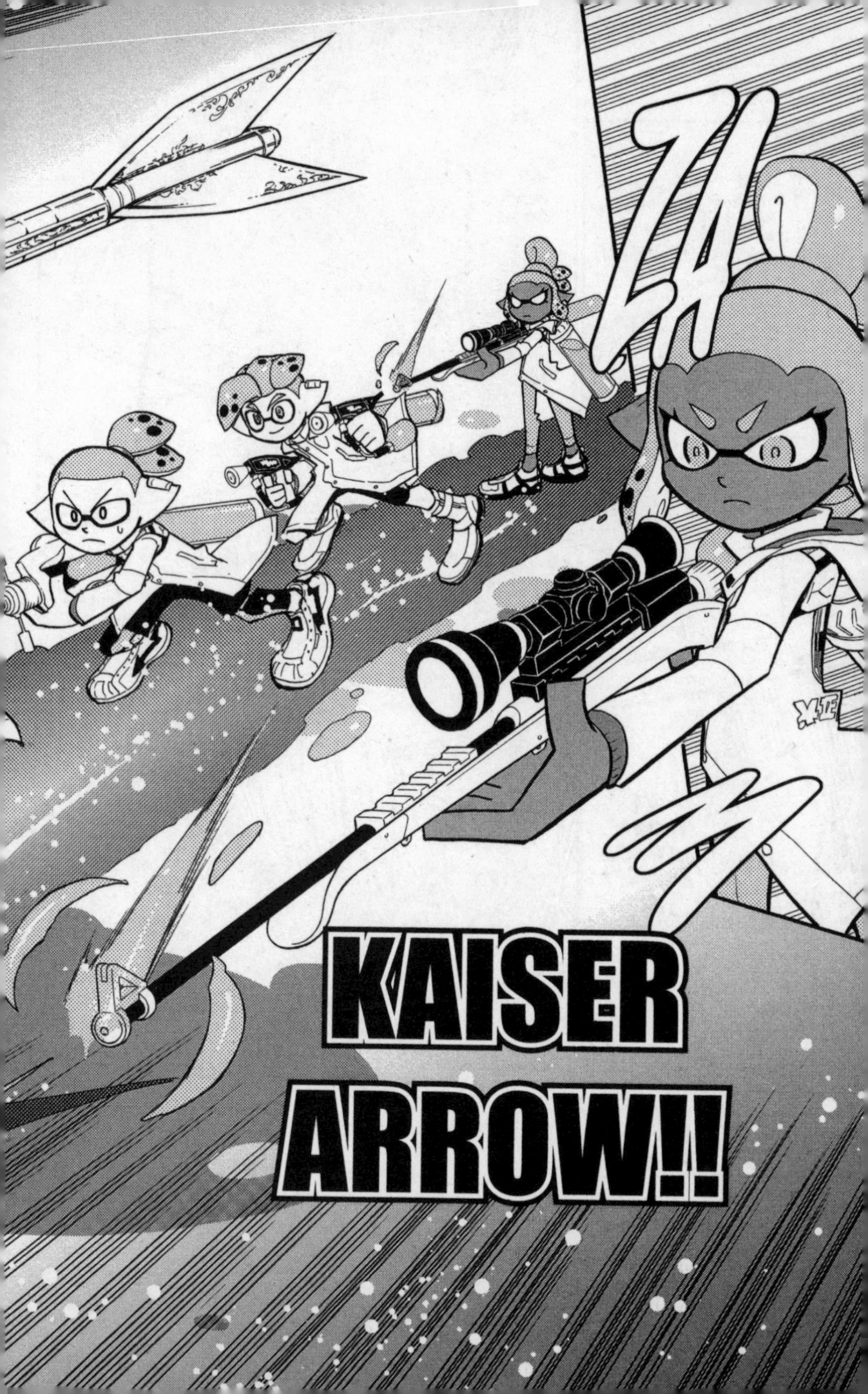
ZAM
KAISER ARROW!!

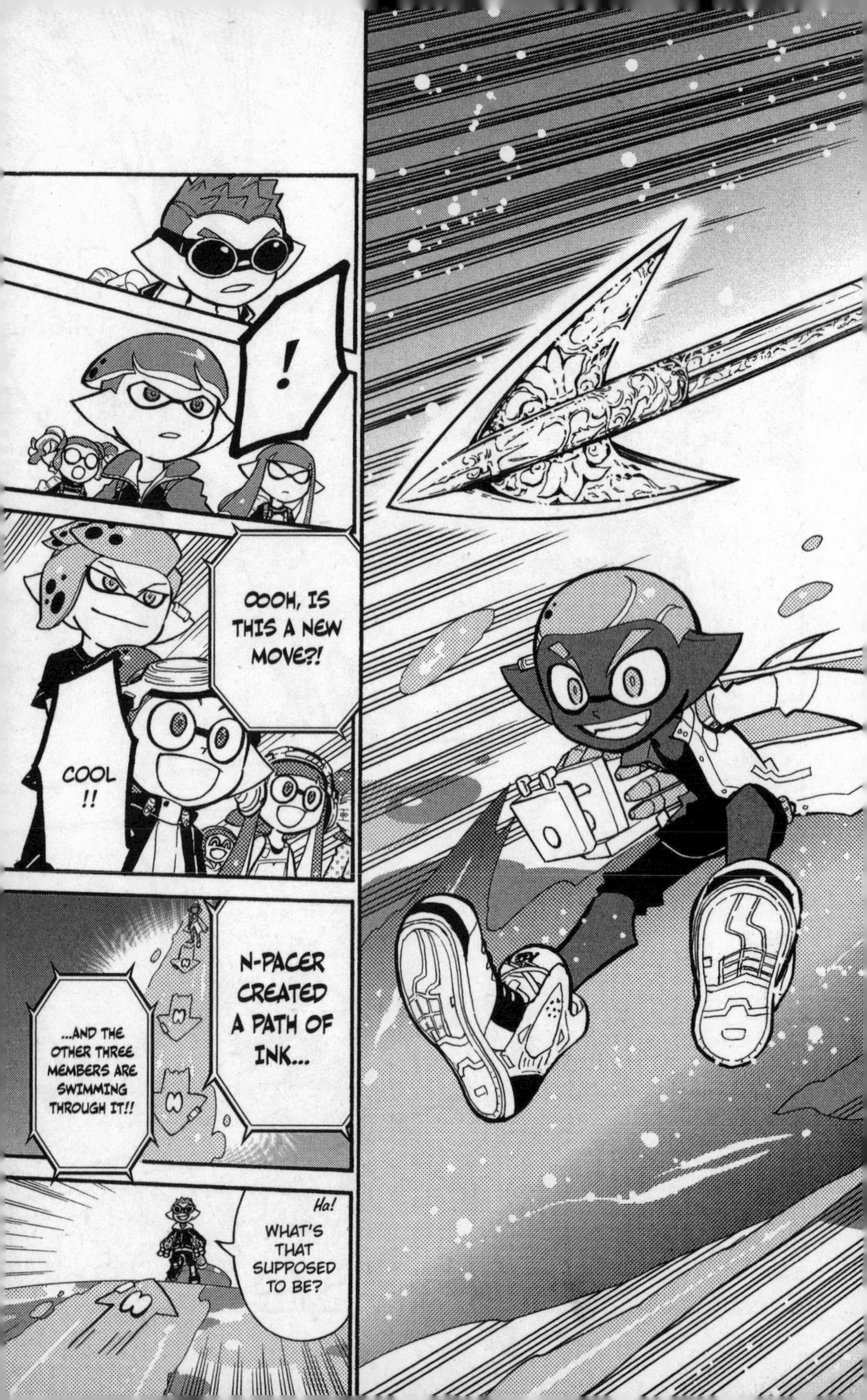
!
OOOH, IS THIS A NEW MOVE?!
COOL !!
N-PACER CREATED A PATH OF INK...
...AND THE OTHER THREE MEMBERS ARE SWIMMING THROUGH IT!!
Ha! WHAT'S THAT SUPPOSED TO BE?

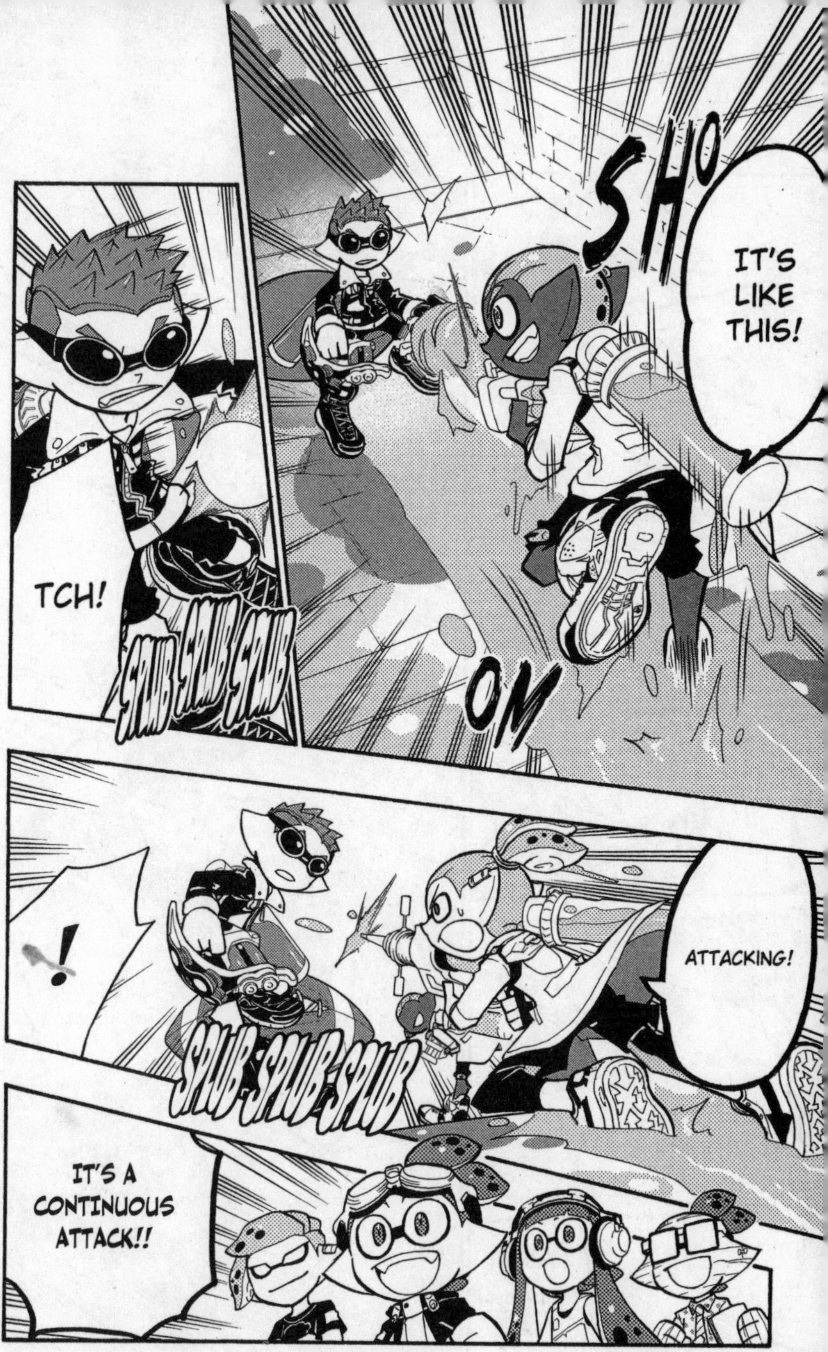
SHO
IT'S LIKE THIS!
OM
TCH!
SPLUB SPLUB SPLUB
ATTACKING!
!
SPLUB-SPLUB-SPLUB
IT'S A CONTINUOUS ATTACK!!

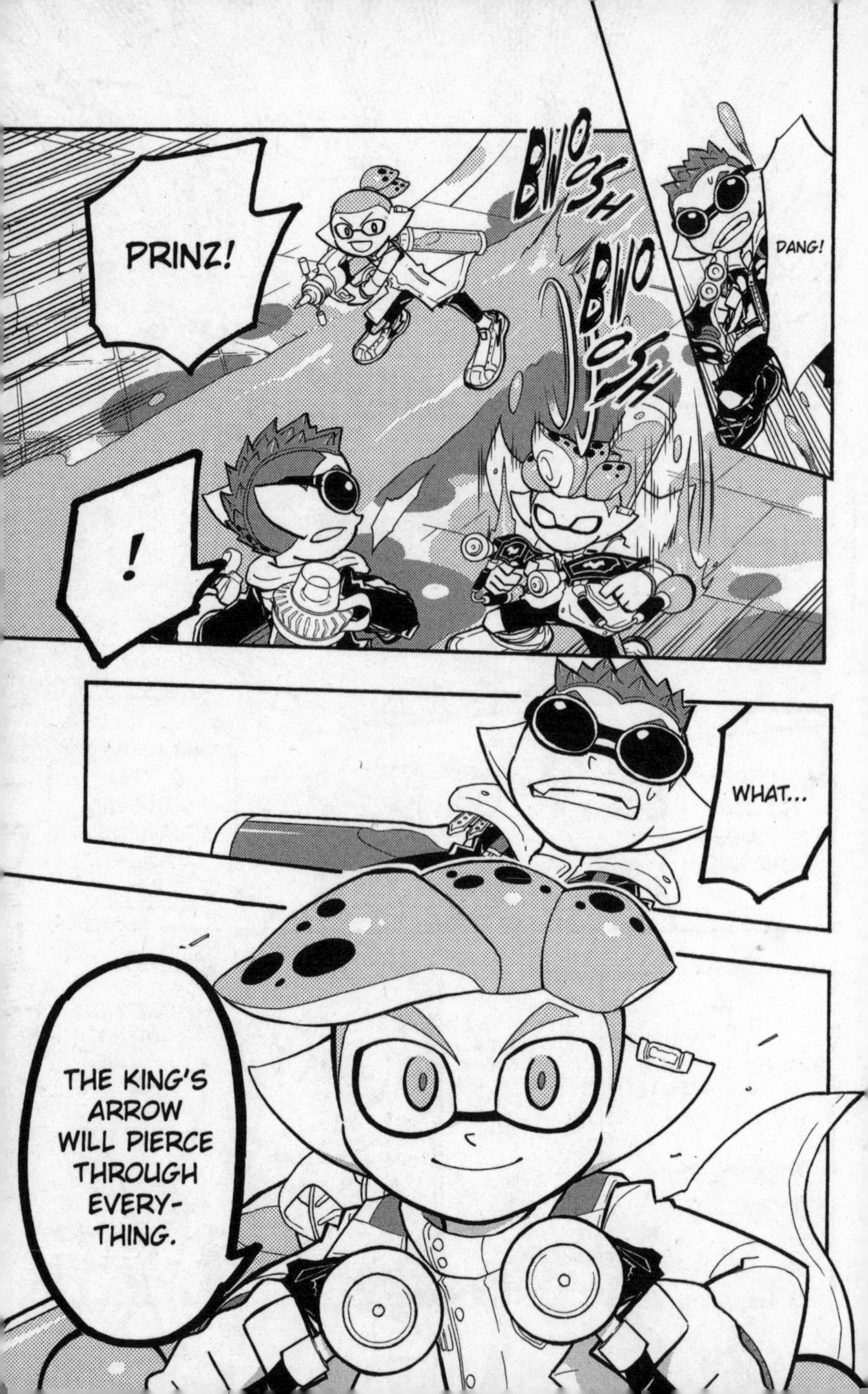
DANG!
BWOOSH
BWOOSH
PRINZ!
!
WHAT...
THE KING'S ARROW WILL PIERCE THROUGH EVERY-THING.

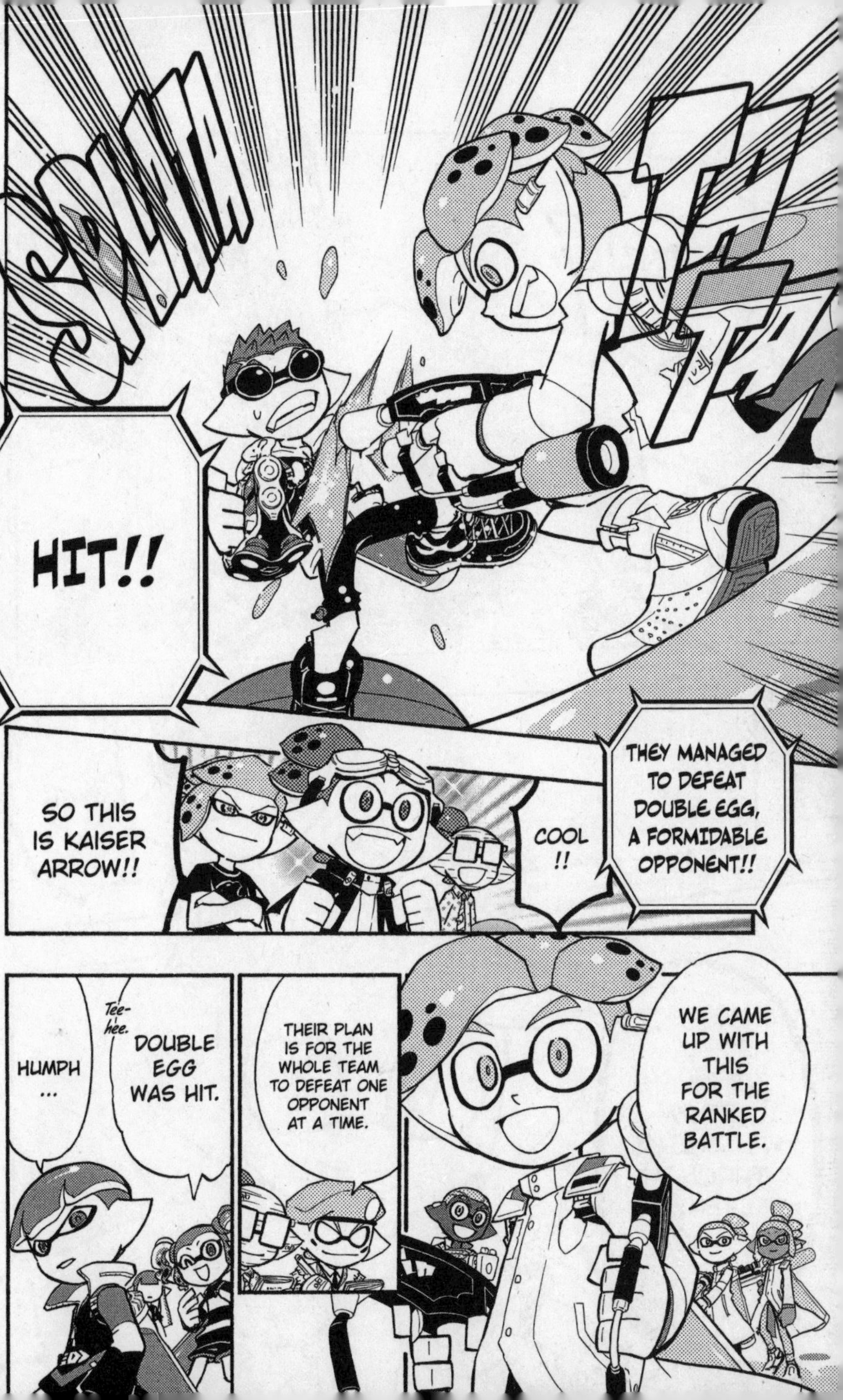
HIT!!
THEY MANAGED TO DEFEAT DOUBLE EGG, A FORMIDABLE OPPONENT!!
COOL !!
SO THIS IS KAISER ARROW!!
WE CAME UP WITH THIS FOR THE RANKED BATTLE.
THEIR PLAN IS FOR THE WHOLE TEAM TO DEFEAT ONE OPPONENT AT A TIME.
Tee-hee.
DOUBLE EGG WAS HIT.
HUMPH ...

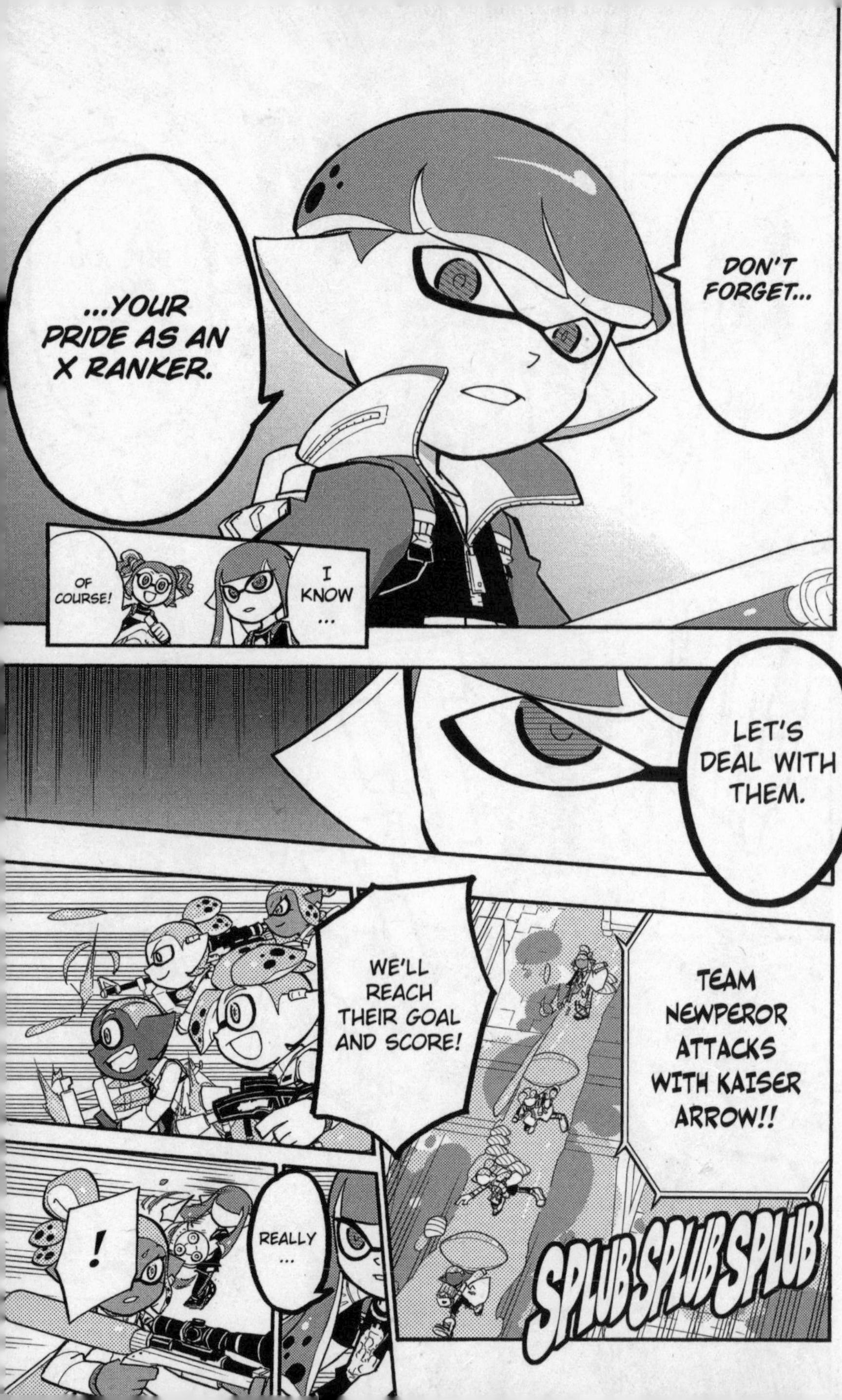
DON'T FORGET...
...YOUR PRIDE AS AN X RANKER.
I KNOW ...
OF COURSE!
LET'S DEAL WITH THEM.
TEAM NEWPEROR ATTACKS WITH KAISER ARROW!!
SPLUB SPLUB SPLUB
WE'LL REACH THEIR GOAL AND SCORE!
REALLY ...
!

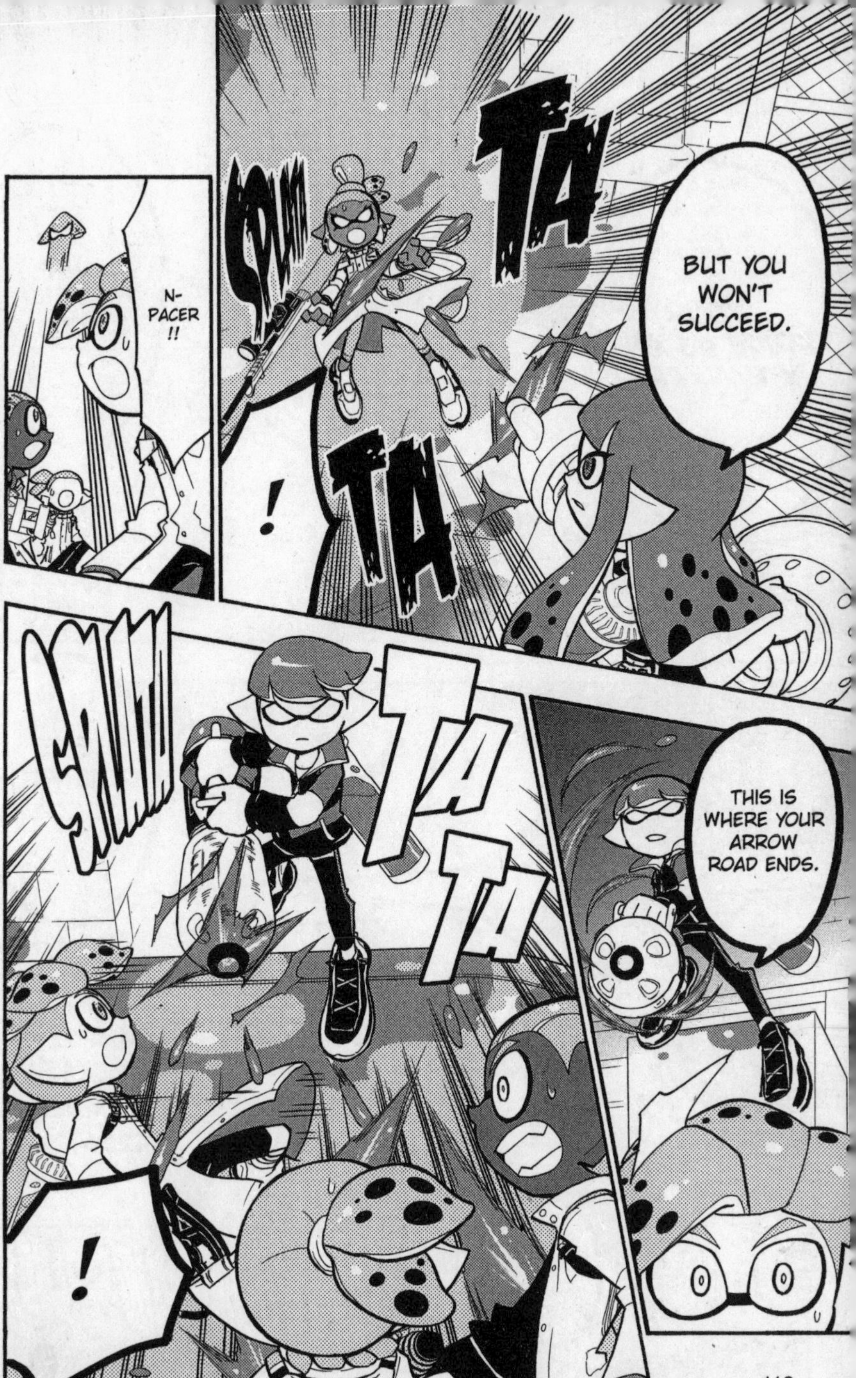
BUT YOU WON'T SUCCEED.
TA
TA
!
N-PACER !!
THIS IS WHERE YOUR ARROW ROAD ENDS.
TA
TA
TA
!

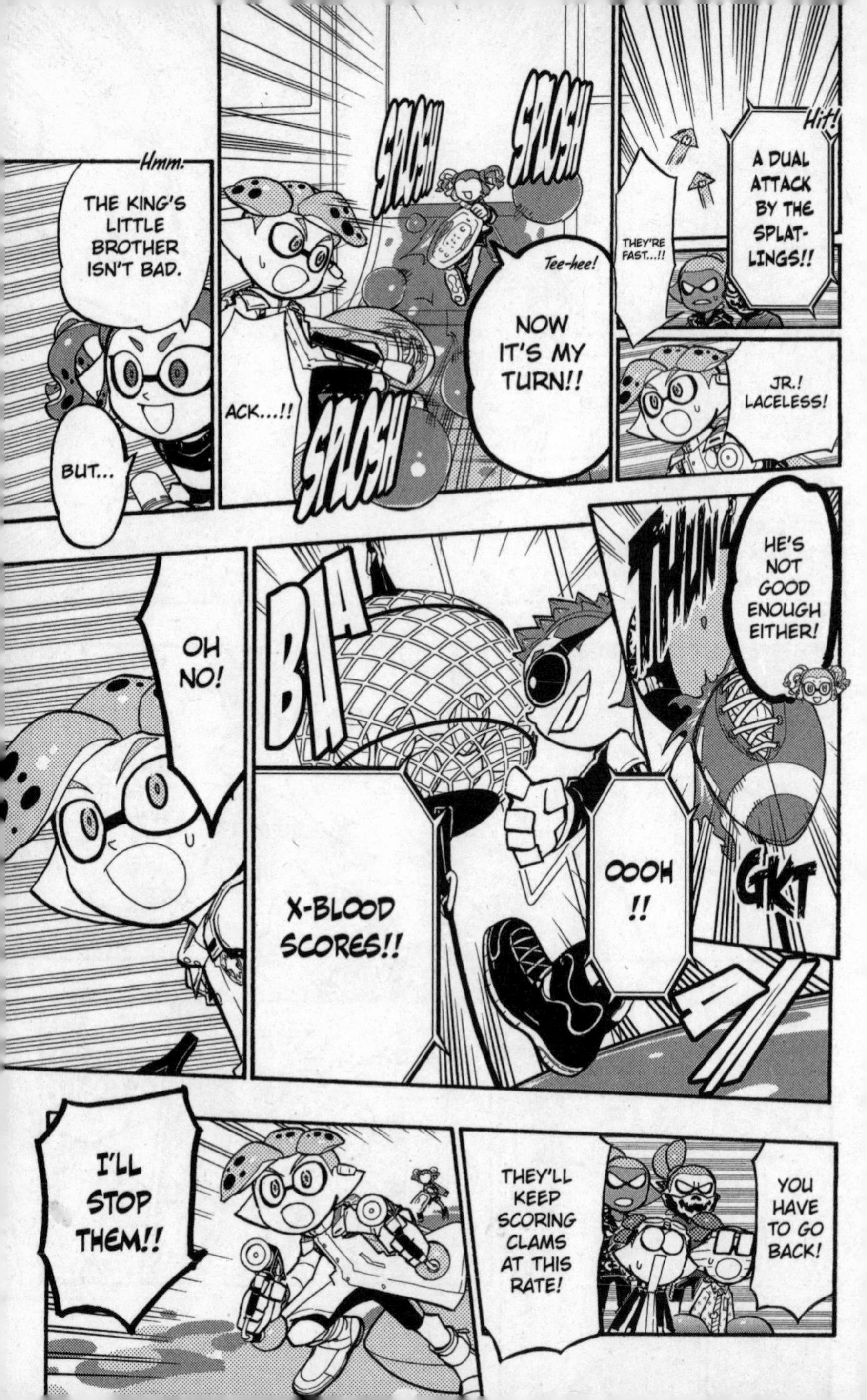
Hit!
A DUAL ATTACK BY THE SPLATLINGS!!
THEY'RE FAST...!!
JR.! LACELESS!
SPLOSH
SPLOSH
Tee-hee!
NOW IT'S MY TURN!!
ACK...!!
SPLOSH
Hmm.
THE KING'S LITTLE BROTHER ISN'T BAD.
BUT...
HE'S NOT GOOD ENOUGH EITHER!
GKT
OOOH !!
X-BLOOD SCORES!!
OH NO!
YOU HAVE TO GO BACK!
THEY'LL KEEP SCORING CLAMS AT THIS RATE!
I'LL STOP THEM!!

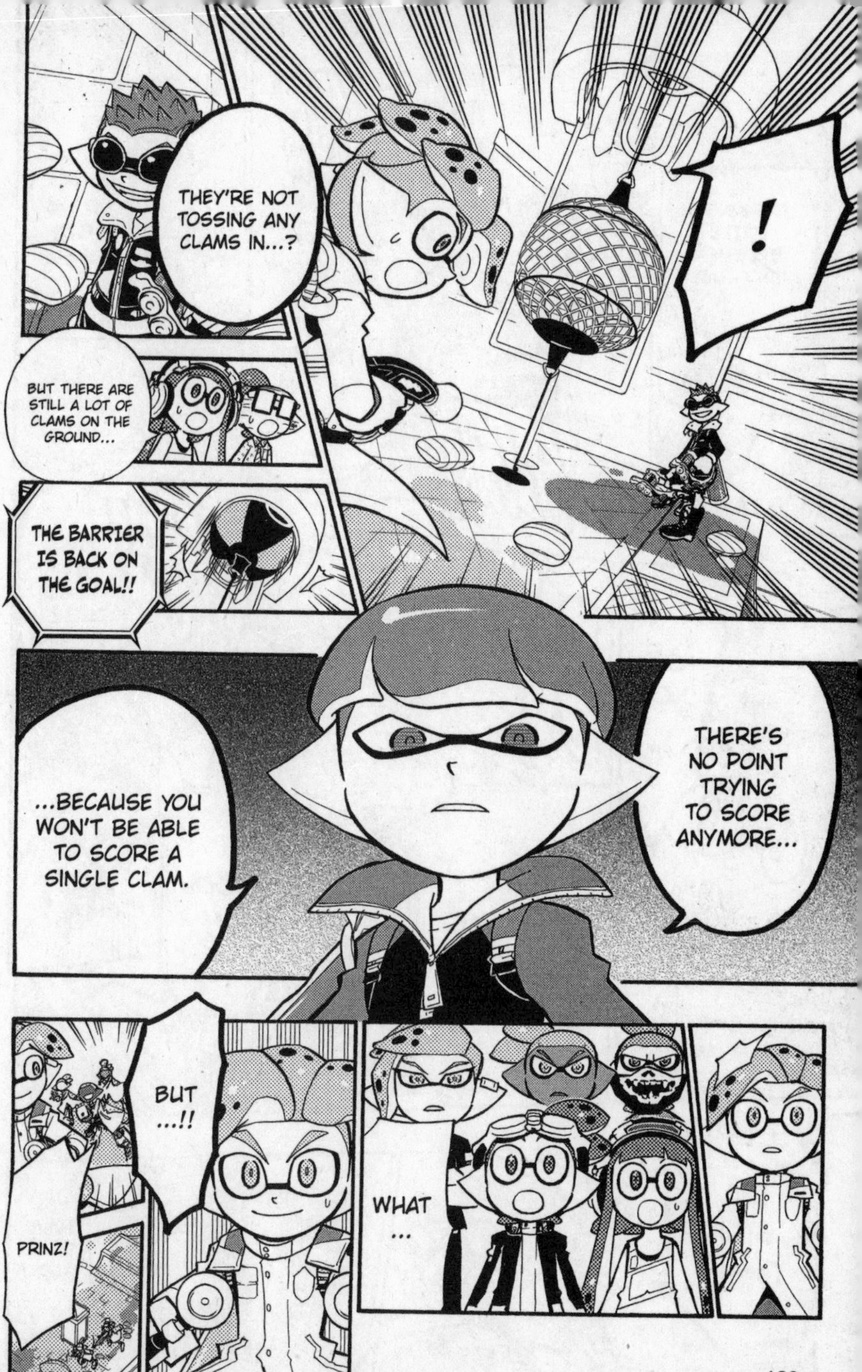
THEY'RE NOT TOSSING ANY CLAMS IN...?
BUT THERE ARE STILL A LOT OF CLAMS ON THE GROUND...
!
THE BARRIER IS BACK ON THE GOAL!!
THERE'S NO POINT TRYING TO SCORE ANYMORE...
...BECAUSE YOU WON'T BE ABLE TO SCORE A SINGLE CLAM.
WHAT ...
BUT ...!!
PRINZ!

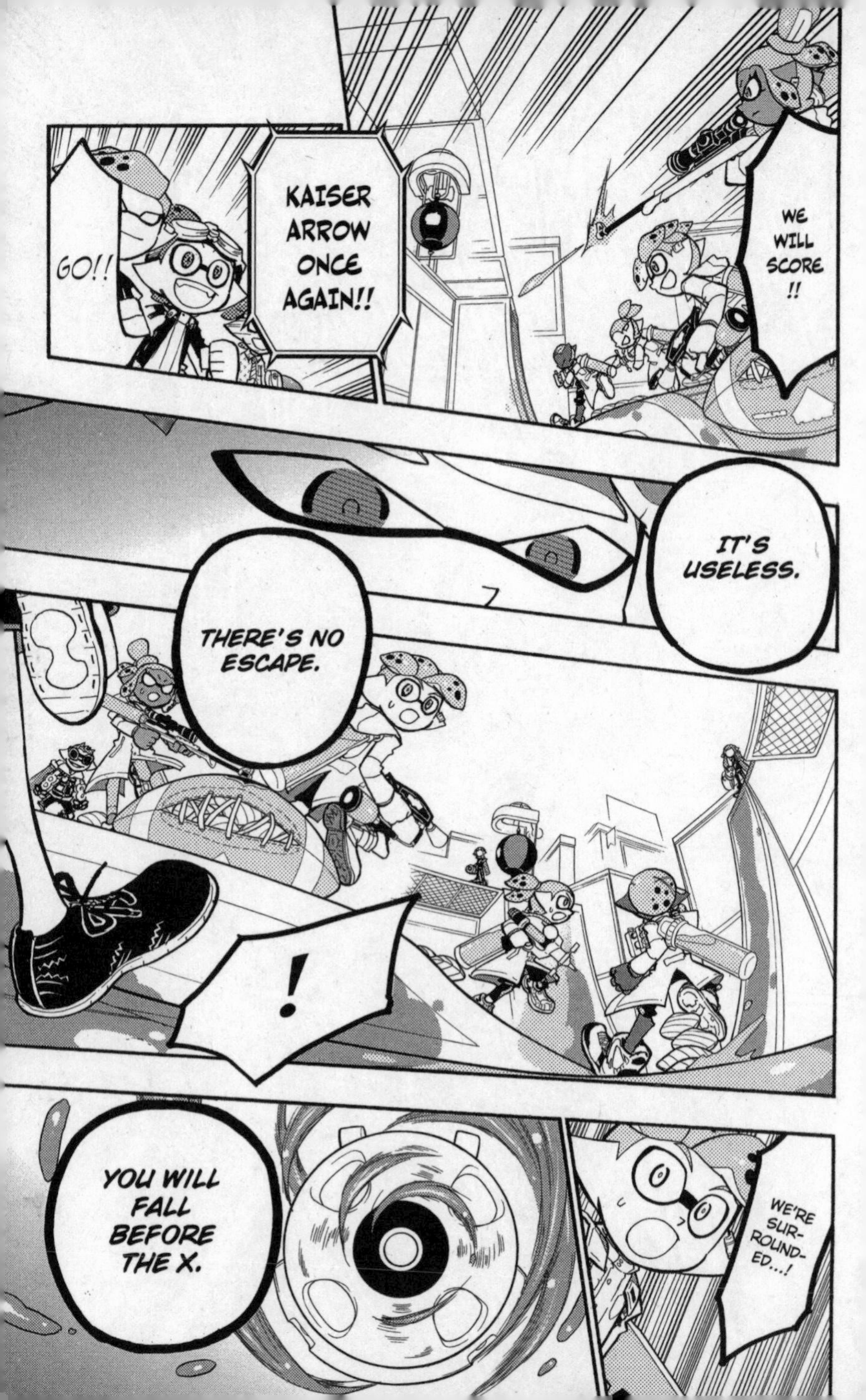
WE WILL SCORE !!
KAISER ARROW ONCE AGAIN!!
GO!!
IT'S USELESS.
THERE'S NO ESCAPE.
!
WE'RE SUR-ROUND-ED...!
YOU WILL FALL BEFORE THE X.

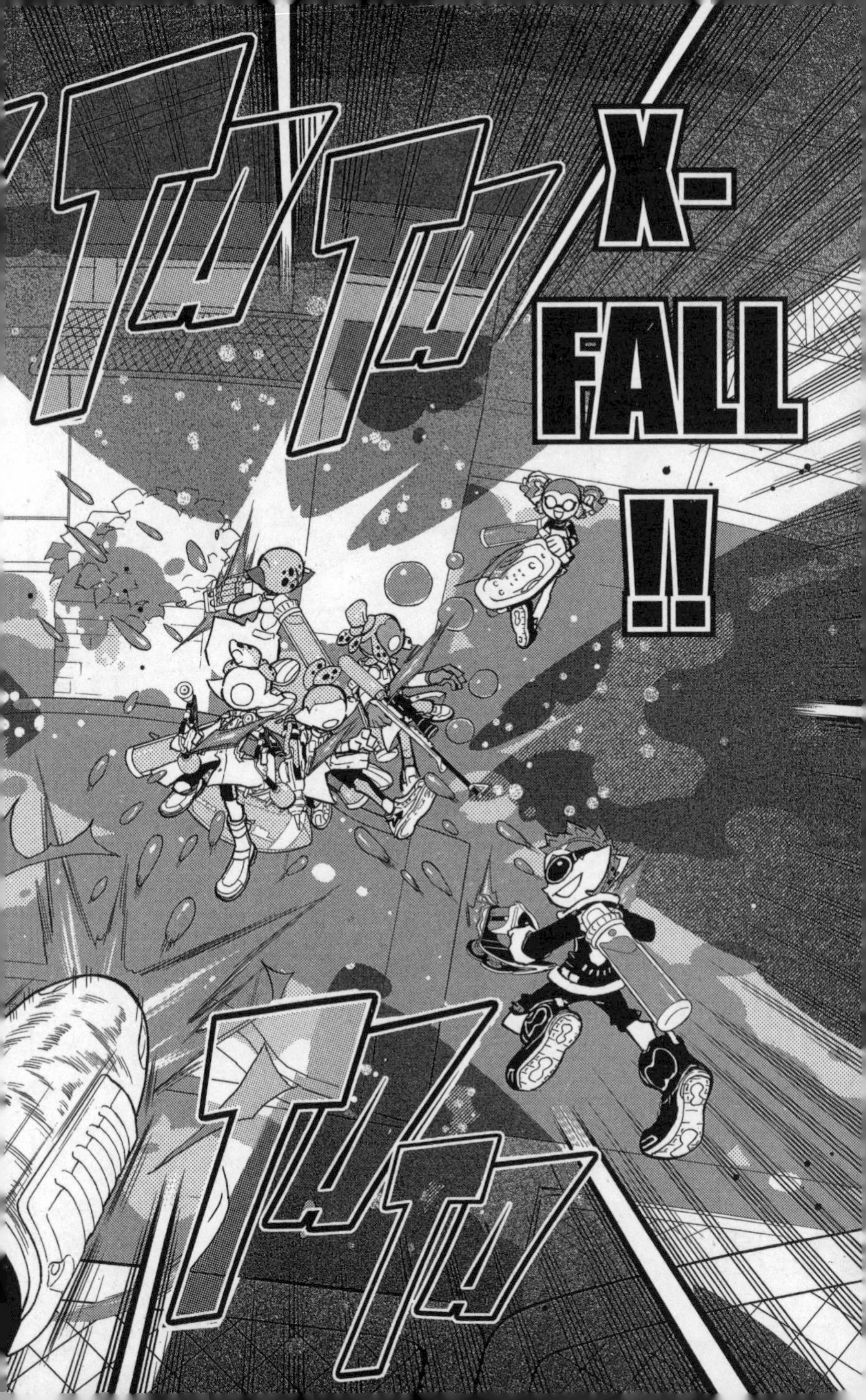
X-FALL!!

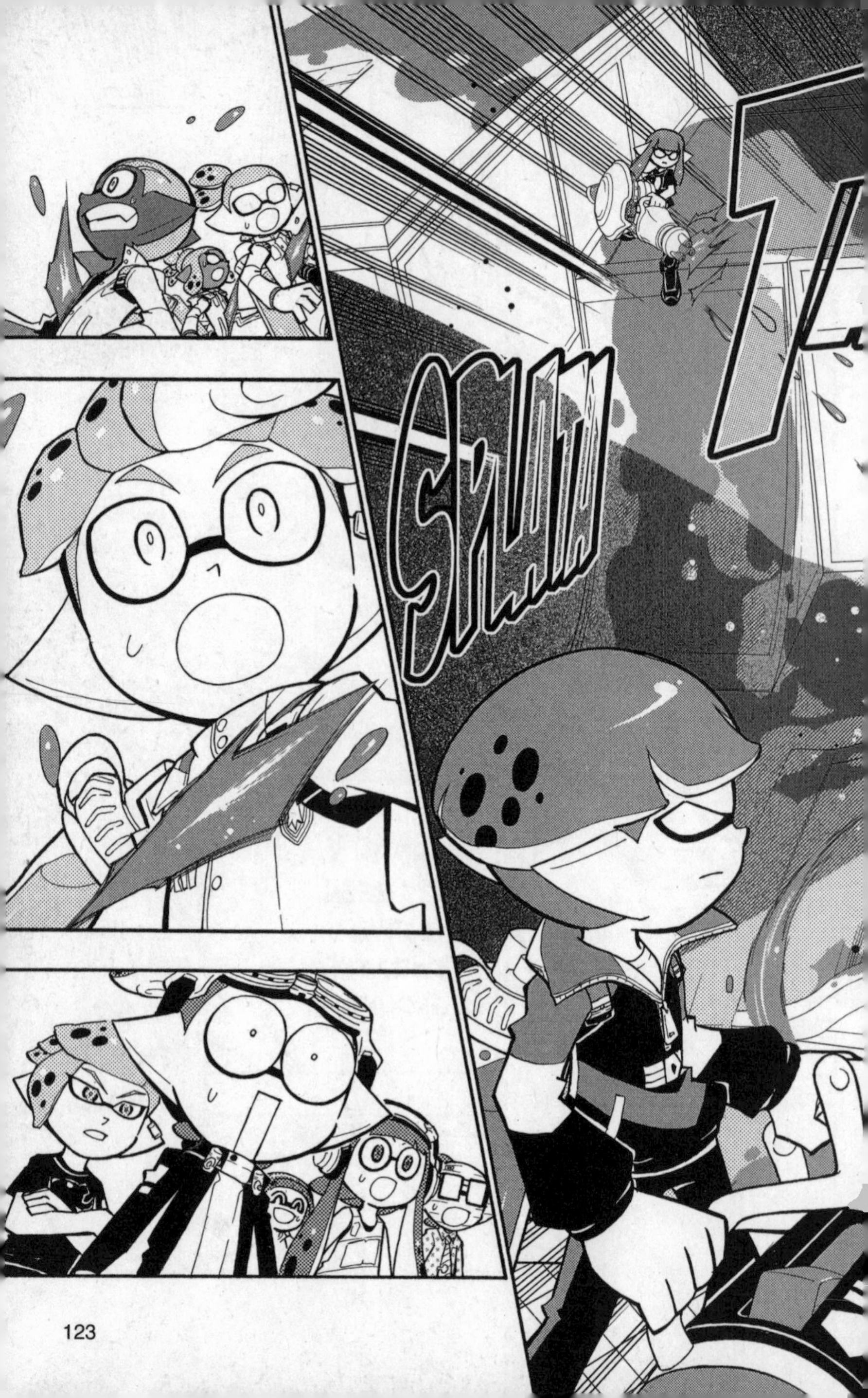

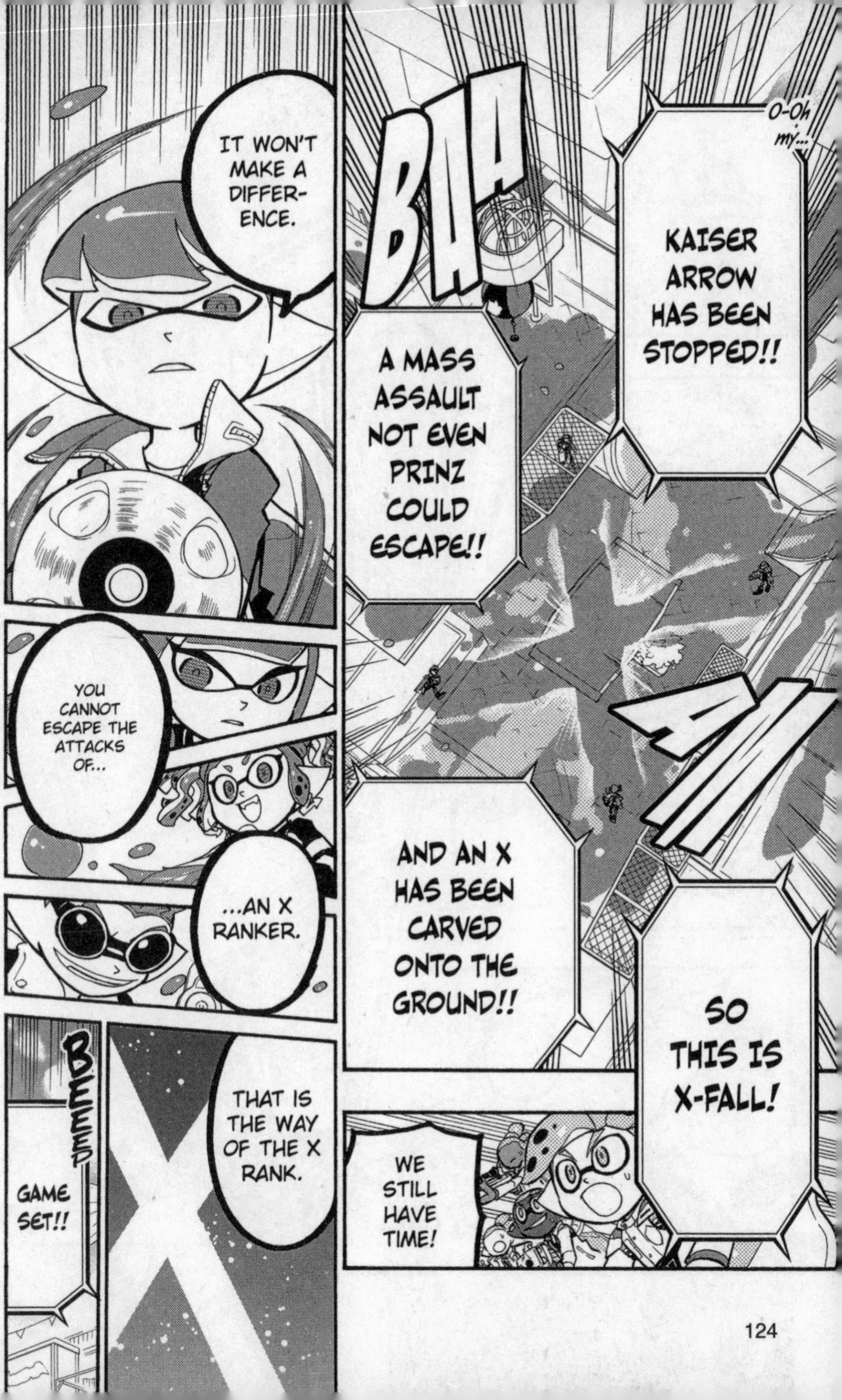

O-Oh my...
KAISER ARROW HAS BEEN STOPPED!!
BAA
A MASS ASSAULT NOT EVEN PRINZ COULD ESCAPE!!
AND AN X HAS BEEN CARVED ONTO THE GROUND!!
SO THIS IS X-FALL!
WE STILL HAVE TIME!
IT WON'T MAKE A DIFFER-ENCE.
YOU CANNOT ESCAPE THE ATTACKS OF...
...AN X RANKER.
THAT IS THE WAY OF THE X RANK.
GAME SET!!

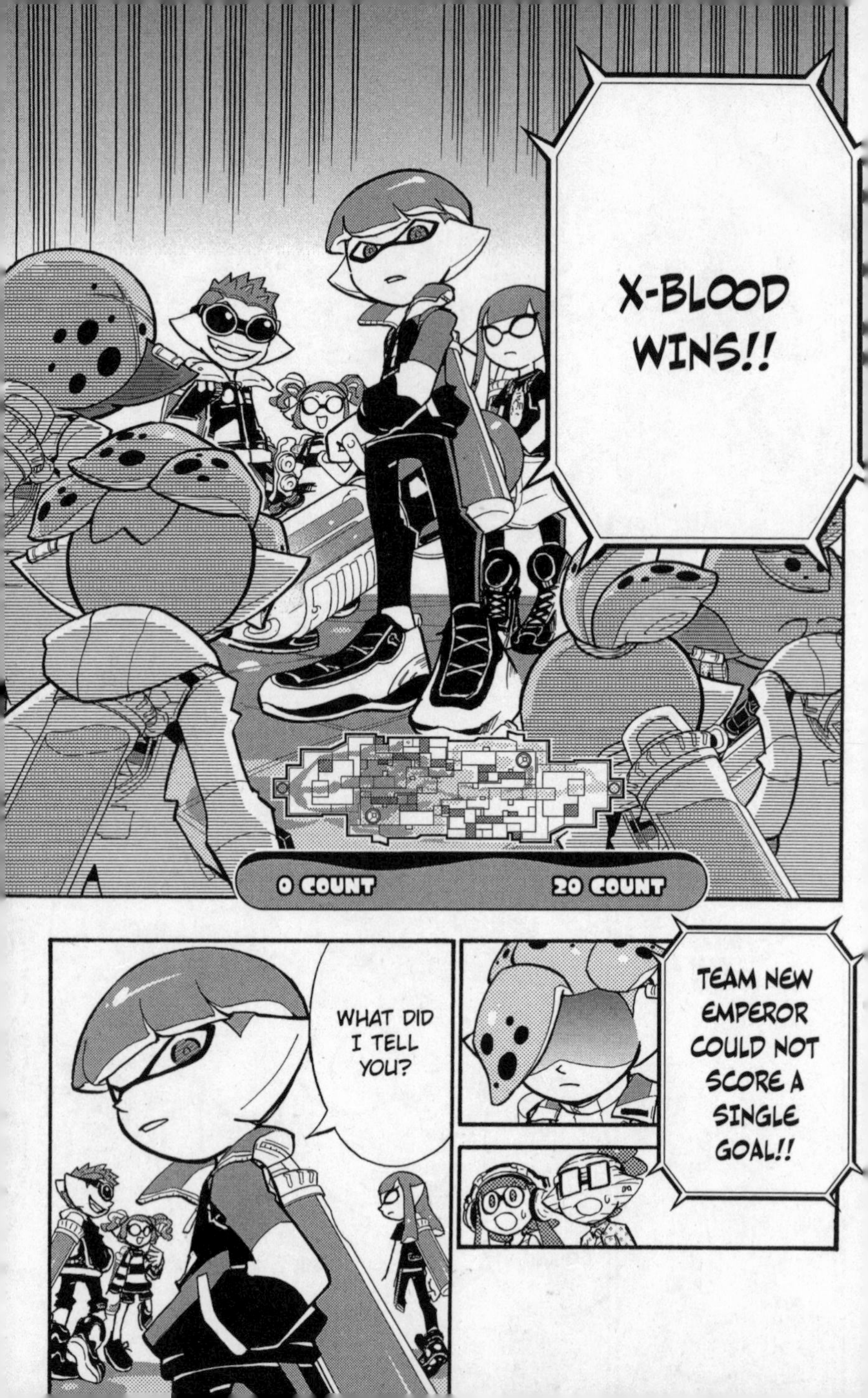
X-BLOOD WINS!!
0 COUNT
20 COUNT
TEAM NEW EMPEROR COULD NOT SCORE A SINGLE GOAL!!
WHAT DID I TELL YOU?

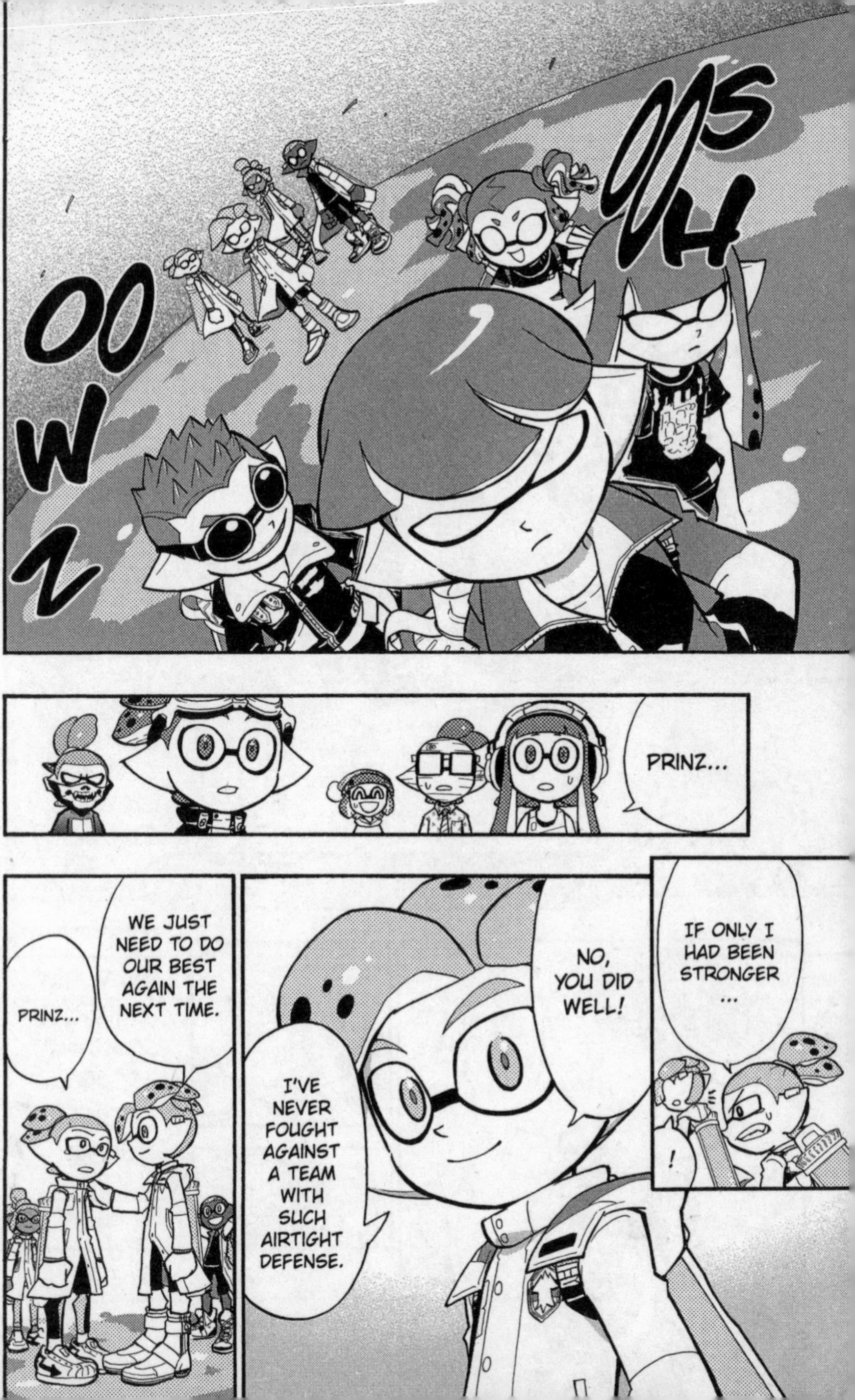
OOSH
OOWN
PRINZ...
IF ONLY I HAD BEEN STRONGER ...
!
NO, YOU DID WELL!
I'VE NEVER FOUGHT AGAINST A TEAM WITH SUCH AIRTIGHT DEFENSE.
WE JUST NEED TO DO OUR BEST AGAIN THE NEXT TIME.
PRINZ...

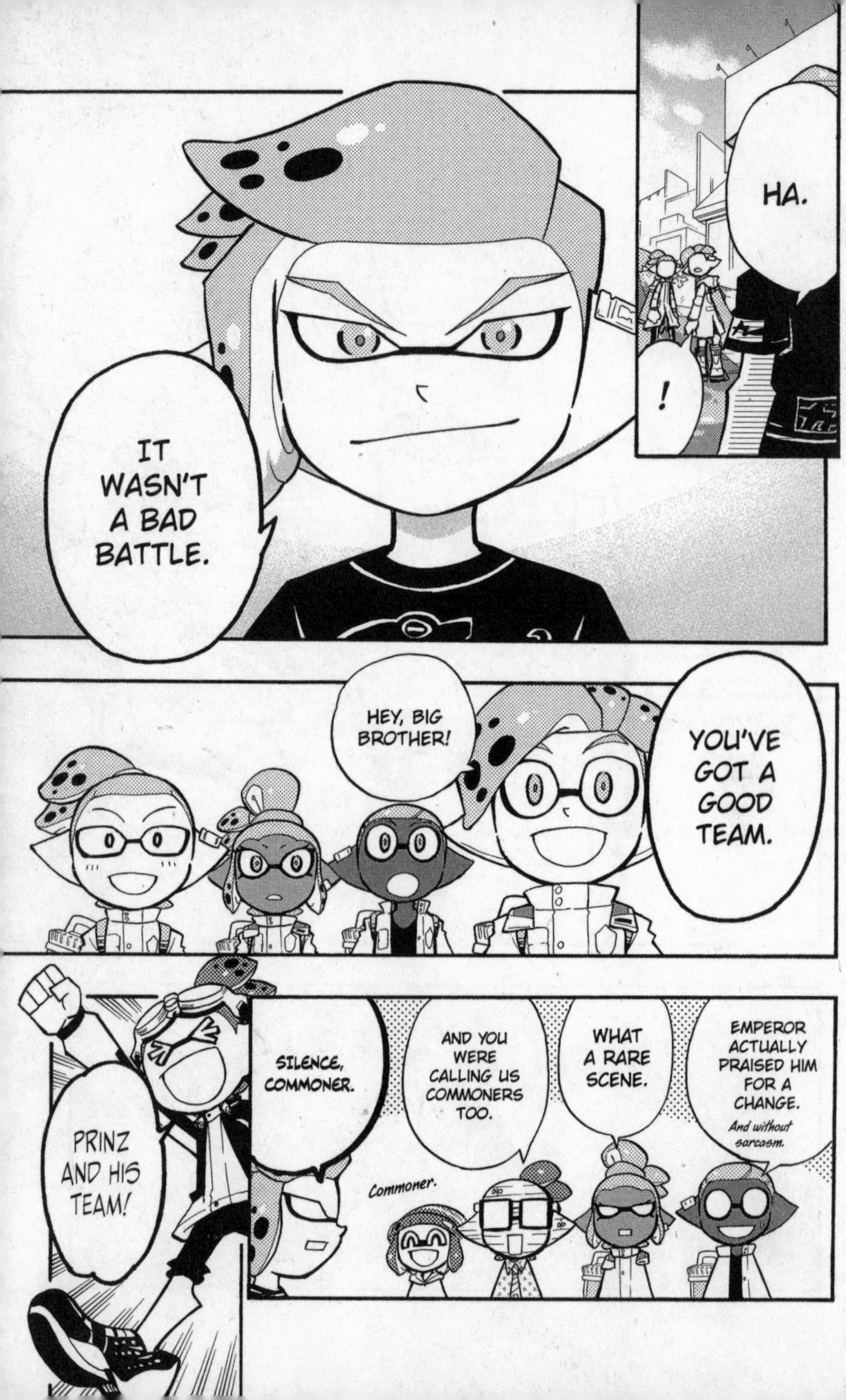
HA.
!
IT WASN'T A BAD BATTLE.
YOU'VE GOT A GOOD TEAM.
HEY, BIG BROTHER!
EMPEROR ACTUALLY PRAISED HIM FOR A CHANGE.
And without sarcasm.
WHAT A RARE SCENE.
AND YOU WERE CALLING US COMMONERS TOO.
SILENCE, COMMONER.
Commoner.
PRINZ AND HIS TEAM!

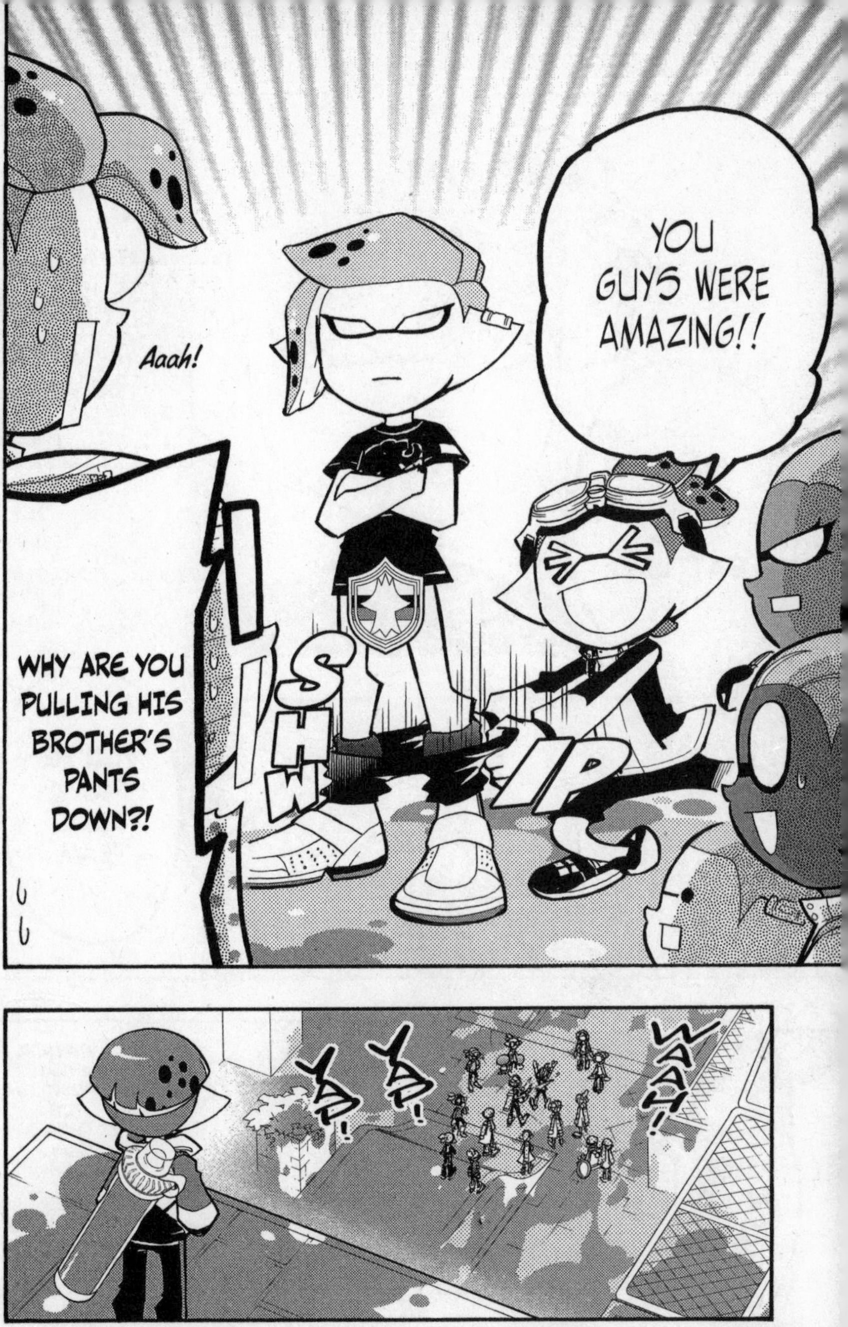
YOU GUYS WERE AMAZING!!
Aaah!
SHWIP
WHY ARE YOU PULLING HIS BROTHER'S PANTS DOWN?!
WAAH!
YAY!
YAY!

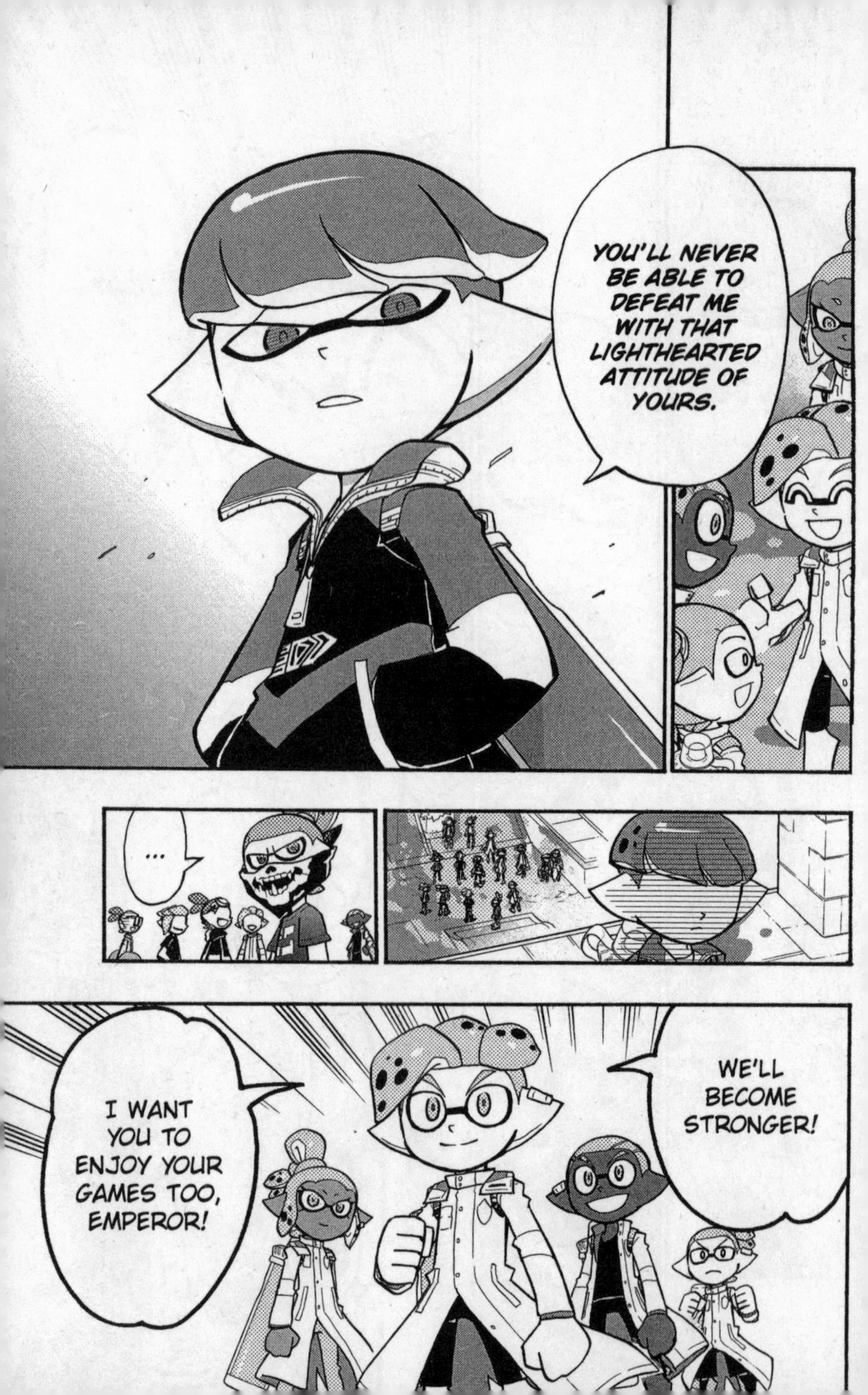
YOU'LL NEVER BE ABLE TO DEFEAT ME WITH THAT LIGHTHEARTED ATTITUDE OF YOURS.
...
WE'LL BECOME STRONGER!
I WANT YOU TO ENJOY YOUR GAMES TOO, EMPEROR!

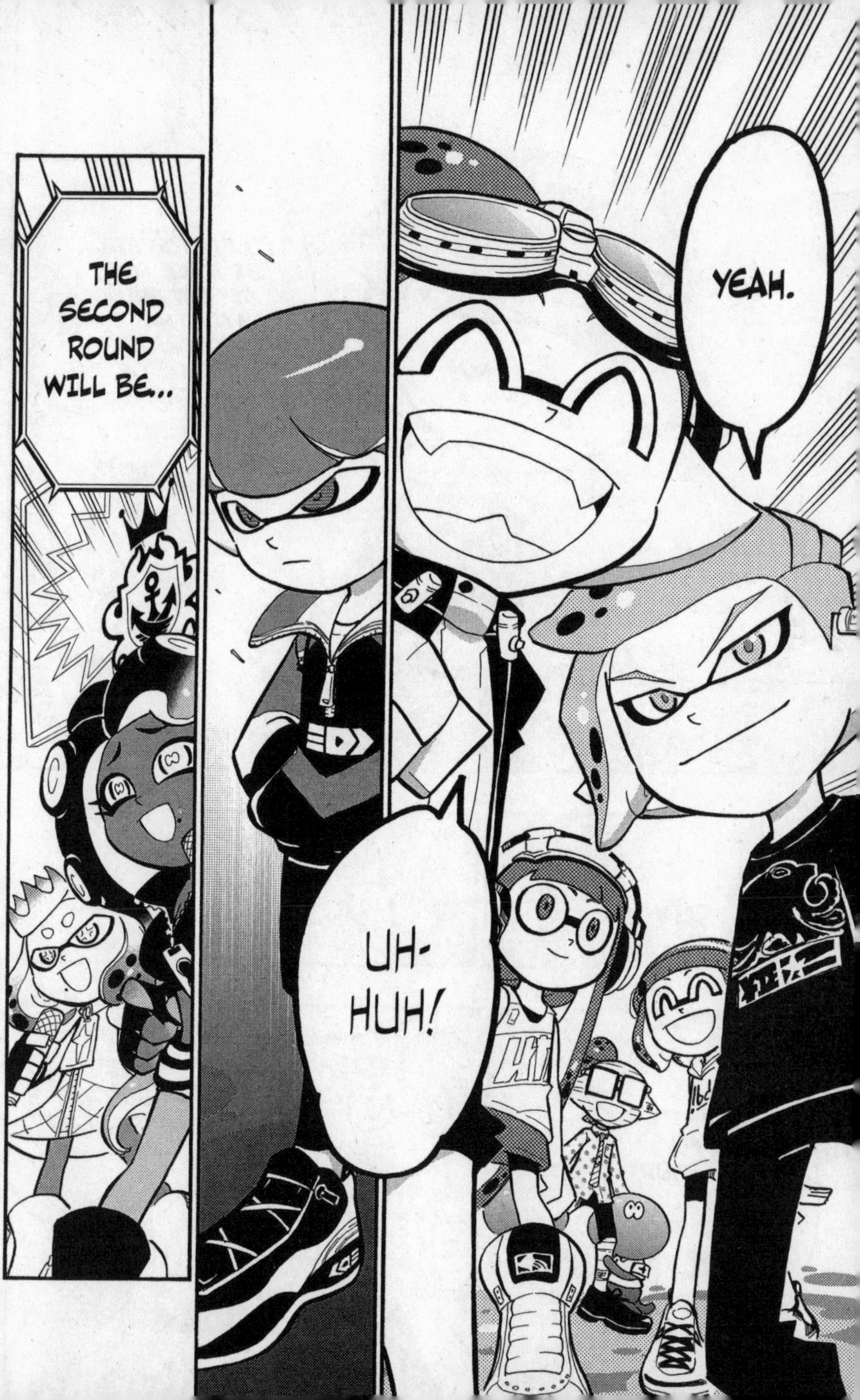
YEAH.
UH-HUH!
THE SECOND ROUND WILL BE...

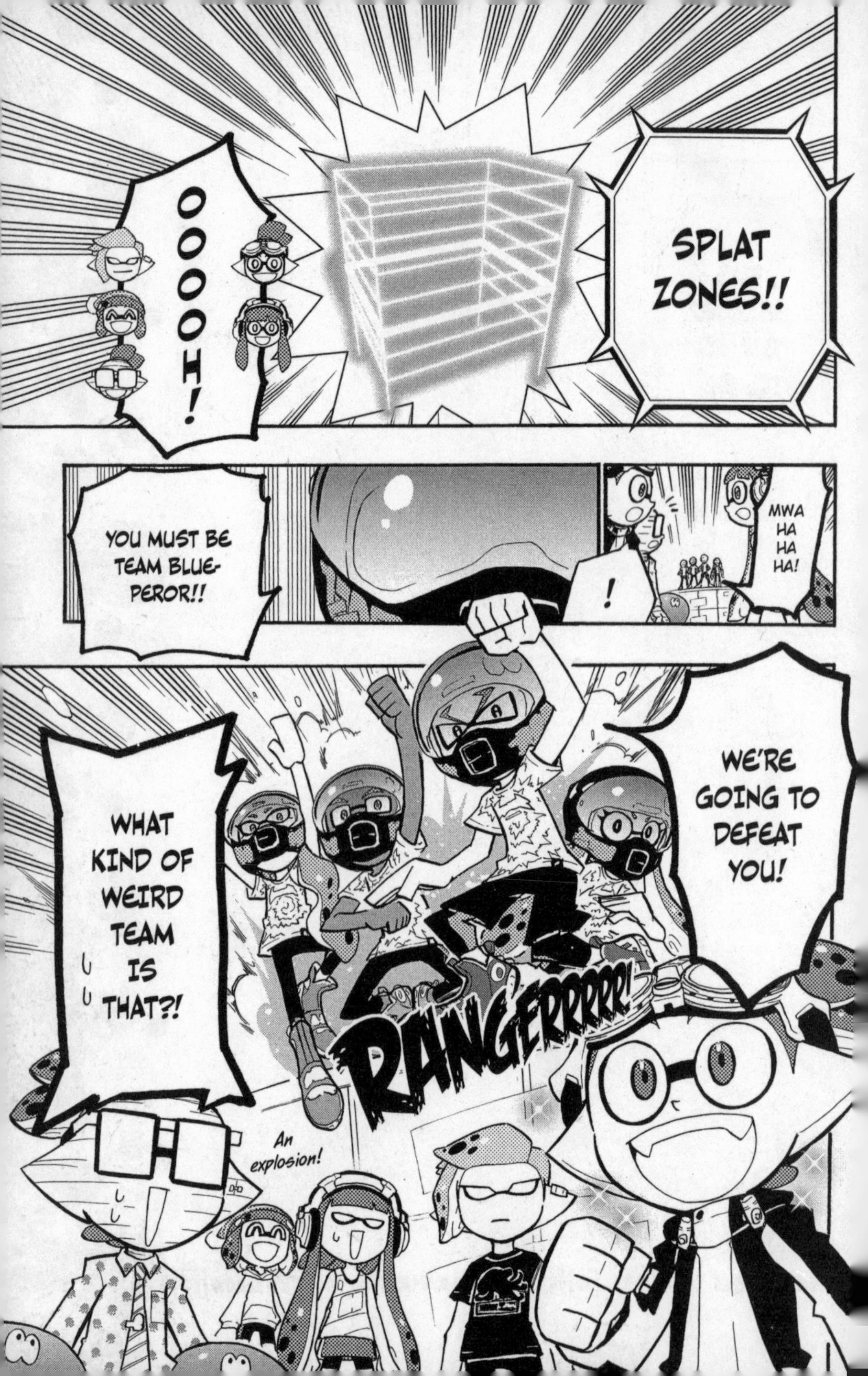
SPLAT ZONES!!
OOOOH!
MWA HA HA HA!
!
YOU MUST BE TEAM BLUE-PEROR!!
WE'RE GOING TO DEFEAT YOU!
RANGERRRR!
WHAT KIND OF WEIRD TEAM IS THAT?!
An explosion!

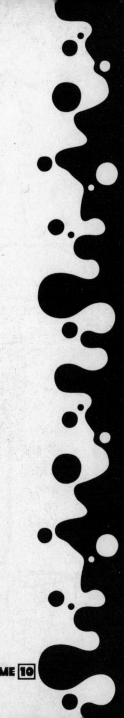

SPLATOON VOLUME 9 END / CONTINUED IN VOLUME 10

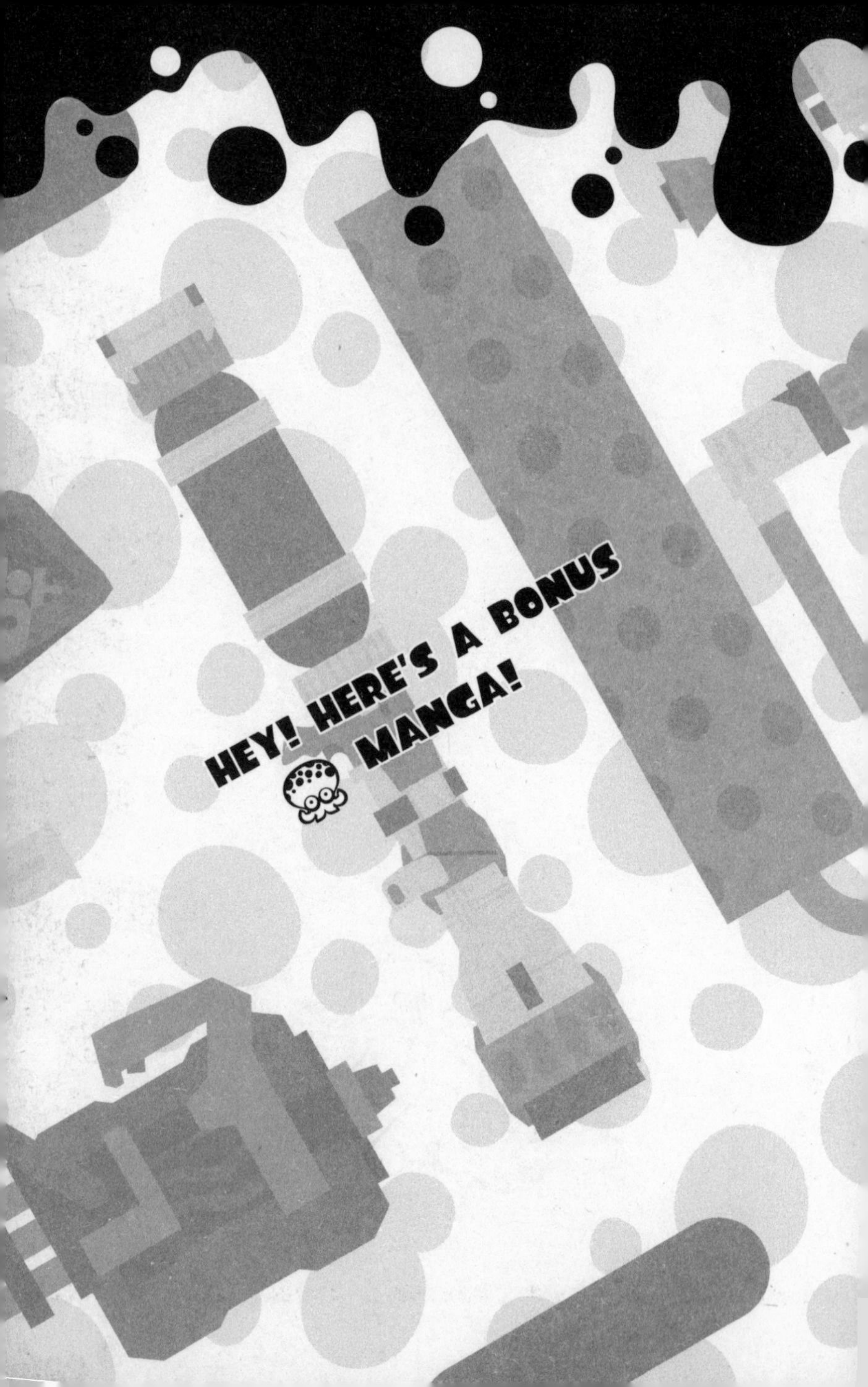
HEY! HERE'S A BONUS MANGA!

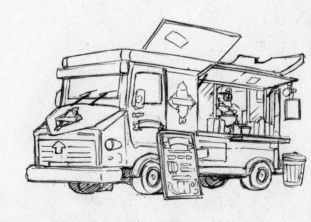

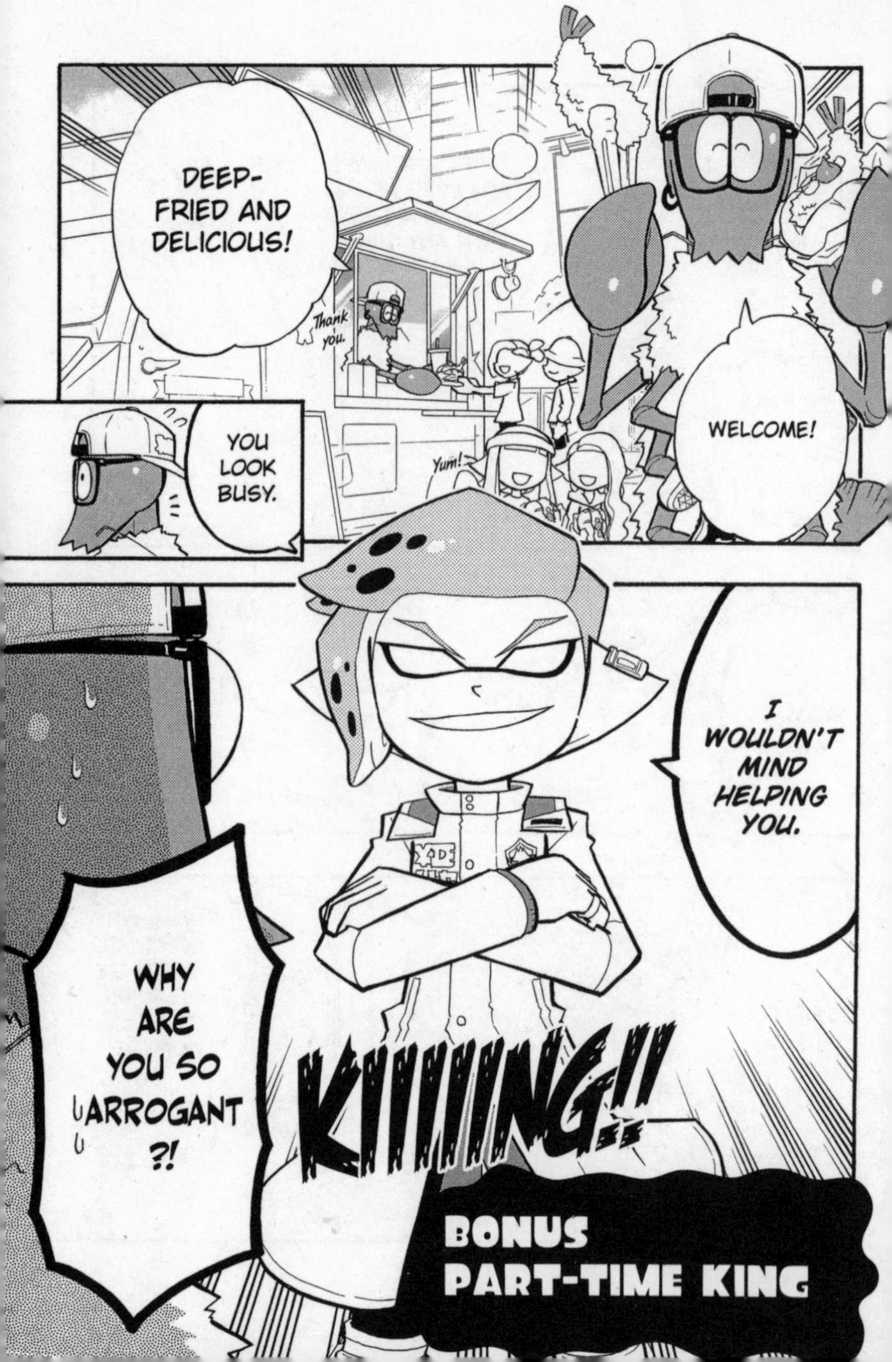
WELCOME!
DEEP-FRIED AND DELICIOUS!
Thank you.
Yum!
YOU LOOK BUSY.
I WOULDN'T MIND HELPING YOU.
KIIIING!!
WHY ARE YOU SO ARROGANT?!
BONUS
PART-TIME KING

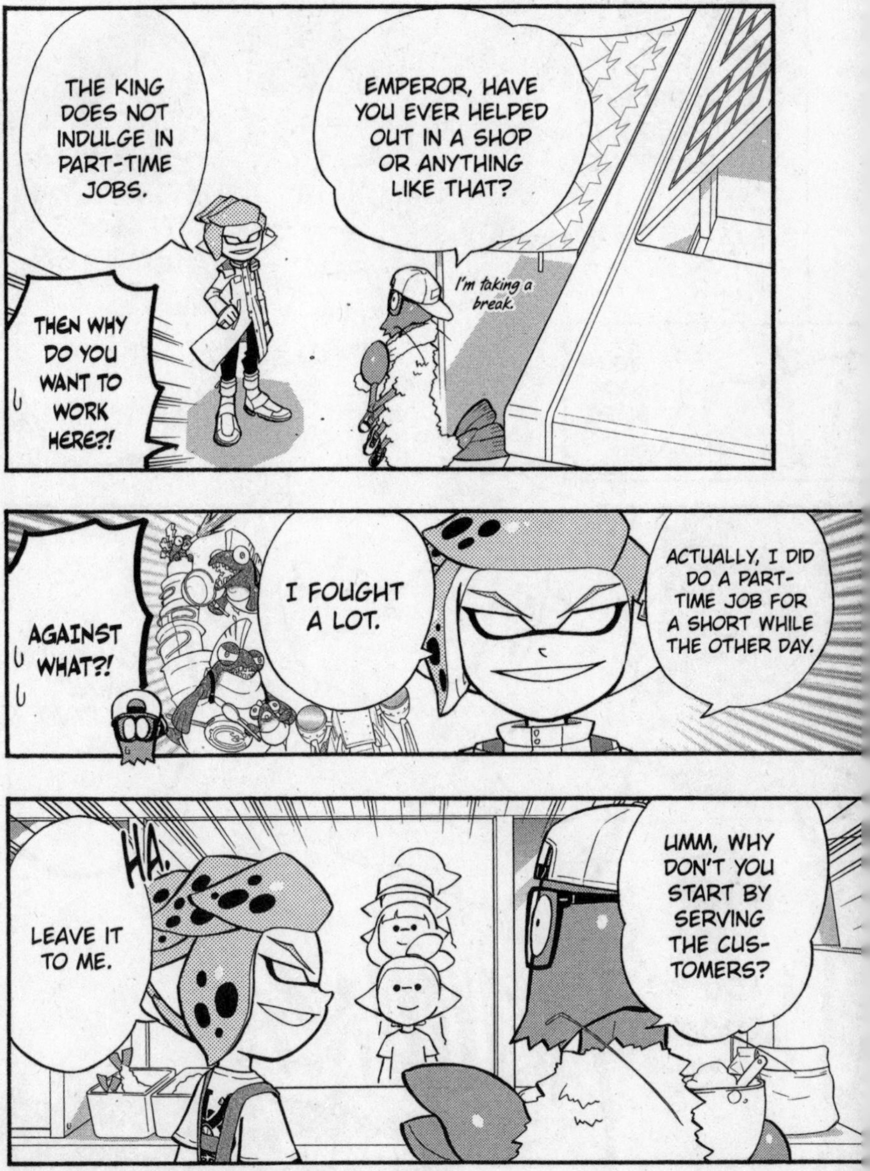
EMPEROR, HAVE YOU EVER HELPED OUT IN A SHOP OR ANYTHING LIKE THAT?
I'm taking a break.
THE KING DOES NOT INDULGE IN PART-TIME JOBS.
THEN WHY DO YOU WANT TO WORK HERE?!
ACTUALLY, I DID DO A PART-TIME JOB FOR A SHORT WHILE THE OTHER DAY.
I FOUGHT A LOT.
AGAINST WHAT?!
UMM, WHY DON'T YOU START BY SERVING THE CUS-TOMERS?
HA.
LEAVE IT TO ME.

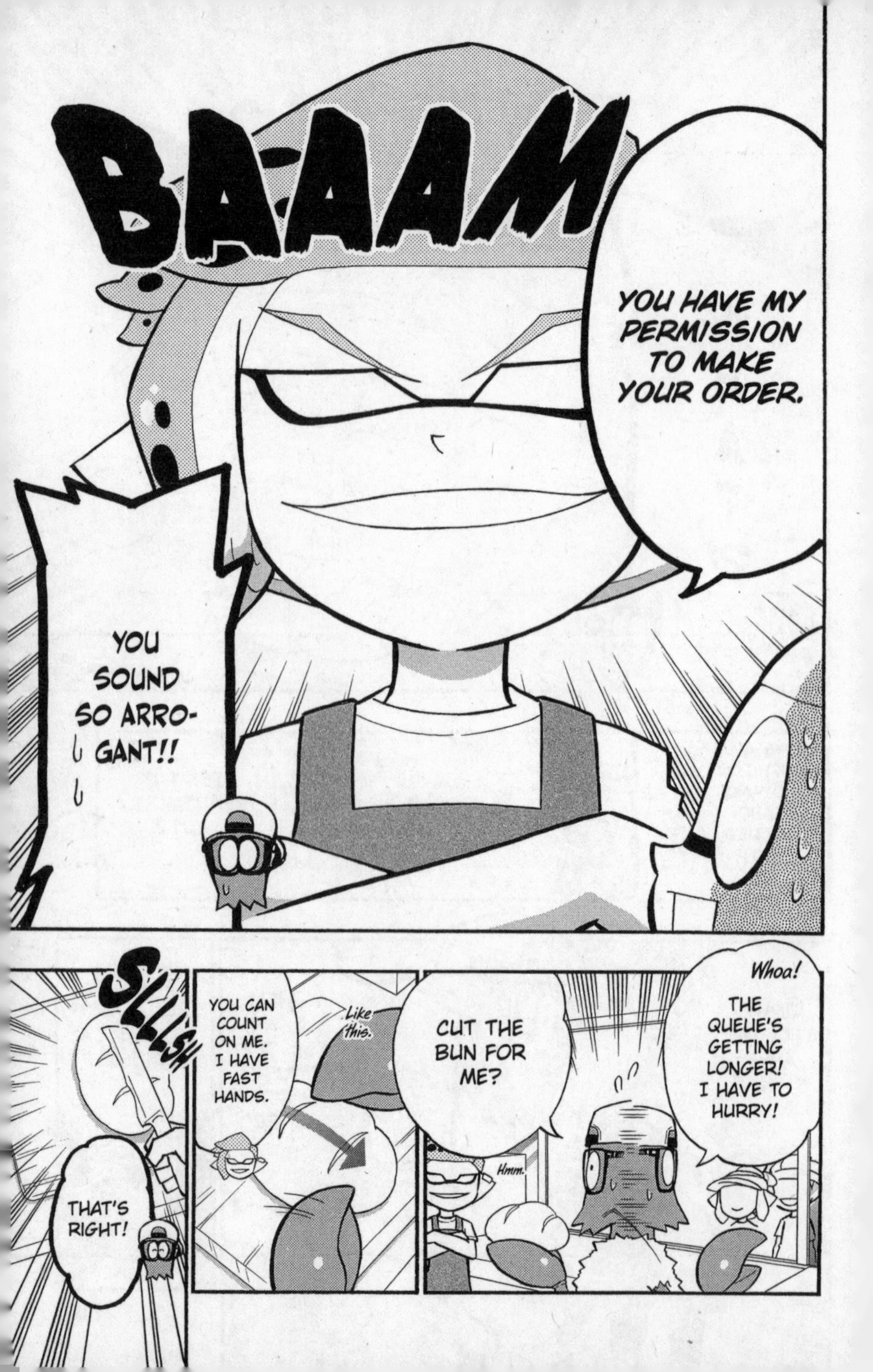
BA-AM
YOU HAVE MY PERMISSION TO MAKE YOUR ORDER.
YOU SOUND SO ARRO-GANT!!
Whoa!
THE QUEUE'S GETTING LONGER! I HAVE TO HURRY!
CUT THE BUN FOR ME?
Hmm.
YOU CAN COUNT ON ME. I HAVE FAST HANDS.
Like this.
SLLISH
THAT'S RIGHT!

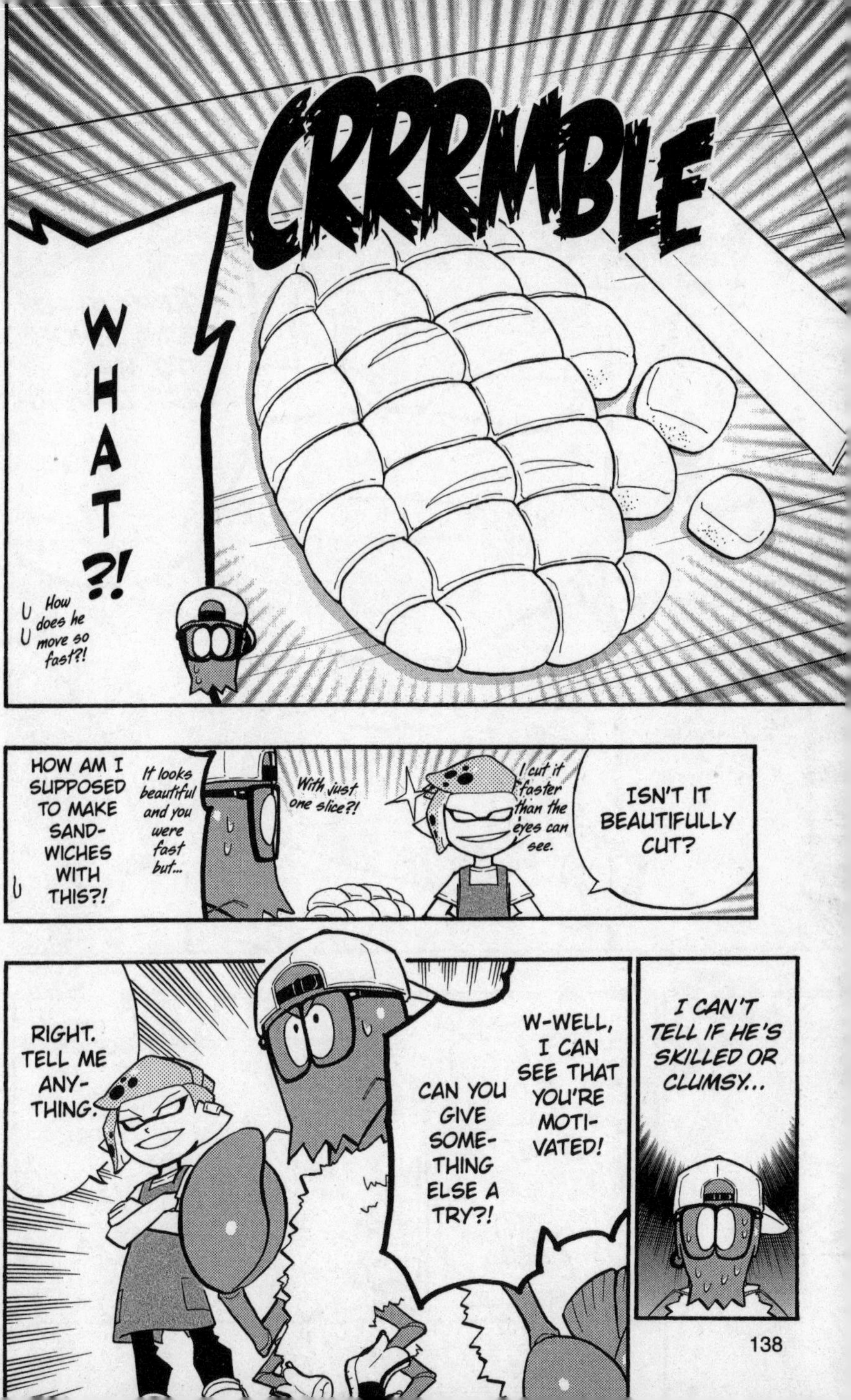
CRRRMBLE
WHAT?!
How does he move so fast?!
ISN'T IT BEAUTIFULLY CUT?
I cut it faster than the eyes can see.
With just one slice?!
It looks beautiful and you were fast but...
HOW AM I SUPPOSED TO MAKE SANDWICHES WITH THIS?!
I CAN'T TELL IF HE'S SKILLED OR CLUMSY...
W-WELL, I CAN SEE THAT YOU'RE MOTIVATED!
CAN YOU GIVE SOMETHING ELSE A TRY?!
RIGHT. TELL ME ANYTHING.

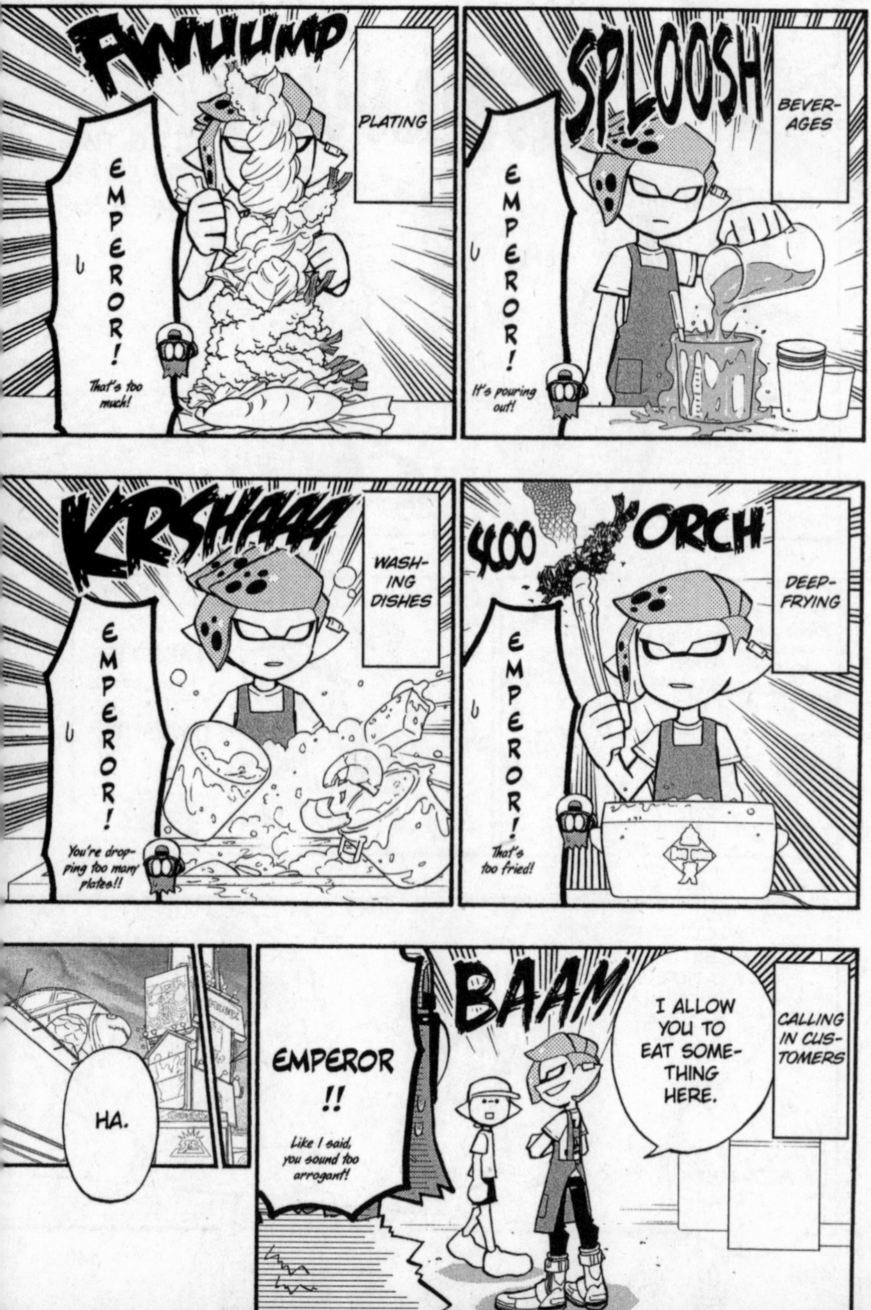
BEVER-AGES
SPLOOSH
EMPEROR!
It's pouring out!
PLATING
FWUUMP
EMPEROR!
That's too much!
DEEP-FRYING
SCOO
ORCH
EMPEROR!
That's too fried!
WASH-ING DISHES
KRSHAAA
EMPEROR!
You're drop-ping too many plates!!
CALLING IN CUS-TOMERS
I ALLOW YOU TO EAT SOME-THING HERE.
BAAM
EMPEROR !!
Like I said, you sound too arrogant!
HA.

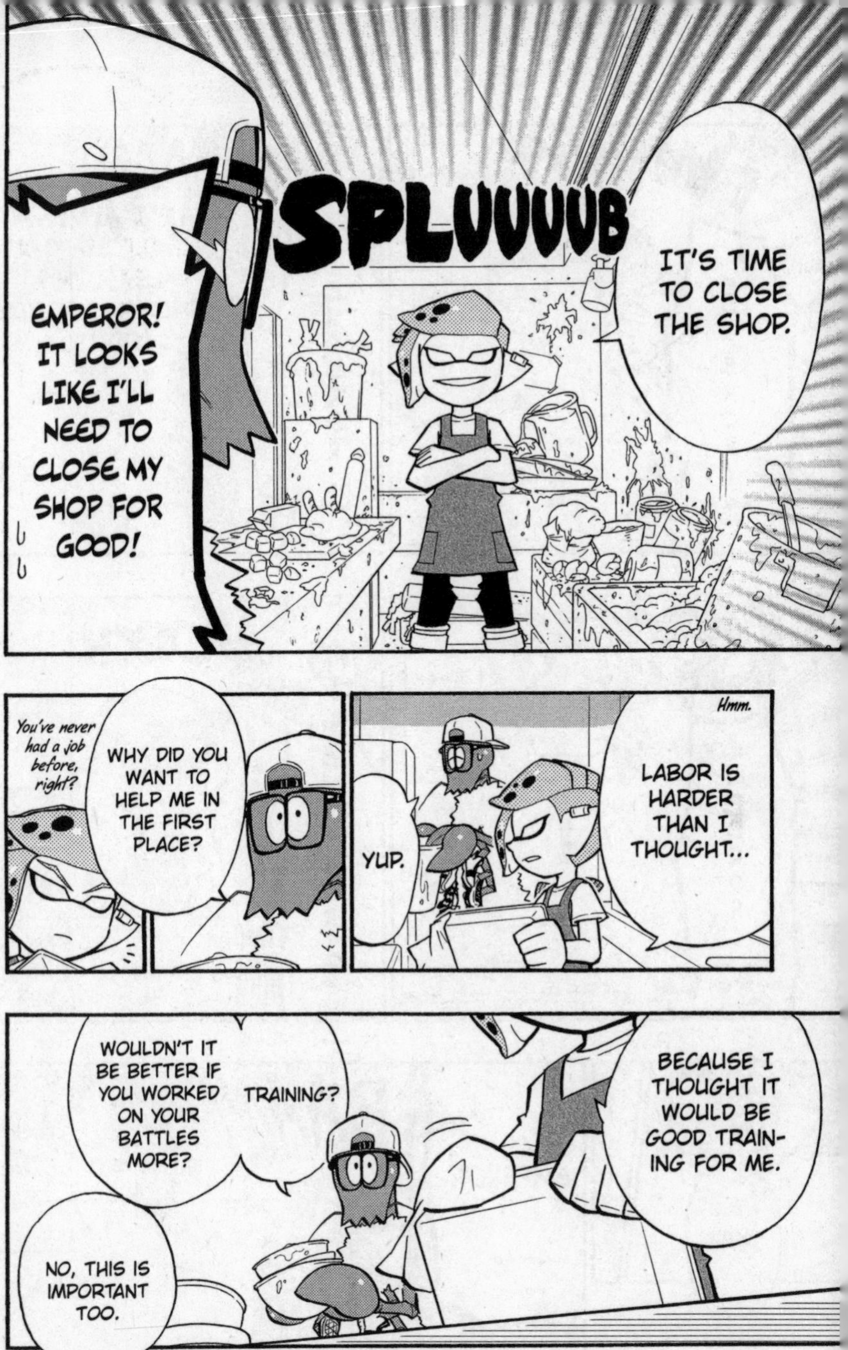
IT'S TIME TO CLOSE THE SHOP.
SPLUUUUB
EMPEROR! IT LOOKS LIKE I'LL NEED TO CLOSE MY SHOP FOR GOOD!
Hmm.
LABOR IS HARDER THAN I THOUGHT...
YUP.
WHY DID YOU WANT TO HELP ME IN THE FIRST PLACE?
You've never had a job before, right?
BECAUSE I THOUGHT IT WOULD BE GOOD TRAINING FOR ME.
TRAINING?
WOULDN'T IT BE BETTER IF YOU WORKED ON YOUR BATTLES MORE?
NO, THIS IS IMPORTANT TOO.

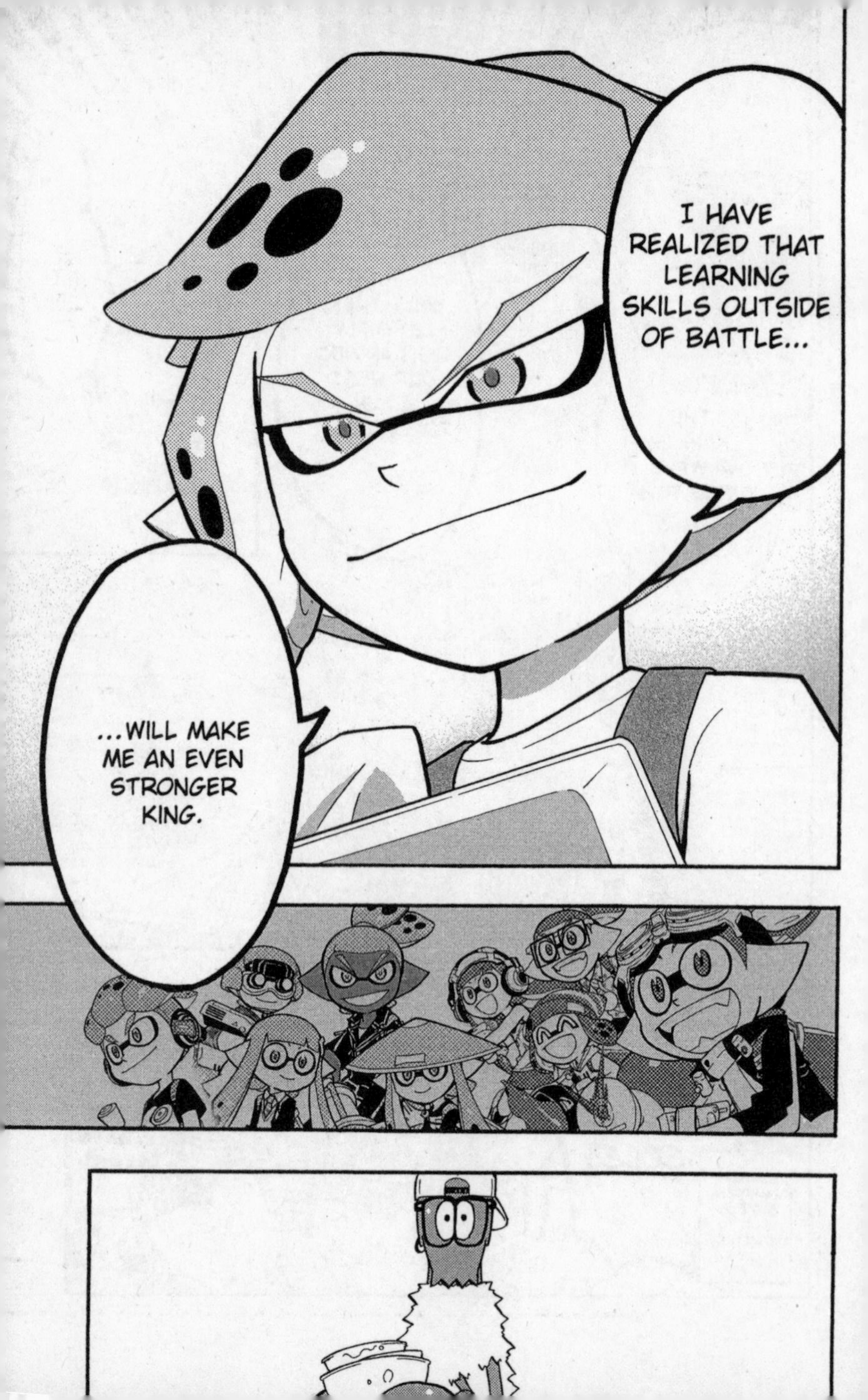
I HAVE REALIZED THAT LEARNING SKILLS OUTSIDE OF BATTLE...
...WILL MAKE ME AN EVEN STRONGER KING.

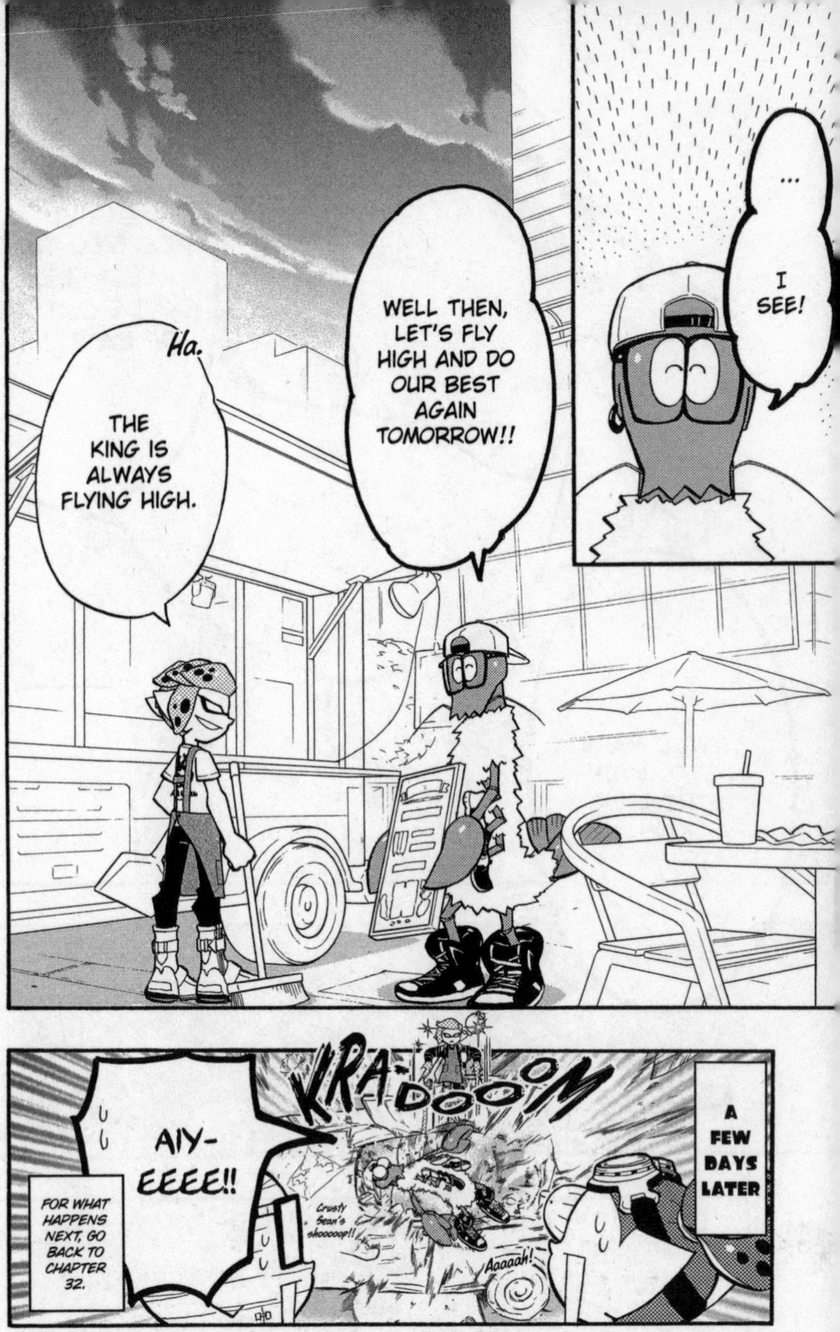
...
I SEE!
WELL THEN, LET'S FLY HIGH AND DO OUR BEST AGAIN TOMORROW!!
Ha.
THE KING IS ALWAYS FLYING HIGH.
A FEW DAYS LATER
Aaaaah!
KRA-DOOOOM
Crusty Sean's shoooop!!
AIY-EEEE!!
FOR WHAT HAPPENS NEXT, GO BACK TO CHAPTER 32.

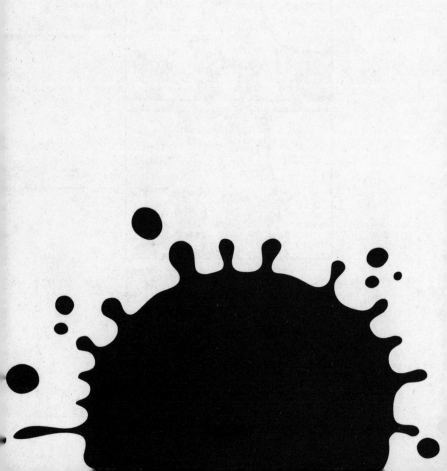

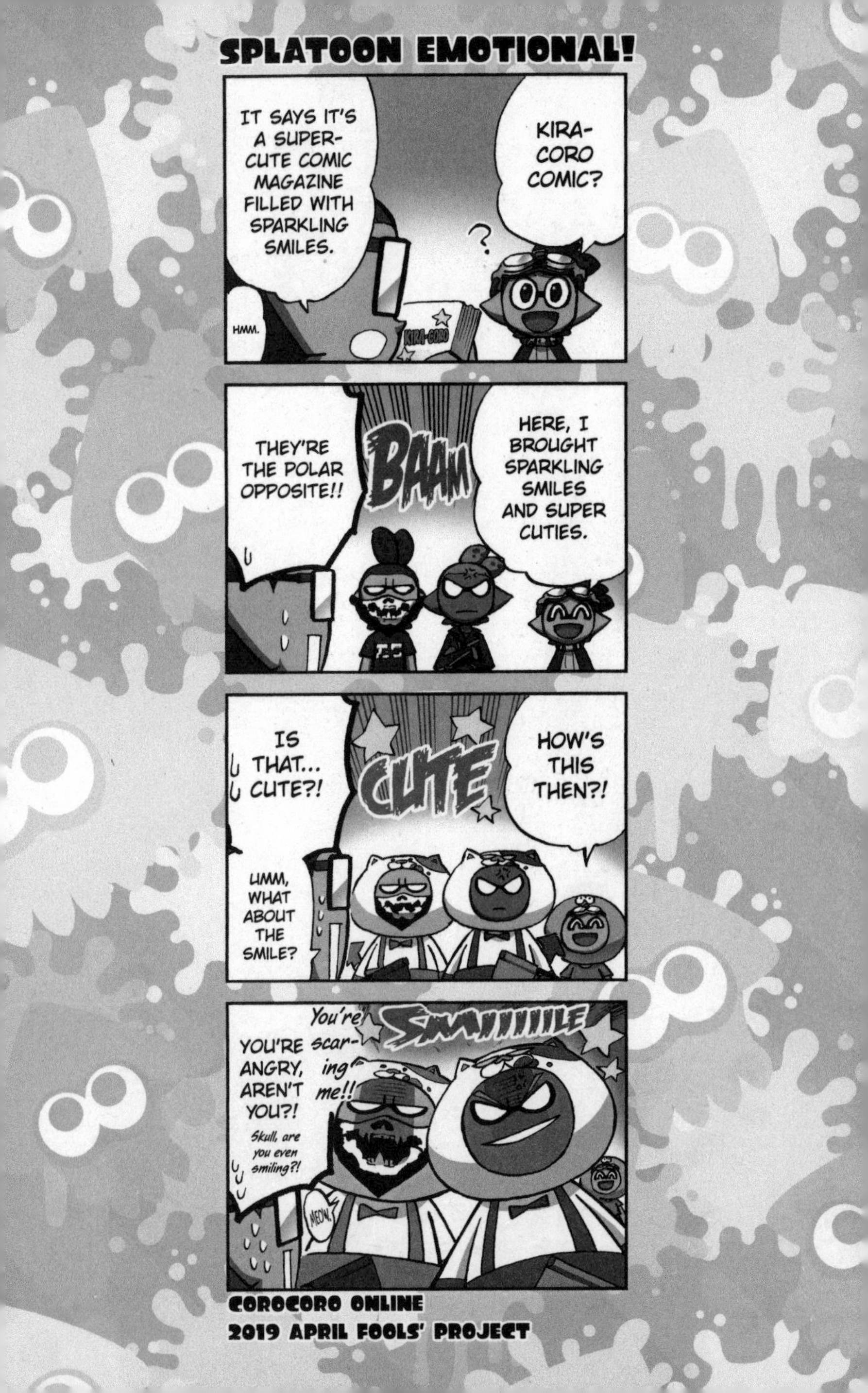
SPLATOON EMOTIONAL!
KIRA-CORO COMIC?
IT SAYS IT'S A SUPER-CUTE COMIC MAGAZINE FILLED WITH SPARKLING SMILES.
HMM.
KIRA-CORO
HERE, I BROUGHT SPARKLING SMILES AND SUPER CUTIES.
BAAM
THEY'RE THE POLAR OPPOSITE!!
HOW'S THIS THEN?!
CUTE
IS THAT... CUTE?!
UMM, WHAT ABOUT THE SMILE?
SMIIIIIILE
You're scar-ing me!!
YOU'RE ANGRY, AREN'T YOU?!
Skull, are you even smiling?!
MEOW.
COROCORO ONLINE
2019 APRIL FOOLS' PROJECT

GRAND TRANSFORMATION!!

HELLO!
WE ARE INKLINGS!!
WE CAN TRANSFORM INTO HUMANOIDS AND SQUIDS!
OKAY! I'M GOING TO DO IT TOO!!
TRANS-FORM!
SQU ID!
HUH?! MY FACE HASN'T TRANS-FORMED!!
FLIP FLIP FLIP
FREAKY...

CoroCoro Comic, MAY 2015
(THIS FOUR-PANEL FUNNY APPEARED IN THE MAGAZINE BEFORE #0!)

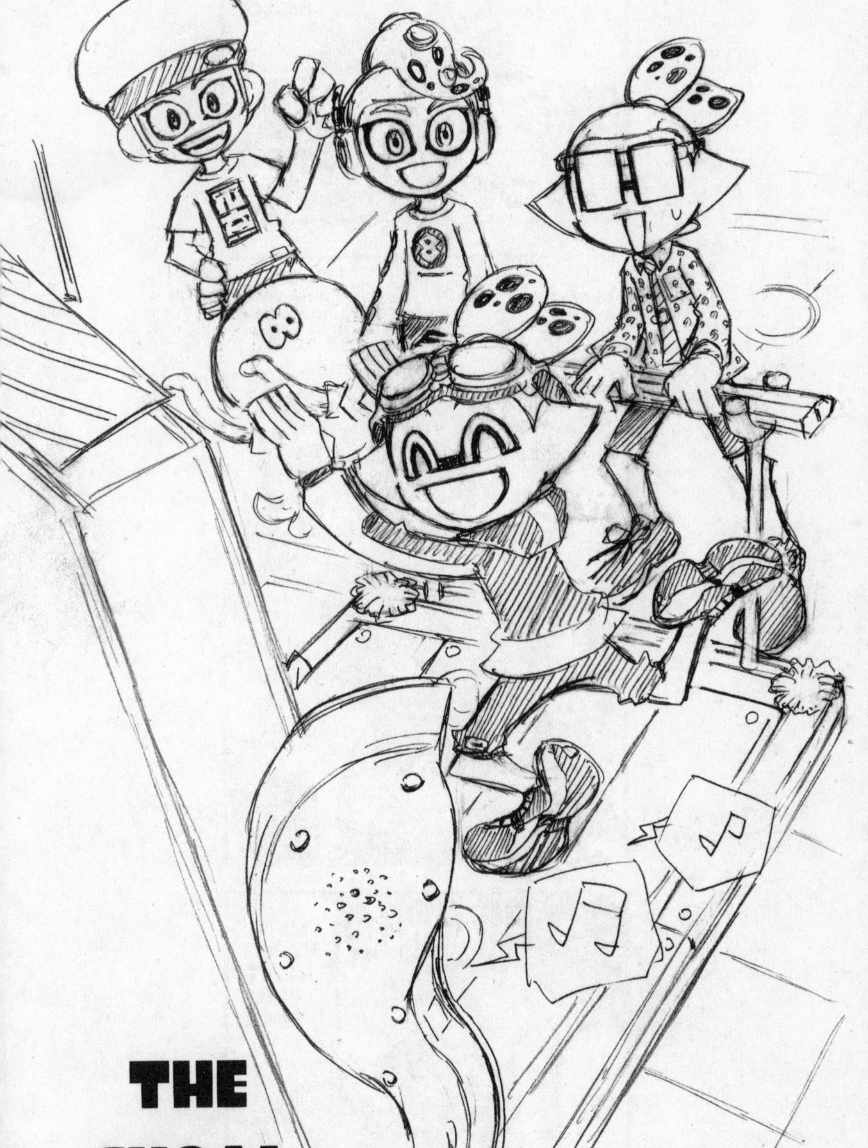

THE SHOAL

HEADSPACE

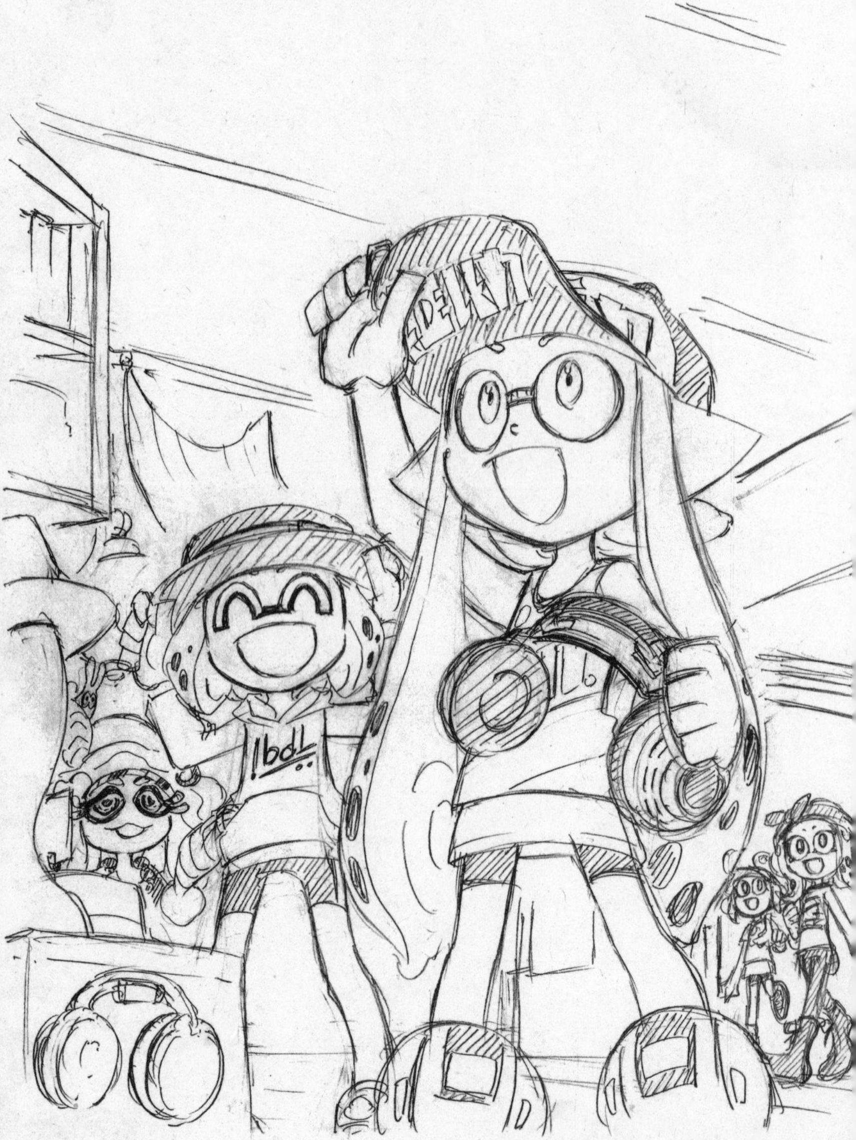

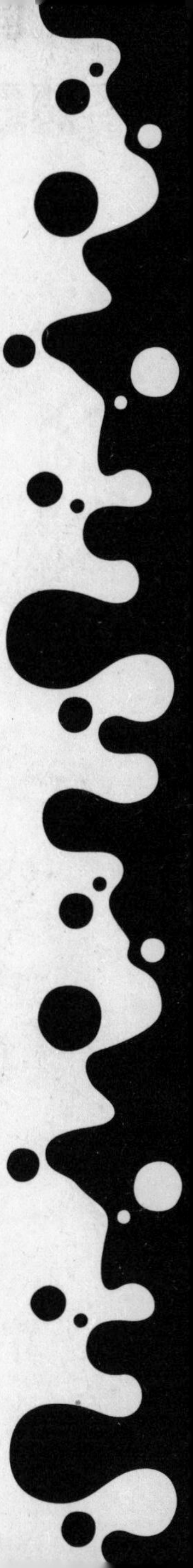

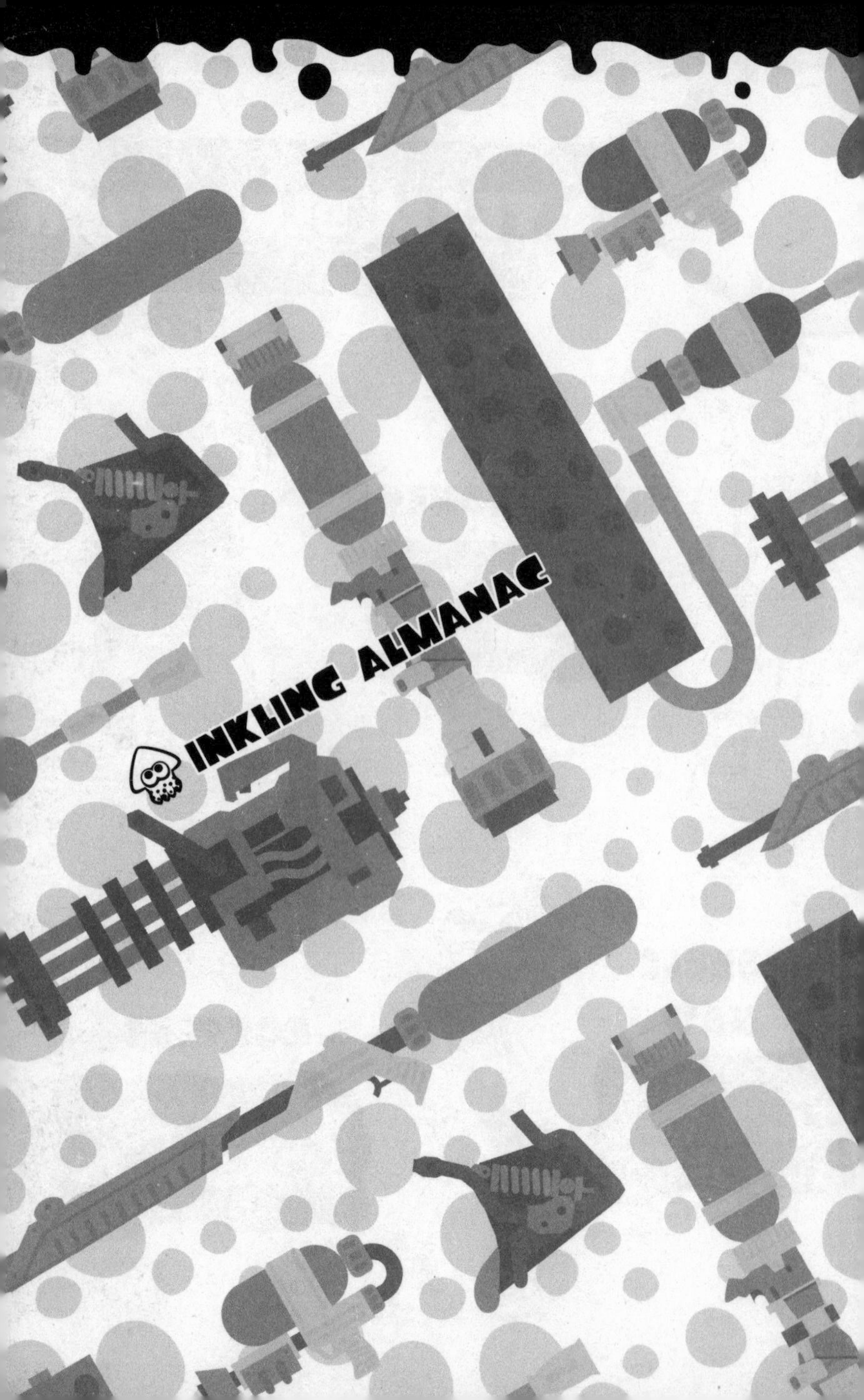
INKLING ALMANAC

TEAM BLUEPEROR

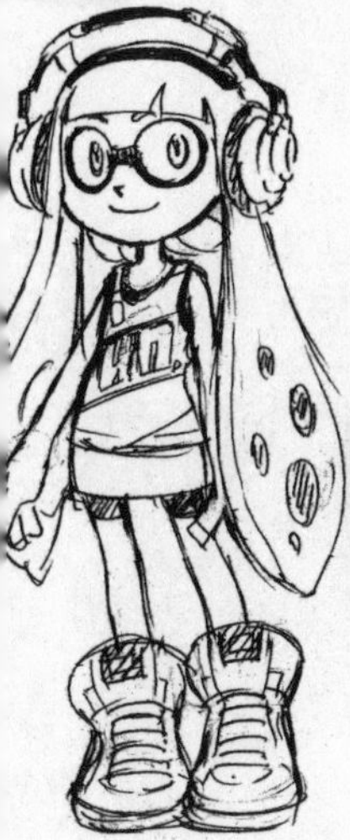

HEADPHONES

Weapon: Splat Charger
Headgear: Studio Headphones
Clothing: Slash King Tank
Shoes: Red Hi-Horses

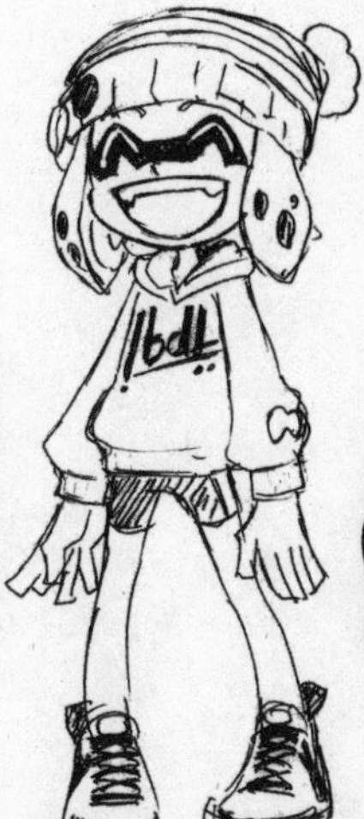

BOBBLE HAT

Weapon: Slosher
Headgear: Bobble Hat
Clothing: Gray Hoodie
Shoes: Purple Sea Slugs

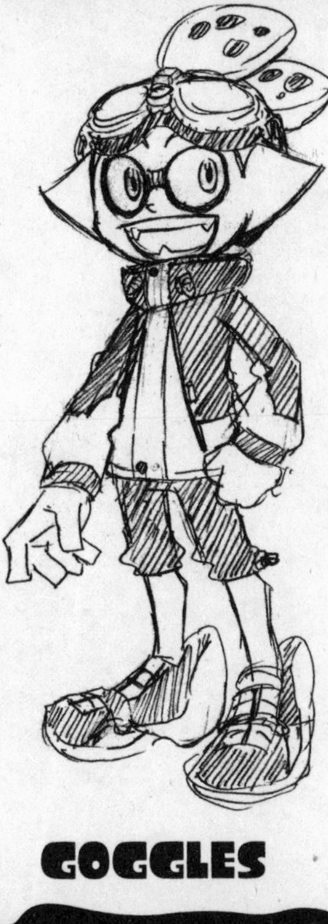

GOGGLES

Weapon: Splattershot
Headgear: Pilot Goggles
Clothing: Eggplant Mountain Coat
Shoes: Hero Runner Replicas

EMPEROR

Weapon: Enperry Splat Dualies
Headgear: Eminence Cuff
Clothing: Black Velour Octoking Tee
Shoes: Milky Enperrials

You can do it!

BUZZCUT TOWEL

Weapon: Tenta Sorella Brella
Headgear: Worker's Head Towel
Clothing: Garden Gear
Shoes: Angry Rain Boots

Hairstyle: Buzzcut

INFO

• The bandage on his forehead was placed there by his little sister as a good-luck charm so he won't get hurt.

TEAM WORKER'S HEAD TOWEL

(INK COLOR: LIGHT ORANGE)

SLICK TOWEL

Hairstyle:
Slick

Weapon:	Explosher
Headgear:	Worker's Head Towel
Clothing:	Garden Gear
Shoes:	Angry Rain Boots

HIPSTER TOWEL

Hairstyle:
Hipster

Weapon:	H-3 Nozzlenose
Headgear:	Worker's Head Towel
Clothing:	Garden Gear
Shoes:	Angry Rain Boots

TOPKNOT TOWEL

Hairstyle:
Topknot

Weapon:	Glooga Dualies
Headgear:	Worker's Head Towel
Clothing:	Garden Gear
Shoes:	Angry Rain Boots

INFO

- They sweat a lot, so they wash their clothes often.
- They are very picky about the fabric softener they use.

TEAM NEW EMPEROR

(INK COLOR: SUN YELLOW)

SQUIDKID JR.

Weapon: Crash Blaster
Headgear: Eminence Cuff
Clothing: Milky Eminence Jacket
Shoes: Red & Black Squidkid IV

N-PACER

Weapon: Splatterscope
Headgear: Eminence Cuff
Clothing: Milky Eminence Jacket
Shoes: N-Pacer Ag

PRINZ

Weapon: Enperry Splat Dualies
Headgear: Eminence Cuff
Clothing: Milky Eminence Jacket
Shoes: Milky Enperrials

LACELESS

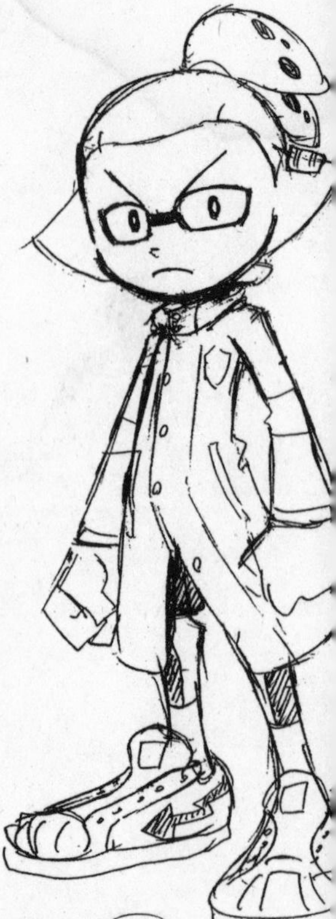

Weapon: Splash-o-matic
Headgear: Eminence Cuff
Clothing: Milky Eminence Jacket
Shoes: White Laceless Dakroniks

INFO

• He is the son of the gardener at Emperor's house.
• He knows the Emperor brothers well, but he's friends with Jr. and N-Pacer too.

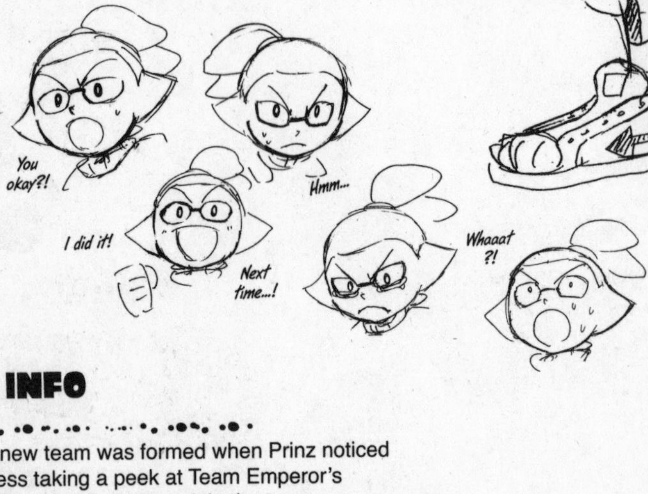
You okay?!
Hmm...
I did it!
Next time...!
Whaaat ?!

INFO

• The new team was formed when Prinz noticed Laceless taking a peek at Team Emperor's practice and asked him to join the team.

Splatoon 9

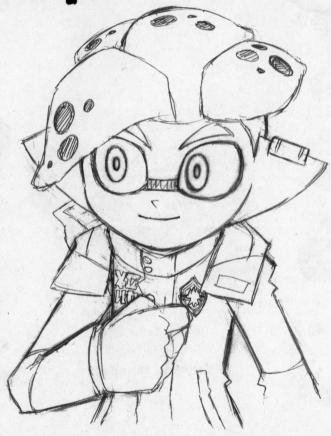

THANK YOU!

It's time for the Square King
Ranked Battle Cup!!
I want to collect clams!

Sankichi Hinodeya

Volume 9
VIZ Media Edition

Story and Art by
Sankichi Hinodeya

Translation **Tetsuichiro Miyaki**
English Adaptation **Jason A. Hurley**
Lettering **John Hunt**
Design **Kam Li**
Editor **Joel Enos**

TM & © 2020 Nintendo. All rights reserved.

SPLATOON Vol. 9 by Sankichi HINODEYA
© 2016 Sankichi HINODEYA
All rights reserved.
Original Japanese edition published by SHOGAKUKAN.
English translation rights in the United States of America,
Canada, the United Kingdom, Ireland, Australia and
New Zealand arranged with SHOGAKUKAN.

The stories, characters and incidents mentioned
in this publication are entirely fictional.

Original Design **100percent**

Printed in the U.S.A.

Published by VIZ Media, LLC
P.O. Box 77010
San Francisco, CA 94107

10 9 8 7 6 5 4 3 2 1
First Printing, May 2020

PARENTAL ADVISORY
SPLATOON is rated A and is
suitable for readers of all ages.

Splatoon
reads from
right to
left!

This is
the end
of this
graphic
novel.